AN END TO ETCETERA

AN END TO ETCETERA

B. ROBERT CONKLIN

Skip the Preface
publishing

Columbus, Ohio

AN END TO ETCETERA
Copyright © 2023 by Robert B. Conklin

ISBN: 979-8-9872301-3-8 (Paperback Version)

Library of Congress Control Number: 2022921895

Cover photo:
Jeffrey Schreier, Pier at Night in Guntersville Lake
iStock by Getty Images

First Edition

For more information, visit:
www.skipthepreface.com

For Miona,
for all you do!

"But certain favourite parts are played by us so often before
the public and rehearsed so carefully when we are alone that we
find it easier to refer to their fictitious testimony than to that of
a reality which we have almost entirely forgotten."

—Marcel Proust, *In Search of Lost Time*

Tell all the Truth but tell it slant—
Success in Circuit lies
Too bright for our infirm Delight
The Truth's superb surprise

—Emily Dickinson

Thuster night, and com'th the day

—Anonymous (c. 1300), *Hymn to the Virgin*

Chapter 1

By the end of the summer, he would drown his only friend in a lake, but it started, he claims, by a fountain.

Selena knows just the fountain her 13-year-old patient is describing. A trio of mermaids stretches tall and naked above it. Water bubbles over their shoulders, runs around their breasts and scales. Splashes, trickles, over the tips of wide tails into a shallow pool. Arms reach skyward, fingers interlocked, as though caught in a secret dance. She used to play around it with her little brother—splashing, wading, pulling toy boats made of bars of soap by a string. But she had been much younger than the boy seated across from her.

White as a loaf of Wonder Bread, compared to her own light brown skin, Leal Porter could be any one of dozens of adolescents she has tried to help over the years. Spindly as a sapling, his body type reminds her of how tall and lanky she was when she was his age. Washed-out jeans, black T-shirt with a faded logo of some rock group, untied grass-stained tennis shoes—he doesn't look like the murderer he purports himself to be. Again, she has to remind herself that he hadn't been charged with anything more serious than creating a disturbance—and even that charge had been dropped once the detectives were through with their investigation.

It's his expression, though, as inscrutable as a walnut, that's difficult to read. A half smile, not quite a smirk, is perpetually pasted to his face, but his eyes are elsewhere, turned inward, maraschino cherries sunken in cream. A thin white scar with an imprint of stitches slants across his forehead beneath a disheveled outcropping of brown hair. Insignia of a duel? She'll have to ask him how he got it sometime.

As Leal tells it from the couch on his side of the office, a woman stepped magically out of a slant of sunlight. He found out later her name was Diana. Long and tall, she seemed like one of the mermaids herself, leaving the palm of a seashell to join the world of mortals. Bare thighs emerged from frayed ends of shorts. Sloping breasts filled an orange midriff. A butterfly spread its wings on soft white flesh below her shoulder. A snake curled around her ankle.

Selena has to admit, he makes it all sound so very real, the delicate gold veins of the butterfly interweaving through purple wings glistening bright and vivid in morning sunlight. An orange snake coiling around the silver shaft of a dagger, seeming as though it might slither up her body to snatch the butterfly with slick fangs, as she knelt to plop a coin in the fountain.

Right away, the boy Leal was looking after drew his hand through the water, plucking out her nickel from the bottom of the pool. The boy was only half Leal's height with a tangle of dark hair and black jellybeans for eyes.

"It's not polite stealing other people's wishes," Leal reprimanded him, just like a parent might do, but Thuster pretended not to hear. Pretended? No, he could hear other things well enough: bird in a tree, exhaust of a truck, police whistle. Just not Leal's voice, not all the time. Selective attention: this is what Father Mac, the neighborhood priest, has called it.

"It's all right," Diana said. "He can have my wish if he wants it."

"No, ma'am. It's not all right."

He tugged at Thuster's wrist but pulled too hard. Together, they succeeded in knocking over a paper bag of groceries that Leal hadn't even realized was there, sitting on the edge of the fountain.

Leal watched as a carton of eggs spilled out of the bag, brown farmer's eggs—not white. This was one of the things he noticed.

Immediately, he knelt down, helping Diana place the eggshells back in the carton one at a time. Seven eggs were smashed, broken beyond repair—not all the king's horses nor all the king's men—leaving a yellow mess on concrete slabs. Using the jagged crowns of the shells, Diana scooped up as much goop as she could manage. Leal must have apologized a hundred times.

"Sorry," he said.

Hundred and one.

Long amber hair fell across her forehead, slanting across her face, not quite able to conceal a green and purple circle of swollen flesh surrounding one of her eyes. And this was the other thing he noticed.

"You're staring, aren't you?" she said, softly, voice like autumn leaves, even though it was early summer.

"No, ma'am," Leal said. "I'm not staring."

"It's all right. Everyone's been staring."

"No one is staring. I don't think anyone is staring."

But it was true. He was staring. It's a bad habit, hard to give up—like coffee or cigarettes, his mom's twin addictions. Everyone has a bad habit, he presumes.

They formed a loose circle around the paper sack of groceries—he and Thuster and Diana.

She made a move to pick up the bag, but Leal reached down quickly.

"Let me carry them for you," Leal offered.

"No," she said, "you don't have to do that."

"It's no trouble," he said, looking up.

And then he saw her smile.

*

Leal didn't recognize any of the street signs along the route they took to get to Diana's house. Most of the streets were named after trees—Oak and Elm and Maple—with a couple of presidents thrown in. Obscure ones, too: Fillmore, Harding, Polk.

White picket fences enclosed immaculate yards, ivy climbed tall arbors. Swing-sets and jungle gyms turned back yards into playgrounds. He envied these people their aquamarine lawns, their pillared porches, their ornamental gnomes and geese.

"Ovid—well, you know what Ovid is like," Leal prompts Selena from the comfort of his couch in her office, twining his fingers, studying a row of bruised knuckles, purplish and tender—another hint of something not quite kosher in Denmark. "I mean, you live here, too, don't you?"

The question catches Selena off guard.

"Yes, Leal. Yes, I do."

"Have you always lived in Ovid?"

She peers into half-lidded eyes.

"No. Not always. I lived north of here. In Chicago. But I grew up in Ovid. When I was younger."

"Is that why you moved back here? Because you grew up here?"

Again, she hesitates. She knows better than to tell him about the separation. Her father's stroke. The pregnancy. She makes it a general rule not to divulge her personal life to her clients. Yet there's something about his posture. Not expectant, not indifferent.

"No, not really. My parents—a couple of years ago my mother died, and my father … well, he needs someone to be with him. But that's a long story."

"Oh. Well, then, you're pretty lucky. I mean that you didn't have to spend your whole life here."

*

Eventually, Diana led them down a sidewalk to a white sugar cube of a house tucked behind a row of pine trees. Once on the porch, she brought them lemonade. One glass she handed to Leal and the other to Thuster, but he didn't take it, of course, and so she set it aside.

Before long, a dark blue car—big as a limousine—buckled around the curb, pulling long and sleek onto the driveway.

Diana frowned at the driver: dark gray suit coat, red tie loosely knotted below an unbuttoned collar. Black hair, just a line of gray at the sideburns, rose from his forehead slicked back on a wave of gel. Sunshades blotted his eyes.

The man stooped to pinch a stalk of pink clover before jostling up the steps to the porch. He set aside a leather briefcase and offered the flower to Diana.

"You're home early," Diana said, wrapping the clover inside a fist.

"Aren't you glad to see me?" He made a move to kiss her, but Diana turned her head.

"Not in front of the kids."

He turned back around to consider Leal at an angle over the bridge of his sunglasses.

"Hello, boys," his voice came out of the side of his mouth, like loose gravel. "Here to collect for the paper, already?"

Leal recognized him from late-night commercials, even without his crown and scepter, his floor-length robe of fur: Saul Solomon, the Chinchilla King. *Two-Fur-One Special Offer. Look Like a Queen Fur a Day. My Kingdom for a Fur.*

Diana, too, now that he saw them together—she would appear in them. The "lovely Diana" would twirl around in a brand-new fur coat, opening it at the end of the commercial to reveal a bikini inside. And there would be her two tattoos.

*

Oh, Selena thinks. *That* Diana.

She has seen the commercials, too.

"This friend of yours," she says, looking down at her notepad. "Thuster. Sort of a strange name, wouldn't you say?"

"It was just his name."

"His nickname?"

"Yeah. Sort of."

"Do you know how he got it?"

"Used-ter know," he confides with a shrug, "don't anymore."

Inwardly, she voices a groan at the rhyme. She wonders how long he's been waiting to spring this one loose. Her soon-to-be ex was full of bad puns, too.

*

"Saul, these boys helped me carry my bag of groceries home today." Diana's voice sounded flat, even.

"Is that so?" Saul said. "Did she give you anything for your trouble?"

"She gave us lemonade, sir." Leal felt obliged to defend her good deed.

"Well, in that case." Saul reached a hand deep into a pocket and pulled out a thick wad of green bills. Peeling back bill after bill—the first bill was a hundred that made Leal drool—he arrived at a couple of crumpled dollars. Thuster didn't take his dollar, just stared back at it in a way that only Thuster would do.

"Thank you," Leal said, stuffing both dollar bills into his pocket.

"What's wrong with your friend?" Saul asked, bending down to squint into each of Thuster's eyes, just like an optometrist might do.

"Are you a doctor?" Leal asked. He was thinking *veterinarian*, because of his interest in chinchillas. In his commercials, he always had a chinchilla perched on his shoulder, like a pirate with a parrot. He thought it possible that selling fur coats was just a sideline.

"Saul, a doctor," Diana laughed. "That's a pretty good one. I'll have to remember that."

Saul confronted Diana bearing his briefcase like a shield.

"Drink ready?" he grimaced, and Diana backed away inside the house.

"Take care of Thuster," she said through the screen.

Selena could picture them leaving the porch on their way back to the parsonage where the priest would be waiting, cooking an Irish stew. The wind blows a pink cloud through the branches of a tree. A boy rides past on a bicycle throwing newspapers. And Leal takes Thuster by the hand, walking along the sidewalk in silence, all the way down Lambeth Street, to the very end of the block, where he takes another look at the street sign, just to make sure he remembers its name.

*

Selena glances at the clock. Almost out of time.

"Leal," she says quietly, "you said in your confession—"

"Confession?"

He didn't know they were going to call it a confession. But he guesses that's what it was. He just needed to tell someone. That's all. And he didn't know who else to tell. He knew he couldn't tell his mom. She wouldn't understand any of it. And as for Father Mac—

Selena looks through her notes, flips a page.

"Father MacDougal?"

He supposes he could have told Father Mac about it, except he left for Florida at the end of the summer. So, when it comes down to it, there was no one really left to tell. He could have told God. He could have walked off into the woods or locked himself in his bedroom and told God all about it. Except he's not so sure he believes in God anymore.

"Let's call it a statement," she suggests. "In your—statement, it says that a young boy—this friend of yours—Thuster— drowned. Is that right? Is that how you remember it?"

"He was more like a shadow. The way he would follow me around half the day. But then, I guess you could look at it the other way around and say that I was his babysitter. That's how Father Mac must have looked at it. It was like he made me Thuster's babysitter for the summer so he would be free to do other things."

"Other things?"

"Like basketball. He was always hanging out on the basketball court. The one outdoors next to the parish house with the rusted hoop?" He makes it seem as though Selena should know the one he is describing. "Oh, and confessions. He liked hearing confessions. He was always good about that. Ministering to his flock. That's what he called it. He was like Jesus in a way. The only thing he couldn't do was walk on water. Only, now that I think about it, it would've been nice if he could have done that, too. Then maybe none of this wouldn't ever have happened."

Selena closes her folder of notes: news clippings, school files, photocopies of police reports.

"Listen, Leal, it's fine if you want to tell me this story," she says, leaning forward. She already knows not to call him Leland—his father's name, too, dead these past six years. He was only seven years old when he died. Took his son along on a business trip and came back in a body bag. His mother had already warned her. He won't want to talk about it. And she was right. He didn't. "There's nothing wrong with that. But you're going to need to give me something more. Something more to go on."

"You mean, you don't want to hear about this?"

"No, Leal. That's not what I'm saying. It's fine to talk about this. It's very good."

"You mean, this isn't what you want me to do?"

"Anything you want to tell me is what I want you to do. This is how it always starts. I normally work with young people, like yourself—who are going through a crisis. You know what a crisis is?"

"Yes, ma'am. My mom has them all the time."

Selena suppresses an urge to smile.

"Well, this is how they normally start out. They start out by telling me a story. And that's fine. It's really quite natural. But at some point—there's really no pressure here. I don't want you to feel there's any pressure, at all. But at some point, you'll need to tell me what's troubling you."

"What's troubling me?"

"And there's something else you should know. Anything you say here is confidential." This isn't quite true, but she decides to skip over the technicalities. "You can say anything to me, and it will stay here. Do you understand what I'm saying?"

"Yes, ma'am. I mean, I think so. Just like Las Vegas, right?"

This time she lets a smile curl her mouth.

A minute goes by, silently. Selena uses the minute to push herself from her chair cushion, using two fists, feeling a slight pull of her stomach muscles. At six months, she's only starting to sense vague movements, a fish swimming through her belly. Leal rises, too, reaching out a hand, as though to steady her.

"You're pretty," he says as she goes over to open the door for him. "I didn't know you'd be so pretty."

"Excuse me?" Selena asks, pulling the coils of her long, black hair behind her neck into a ponytail, a reflexive habit whenever she's caught off guard. She can feel herself blush all the way to the base of her skull. *So much for transference!*

This isn't the first time a patient has remarked on her physical features: hair, height, eyes, even skin tone. In a town like Ovid, blackness is an anomaly. And Black therapists are not only rare but unique. Her father is Black, her mother was white. Her husband—almost ex-husband—is white, too. She still likes to tell the story of the little white girl who scrutinized her in silence for several minutes to the point of making Selena feel uncomfortable, worried she had a crumb lingering on her face from breakfast or insect crawling in her hair, before blurting out her sudden epiphany: "You're Black! Like Princess Tiana!"

Younger patients are like that—open and direct, unpremeditated, without the subliminal uneasiness of an older clientele. That's one reason she likes working with kids.

And now standing in front of her is yet another patient delivering an assessment of her appearance.

"Not as pretty as Diana, of course," Leal tells her, eyeing her up and down, "but you're definitely a close runner-up."

"Thanks for the compliment," Selena replies drily, forcing her therapist's smile.

"Well, B-F-N."

"Right," she says, taking a moment to interpret, "bye for now."

And then he steps past her out the door.

***

She brings take-home Chinese for her father, but this time she doesn't feel hungry—just nauseous. Late-afternoon sickness, she thinks. Symptoms of morning sickness dissipated months ago.

In her bedroom, she scans an email from Lori reminding her about the upcoming high school reunion, their twentieth. *You're still going, right? Don't leave me stranded!* Another confirming her reservation at a conference in Montreal. It will be good to see Henri again.

Henri—she lets herself think about Henri, their last encounter, shortly after her husband left her for that woman in L.A. She pictures a row of candles, like votives in a church. She closes her eyes and feels again the softness of hands, the light pressure of lips. She hears murmurs, moans, confessions of doves. It had only been one night, but as in soap operas and daytime talk shows, one night had apparently been enough.

Lighting a cigarette, she creates a new email message:

Dear Henri,

Will you be at the conference? The one in Montreal? It will be so good to see you again—both of you, I mean.

She takes a short puff on her cigarette without inhaling. Newport Lights have been her therapy of choice since she would sneak them out of her mother's purse.

Fingers pause on the keyboard. Henri and Genevieve must be touring the south of France by now—a trial honeymoon, Henri called it.

She thinks about her own honeymoon with Thomas. They'd gone to Cancun. The undercurrent had carried them out to sea on their inflatable raft. Two Mexican boys rescued them only after Thomas promised them $50 US each when they got back to shore. It had been a bad omen.

I met with my new client today.

His narrative presents some unusual difficulties, as I'm sure you'll appreciate based on your work with similar cases (please see attached file).

For the record, the client's mother told me what she told the detectives: that she had prior knowledge of the primary subject of her son's narrative. I spoke with her on the phone beforehand.

Customarily, she would have suggested having the parent sit in on the first couple of sessions—often, she didn't even have to go that far; the parent simply assumed—but Sandra conveniently had an excuse for any time Selena proposed, vaguely postponing their face-to-face for another date. All the paperwork, she completed online, including the checkbox granting Selena permission to consult as needed with a supervising psychiatrist, who just happens to be Henri.

She knew all about his imaginary friend. He's had him for a very long time, she said. Ever since his father died. She just didn't think he would go so far as he did. She was as surprised as anyone when Leal confessed to the murder—the drowning—of a small boy named Thuster.

She wanted to know how long it would take to make my determination.
I told her it all depends on the client—some sooner, others longer.
She said she just wants it to end—the etcetera.
The etcetera? I asked her what she meant.

You'll find out soon enough, she told me. With Leal, there's always one more thing—one damned thing after another to worry about.

Bottom line: she doesn't want any more trouble with the school authorities. And so she'll keep him coming to see me—at least for as many visits as her insurance allows a dependent. It's not as though she has much choice. He's on probation at school. Attending our sessions is one of the conditions he has to meet to stay enrolled.

Her friend Lori made sure about that. Lori worked as a guidance counselor for the Ovid school system, rotating among two elementary schools, a middle school, and the high school. About once a week, she called Selena with a case she labeled "just too damned complicated for a country mind like mine." Privately, she suspected that Lori was only trying to lighten her workload. Still, she ought to be grateful for the extra business. It was hard setting up practice all over again—especially in a small town like Ovid.

Preliminary diagnosis: magical thinking; false beliefs. I should stipulate the qualifier 'possible,' as the client is both lucid and coherent. Or maybe he just lacks attention. After all, his disruption at school made him a celebrity for a day, even if his name was withheld from the evening news.

She could picture students' mouths opening like sirens without sound, as each received the message in turn and then passed it along in a growing chain:

i killed thuster. i can kill u 2

Zero tolerance. The school went into lockdown. The police were called in. Leal was escorted out the door—all because he had sent a threatening message to the cell phone of a student who had been bullying him.

At this point, all I can really do is probe for hidden trauma.

She takes a moment to snub out the long, lingering ash of the cigarette she has left smoldering in the ashtray, untouched. Idly, she spins the globe of the world that rests on her desk until her finger comes to rest on a group of islands at random: the Seychelles. "Seychelles" rhymes with "seashells," and she can picture playing in the sand on the seashore with her baby-to-be, filling buckets, digging trenches, building castles.

"So what do *you* think, Henri?" she asks aloud.

Any recommendations?

Chapter 2

She observes her roundness in the bath, stomach rising above the surface of the water like a low-lying island. She reviews the rest of her body with dissatisfaction: too long, too angular. With every breath, the water ebbs and flows gently beneath swollen breasts to match her swollen ankles.

She studies her birthmark, a wide, irregular oval above her navel, color of a red, rich wine, imprinted upon the warm brown canvas of her belly, taut and tawny.

Sinking into her tub, she submerges her head, listening to the submarine beating of her heart in her eardrums. She blows out a series of bubbles, feeling her back settle onto the smooth ceramic bottom of the tub.

She can only hold her breath so long.

She imagines a small boy descending through water beneath wavelets moved by wind across the surface of a lake like palm fronds. As he descends, he regresses through time, becoming small and round and dark. His eyes beckon to her bleakly, black pupils like saucers within dark irises. His hands reach toward her, tiny fingers clutching as though at filaments of insubstantial light. Tight, black curls of hair cling closely to a misshapen scalp—the bones crunched by forceps.

And what would he have been like if he had lived? If the doctors hadn't had to extract him out of her—as though excising an overlarge tumor—if he hadn't died in the womb. Months early, he would have been a preemie, but he could have survived. She'd waited until she was ABD with her doctorate, so that would make him seven going on eight years old in just another— she does a minor calculation in her head—three months and thirteen days. Presumably a similar age as this small, silent boy that her new patient is starting to tell her about, so confident that he had been someone real. How terrible that his birth day had been his death day—all in the same instant.

A steady tapping, as of a spoon on a tin can, intrudes upon her consciousness. She brings her head above water, and the vision dissolves. It is only her father, standing outside the bathroom door, knocking gently to come in.

"Helena? Are you in there?"

"It's Selena, Dad."

"Are you going to be much longer? You're going to be late."

Helena had been his wife, her mother. She hates these moments of confusion, even though they never last very long.

At breakfast, his mind is back to an even keel.

"You seem preoccupied," he observes from his side of the round table. And she realizes she's let her bowl of Special K go soggy.

"Sorry, just thinking about a new client."

"The boy from the school? The one who—"

"Yeah, that one."

She takes a sip from her mug and discovers she's let her coffee cool too long, as well.

"Well, don't get your head too wrapped up in it," he advises. "You know how you can get sometimes. Like with that last one—"

"You don't have to remind me." She pours her cereal down the disposal, reheats her coffee in the microwave. It hurts to be forced to recall a case when you lose one, especially one so recent. Paula, the patient in question, a bright girl with curly red hair, her cheeks sprinkled with freckles, was only eleven, bullied and taunted and teased until the pain of change was less than the pain of staying the same. Except the change in this case had involved a bottle of prescription opioids from her mother's shelf of the medicine cabinet. That she had only taken ten pills meant it as a proverbial call for help, but her mother blamed Selena and used the incident as an excuse to pull her daughter out of therapy.

"You should have your license revoked, if you can't prevent an episode like this." These had been the mother's opening words when Selena came to check on her patient at the hospital.

She feels a movement—sharp scissor kick that makes her wince—something definite, something real.

"You all right?" her father asks, knocking his chair back to stand up.

She nods her head, then lowers it toward her belly. She intertwines her fingers below the bulge in her waist.

"Well, hello in there," she whispers in welcome.

***

He likes the idea of the recorder. It makes him think that all of these words won't be wasted. They won't be flying through the air like birds. It would mean all of his words wouldn't come back home. They would be somewhere else. They would be out of his head forever.

As though to underscore the point, a formation of geese bends past the window, angling against a dull gray sky, like the distant wake of a boat. The volume of their *honk-honk-honking* registers on the digital screen of the recording device propped on her desk, as the sound recedes.

"Last time," Leal says, "when I first came here. This room— I thought it would be like a prison. But now—it feels different. It feels more like a cell."

"You mean a jail cell?"

"More like the kind where monks live. You even have pictures. I didn't think there'd be pictures."

Selena wonders if he can tell the Monet from the Bonnard. Probably not. Ovid isn't what you would call a cultural town. No art museum, for one thing. Its closest approach to Broadway: the annual high school play. Her husband had helped her select the paintings from an art gallery when they lived in Chicago. "The Impressionists will make an impression," Thomas had joked. She hadn't corrected him: Bonnard is not an Impressionist. Monet's bridge over lily pads: too symbolic. Maybe replace it soon. She has in mind a Chagall or something more "cultural" to satisfy her brother: maybe that print by Jacob Lawrence of children doing cartwheels.

"I guess I can see how you might think of this as a sort of cell. But you know you're not confined here. You're always free to leave. If you want to, that is. Let's say you didn't like me, or you didn't feel comfortable with how things were going—"

"You mean I could leave?"

"Yes. That's your prerogative. Your—option."

"I could leave right now if I wanted to?"

Of course, she would have to help him find a different therapist, if he wanted to stay in school. This is one of the terms of his probation—for the time being, at least, until she makes her assessment of his ability to keep himself and others safe. But she doesn't feel the need to remind him of this. She figures he already knows.

"Do you want to leave? Would you rather not be here?"

He shifts his position, tucking one leg under the other on the cushion.

"No, ma'am."

"Leal, you know you don't have to call me 'ma'am.'"

He looks at her—direct eye contact this time.

"That's funny," he says.

"What's funny?" Selena asks.

"That's just what Diana told me. She said she didn't like me calling her 'ma'am.' She said it made her feel old."

*

On the banister, a sparrow cocked its eye at them, as they stood side by side on the welcome mat.

"Are you sure this is the house?" Father Mac asked.

Leal pushed the doorbell again.

"Maybe it's broken," Leal suggested.

The sparrow seemed trying to tell them something, a spirit in disguise.

"Do you know where Thuster went?" he asked it before it flew away.

"Maybe we should be going," Father Mac said. "He's probably already back at the parsonage by now."

Now Leal felt doubly guilty. Not only had he lost track of Thuster, he had dragged Father Mac from his duties unnecessarily in an attempt to retrieve him.

"We could try knocking," Leal suggested.

Father Mac sighed. Curling long fingers into a fist, he pulled back his forearm, but the door swung open instead. Diana stood behind the screen, wrapping the ties of a bathrobe around her waist. Uncombed hair hung about her shoulders. Her eyes focused on Father Mac, then dropped to Leal.

"Oh, hello. It's Leal, isn't it?"

"I'm sorry if we woke you," Father Mac apologized.

"Oh, you didn't wake me. Nothing could wake me if I was really asleep. I just thought you were a couple of Jehovah's Witnesses. They've been coming around lately. Don't tell me, Leal, you've taken up saving souls for a living."

"No, ma'am." He wanted to tell her that was Father Mac's job.

"Are you sure about that? Are you sure you're not going to hand me a pamphlet the second I open the door?"

"No, ma'am."

"Leal, you don't have to keep calling me 'ma'am.' It makes me feel old."

*

"So you see?" Leal says to Selena. "She told me the same thing you told me—not to call her 'ma'am.'"

Selena nods her head. She thinks she sees—but not clearly.

*

I didn't know you were a reverend," Diana said when she stepped out onto the porch.

"Priest, more accurately," Father Mac corrected her, giving his collar a tug.

"I should be better dressed. If you want to wait here for a second."

"Don't even think of it," Father Mac said. "You're fine the way you are."

"That's very nice of you to say so." Diana brushed her hair from her forehead. "I'd love to invite you inside, but the place is kind of a wreck. I'd have to clean up a little. I could make some coffee. Or lemonade?"

"That's quite all right," Father Mac said. "We only stopped by because Leland—Leal—had this idea that the boy he was with when he met you—the boy named Thuster—might be here, that's all."

"Thuster," Diana said. "Why would Thuster be here?"

"That's a very good question," Father Mac said.

"Is he missing?"

"No, I wouldn't say that he is missing, exactly. He usually turns up sooner or later."

"But that sounds serious," Diana said. "A boy like Thuster, out on his own."

"He should be fine. Like I said, he usually turns up. He's never away for very long."

"Actually," Diana said, "I'm not really doing anything today.

I'm not saying there aren't things I could be doing, but I wouldn't mind postponing them." She gave Leal a smile. "I could help you look for him. It would only take a couple of seconds to throw on some clothes."

"No," Father Mac rebuffed her. "Thank you for your offer, but I'm sure the boy will turn up, if he hasn't already."

"I can be down in just a second, if you don't mind waiting. I'd like to help."

"Well, I think it would be best if we were to return to the parsonage." Father Mac wrapped an arm around Leal's shoulder. "That is the first place he'll show up when he decides of his own accord to return."

"I'll wait," Leal said adamantly.

Father Mac squeezed Leal's shoulder.

"Leal, I think it would be better if you were to come back with me."

"Great!" Diana said. "I'll be right down."

Father Mac looked around the porch with a critical squint: clay flowerpot with wilted geraniums, rolled-up newspaper on the welcome mat, cross-legged brass Buddha beneath the rusting legs of a barbecue grill. He took in a deep breath, let it rattle free of paper lungs.

"Leland, I only hope you know what it is you're doing."

"Excuse me?"

Father Mac sighed.

"There are many thresholds in life. Some you cross as you come to them. Others are thrown directly in front of you. I'm afraid this is one of the latter."

"Huh?"

Leal still didn't quite get what Father Mac was rambling on about. It sounded like the prelude to a sermonette. The only threshold he was aware of was the one he was waiting for Diana to cross.

"Let me put it another way," he said, sighing. "There are some tests, Leland—I'm sure you can appreciate this—there are some tests that are much harder than you might anticipate. Then there are other tests that you begin to take, and the questions— they just become too hard to answer, no matter how well you think you've prepared, no matter how long you've studied. Your mind goes blank, and you don't have the answers you thought you started with."

"Like math?" Leal suggested.

"Oh, no, Leland. Not like math. Much harder than any math test."

Harder than math? Leal tried to think what could be harder than taking a math test. It's why he was stuck in summer school one never-ending hour three mornings a week.

They studied the street in silence. A car passed by. A boy rode by on a bicycle slinging newspapers onto porches.

"I'll be at the parsonage if you need me. Or else the basket-ball court. All right? I'm sorry I can't wait with you."

He offered a gentle, moist-eyed smile, placing his hand on top of Leal's head, like a blessing. Leal watched him walk slowly down the steps toward the street, left leg limping, right arm stiff at his side.

"What happened to your friend?" Diana asked, coming back.

Leal told her that he had to go back to the parsonage.

"Oh, that's too bad," she said. "I've never really talked with a real, live priest before. Not up close, anyway. Although I must say, there's plenty I could confess."

Leal waited until she tied her hair back with a purple scrunchie.

"Ready?" she said. Her smile showed a half-moon of white teeth, her eyes were dark and shining. She placed her hand on Leal's head and scratched his scalp. He liked the feel of her fingers running though his hair better than he liked Father Mac's blessing. And then they walked off looking for Thuster hand in hand.

*

"Hand in hand?" Selena asks. "Really?"

"Well, maybe not hand in hand exactly," Leal tells her. "But that's how it started to feel. I mean, it's not like I've ever had a girlfriend or anything."

"Is that how you thought of Diana? As a girlfriend?"

"Well, no. Not really." Leal grins with the thought. "I doubt my mom would approve. She keeps telling me I'm going to become girl crazy in a year or two—but there was something about Diana that was driving me crazy right then. I definitely felt something weird going on as I walked with her."

"Weird? How so?"

"It's hard to describe. It felt like an electric current running up my leg like a wire. I'd look at her every now and then, and she'd give me this strange, soft smile. I liked it that her teeth weren't perfectly straight. She had this slight overbite and a tiny gap between her two front teeth. It meant she'd never been forced to wear braces."

Typical adolescent crush, Selena thinks, feeling relieved. At least this aspect of her patient's personality seems within normal parameters.

"Had you ever felt these changes before?" she asks.

"Our first stop was the city park," Leal gushes, racing ahead of the question, "and we went to the fountain—you know the one I mean, where Thuster dipped his hand in before to steal her wish? Well, Diana held out these two shiny pennies, flat on her palm. Her mouth was very close, and she kept saying something over and over, but it took a while for me to make out the words. 'Go ahead,' she kept telling me. 'Make a wish.' And I have to tell you, with her standing so close, I couldn't think of anything else I wanted to wish for. She seemed so much prettier than the three mermaid statues there at the fountain. She placed one of the pennies in my hand and told me to close my eyes. I kept them squinted, though. And looking at her, through my eyelashes, with the sun playing on her hair … I could just imagine her standing there naked like one of the mermaids without wearing any—"

He stops abruptly, turning off the spigot of words.

"Sorry, guess I got a little carried away," he admits, ducking his head sheepishly. "You'll probably want to delete all that." He points out the digital recorder on the desk beside her.

"It's quite all right," Selena reassures him with a smile. "You know, what you were feeling, what you were imagining—it's all perfectly normal for a boy your age."

"That's just the thing," Leal tells her, leaning forward, as though confiding a secret. "I didn't have to use my imagination for long."

*

Their search led them to a crossroads somewhere outside of town, past the town limits sign. Empty, narrow, gravel road with a line of weeds growing between the tire tracks. Woods lined the left-hand shoulder, an open field spread out to the right. A lake glimmered like paint by numbers through a web of branches beyond.

"I don't know," Leal said.

"What don't you know?"

She was standing beside him now, but she wasn't looking where he was looking. She was looking far down the gravel road where it disappeared around a curve.

"I just don't think he would have come down all this way."

"Listen, I know you're worried about your friend. But I have this idea."

"Yeah?" Leal said.

He can't say he likes it when other people have ideas. Especially when they *say* they have ideas. Take his mom, for instance. She comes up with these ideas all the time about moving to a nicer neighborhood where he can go to a better school or quitting her job at the diner so she can spend more time with him or even the two of them taking dance lessons someday, but nothing ever comes of them. No, he can't really say he likes it when other people have ideas.

"There's this friend of mine. He lives only a little farther down this road. And it's a beautiful place that he has. It's this little cottage by a lake. You wouldn't mind seeing where he lives, would you? This little cottage by a lake?"

"I don't know," he said.

Hansel and Gretel, he was thinking. Look what happened to them.

"I haven't seen him in, oh, I really don't know how long it's been. And I know he wouldn't mind us just dropping in like this. I mean, if he's still there. What do you think?"

Leal wasn't sure. He wasn't sure what to make of this whole situation.

"Come on, I'll race you."

And before he knew what she was doing, he saw her running down the middle of the road. And before he knew what *he* was doing, he was running down the road after her. She was a good runner. He's seen other girls run, on the playground, and their arms move side to side like windshield wipers. But she wasn't like these other girls, not at all. She held her arms close to her body, like a track star, and she ran in a straight line, and there was just no way he could catch up with her. But then she lurched forward, and Leal trotted up to where she was a little heap of blue and green holding her knee.

"Looks like you win," she said, looking up, wincing.

"Are you all right?"

"Well, my knee's bruised, as you can see."

And this much was true. Her knee was scratched, pock-marked with flecks of coarse gravel.

"Can you walk?"

"I don't know. I can try."

Leal helped her up. She took a small step and said, "Ow!"

"Is it bad?" he asked.

"I'm not sure," she said.

She took a number of baby steps. Her right foot seemed tender. She didn't want to put much weight on it.

"Not too good, huh?" she asked, coming to a standstill.

She stood in place and shifted more of her weight to the sore ankle. She winced, vertical lines forming between her eyebrows.

"Well," she said. "I know this friend of mine is close by."

This friend again, always this friend.

"That's not too far, is it?" Leal asked. "It's not too far to walk?"

She put her arm around Leal's shoulders, and he put his arm around her waist. His hand on her skin. On her bare hip. He liked the feel of her skin—very soft, like goose down. And then it felt like they were Siamese twins, sharing one leg, and now he knew how hard it must be for Siamese twins to move in a straight line. You'd really have to like your twin.

Around a bend and down a hill, they arrived at a small scrap of a yard, where a man emerged from behind a sheet attached to a clothesline blowing like a flag in the breeze from the lake.

"Diana?" he said, coming up to her.

He wrapped his arms around her. They weren't like Leal's arms—helpful arms, Boy Scout arms. Keeping his hands on her shoulders, the man took a step back, a thin man with a narrow face. An unbuttoned shirt revealed a bony, hairless chest.

"I can't believe it," he kept saying. "I just can't believe it's really you. What are you doing here? How did you get away?"

"Oh," Diana said. "I was walking with my friend here, and it looks like I took a little spill in the roadway."

"What? Are you hurt? Well, let's move you inside, then. What is it? Your ankle? It's not broken, is it?"

"No, it's not broken."

"Well, let's go inside, anyway. Before you disappear on me again, like last time."

"It's only been a couple of weeks."

"Thirteen days to be exact, but who's keeping track?"

"This is the first opportunity I've had to get away."

He helped her up the steps to the cottage, while Leal waited at the bottom—useless. But then Diana turned at the threshold.

The man gave Leal a distant, half-smiling look while holding the door open for Diana.

"I really should introduce you," Diana said. "Leal, this is my friend, Jay."

Leal followed them inside. The first room was a kitchen where Jay seated Diana at the table. He filled a bread wrapper with ice cubes and pressed it against her ankle.

"Ow!" Diana said. "Too hard."

"I'm sorry, dear," Jay said. "I didn't mean to hurt you. That's the last thing on earth I'd want to do."

Dear, dear, dear. He kept fussing over her like an overprotective pigeon.

"I've been meaning to call. I've been after the landlord to install a phone jack, not to mention wi-fi. The cell service out here in the boonies, it's simply atrocious!"

Diana shrugged.

"Not that it would matter," she lamented, with a sad pout of her lower lip.

"What? You mean that brute of a husband still won't let you have your own phone? Couldn't you just purchase a plan in secret?"

"I would if he let me have a credit card to my name. Besides, I'd have to keep it somewhere private."

"What, like a locker at a Greyhound station?"

Diana let out a laugh.

"He rummages through my belongings each night—my drawers, my closet. I don't even bother with a purse anymore. He'd just empty it out, like a prison guard searching for contraband. He scrutinizes the phone bill each month for unknown numbers, so the land line's out."

The conversation was getting too adult for Leal, and no one seemed to notice when he wandered into the other room.

Rows of windows rinsed the room with sunlight. White curtains wavered in the breeze. The room contained only a few pieces of furniture: armchair, easel, table of brushes and paints.

Leal looked at the painting on the easel, a large canvas streaked with blues and purples. He can't say he is very good at art. He only earned Cs in art class. Last school year, an art teacher looked at one of Leal's watercolors and commented, "Your puppy dog looks too much like a puppy dog." Leal asked, "What *should* it look like?" And the teacher had responded, "Exactly. That's the question."

So it took him a while to realize that he was looking at a human shape, but when he saw that it was human, he could see right away that it was a painting of a woman. And after he knew it was a woman, he came to see that she was naked, and suddenly he saw Diana staring out of the painting. It happened all very slowly in his brain, like an optical illusion, one of those cubes that changes its shape depending on which way you stare at it.

"What do you think of it?" Diana asked, coming up behind him.

Leal couldn't say anything. He couldn't make his mouth open or close.

"It's beautiful, don't you think?"

On the lip of the easel sat a 5 x 7 glossy print of Diana in real life. In the photograph, she held much the same pose as on the canvas. Her hair ran like rainwater over her shoulders. Her head was bent, eyes looking out from under long lashes at the camera.

Her breasts were full and white, the nipples dark as plums. Her lips were puffy and pouting like those of a little girl. One hand was on her hip, thrust out in an attitude of defiance. At the same time, she looked young, innocent, like a Girl Scout inviting the viewer to join her in milk and cookies. Except for the two tattoos.

"It doesn't bother you, does it?" Diana asked.

"I'm sorry?" Leal said.

"Seeing me nude?"

"Well," Jay said, lifting the photograph from its resting spot. He measured the photograph of Diana against the painting, closing one eye, as though sighting along the barrel of a gun. Then he tore it down the middle, separating Diana into halves. He dropped the halves into a wastebasket. "I guess I won't be needing this anymore."

*

"And Thuster?" Selena asks.

"What?" Leal responds, coming out of daydream.

"You were looking for Thuster."

Leal blinks twice, as though batting away a piece of lint with his eyelashes.

"Oh. Well, when we went back to Diana's house, Saul was playing with Thuster in the front yard. He was pushing Thuster in a tire swing hanging from a tall branch of a tree. A cigar tree, I think. You know, a catalpa. There's a story about how it got its name. This little Italian woman had a cat that was stuck in a tree, and when the firemen arrived, she kept running around shouting, 'Helpa, helpa, helpa the cat. Cat helpa!'"

Selena can tell he's waiting for a reaction, but she doesn't give him what he's seeking. She withholds even the hint of a smile.

"Anyway," he continues flatly after letting out a breath,

"Thuster was sitting in the hole in the tire, holding onto the rope with both hands, and Saul stood behind him giving him push after push."

"Were you happy to see him?"

"Thuster? Sure. I mean, yes. I was."

Leal tilts his head against the back of the couch. He stares at the ceiling.

"The first thing I did, though, was look into his eyes to make sure there was nothing wrong."

"What did you think might be wrong?"

"There didn't seem to be anything wrong. In fact, it was just the opposite. I couldn't remember when I had ever seen his eyes so bright and shining. It almost seemed like he was smiling."

"What did you think might be wrong?" she asks again, and Leal straightens up into a sitting position.

"You know how it is. All the moms are always telling you never to play with strangers."

"And Saul was a stranger?"

"It didn't look like there was anything wrong. It would've been hard to tell with Thuster, anyway. But he seemed all right. It's just that I'd never seen his eyes look so bright as they did that afternoon. I didn't know what to make of it, and then I saw Saul's eyes."

"Saul's eyes?"

"I can't really explain it. He was staring at the whole scene with bright eyes, too. Except in his case it was like there was a bomb ticking away behind them."

***

It's only eight o'clock, but she's already changed into her sleeping clothes, a baggy, cottony thing with imprints of flowers. She'll have to start buying onesies and booties soon. Against her wishes, Lori wants to throw her a baby shower, so maybe she'll wait until after to shop. There's a space she's cleared out in a corner for the crib, on order through Ikea. She hasn't decided on a décor. Lion King, she'll think one day. Winnie-the-Pooh, the next. There's a third bedroom in the house, unused, but it's on open reserve for her brother whenever he drops in.

Without inhaling, she takes a quick puff of her cigarette and sets it aside.

Dear Henri,

It is too early to call it progress, of course. But I feel we made head-way today.

She types slowly, feeling the keys the way a pianist might tinker with fragments of a song. It's difficult maintaining a professional tone with her former mentor. At first, they had been no more than professor-student, a relationship that within two semesters mu-tated into lovers minus the *quid pro quo*. Before she finished her coursework, however, she started dating Thomas, Henri obtained a tenured position in Montreal, and their sexting devolved into mundane emails about her work in progress on her dissertation.

How should I describe it? Delusional syndrome? False memory? Antisocial defense mechanism? Sociopathic power play? The conditions for transference are still insufficient at this point, although I can feel an easing of barriers as he begins to view me as an actual person, rather than a sounding board. My primary suspicion is sexual trauma. I need to talk to Leal's mother about his early relationship with his father. The father may be the key.

The detectives assured me once more that the case has been perma-nently closed.

She had stopped by the police station after her session with Leal. She asked one of the detectives, a bleach-blonde woman who had handled Leal's case, if he had mentioned Saul and Diana Solomon when she interviewed him.

"You mean, the Chinchilla King and Queen?" she laughed.

"We would have remembered that."

"Funny you should mention him," her partner, an older man with a gray goatee masking a weak jaw, pitched in.

It turned out Saul had been served a subpoena to submit his ledgers to a grand jury. His alleged criminal activity: embezzlement of his company's retirement fund.

Here's something else: I will be unable to verify the client's testimony—at least for the time being—with Father Timothy MacDougal, emeritus, semi-retired. According to the diocese, he is in the process of establishing residency with a small parish in Florida. The number they gave me, however, was unavailable. I couldn't even leave a voice message.

Personal note: I believe Leal believes his own narrative. I must, however, consider the elements of his narrative as a symbolic representation of deeper trauma. He is hiding something. The narrative is only a thin veneer.

Strategy: Everyone has a story to tell, as you're so fond of reminding me. Should I just let him tell his?

*

Her father's voice calls her from his room.

"Coming!" she shouts across the hallway.

She has forgotten to help him refill his pill organizer. There are too many pills, even though color-coded, to keep straight in his mind. And some of them need to be cut in half to avoid a double dose. It is time for his medication.

Chapter 3

In a clinic in town, a nurse hands Selena a backless gown into which to change. He points out a privacy screen to the right of the small lime-green room that smells as sterile as a bottle of formaldehyde. Selena contemplates the examination table, its two steel stirrups looking like the relics of a medieval torture chamber.

As the nurse leaves the room, Lori barges in.

"Whazzup, homeslice? How's my bae today?"

Selena has to smile. Lori always tries just a little too hard to connect with what she assumes is universal Black vernacular. Or is she just playing? It's hard to tell with her sometimes. Just like Selena, she is so *not* ghetto.

Fist bump concluded, Lori plops into a bright orange plastic chair without legs shaped like half a bucket—a cheap attempt at Art Deco. Symbolically, it looks like a womb, and she has to wriggle to make herself fit its contours. It has an empty twin next to it that looks oddly inviting, even though it must be an ant trap for pregnant women.

"I'm not looking forward to this," Selena says, unpackaging the paper gown and holding it up to view as though it represents a flag of surrender.

Lori suspends her gyrations for the moment.

"If you're going to be embarrassed, I can leave."

"You know what I mean," Selena frowns.

"Just when I was starting to feel comfortable. I don't suppose they let you smoke in here."

This time, Selena lets out a laugh.

"That's better," Lori says. "I was afraid you'd lost your sense of humor."

"That's not what I'm afraid of losing," Selena says, stepping behind the changing screen. She's tall enough to peek over it to maintain eye contact with Lori.

"You'll be fine. You're too old to be worried about something like that."

"That's just what I'm afraid of—I'm too old."

"If you're too old, then I'm too old, too."

"I'm considered high risk."

"I like what you've done with your hair." Typical Lori—changing the topic before it gets too deep.

Selena decides to play along, relieved in a way to contemplate a more commonplace subject.

"I'm thinking of letting it frizz."

"Too hard to manage?"

"Wash-and-go would be so much easier."

"Listen to us. We sound like a commercial for salon products."

"That's us. Two talking heads."

They had been friends since high school. Selena had played center in basketball. Lori was a cheerleader, shaking her pom-poms from the sidelines. And this about summed up their relationship to each other—the one always cheering the other one on, as first, Selena left Ovid, then graduated from college, not just once but thrice (while Lori stayed behind to go to community college), and somewhere in there got married, and then pregnant, and then—well, that was another story altogether.

"Listen," Lori says. She opens her purse and prods through its contents with the tips of long red fingernails. "I know what you went through in Chicago. This time, things will be different. You'll see."

Selena isn't so sure. Back in Chicago, she underwent an ultrasound on three separate occasions. The first time around, the results had been fine: normal heartbeat, normal growth, normal movement. The second time had identified the fetus as a boy. But the third visit had failed to detect a heartbeat, confirming what she already knew. And then the doctors had "evacuated" the contents of her uterus—their term for the procedure, making it sound as glamorous as suctioning a septic tank.

It had taken her five years to work up the courage to try again, an experiment with embryology that resulted in a miscarriage—not to mention the eventual death of her marriage—and here was Lori, trying to convince her about the charm of third chances.

"I wish I had your confidence."

"I wish I had your figure. What? No cravings?"

"Plenty."

"Chocolate and pickles?"

"More like meatballs, mozzarella, and mini marshmallows by the handful."

"Not your usual macrobiotic diet."

"This little fetus is so not vegan."

"It's still hard to tell you're pregnant."

"Only when I wear loose clothing." She comes out from behind the screen and performs an awkward twirl. "Ta-da! This gown isn't too suggestive?"

Maybe Lori was right. Maybe humor *is* the answer. If only she could use it to tuck away images that have been swarming through her imagination for weeks: fetuses with every imaginable defect possible, an aquarium filled with mocking, twisting specimens, like jellyfish in a jar.

"How are things going with your new patient?" Lori asks.

"You mean Leal?"

"That's right. Leal the Eel."

"Oh, are they still calling him that?"

Lori lets out a laugh, but Selena doesn't smile. All through grade school, she had been subjected to the occasional shove from behind or slur—usually uttered in an undertone when passing in the halls—from some of the meaner kids. Even the nice kids treated her differently as though she were something fragile they were given to handle, like a raw egg. Or else she was regarded as something exotic, rare. She remembers the girls, and even some boys, who always wanted to touch her hair to feel its springiness, no matter the efforts she begged her mother to make at home to straighten it.

"About as well as can be expected," she responds, checking out her figure in the mirror, as though evaluating a new dress she's tried on at a department store.

"No breakthroughs yet?"

"Not yet."

"I'm not surprised. He's a tough case. Slippery, he is. Squirms his way out of trouble."

"Like an eel?"

"I'm half tempted to place him in special ed whether he qualifies or not. Just to get him out of my hair."

As though acting on a subliminal impulse, she stands up to check her appearance, joining Selena in the mirror. Before Selena can ask her if she's truly serious, the door swings inward admitting the doctor—a specialist provided by the hospital, not her usual OB-GYN, who is on vacation.

"Hello, Mrs. Harris, is it?"

She looks at Selena critically over the tops of her black-framed glasses.

"No," Selena corrects her. Technically, she's a doctor, but in this situation, she prefers, "Just Ms."

Better to start thinking of herself as completely separated, even though the divorce hasn't gone through. At least she had the foresight to retain her maiden name, which makes it easier.

"What about the ring?" Selena asks, holding up her wedding band for inspection.

"It's sound waves," the doctor explains, as Selena hefts herself up on the table, "not magnetic imaging."

"Oh," Selena emits a sigh, as the procedure begins. She was hoping for an excuse to remove it altogether. "Let me take it off anyway." Better now than later, when her fingers would get too thick to allow it to come off short of amputation. Even so, it takes her an impatient minute to wriggle it free.

***

In her office, she is still studying the ultrasound photograph as Leal takes his seat. The technician had used a computerized stylus to draw a thin, white arrow aimed at its head, as though to label it "This Side Up." She keeps trying to make out its face: eye sockets, nostrils, seam of its mouth.

The photo, slick and grainy, is curled about the edges, the fetus curled tightly, too. So small, so tiny—the size of her thumbprint. A girl is what the doctor suspected based on the hamburger-in-a-bun. A boy would be a clear hot dog. But the outcome was still inconclusive. She told her about cases that had turned out to be a boy—not so much the other way around.

"What's that?" Leal asks, settling into his couch.

"Just a photograph," Selena replies, setting it on the desk beside her chair, face down.

"Family photo?"

"Yes," Selena smiles, "you could say that."

"Oh," Leal says, studying the back of his hand.

Selena waits for his eyes to come back to her, but they drift away like lily pads on a pond.

"About last time," he says. "What I was telling you—about Diana's picture?"

Now he is looking at the carpet, narrowing his eyes, as though tracing the path of an insect across the floor.

"There's something I left out. I didn't tell you I stole it."

"The picture?"

Selena's eyes go to the floor, as well.

"Not the painting. The photograph. Out of the trashcan."

She tries to see what Leal is looking at.

"Really? On impulse?"

"Yeah, but I didn't feel too good about stealing it—afterward."

"Oh? And how *did* it make you feel? At the time?"

She squints more closely, wondering if she should renew her contacts prescription.

"Guilty," he admits. "I guess I felt guilty."

Good, Selena thinks. Now we might be getting somewhere. But why would he feel guilty?

"You know, picking something out of the garbage isn't exactly stealing."

"Oh, I didn't feel guilty about taking it," Leal clarifies. "I felt guilty about looking at it."

*

Leal couldn't get over the fact that she was naked.

"Nude," he said aloud, correcting his thought, using the term Diana had used, passing the photograph to Thuster. "The correct term is 'nude.'"

Thuster didn't seem to care, and when it came down to it, neither did Leal. The fact of the matter was she didn't have any clothes on.

Leal crouched next to a fire he had built on the edge of a garbage dump, adding pieces of cardboard. It was a local dump with trash delivered weekly, so there were always fresh pickings.

He watched Thuster walk off, carrying the photograph of

Diana, studying her heavenly form. He wouldn't let go of her, after Leal had passed it to him. But that didn't matter. He would get it back. He could easily take it back from someone like Thuster.

Leaving the fire, Leal prodded through piles of garbage with the tip of a stick. Finding a broken pair of eyeglasses, he closed one eye and looked through the lens that was still intact. It made Thuster seem even farther away and very small. Poking around, he pulled out a strand of pearls. He looped the string around his neck.

Looking through the single lens, he tried taking a couple of steps but tripped and plopped onto a fresh pile of junk. Reaching around to find what had tripped him, he produced an umbrella. He opened it over his head, long metal legs of a spider, shreds of fabric clinging like cobwebs on a skeleton.

He felt something sharp that turned out to be the metal clasp of a yellow rubber boot. For a lark, he pulled the boot over a tennis shoe to see if it would fit.

"Thuster!" Leal called out. The sun was setting pink and gold behind a stand of trees flattened black against the sky like a row of fence posts. He could only make out Thuster in silhouette, as quiet as a sentinel, standing next to the outline of an abandoned refrigerator. "Come over here! By the fire!"

By the time Thuster returned, the moon, a thick wedge of silver, had risen above the trees, as though on a wire. In the moonlight, he stared at the photograph of Diana, holding it in both hands by its edges. Leal peered over his shoulder to make sure the photograph was still intact. The two halves of her face were slightly mismatched along a jagged seam where he had taped it back together.

Leal bent down and added another piece of cardboard to the fire.

Wearing the string of pearls and the broken eyeglasses, holding the umbrella over his head, his foot in a yellow rubber boot, he gave his impersonation of Ms. Jacobson a try, doing his best to imitate one of her across-the-desk harangues: "You need help, young man. Serious help. More help than I can give you here in this office."

*

Selena makes a mental note of his impersonation of Lori. She wonders if it would be an ethical violation to tell Lori about this part of her patient's narrative when she sees her next. They might enjoy a laugh over it—or not. Lori is always so sensitive about her appearance. She might not like knowing that Leal was making fun of her behind her back.

*

Leal looked down at Thuster to see if his lecture produced any impression, but Thuster, cross-legged before the fire, kept his eyes on the photograph, presumably studying the contours of Diana's body.

"Thuster," he said, very softly, very quietly, crouching next to him. "Thuster, is it okay if I look at the picture, too?"

But Thuster didn't look up. He didn't look at Leal. It was hard to tell if he even heard the question.

Leal stared into the fire. After a while, he said, again very softly, "Can I have the photograph back now, please?"

The fire crackled. A tall green flame shot out, making a popping sound. Leal lurched backward, in case something in it decided to explode—like a battery full of acid—but Thuster remained stationary, unflinching.

Turning back toward Thuster, he took hold of the photograph by its top edge, fingers like a pair of tweezers.

"It's all right, Thuster. It's okay. I'll give it right back. I promise."

He tugged at the picture, applying gentle pressure, and gradually, gradually—ever so slightly less than gradually—Thuster let it slide out of his fingers … fingertips …. until he was left staring after it through his empty hands.

And then, before Leal could react, Thuster reached out for the photograph again and grabbed it.

"No, Thuster. No!"

In the tug of war that ensued, Diana—naked, nude—stared at the contest, her eyes separated by the uneven fault line where the photograph had been put back together. Her eyes seemed to reprimand Leal, making him feel guilty for trying to take her away from Thuster. As though letting Thuster choose a card in a game of Old Maid, he reluctantly let go of the photograph.

"It's all right, Thuster. You can have it."

Quietly, Thuster turned the photograph over in his hands. He looked at the back of it. Then he turned it around to the front side. Over and over.

"But just for a little while," Leal added.

The shadows of the trees closed in. The twilight was quiet and still.

Thuster held the photograph low over the flames of the fire, dancing above a bed of hot coals.

"Careful," Leal said. "Don't get it too close."

Still staring at the photograph, Thuster's eyes reflected sharp orange points of flame.

His hands jerked once—twice.

Leal reached his hand toward the photograph, but he was too late. The flames were too high, the fire too hot.

As Leal watched, the photograph bubbled, flames curling around the edges. Diana still smiled her soft, crooked smile, but her eyes were very far away and lost. It seemed as though she were looking at someone that she loved very much but whom she would never see again. Flames tickled through the center of the photograph and peeled away her face. The eyes stared out at Leal very calmly until all that was left was her smile, and then even that was gone.

As Thuster stood up from the fire, Leal flopped down on a mound of compressed tin cans. He set aside the spidery umbrella, took off the broken eyeglasses, removed the strand of pearls.

He struggled with the yellow rubber boot, and his shoe came off inside it, as he suspected it might.

He sat until the fire faded into red embers and the shadows of the trees stretched across the mounds of trash. He couldn't be absolutely sure, but it seemed to Leal, sitting there in the darkness, that Thuster might have been crying.

*

"Thuster was crying?" Selena asks.

"Yeah. I believe so."

"And what were you doing when Thuster was crying?"

"Doing?"

"What was your reaction? How did you react when you saw he was crying?"

"Oh, I was crying too. Not right then. I cried later. At least, I think I cried. I'd have to think to remember. But any crying I ended up doing would've been put on hold. I had to take a phone call first."

"A phone call?"

"Yeah, my phone buzzed. In my pocket. It was Father Mac. Inviting me to spend the night."

This information makes Selena sit up as straight as she can manage with a fetus inside her as though jolted by an electric current beneath her seat.

"He thought I might enjoy a hot breakfast in the morning instead of the usual cold Pop-Tart I'd eat at home," Leal continues nonchalantly, as though this makes obvious sense. "Besides, my mom wasn't going to be home. She was sleeping overnight at one of her boyfriend's."

"And where did you sleep … overnight?" Selena can't help but wonder.

"Next to Thuster. On a mat. On the floor."

"Which floor? In which room?"

"The bedroom, of course." He gives her a cockeyed look, as though she has asked the most absurd question ever. "The parsonage only has the one."

"This was your first time?"

"Oh, no. I'd been staying overnight for as long as I can remember. Well, almost as long. Ever since my dad died."

"And your mother approved?"

"She's the one who suggested it. It saved her the cost of a babysitter. She liked it when I stayed over. It meant she didn't have to worry about me being home all alone."

Selena can't help but give him a dead-on look, as though inspecting a precious vase for imperfections, thin-veined rifts, shallow clefts. But Leal returns her gaze calmly, serenely, without flinching.

Internally, she scolds herself. Maybe she's jumping to conclusions on the basis of stereotypes fostered by a slew of outbreaks in recent years. You can't scroll through a newsfeed these days without running across an item involving a priest and a minor, however cold the case.

Nevertheless, this is the kind of revelation that would normally motivate her to contact Social Services, just to have them check on the situation and make sure everything was above board. But with the priest having relocated, there doesn't seem much point to the exercise.

Besides, it isn't as though her patient is making an allegation. And with his only being thirteen years old, she can understand his mother being a little leery of leaving him alone overnight at home unsupervised.

"It must have been quite the adventure for you," Selena comments, still scrutinizing Leal's expression, his demeanor, for cracks, fissures, points of entry. "Spending the night."

"Yeah, maybe. When I was little. But then it got to be pretty routine."

"Do you miss those nights? Sleeping over?"

"Sort of," he remarks and squirms in his seat. "Can I go now?"

There, she thinks. *Just the chink in his exterior I was looking for.*

***

This night, Selena plays a game of backgammon with her father. She moves her pieces carelessly, without hesitation, as soon as she rolls the die. In contrast, her father studies his moves carefully, scrutinizing the board, considering and reconsidering various combinations.

His movements are slower because of the stroke, but it could have been worse. A slight droop of an eyelid, a hairpin curve of his mouth, a stiffness from his shoulder to his fingers—these are the only telltale signs. Several weeks of physical therapy erased the rest of the evidence of an illness that had initially immobilized the entire left side of his body.

Growing up, she had always thought of her father as a Cosby Dad. Of course, a criminal conviction had ruined that association forever. Plus, it had been her mother who was the physician—although one who couldn't "heal thyself."

Nevertheless, her father had always been calm, kind, compassionate—ready to applaud his son as he fumbled at chords on a toy piano or play a game of H-O-R-S-E with his daughter on the driveway half-court or tape up a wounded knee whenever their mother was on call at the hospital. But that was then.

Now, following the stroke, with the rewiring of his brain making his thoughts a bit of a jumble, he often seems a stranger.

"You shouldn't be smoking," he reminds her between moves, even though she never smokes in front of her father, keeping her pack of cigarettes locked in a drawer in her bedroom. And now with a baby on the way—she's reduced her intake to a stingy single cigarette a day. Nothing to harm the baby. In fact, she snuffs it out in an ashtray almost as soon as she's lit it. A portable fan on her desk dissipates secondhand smoke. It's just that after the separation, cigarettes had been her main source of comfort. And when she found out she was pregnant, it was like giving up a beloved helpmate or friend. "What would your mother have to say about it?"

Selena winces at one of his favorite refrains ever since his wife, their mother, had died. Maybe it still produced an effect on her brother, who ever since he dropped out of high school, post-GED, used their childhood home as a way station, a safe haven, between gigs.

Besides, he had ten times the bad habits—and smoking cigarettes was the least of them. The last she heard from him, he was recording with a garage band he had joined in St. Louis as a replacement bassist—not his instrument of choice, but when opportunity knocks …

"I shouldn't have to breathe your secondhand smoke. I can smell it from under your door, you know." Obviously, the air freshener isn't doing its job. "It's bad for the baby."

He makes his move, taking out three of her pieces, removing them to the bar dividing the board. Sensing victory, he runs his fingers across a Brillo pad of graying hair. Not for the first time Selena wonders how he ever got so old. The stroke seems to have aged him even further.

Passing Selena the die, he studies the backs of his hands, assessing, it would seem, their steadiness.

"You know what, Dad? We should go on a cruise."

Her father regards her with skepticism hurdling the top of his eyeglasses frame. "What kind of cruise."

"There's this one I checked into. It's only three days. It leaves from Ft. Lauderdale and goes around the Caribbean, stopping at Grand Cayman and—" She takes a second to open a saved screen on her phone. "Cozumel."

"One island rich, the other one poor," her father surprises her with knowledge of the economies of islands.

"I suppose, but I was thinking it would be nice for us to get away somewhere."

Plus, talk about two birds with one stone, she could check the residence the diocese gave her for Father Mac, find out from the source about Thuster, dispel from her brain the notion he might actually have been someone real.

"You wouldn't like it," her father says, frowning, lowering his eyes to the board and picking up the die for another roll. "They don't allow smoking on board those kinds of ships anymore."

***

Dear Henri,

I believe my father's condition is worsening—his mental condition, I mean. More and more, I have the sense he is moving farther and farther away. I feel I am playing games with a stranger.

Fathers: they're always the key, aren't they?

Speaking of fathers, Leal's mother Sandra called tonight with some information about Leal's. She called earlier this time, around eleven o'clock—if you can call that early. I always feel so tired these days—run down—obsolete, like an antique clock. And like clockwork, she makes sure to call after every session.

She asked how this one had progressed, and I told her I needed more time to work with him. This seemed to annoy her, and she told me she would remove him from the school altogether if she could. But what would she do, home school him? Working double shifts at the diner, she didn't have time in her schedule for that.

I told her it is too bad Ovid doesn't have any charter schools nearby. Has she considered the private academy here in town?

At this, she sniffed in contempt. Just like us high-paid professionals not to know the salary a waitress brings home. It was the same reason she couldn't just pick up and move to a different town—money.

I was so tempted to ask if this was the reason she let Leal spend the night at Father Mac's from time to time, but I refrained. I didn't feel the moment was apropos.

She described her son as a loner. He was always very private, even as a small child. He had been known to create stories before. For example, in kindergarten, for show and tell, you know what he did? He told his classmates his mother had murdered his father, sabotaged the brake lining of his car, causing a fatal accident. Isn't that something?

In fact, she claims she had been the subject of an investigative probe by Child Protective Services, but insufficient evidence had been produced warranting intervention.

Selena understood the hidden message. Sandra didn't want a repeat experience. She didn't want to go through this kind of ordeal all over again. But just in case Selena didn't get the hint, she came out point blank and called her son a "little boy who cries wolf."

Take the alleged accident, for instance. It never happened. Did Selena want to know the truth? Well, her husband had been a traveling salesman, and whenever Sandra had to work late shifts at the diner, he'd sometimes offer to take young Leal on the road with him to avoid the cost of a babysitter. It was always an adventure for Leal. He loved traveling with his father, going from town to town, staying in cheap motels. The last time he went along, however, only the boy came back alive.

"What happened to his dad?" Selena asked.

"He was electrocuted," was the straightforward reply.

"Electrocuted? How?"

"Apparently, the fool was drying his hair while taking a bath."

What possessed him to do something so risky, so life-threatening, Sandra didn't know. But there you have it. And it wasn't even Leal who found him that way. He was under the covers asleep when in walks some strange woman, some trollop or other, who discovered him and called the police.

"Well, that created quite a scene for Leal, let me tell you. Waking up to find out his father just died in the very hotel room he was sleeping in. It changed him, Dr. Harris. It changed him somehow. He wasn't the same boy after that. And he's never been the same since."

"Who was the woman?" Selena asked.

"Who knows? Some tramp. Some whore, excuse my expression. I'd long suspected my husband was having affairs on the road. But to actually have a woman in the same room with Leal. I can't tell you how that made me feel. I can never forgive the bastard—again, pardon by French. But I could never forgive him for doing something like that—never."

"And the woman?"

"She told the police her story and stuck to it—that she just happened to be passing by, noticed the lights flicker, heard a loud scream—so there was no suspicion of foul play."

"Almost like Willy Loman," Selena said her thought aloud, conjuring in her mind a scene from the play.

"Willy who?"

"No one," Selena apologized.

"Moral of the story: You can't believe anything he tells you."

"Not even in the privacy of my office?" Selena asked, begging the question.

Sandra paused on her end of the conversation for a moment, exhaling a long stretch of breath.

"Especially not there. Just what has he been telling you anyway?"

"Nothing significant so far. We're still in a getting-to-know-you phase."

"Good," she said, "good." But Selena could tell by the tone of her voice that her answer hadn't completely reassured her.

*

So, tell me, Henri ...

Selena takes a moment to pull a cigarette out of its pack. She rolls it between thumb and forefinger, studying the computer screen, then sets it aside, unlit, and goes back to her message.

How are things with you?

Chapter 4

When he takes his seat this time around, he opens a magazine he carried in from the lobby, an outdated copy of *Highlights for Children* she had set out for the perusal of much younger patients. She wonders what he can possibly see of interest. Or is he regressing to early childhood as he flips through the pages?

She has a rule about cell phones, but aside from the first visit, when she asked him to put an outmoded flip-phone away, he hasn't attempted to challenge her as other young patients have done on subsequent visits. She hasn't implemented the same rule about magazines—yet.

"I was wondering if we could talk about Father Mac," Selena suggests.

She waits for a response, but Leal turns to another page, magazine flat on his lap.

"Leal?"

"Yeah," he says without looking up, "I heard you."

"Would you say that you had a close relationship with Father Mac?"

Again—silence. No response, as he studies the Hidden Pictures puzzle.

"Leal?"

"Yeah. I guess so."

"How did you view Father Mac?"

"View him?" he asks, eyes glancing up like fencing swords.

"What I mean to say is—did you see him as a friend?"

"No. Not really." His eyes return to the puzzle on his lap. "I mean, he was pretty old."

"Maybe you saw him as a father figure?"

"Figure?"

He sets the magazine aside, spread out on the couch, but he keeps his eyes on the puzzle. Selena has to admit, she's curious, too, about the objects that might be hidden there—in plain sight but camouflaged within the surrounding scene.

"A substitute father? Someone who could replace the father you lost?"

"I don't know. Maybe. I do know one thing, though."

Selena leans forward, as he lowers his voice.

"He didn't like me spending time with Diana."

"No?"

Leal looks up.

"He called it fraternizing."

"Fraternizing? Really?" Selena represses a smile.

"I think that's the word he used. He said I shouldn't be fraternizing with a woman almost twice my age."

Privately, Selena agrees.

*

Every morning, he stopped by the parsonage to pick up Thuster, but they didn't go to the fountain in the park anymore. One day became two, then two days became three. Two more days, and Leal began measuring time in weeks. After the second week, he could label it a new routine.

There was summer school to attend. He needed to make up a math class. But it was only one class, and Thuster waited for him outside on the school steps. If Leal looked out the window when the teacher's back was turned, he could still keep his promise to Father Mac by keeping an eye on him—just one eye—while Mr. Birch scribbled endless formulas on the whiteboard, adding and subtracting and multiplying until he was literally out of breath, bringing out a handkerchief to wipe a bead of sweat from his brow, his fingers smeared with red and green marker ink. Leal pretended to jot them down.

Secretly, though, he was composing notes for Diana. Love notes that he crumpled and threw away as soon as the class was over. And Thuster would always be waiting for him, sitting with his knees drawn up to his chest, hands clasped about his legs. He was good that way about waiting—like a loyal dog.

After Leal's class, they would go to the lake. They would play outside while Diana posed for Jay. Leal would peer through the windows, but he could never find cracks wide enough between curtains, and the translucent fabric would tease the senses, permitting him to perceive only dim outlines, wavering shadows. So they waded along the shore or tossed rocks in the water. Sometimes Leal would idly flip through photos on his phone, looking up from time to time to make sure Thuster hadn't waded too far into the lake or disappeared into the woods. None of the photos, he's sad to report, were of Diana—clothed or unclothed.

Diana and Jay would break for lunch, and they would have a picnic near the cattails, except on rainy days, when Leal and Thuster would be invited inside, but the canvas was always covered with a burlap sack, and if Leal asked to see the painting, Diana and Jay would exchange looks, and Diana would tell Leal maybe next time—it was always next time.

"It's because he's an artist," Diana explained to him once. "You know, a sensitive type. He doesn't like displaying his work to the pubic before it's finished."

"And I'm the public?" Leal asked.

"John Q.," Diana confirmed.

Two weeks turned into three, and then one morning, Leal noticed something different when he stopped by the parsonage to pick up Thuster.

Brochures were scattered atop the kitchen table showing

photos of pink magnolias, ice-blue lakes, white-capped waves, tan beaches, bikini-clad women. A map was Scotch-taped to the wall showing the coastline of Florida. A string of beaches had been marked with color-coded straight pins: Boca Raton, West Palm, Delray, Juno, Jupiter; as though the Good Father was playing connect-the-dots with the pinpoints of beaches.

Thuster sat silently at the table, unmoving, staring at the cover of one of the brochures with empty, hollow eyes—not lifeless eyes, like a toad's, but steady eyes, full of a distant, strange life of their own. Leal could only stand outside the barbed-wire fence of Thuster's mind, his inner world, watching his own reflection in the circles of dark irises and even darker pupils.

"Father," Leal asked, "are you taking a trip?"

Father Mac was busy at the kitchen counter, slicing an onion with a long, sharp knife. The aroma filled the room, stinging Leal's eyes. He waited patiently while Father Mac poured a swig of olive oil into a pot on the stove. It wasn't until he scraped the slices of onion into the bottom of the pot so that they sizzled and popped that he turned to face Leal.

"Oh, the brochures?" Father Mac replied. "Yes, they all came at once in the mail today. Federal Express. My brother-in-law sent them. Did I tell you I have a brother-in-law living in Florida? Boca Raton. My sister, dear soul, died three years ago this coming Thursday."

He took a package of roast beef from the refrigerator, began carving it into strips. Then he added the strips to the pot, building his infamous Irish stew one layer at a time. In fact, Leal couldn't remember a time when he had stopped by and a pot of stew wasn't bubbling on the stove.

"I'm sorry, Father."

"Please don't be. She lived a good life. The cancer went into remission seven years, then came back with a vengeance. God's will, you know."

Leal crossed his heart and hoped to die. If his mom had been here, she would have teased him: "You're not even Catholic." And he wasn't—not really. St. Mary's had been just a convenient place to dump him on her way to the diner when she had to work a Sunday shift. "Will you be leaving soon?"

"No, not too soon. Hopefully, by the end of summer. I have a few loose ends to wrap up."

Opening a cabinet, he selected four or five spices, sprinkling their contents onto the steaming onions and meat.

Leal listened to the time on the kitchen clock, studied the plastic Jesus on His nail above the stove.

"There's something I need to tell you before you go," Father Mac said, cutting up a potato into quarters and eighths. "I've recently had an opportunity to speak with your mother."

"My mother?"

"You turned out to be the subject of quite a little conversation. I don't mind saying that your mother is just a little worried about you. I tried to reassure her, but you know how mothers can be. We talked about the state of your soul."

"My soul?"

He was a little surprised that his mom and Father Mac had spent any amount of time talking about his soul. They could have discussed the state of his liver just the same.

Father Mac dumped the plate of potato wedges into the pot, then focused his attention on a green pepper, defenseless on the cutting board.

"Please, Leland. Don't look so forlorn. Is that a tear I spy?"

"It's just the smell of the onion." Leal wiped his eyes with his shirtsleeve. "I'll try to be in Church this Sunday, Father. I really will."

"That's not what I meant when I said we were worried about your soul. The Church is only an Institution. Your Soul, on the other hand, is a living, breathing, personal part of your being. It's the functioning of your Soul, in conjunction with the operation of your Body and Mind, which gives us the most reason for concern."

He turned back to the stove to dispose of the diced green peppers.

"Don't you think this has gone on long enough?"

"Father?"

Father Mac began agitating the pot with a long wooden spoon.

"This business with Diana."

"Diana?"

Even Thuster looked up at the mention of Diana, but Father Mac continued stirring the pot without interruption.

"I believe you introduced me to her as Diana."

"Father, you didn't tell my mom about Diana?"

Father Mac set the ladle aside. Leaning over to study the gas flame, he made a small adjustment of a knob on the stove.

"Let me just say that it came up in conversation, in passing. You see, it's the people with whom we surround ourselves that help make us who we are. We must always choose our friends, our playmates, carefully, very carefully."

"Yes, Father."

Diana—he couldn't believe Father Mac had narced on him to his mom about Diana.

Leal watched as Father Mac pulled a bottle of rum from the top shelf of the cupboard and poured a quarter of its contents into the bubbling pot of stew.

It was the secret ingredient—one he kept from the rest of the civilized world—that gave the stew its flavor, Father Mac had explained. A secret only he and Leal shared, like Thuster. But this time, watching the priest tend to his stew as he had on dozens of occasions, rather than anticipation, Leal felt nothing but nausea and asked to be excused.

*

Late that night, he heard his mom's car pull up to the curb. A second car with a louder engine followed, so there was a chance she would be too busy in the bedroom to bother him tonight. Car doors banged shut like garbage can lids, and then he heard their laughter, his mom's fluttering flutelike, the man's a bellowing bassoon.

As they climbed the stairs, he pulled the covers around his shoulders. He heard a soft knock at his door. "Leal?"

She knocked again, more loudly. Her voice was louder, too. "Leal? Okay to come in?"

He didn't respond. He lay rigid as any corpse, until she opened the door a crack and yellow light bled into the room from the hallway.

"Are you awake?"

He sat up in bed, rubbing his eyes, looking around the room. Using a little lamb's voice, he bleated, "Mom?"

"Is it all right if I turn on the lamp?"

Squinting at the shock of fresh light, he sat up in bed, the covers drooping around his waist like a petticoat. The man she brought home peered through the doorway over her shoulder.

"You coming or what?" he asked, his voice as heavy as a foghorn. He let out a couple of ragged coughs.

"Would you mind leaving us alone for a couple of minutes?" his mom asked, using her polite waitress's voice. "I'll be down in a second. There's a beer in the fridge."

His mom sat on the edge of his bed and, taking his hand, petted it as though it were a stray kitten. She was still in her pink uniform, a fresh ketchup stain on her chest.

"I had a long talk with Father Mac today."

"You did?" Leal responded, all innocence.

"Yes, I did. Mind if I smoke?"

"No, go ahead." Leal wouldn't have minded a cigarette himself. He had built up a cache he had stolen from the packs his mom left lying around the house, stashing them in his underwear drawer.

A puff of white smoke formed a wreath around her head.

"Father Mac says he's worried about you. Do you know why he's worried?"

Leal rolled his eyes into his forehead, searching for an answer. "No, I don't know why he would be worried."

"Well, I was hoping you would tell me. I was hoping you would tell me, so I wouldn't have to tell you what he told me."

"What did he tell you?" Leal wrapped his arms around his knees. "I mean, why would he be so concerned?"

"You don't know? You can tell me that you honestly don't know?"

"I can't think of anything. Nothing comes to mind."

She took another drag on her cigarette, like she meant business this time. She looked around for something she could use as an ashtray.

"He told me about a woman. Some woman you took him to see."

"What woman is that?"

"He said her name is Diana. Do you deny you took him to meet a woman?"

"Well, no. I did take him to this woman's house, but I didn't know what her name was or anything."

"He distinctly told me that her name is Diana."

"Well, maybe she did introduce herself to us as Diana. I couldn't be sure. I mean, a name's just a name, isn't it?"

"But that's not all he told me." She blew out a short, nervous stream of smoke. "He said he saw you afterwards. He said he observed you walking through the park with this woman. And that's not the worst of it, Leal. He said you were walking with her hand in hand."

Leal closed his eyes. His face felt warm and red. A wave seemed to crash against rocks in his head.

"All I want to know is why you were walking with a strange woman hand in hand."

"Well, maybe he thought he saw me walking with this woman."

"You're not going to sit there and contradict the word of a priest, are you?"

"Well, no. Of course not. Not if you put it that way."

"So you admit to knowing her?"

"Yeah. I know her. Not that well. But I know of her."

"And the holding hands? You actually held hands with this woman? A woman old enough to be your mother?"

"I don't know. I mean, maybe, I guess. Maybe it looked like we were holding hands. I didn't see Father Mac around any-where. So maybe it looked like we were holding hands. To him."

"Were you or were you not holding hands? I want a straight answer from you this time."

Leal pictured Father Mac as a spy, a character out of James Bond, peeking around tree trunks, crawling on his belly through tall grass.

"Look me in the eyes, Leal."

There was nowhere he could turn to hide. Of course he had to bring his head up and look his mom in the eyes, but he couldn't seem to move his neck.

"Look me in the eyes and say you weren't holding hands."

She placed her fingers under his chin, lifting his head into place. She did this slowly and gently, and her voice became softer, too.

"Leal, look me in the eyes, please."

He looked her in the eyes.

"Yeah," Leal mumbled. "I guess maybe he's right. I guess we were holding hands."

Her fingers trembled under his chin, her mouth twitched in one corner. She stood up, paced a tiny circle, tripped over a baseball mitt, avoided a disabled drone, sidestepped a half-assembled LEGO kit.

"Why, Leal? Why? Who is this woman? I don't understand."

Leal sat still, watching her pace in circles. A spring felt tightly wound up inside him.

"Why were you holding hands with this woman? Can you tell me why?"

The spring popped loose, a weasel leaping out of its box.

"It was for Thuster."

She stopped in mid-step, spinning on her heel.

"Thuster? What's Thuster have to do with any of this?"

"Didn't Father Mac tell you? She was helping me look for Thuster. He was missing, and she was helping me look for him. That's all."

She stared at Leal, reading what lay behind his eyes. And then it all came out in a rush.

"I was worried about Thuster. I thought he might have gone to this woman's house. And when I went back for him, he wasn't there. So I knocked on her door to be sure he wasn't inside and when she came out, she said she would help us look for him—Father Mac and me—but Father Mac said he couldn't stay around. He said he was going back to the parsonage to wait for him there. So I guess I was worried about where Thuster could be, and she told me not to be so worried, and that's when I guess maybe she must have taken my hand."

Leal put his head on his knees, rising beneath the covers like two hillocks. He didn't like the sound of his voice. His mom put her arm around his neck, pulled his head onto her shoulder, stroked his hair.

"It's all right," she soothed. "It's all right. I just had to know. I had to know for sure. I mean, there are some women out there—and I'm not saying this Diana is one of them—that take advantage of young boys. They're like—tarantulas. I don't really know how else to put it. You're getting to be of an age when you'll start to understand what I mean. I just want you to find out the right way, that's all. I just don't want anything bad to happen to you, do you know what I'm saying?"

"Yes," Leal said, "yes." His voice didn't sound quite right, though. It didn't sound like his voice.

"I'll talk to Father Mac again. I'll tell him it was all a misunderstanding, if you want me to."

"No, that's okay. You don't have to talk to him."

"I'll tell him this woman was just trying to help you, that's all. She sounds like she could be a nice woman. She was just trying to help you find your friend. I mean, that's all that happened, isn't it?"

"It's all right. You don't have to talk with him."

"And Leal?"

His mom placed her hand on his shoulder, leaning close.

"This woman. You won't be seeing her again? I mean, there's no reason to see her again, is there?"

"No, ma'am."

She took his head in both hands, turning it slowly until he was facing her again. Her fingers held his head like a block of wood in a vise. She stared as if trying to make her eyes move behind his eyes.

"Promise me you won't be seeing her again."

Leal nodded his head between her hands.

"Good. That's good."

Letting his head drop, she stood to go to the door.

"Leal?"

He didn't look up.

"I want us to go to Church this week. We'll go to the early mass. Is that all right?"

"Yes," Leal said.

"Good."

She turned off the light and opened his door. Pausing at the threshold, she exhaled a cloud of white smoke that streamed against the moonlit ceiling. Snores of the man downstairs climbed the steps like a chainsaw cutting through the night.

Exchanging a glance, they both laughed at once. This time the laughter was just theirs. There was no one else around to share it.

***

Dear Henri,

I am still perplexed by Leal's style of delivery. At times, his story proceeds quickly, a race to the end. At other times, it dawdles like an old man with a cane. Sometimes, his voice is full of emotion. At other times, the narrative seems an exercise in pure objectivity, the therapeutic equivalent of a nature documentary.

While telling his story, he will sometimes close his eyes, sometimes look at the ceiling or down at the floor. Rarely, if ever, does he maintain eye contact with the listener—in this case, his therapist. Only when a segment of his story is over will he give me a direct look, eye for eye, as though to measure my response to this episode, this portion of his evolving narrative.

And yet, all the while, I have the feeling there is more going on inside his head than is coming across verbally. His focus is perpetually inward. It's as though there is a feature-length movie unfolding in his imagination, complete with dialogue, pans and zooms, soundstages— who knows, even CGI—and I am like a hungry dog, grateful for tidbits, leftovers, thrown from a table holding a smorgasbord out of my reach.

Has he memorized this narrative? Does he rehearse it at night— in his bedroom, in his sleep? Or is it impromptu, completely improvised, an on-the-spot recitation? Is this story the product of his unconscious? Is it swelling into being like a geyser through a hot spring? Or is it a conscious ploy—a way to gain and maintain attention? I am struck, impressed, mainly by the small details: the tiny elements and visual effects that constitute his narrative. He is adding ingredients the way he described Father Mac assembling a stew, one layer at a time. There is an old adage: if you want to make up a lie, be specific. And Leal's narrative is very specific.

Take the bit about Father Mac's secret ingredient. If inviting a minor to sleep overnight in an adult's bedroom isn't enough cause to bring in Child Protective Services, certainly intoxicating said youth would justify bringing investigators to the priest's front door. If only the parish would supply me with a working phone number or email address so I could get Father Mac's side of the story.

But what if the quart of rum is all make-believe, a fabrication, a spur-of-the-moment addition to Father Mac's recipe for the sake of provoking the listener—me?

I can't help but suspect that my client is teasing me, luring me, with this narrative. He is hoping for something … inviting me into his world of play. It goes without saying that I must resist this invitation at all cost.

She pauses to snuff out the ash of her cigarette. She wishes to add a postscript. She feels the need to tell Henri about Thomas—about how close they are to the end of their marriage. But what good would it do? Henri is still engaged to Genevieve.

Why, oh why, must there always be another woman in competition with her affections?

***

Earlier that evening, Selena had taken a phone call from Thomas on the landline. Long distance. L.A. No caller ID, so she fell into a trap of discourse.

He took the liberty of setting up a hearing—six weeks from today. But she could bypass the formalities, if she chose. He wouldn't even have to be there. His part was already signed. All she would need to do is sign the papers and turn them in. It would all be very easy for her. The paperwork was already in the mail—Federal Express—so she could look it over, review the fine print with her lawyer.

"I don't have a lawyer."

"Selena," Thomas said, sympathetically, like an uncle doling advice, "of course you need a lawyer."

"You were my lawyer," she told him.

"What about your dad?"

"He was a tax attorney, not a divorce lawyer." There—she uttered the word.

"Selena, please." His voice sounded suddenly stern, impatient. "We've been over this before. It was different when I was living in Chicago. But if I fly all the way back for another hearing and you aren't there again …" His voice weakened, the sternness subsided, as he switched tactics. "What are you hoping for?"

She heard a woman's voice in the background: "Tommy-boy, are you going to be much longer?"

Tommy-boy?

Only his lover would call him that. *Susy-q.* Selena imagined a small, impish figure, like that of a pixie.

She reflected on that afternoon when she found out about Thomas's affair. She had suspected it for some time—all those late-night hours he spent at his PC terminal in his basement office after she had gone to bed. Catching up with correspondence—this is all he ever said about it on subsequent mornings at breakfast.

She truly believes he wanted her to find out. He wanted her to be the one to ask for a divorce.

Normally, Thomas shut off his computer when finished, effectively locking her out with his password—not that she ever had reason to access his programs. This time, though, a simple touch of the keyboard dissolved his screensaver without fanfare. She clicked on his email account and sat for some time in his padded swivel chair scanning reams of incoming and outgoing messages saved to his hard drive, an erotic dialogue spanning months with a woman named "susy-q," becoming more and more intense, like a steamy, sleazy romance novel.

At first, she tried to reassure herself: it's only cybersex, a harmless outlet, trivial fun. But the last set of messages confirmed her fear. Two days before, Thomas had told Selena he was flying to L.A. to attend a three-day legal seminar. He even showed her the website. But susy-q's latest email suggested something less professional: "cant wait to see you honeybuns. pick you up at LAX at 3:15. cant wait to do it to it in the flesh baby."

She didn't believe for a moment that Thomas had been this slipshod with security. For whatever reason, he had wanted her to find out about susy-q.

And now?

Really, she just wanted to be done with it all—as quickly and painlessly as possible—the same way she would feel if getting a cavity filled.

"Selena? Are you still there?"

"Yes, I'm still here."

"Good. For a second, I thought—"

He said something else, but his hand must have been covering the transmitter. His voice sounded muffled. But Selena could tell he was talking to someone in the background: Susy-q.

This Susy-q must be something for Thomas to pull up roots, give up his practice, move out to L.A.

Again, Thomas asked: "Selena, what are you hoping for?"

"Nothing ... Tommy-boy," she said and hung up the phone.

Chapter 5

"I'm sorry I wasn't able to meet with you last time," Selena apologizes as Leal takes his seat and stares at the trees out the window. Leaves etched in amber droop beyond the sill. "I had an emergency."

"What kind of emergency?" he asks, without turning his head.

"A girl—about your age. She's a patient of mine, too."

She hesitates. Wind plays with the leaves. Leal's pupils follow the movement.

"She's in a hospital right now," Selena explains. "She had to be hospitalized. It happens sometimes."

"Do you mean Paula? The girl who tried to kill herself?"

This makes her frown. Does he somehow know her schedule? Has he hacked into her computer to access her appointment log?

"Oh, do you know Paula?"

"No, but it's all over school. The attempts she made."

Of course it would be. Someone at school would confide in a friend, pinkie-swearing strict confidence, double-daring not to tell, and before long, it would become common knowledge, spreading like a virus. She only hopes this knowledge isn't turned against her patient in the form of bullying—cyber or otherwise.

"Let's not worry about Paula for the moment."

It was her second attempt in as many months. Her overdose failed to produce the desired effect. She is still among the living, even though lying in a hospital bed, unconscious, in critical care with an IV in her arm. This is a patient—with a real problem, a serious problem. And here is a boy, sitting quietly on her couch, staring out the window.

"What did you want to talk about today?" Selena asks.

"Diana," he says promptly. "The next time I saw Diana."

"Didn't you say you promised your mother you wouldn't visit Diana again?"

"Yeah," Leal answers. "I did."

"But still you went back to the lake?"

"Well, you know what they say about promises," he says, revolving his head and body to face her.

Selena thinks about her own promises.

"Yes," she admits, "I do."

*

Frogs sunned themselves on lily pads beneath the willows. Ducks paddled along the shore. The head of a snapping turtle punctured the calm surface of the lake.

Diana kept a branch from bending back until Leal could step through along the path. He took the branch from Diana so it wouldn't swing back and hit Thuster.

Diana lifted herself onto a thick white limb of a tree stretching low over the water. Kicking off her sandals, she dangled her feet, while Jay steadied her with thin, white arms.

They had never come this far around the lake before. Leal picked up a flat black stone and skipped it across the water. Then he placed a stone in Thuster's hand, but he dropped it listlessly onto the ground.

"What do you think?" Diana asked. "Would you like to go for a swim?"

"Oh, I don't know," Leal said.

"Come on. Don't be a spoilsport."

"I don't have a suit."

"You don't need a suit. Not here. How about you, Jay?"

"Sure," Jay said. "Why not?"

Diana untied the knot of her blouse above her bellybutton. Sliding out of her pants, she tossed shirt and shorts to Jay. Then she squiggled out of her undies—a sliver of silk like the tip of a handkerchief—and flung these playfully at Jay as well.

Leal tried not to look at her, but he couldn't help it.

She unclipped her bra and snapped this into the leaves like a slingshot, leaving her all white and naked on the tree limb, her legs dangling, breasts swaying. Then Jay pulled off his clothes: gray painter's pants, splattered yellow and orange. White T-shirt a canvas of color. But Leal didn't look at him. It was like he wasn't even there.

Diana slid into the lake, water rising around her thighs. Jay waded in after her. Both were up to their shoulders. Her breasts floated like dead fish, purple butterfly staying dry on top. She splashed Jay, and he splashed back, like kids in a swimming pool. Then Diana dove under the water and sprang back to the surface, breasts bouncing freely, nipples hard and stiff. All Leal could do was stand there and stare without trying too hard to stare.

"Come on in," she said. "The water's fine."

Leal shook his head. He glanced at Thuster, staring through the overhanging branches of the willows, looking back at the cottage on the farther shore.

Scooping handfuls of lake, she splashed water at Leal, but it fell short.

"You don't know what you're missing," Diana laughed.

"Okay," Leal gave in. "But don't look."

"We're not looking," she said. But she looked straight at him, so he had to make his request all over again.

"Okay, okay," Diana said. She turned around so all Leal could see was her back, auburn hair streaming between her shoulder blades. Jay turned around, too. He came up behind her, pressing his body against hers, wrapping his arms around her, as

Leal waded into the water.

He doesn't want to say that Diana lied to him, but the water felt very cold.

*

Wearing only their shoes and sandals, they walked back to the cottage, carrying their clothes. Jay led the way, and Leal followed Diana, with Thuster bringing up the rear. He liked walking directly behind Diana. He couldn't keep his eyes off the round, white half-moons bobbing along in front of him.

Leal paused with Thuster outside the door to the cottage.

Diana turned to him.

"Aren't you coming in?"

Leal shuffled at the threshold.

"Well, sure. It's just that—"

"Come on in, Leal"—a firm invitation.

They walked through the lakeside door of the cottage single file. The painting this time was on full display on the easel. Diana was spread naked—nude—across the canvas. It seemed strange seeing her naked in real flesh and painted flesh, too—as though looking in a funhouse mirror, one that transformed her into a new shape full of squares and triangles and cubes.

"Well," Jay said, "what do you think? I could finish it probably today, if you feel you have the time."

"Leal," Diana asked, "you wouldn't mind? You wouldn't mind it if I posed a little longer for Jay today?"

"No," Leal said, "I wouldn't mind."

She moved behind the canvas to a soft-cushioned armchair—velvety purple.

"It's all right if Leal watches, isn't it?" Diana asked.

Jay shrugged his shoulders. He was back in his painter's clothes, concentrating on squeezing orange paint from a tube.

Leal put his clothes back on and sat cross-legged on the floor.

Thuster looked out one of the windows at the lake. Life slowly seeped out of the afternoon, quiet and still, as Jay mixed his colors, brushing them quickly onto the canvas, adding shadows of blue and purple, overlapping a hint of lemon with a square of crimson.

Leal became lost inside his own head. His thoughts drifted like water lilies. He thought about life in a strange, new way, like he was not the one living it but someone looking at himself the way Jay was looking at Diana and the painting of Diana at the same time. He started to feel very calm inside. It felt strange to feel this kind of calm. Then he thought about Thuster, and it seemed to him that Thuster was moving farther and farther away.

*

Ordinarily, Leal and Thuster parted company with Diana after Jay dropped them off at the parsonage from his clanking red Mazda coupe with Diana up front and Leal and Thuster stuffed in the back seat. Lately, however, Diana had taken to inviting them back to her house after their time at the lake—just Leal and Thuster, that is. Jay always played it safe, pulling up to a bus stop far down the street on the corner, forcing his passengers to walk the rest of the way so he could speed off unobserved.

This time, Saul arrived home just as Leal and Thuster were leaving for the parsonage. After he pulled in the drive, he removed a large wooden crate from the trunk of the Lincoln.

"What is it?" Leal asked, coming up close, Thuster behind him.

Saul set the slatted crate carefully on the blacktop. Kneeling down, he opened the lid, and Leal peered inside.

Inside the crate was a tiny world for miniature prisoners: a little house with thatched roof and shutters, a bonsai tree, a large clay pipe, a tiny Ferris wheel. He wondered whether Saul had discovered a way to trap leprechauns or elves.

"She's still sleeping," Saul whispered, close to Leal's ear. He could smell alcohol on his breath, but that didn't bother him. From what he remembers of his father, he was a drinker, too. A social drinker, his mom would claim. There's a big difference between a social drinker and a flat-out drunk.

They waited in silence, barely breathing. A square of sunlight crept across the drive.

Saul lit a cigarette, and a whiskered nose poked out of the toy house.

Holding his cigarette in one hand, Saul reached inside with his other. A tiny dust-mop of fur hopped onto his palm. It was nibbling a pellet, holding it between furry forepaws.

"Say hello to Cressida," Saul said.

He held out the gray ball of fuzz to Leal for a closer view.

"What is it?" Leal asked.

"You got to be kidding me," Saul said. "You mean to say you've never seen a live chinchilla before?"

Diana came up behind them.

"Oh, Saul," she said, "be honest. You didn't know a chinchilla from a bison when you first started the business."

"Business?" Leal asked without thinking.

"Owner of a haberdashery," Saul said.

"He sells fur coats," Diana said.

"You mean to tell me you haven't seen my commercials?" Saul sounded offended.

"He keeps taking pity on the poor, little furballs," Diana explained. "Second one he's brought home this week."

"Troilus is upstairs," Saul said. "I'm going to try to get them to start a family together."

"It's like he keeps rescuing prisoners from the Holocaust," Diana said. "It makes him feel all warm and squishy inside."

"What do you think, Leal?" Saul asked, ignoring Diana. "Think your mother might like a genuine chinchilla fur coat?"

"I don't know," Leal said. "She's allergic to fur."

"Saul, leave the poor boy alone," Diana said.

"All right, all right," Saul said. "It's just that business has been bad lately. All these anti-fur nuts."

Leal asked to hold her.

"Sure," Saul said. "Just be careful. They're very delicate."

"Hard to mate, too," Diana said.

"That can be caused by stress, anxiety—any number of reasons. That's what a psychologist would tell you, anyway, if you believe what those shrinks have to say."

*

"I'm sorry," Leal apologizes to Selena. "I'm just telling you what he said."

"Don't worry about it," Selena assures him. "I'm used to it. Really."

"I don't think he meant anything bad by it."

"It's fine. I know there are a lot of people who are—suspicious—about what goes on behind the closed doors of a psychologist's office. Do you think your mother is suspicious?"

"I don't think so. But she always asks me what we talk about."

"And what do you tell her?"

"Not too much. I just tell her we don't talk about her."

He smooths away a crease in his pants.

"To tell you the truth, I think she's a little disappointed when I tell her we don't talk about her."

"You think so?"

"Yeah."

Selena glances at the screen of the digital recorder to make sure the volume is registering.

"Let's go back to Saul," Selena suggests.

*

Saul put Cressida back in her cage.

Leal took Thuster's hand.

"Time to take him back to the parsonage," he said.

"That's a long walk, isn't it?" Saul asked.

"No, sir," Leal answered. "Not that long."

"How about I take you in my car?"

Leal gave Diana a look, but she didn't seem concerned.

After setting the crate on the porch, Saul opened the back door of his Lincoln. Leal led Thuster by the hand, prodding him inside, while Diana stood on the porch, a mannequin on display. At Saul's behest, Leal took the passenger seat up front.

A beautiful car, black leather seat cushions, the seats softer than the couch in Leal's living room, the interior of the car as big as his bedroom.

A smooth and quiet ride, just like a commercial. If you weren't looking out the window, you wouldn't even know you were moving.

Saul pulled up in front of the parsonage. He looked at the basketball court across the street.

"You know," Saul said. "I used to be an altar boy myself quite a long time ago."

Leal made a move to open the door, but the door was still locked. The lock button fit snugly into the side panel, so he couldn't pry it out with his fingers.

"Just a little scruffball kid, getting all dolled up on Sundays in a long white robe. There's no way you would have recognized me if you'd seen me on the streets. I guess you could say I grew up in a pretty rough neighborhood."

They sat with the motor idling. The windows were rolled up, tightly sealed, with the air conditioning blasting an arctic chill.

"This priest—what's his name again?"

"Father MacDougal," Leal said.

"He treats you all right?"

"Sure," Leal said. "I mean, sure."

"Listen," Saul said, "before you go. I have this little favor to ask you. Maybe more than a favor. Let's call it a proposition."

Saul fumbled with thick fingers inside his shirt pocket, then reached between Leal's legs to open the glove compartment, where he searched through a bunch of papers and receipts. Then he pulled his hand back clean. "You don't happen to smoke, do you?" he asked.

"No, sir," Leal told him.

"Good boy. It's a very good habit not to start. I remember I was about your age, I was already smoking about half a pack a day, just from the cigarettes I could steal from my old man. But listen, getting back to my original proposition, let me run by you what I've been thinking, okay?"

"Yes, sir," Leal said.

"We're going to start working together on this, you might want to consider dropping the 'sir, this' and 'sir, that' routine."

"Yes, s—" Leal suppressed the urge and nodded his head.

"Good. Now this proposition, you'd really have to know a little bit about Diana to know why I'm asking this. I mean, you'd have to know for one thing about my trip to Chicago. That was about three years ago, to bring her back home. Let's just say she wasn't in the best of places she could have been in. I don't know if you're following me or not."

Leal didn't know that he was either, but he nodded his head, anyway. He nodded his head so many times in a row, he started to feel like the bobble head on display on the dash.

"Well, about all I'm trying to say is I think it's kind of cute the way, oh, how do you call it, the way she's sort of adopted you, more or less. In fact, I like the idea so much, I can't tell you how much I like it. Here they are, I left them in here. I knew I left them somewhere."

Saul pulled his cigarettes from the compartment between the two seats and used a silver lighter from his pocket to fire one up.

"Now where was I? All I'm saying is if you're going to be coming over to the house when I'm out working, as it looks like you might be starting to do. All I'm saying is I like you boys, the two of you—your friend back there, Thuster, included."

He took a long drag on his cigarette, expelling a cloud of smoke that filled the interior of the car, making Leal gag.

"Now, what I'm proposing is this. All I want you to do is keep an eye on her. That's all I'm asking. Just keep your eye on her. I'll even make it worth your while."

He dug in his pants pocket and pulled out his fat roll of green bills. This time, he stopped short of reaching the singles. "Here." He handed Leal a five, very crisp and clean, as though it had been pressed at a dry cleaner's. "Go ahead. Don't be shy. Take it."

While Leal was making up his mind, Saul let it drop from between forefinger and thumb. It fluttered like a feather onto Leal's lap.

"Tell you what, you can expect to see one of these the tail end of every week, fair enough? You produce any information I can use, you'll see double. Know what I'm telling you? Just think of it as a little extra allowance, you know, on top of your regular allowance."

"I don't know," Leal said.

He thought about his regular allowance. It all depended on how many tips his mom brought home from the diner.

"What's that you mean, you don't know? Did I just hear you right?" Saul took another drag on his cigarette. "There's plenty more where that one came from, I'm telling you. This is just a little payback, you know, reimbursement for the favor I'm asking you to do."

"I'm not sure what it is I'm supposed to be doing."

"Just keep an eye on her, like I was saying. You know, watch out for her own safety. That's all, like you're her knight in shining armor or something, how should I know? All I'm asking is if you should happen to notice anything that don't seem right, that don't seem like it would be in her best interest, just to let me know, if you would be so kind. Deal?"

"I guess," Leal said. "I mean, I guess I could watch out for her. Like you said, if it's in her interest."

"Sure, that's all you'd be doing."

"But that's the part I don't understand. What exactly would I be watching for?"

"That I couldn't tell you. All I can say is you'll know it when you see it. All I'm really asking is, you should see something strange, something that don't fit, you should tell me about it, that's all."

"But how will I know?"

"You'll know. Diana—how can I put this? She's very private in her own way. She keeps a lot to herself. I'm only a little bit worried about her, okay? The kind of people she might run into on a daily basis. Who she talks to. Who she interacts with. Undesirable types. Know what I mean?"

"Sure," Leal said, "I guess so." He was pretty sure Jay was just the "undesirable type" Saul had in mind.

"Then it's a done deal."

Saul held out his hand. It hung like a great white shark. Leal can't say he felt good about shaking it, but it seemed like the thing to do at the time. In any case, it was an act that sprung him free of the car. And Thuster, too. As soon as Leal shook Saul's hand, the door locks popped up and they were set loose. That's when he knew what it must feel like to spend a night in jail.

*

Selena looks up from her notebook.

There is still time on the clock.

"You mentioned—you started to talk about your father."

"I did? My father?"

"You said he was a drinker. A social drinker."

"Yeah. I mean, I think so. I'm just going by what my mom said. I was pretty young."

"What else can you remember? Do you remember anything else about your father?"

"Not too much. He was on the road a lot. Always going someplace or other. Sometimes he took me with him, but usually he left me at home."

Selena knows all about absent parents. Her mother directed a residency program, which took up most of her spare time, even when she wasn't on call. And now her father, who had always been there for his kids when they were growing up, is fading, his memory fleeting, moving farther and farther away.

"Anything else?" she gives him a nudge.

Leal rolls his eyes toward the ceiling, then looks out the window.

One thing he remembers is the day of his funeral. He remembers standing on a chair to see him inside his coffin. He had this smile pasted on his face. It was like he was having a nice dream. And that's what his mom said. She said that he was just asleep and dreaming about a special place, a very pleasant world with flowers and white robes and harps and rivers of gold. So when they carried him out of the church and put him in the hearse—well, he remembers crying because he wanted to be with him.

"You wanted to be in heaven?" Selena asks.

"No. I wanted to be in the hearse. I wanted to ride with him. To the cemetery. But my mom said I had to ride with her in her car."

"What about when he was still alive?"

There was one time, they went to the ocean. It must have

been the summer before he died. Leal doesn't remember that much about it, except that his father made fun of him because he was afraid to stick in his big toe.

Every time a wave came onto shore, he ran back to his mom on her beach towel. So his dad, well, he carried him waist-deep out to sea and dropped him in. It's funny, but he doesn't think they've taken a family vacation since then. Leal's mom—she's forever promising to take him somewhere. But she's always too busy with the diner.

"I was wondering if you might like to talk about a different memory," Selena prompts. "Before the funeral took place. You were in a motel room. The two of you together. And—"

"—a woman came in when I was asleep, and she started screaming and screaming."

She lets a quiet moment go by, surprised and pleased she's made it this far.

"And then?"

"That's all I really remember," he says, giving her a sad-eyed, puppy-dog look that could make a person with emotional detachment disorder—and she's treated several over the years—burst out in a torrent of tears. "The screams."

"That must have been really hard for you. And scary."

"Yeah, I guess so."

"Do you want to talk about it?"

"Not really." Leal glances at the clock on the wall. "I need to get home. I have a lot of homework."

This is a first. He's never expressed much interest in school before.

Nevertheless, Selena switches off the recorder and walks Leal to the door.

***

Dear Henri,

It will be a pleasure seeing you at the conference. Please save me a seat at your session. Will Genevieve be attending the conference with you?

She raises the unlit cigarette to her lips and pretends to take a deep drag.

I am beginning to think of Leal as my "problem" client. Outwardly, he manifests few indications of trauma. He seemed calm, more relaxed than in former sessions. I believe a level of trust is building between us. Question: does he have a problem at all? Or is this a child—an adolescent—with an overly active imagination? Should I even consider this a therapeutic issue requiring resolution? Maybe he only craves attention.

Here's something you might find interest. I came across a headline in the Ovid Gazette: *"Saul 'Chinchilla King' Solomon Charged with Tax Fraud." Saul Solomon—I still can't believe he's part of Leal's story. He's still putting out these cheesy commercials on Ovid's local cable channel wearing a paper crown and holding a cardboard scepter. He owns a factory outlet in town: mainly men's suits, but he's better known for his apparel for women, especially faux fur coats. In fact, I stopped by the store the other day but didn't find him inside. If possible, I need to arrange a meeting, just to talk with him about Leal.*

Henri, I know you would disapprove. Inference. Induction. Use your intuition you'd say. Everything you need is at your disposal within the client's monologue. There is no need to go outside your office for information, for additional clues.

*

There is only one problem, she thinks. *I'm not you.*

Chapter 6

She admires the updated kitchen, stands in awe of the cathedral ceiling. She finds the view of the lake through the set of French windows spectacular. The house is partly furnished, as the advertisement stated. She notes an armchair in a corner—just as Leal has described it—a paint-stained table, empty skeleton of an easel. A spiral staircase winds to an upstairs loft like the shell of a snail.

She saw the advertisement in the classifieds: 'Lovely 1 BR cottage, lake view, partly furnished, WBFP, DW, cathedral ceiling, newly refurbished HW floors, EZ2C.' She made an appointment with the landlord. Over the phone, he introduced himself as Sid. At the lake, he turns out to be a man in his fifties—lanky, red face, thinning hair.

Fog wafts over the dark surface of the lake. A morning chill makes her wish she had brought a jacket.

Sid gives her the complete tour. He tells her his great-grandfather built the cottage, back in the 1870s. He had emigrated from Ireland and built it as a retreat for his extended family, a refuge against anti-Irish sentiment of the time period.

"Can you imagine three families of aunts and uncles and cousins all crammed inside?" he asks.

"Remarkable," Selena answers.

"I'm just making it up," Sid says, "about my great-grandfather."

Selena reassesses the jovial face, the vaudevillian demeanor.

"You are?" she asks.

"It's just an act," he says. "Just like I know you're not here because you're interested in the cottage."

"You saw right through me," Selena confirms. "How?"

"I'm an actor," he confesses. "I can always tell when someone's acting. Putting on an act. Grew up on Long Island. Moved out here twenty years ago—don't ask why. No regrets, though. Put together a little acting troupe. We rehearse, twice a week, in the basement of the Third Avenue Church. Maybe you've heard of us: the Old-Time Players?"

Selena shakes her head. "I'm sorry."

"Don't be sorry," he says. "If anything, we're the sorry ones. That is, you ever see us perform."

"I'm afraid you're right," Selena admits. "I'm not much of an actress."

"It's too bad," he says, eyeing her up and down, as though measuring her for a jumpsuit. "Otherwise you'd be perfect for this play we're working on. Ever hear of *Medea*? We're doing a musical version. Now, tell me something, Dr. Harris."

"Please, call me Selena."

"All right, Selena. Now, why are you really here?"

The landlord is forthright with his answers. Yes, the cottage has been mostly vacant since the end of August. He blames it on the weather: too rainy for romantic getaways or fishing retreats. Before that? Yes, a man rented the cottage for the summer. He came down in June—from Chicago. No, his name wasn't Jay. It was something else. Gerald. That's right. He went by Gerald. Was he a painter? As a matter of fact, that's one of his paintings hanging above the mantlepiece.

The painting is of a small boy: highly Expressionist—Abstract. Slabs of beige mark cheeks and chin accented with shadows of purple. The eyes seem cut out of a paper mask. Daubs of black and blue compose a coil of hair. As a portrait, it fails to denote anyone in particular. The face, an irregular oval, is generic.

"What do you think?" the landlord asks.

Selena nods her approval.

"You don't collect art, by any chance?" he wants to know.

Selena admits she dabbles.

"You think this will be worth anything some day? You think he'll ever become famous?"

Maybe after he's dead, Selena suggests. That's the case with most artists.

"Except Picasso. Wasn't he famous during his lifetime?"

He's the exception. Not the rule. She does have one more question. This artist who stayed here—Gerald. He was young? Single?

"Oh, no," he says. "I'd peg him just shy of forty. Single? You could say. He was just getting away for the summer. I should tell you, he wasn't an artist by trade. He worked as a schoolteacher. Or maybe a stockbroker. One or the other. In fact, he gave me a good tip on a high-tech stock. You want, I could share this information with you."

Selena politely declines. Aside from a solo 401(k), she doesn't play the market. She takes one last look at the painting before stepping outside.

"There were others," Sid says, locking up.

"Others?"

"Paintings."

"Portraits?"

"Not exactly kid-friendly, if you know what I mean. I put them in storage. Never know, he might come back to claim them some day."

"Close by?" she inquires.

"Boat shed," he admits with a hook of his thumb to indicate the direction.

"Would you mind if I—"

"Take a look?" He studies her up and down with a contemplative frown. "Guess so," he relents. "I just don't want you to think I'm a dirty old man, hoarding them and all. I like to pride myself as a connoisseur."

"Of course," she concurs, as they head toward a rusted corrugated structure slumped against the shore.

Searching through a ring of keys, he finds the one for the padlock and pulls open the door on loud, creaking hinges.

"Got to oil those someday."

No windows, but the sunlight streaming through the doorway is bright enough to see by.

"You wouldn't lock me inside?" she hesitates at the threshold, half joking.

"Don't worry. I keep the bodies well hidden."

His banter only half reassures her, as she takes a step inside. Sure enough, there are two rows of paintings stretched on canvases without frames, four or five per row, raised on wooden pallets, arranged like posters on display in a print shop. It's the first two, the column headers, that concentrate her focus, and she flicks on her flashlight app for a better view.

The one on the left must be Diana. Clearly visible are the orange snake along her calf, the purple butterfly above her breast, colorful imprints on otherwise pale, naked flesh. But the one on the right is different. The hair is shoulder-length, blonde, dyed a greenish tint as though from an overlong swim in a hyperchlorinated pool. A white woman, as well, but with a different set of tattoos: a long string of bluebells or violets—lacking a green thumb, Selena has never been good about flowers—punctuating a vine that winds around the length of an upraised arm from wrist to chest, where it curls around and beneath a breast. One ankle is clasped with a silver shackle, links in a chain, but squinting, Selena can't tell if it represents a tattoo or something tangible.

"All done in there?" Sid calls in.

"Almost!"

She hurriedly snaps two photos, one of each woman, then thumbs through a couple other canvases, but they're of the same women in each respective stack: different poses but the same tattoos.

Sid is standing outside the door like a sentry, a Queen's guard, keeping watch, as she emerges into full daylight.

"Any you'd like to take home with you?" he asks, friendly enough. His demeanor hasn't changed.

"No, I'm good."

As Sid closes and locks the door, Selena gazes at the lake, its surface ruffled like a potato chip with the breeze. Early October, and there's already a hint of winter in the air. It's not only Chicago that can claim Windy City status. Across the way, on the opposite shore, her eye catches a movement and makes out a small oval that resolves into a face with two dark pinpricks of eyes aimed in her direction. She can almost believe they're looking directly at her, locking her in a staring contest. She's the first to blink and the face disappears. It's a boy, no doubt, with a scruff of brown hair, and she has an idea who it might be. Has he been watching her this entire time?

On their way to her car, Sid tells her it's been nice meeting her, even if she isn't truly interested in the cottage.

"By the way," he says, "when are you due?"

"Due?" Selena asks.

"The baby—when's it due?"

"Oh," Selena says. "Not for a while."

She takes a look across the lake again at the same spot she'd seen the face, and there it is again, this time accompanied by the wave of a hand. As she adjusts her eyes, it's gone, branches snapping back into place with a swish.

"Is there a road that goes around the lake?" she asks, but Sid shakes his head.

"Not all the way around," he tells her. "Footpath maybe. Unless it's all overgrown."

She estimates the time it would take to circle the lake on foot versus rowing across in the boat docked at the short wooden pier.

"This may sound strange," she begins, "but would you mind if I borrowed your boat?"

Sid shakes his head.

"In your condition?"

"It's no problem, really. I used to scull," she explains, but Sid gives her a puzzled look. "You know, crew? In high school." In between basketball and fencing, she should add. "Besides, the exercise would be good for me. My OB-GYN is always on my case to do more than I do."

"Well, you look fit enough from my perspective, but you're right," Sid agrees with a quizzical smile. "It does sound strange." But then he gives in with a shrug of his shoulders. "At least let me push you off."

*

The wind is at her back, which makes it longer to cross the lake than she estimated. Plus, she has to look over her shoulder every few strokes to make sure she's steering for the opening in the trees that will provide access to shore.

Within the half-hour, it's land ho! Only one foot goes under water as she pulls the prow of the boat ashore, but not to worry. She's switched her Sarah Flints for tennis shoes, once her ankles began swelling with the regularity of an ebb tide.

The sun is high overhead, but you wouldn't know it for the multilayered branches of trees. The understory is still green, if not lush, but overhead, the leaves form a mosaic of yellow and orange swatches. Autumn peakage shouldn't be too far off.

Pausing, she listens for movement, but the only sounds are from a flock of crows gliding in spirals above the trees. She tiptoes through brambles and fallen branches and withered leaves, navigating back to the spot along shore where she caught sight of the face peering out at her. Maybe she was mistaken. Maybe it was nothing more than an owl or squirrel, but if so, the squirrel was albino, the owl snowy. Solid ground gives way to a patch of mud, which she is averse to treading, until she notes footprints. Deep ones, as though made by a cookie cutter in soft dough. Recently made, too, as they're oozing, not dry.

"Leal?" she calls out tentatively because it has to be him, doesn't it? Who else would it be on a school day, truant from school? The footprints lead her to a clearing where she sees something hanging from the branch of an old, gnarled tree. A few steps closer and she makes out a body dangling from a rope. She lopes across the clearing as quickly as her belly will let her until she sees it is only a mannequin, tied by a noose as though on the receiving end of a lynching.

Reluctant to reach up and touch it, she watches it twirl idly in the breeze until its face rotates into view. The face is generic beneath a wig of long brown hair. Two tattoos are crudely drawn with permanent marker: a purple butterfly above the curve of a breast, an orange snake along her calf. And that's not the only thing: drilled into her naked torso are three distinct holes, grouped together in a compact constellation. A fourth hole has punctured the side of the mannequin's head. She can even guess the caliber. Her father used to take her and her brother to a range for target practice when they were younger to teach them gun safety since he kept one in the house for self-defense.

But these holes hadn't been made in self-defense. They are starkly, sickeningly offensive. The sight of them makes her bend over and retch. And that's when she sees what's been constructed beneath the lifeless corpse of the mannequin: a small shrine made of rocks, piled knee-high, with a plank of splintered wood resting on top like an altar. On the altar someone has left an offering: a bundle of flowers, purple and gold, tied with a bow.

***

The phone rings between patients that afternoon. Whoever it is knows how to time the call just right.

The moment she picks up the phone, she hears a stream of rapid-fire words: "You'll have to meet him at my office today if you want to see him."

This time, Lori's abruptness doesn't take her by surprise. She's readjusted herself to her habit of spilling whatever is on her mind before Selena can generate a simple hello.

"See who, Lori? Slow down."

"Leal—he's serving an after-school detention. Double detention, actually. One for being tardy to class."

"And the other?"

"For getting into a fight."

"A fight? Really?"

This doesn't sound like her patient.

"Just come over as soon as you're free."

Selena double-checks her appointment book. She doesn't make enough to afford a secretary.

"All right," she says. "I'll be right there."

*

Lori greets Selena at the front entrance, snuffing out a cigarette beneath her heel and holding open the door for her.

"Thanks for coming." She walks her halfway down the hall to the administration office. "I don't think I have to tell you. Just one more incident, and he's out."

"Expelled?"

Lori nods her head.

"It took all my persuasion to keep them from kicking him out this time around."

"I'll do my best," Selena says.

"Hey, before you go in—" Lori grabs Selena by the wisp of a sleeve. "You'll be going to the reunion, won't you?"

Selena shakes her head.

"No, I don't think so. I'd be too embarrassed. It's too obvious now."

She can picture herself on the dance floor, lumbering around like an awkward penguin.

"No one will notice," Lori insists.

"My other patients have—all except Leal. In fact, I'm surprised he hasn't mentioned it."

Selena takes a step back as Lori brings her mouth, lips painted grotesquely red, absurdly close. She smells a heavy whiff of double-duty peppermint. "Single moms—they're the 'in' thing now, aren't they?"

"Maybe in big cities, but small towns like this? I'd feel out of place."

"You'd be with me. That'd make two of us."

"Well—" Lori is still hanging onto her sleeve. Selena knows she won't let go until she gets the answer she wants. "Let me think about it. When is it again?"

*

As she steps through the door, she tries to keep her tone lighthearted.

"So young man, you're serving detention?"

"Yes, ma'am."

Selena moves around Lori's desk, cluttered with several piles of manila folders.

She sets her purse on a stack of folders while pushing the swivel chair back far enough to accommodate her abdomen.

Then she finds a place for her recorder.

She feels a movement—a kick to the right, underneath her ribs—sharp enough to make her wince. Time for baby's exercise routine. Fetus, she reminds herself. It's still only a fetus.

"Want to talk about what happened?" she asks.

He's sitting solemnly in a hard-backed chair, leaning forward, elbows propped on knees.

"Didn't Ms. Jacobson tell you?"

"As a matter of fact, she did. But I want to hear it from you."

"I guess I got into a sort of fight."

"Sounds serious."

"Not really. It was just a stupid battle with lacrosse sticks with some kid. You know, PE. At first, it was just for fun, like light sabers. But I guess I took it a little too far. That's what the phys-ed instructor said anyway."

"Too far?"

"I sort of knocked him unconscious."

Another kick—very sharp this time. Selena closes her eyes.

"So things aren't going very well at school?"

"No, not really. I guess word got out somehow that I've been coming to see you. So a couple of kids—they've been making fun of me."

"What kids?"

"Different kids. You know how kids are. They like to whisper things. Talk behind your back when they know you can almost hear what they're saying. They can't help it. It's just how they are."

"What things? What are they saying?"

"That I'm some kind of Frankenstein's monster. You know, a freak. They already think of me as this scrawny no-account kid who talks to himself at his locker. This just makes it a little worse."

"Worse?"

"They must think I'm getting shock therapy or something. It's like they keep looking for bolts coming out of my neck. But that's just how kids are."

"Is that why you weren't in school this morning?"

"Oh, she told you that too?"

"Uh-huh. Do you want to tell me where you were?"

"Just out and about."

"Anywhere special?"

"No, not really. Nature hike, you could say."

The statement shocks her into silence. She takes a moment to regroup by studying his shoes. No mud on them anywhere. In fact, they're spotless, out-of-the-box white.

"Are those your same shoes you always wear?"

"These? My mom bought them for me. I was outgrowing my old ones. Fact, this is the first time I'm wearing them."

He leans back, performing a horizontal leg lift to show them off.

"Nifty, huh?" He gives one of his trademark grins, plops his feet down again. "That's another reason the kids were picking on me. It's embarrassing wearing brand-new Keds to school."

"How does it make you feel? The things they're saying about you?"

"Oh, I don't know. I mean, it would be different if I really liked them or something. Then it might be a little different."

Selena feels another kick and another—then three more kicks in a row, as though transmitting a message in Morse code. Active little thing today, she thinks. During her first pregnancy, the baby had been active as well, until it wasn't. Her second pregnancy had miscarried before she felt anything at all. Her fears about this fetus make her consider a different line of questioning altogether.

"Are you afraid of anything, Leal?"

He looks down at the floor.

"Not that I can think of."

"Everyone has some kind of fear, wouldn't you say? I've treated—I've talked with young people, like you, and they generally admit to having at least one fear. Sometimes they're even funny fears. Like fear of fire hydrants. Or woodpeckers."

Silence. Her subject focuses on the recorder.

"Maybe death," he says softly.

"That's a good one. A lot of people are afraid of death. Although it might surprise you to learn that more people are afraid of public speaking."

"Maybe Saul."

He shifts his gaze to a poster of a cat struggling with a chin-up, pinned to Lori's bulletin board.

"Why Saul?"

"I just don't think he'd like me telling you about what happened."

"Why wouldn't he?"

"I just don't think he'd like it."

"Do you want to talk about it?"

He returns his eyes to the recorder sitting on the desk.

"Would it be better if I stopped recording?"

Leal nods his head.

*

One day—Leal believes it was a Saturday—Saul invited Leal to go for a walk through the woods. As a double agent in Saul's employ, it was an offer he couldn't refuse, despite the looks of concern Diana kept throwing Leal over Saul's shoulder.

They drove in silence in the quiet Town Car until they turned onto a gravel drive to a distant patch of woods sprouting out of an abandoned cornfield.

"I had a part-time job tapping trees here when I was your

age," Saul said, pulling the car into a clearing. "I don't think I've ever seen anything moving in these woods since—not even a chipmunk. It's like when the maple syrup people left, they took all of the animals with them, like Noah's Ark. You think they could have left a chipmunk behind."

Once out of the car, Thuster stooped to pick flowers—white ones and purple ones and yellow ones with brown centers—while Saul pulled a mannequin out of the trunk. Dragging her caveman-style by her hair, he made a beeline through the trees and set her on top of a fallen log. He crossed her leg to give her a more natural posture, like she was resting after a walk through the woods, which was hard to imagine, unless she belonged to a nudist colony. Then Saul marched back, smacking his palms together, smiling, although it was hard to tell with Saul if he was really smiling or just had chapped lips.

Thuster began walking toward the mannequin, weaving his flowers into a wreath, but Leal restrained him by his arm, as Saul brought a gun out of his waistband from the back of his pants, beneath his suit jacket.

"What's that?" Leal asked.

"What's it look like?" Saul replied. "Thought we'd do a little target practice today."

He pointed the gun in the direction of the mannequin. Leal looked at Thuster, then into the trees. Saul was right, these woods were lifeless. There weren't even any birds.

"I got to tell you the truth," Saul said. "I wasn't expecting this cool a reaction. I thought maybe you'd be a little more excited than this."

Saul took a step closer to Leal.

"Here. Just hold it in your hand. Feel the grip. The weight of it."

"No thanks," Leal said. "I'd rather watch."

"Go ahead. You'd think it was a poisonous snake I was

asking you to hold."

Saul held the gun out like a birthday gift, and Leal felt his eyes soften like tabs of butter in the warm light.

"Is it loaded?" he asked.

"Of course it's loaded. There's not much point bringing an unloaded gun into the woods, is there?"

"I wouldn't want to fire it by accident."

"The safety's on."

"All right. How do you hold it?"

Leal took the handgun tentatively from Saul.

"Hold on, don't swing it around!"

Leal brought the gun to a standstill in trembling hands.

"Just hold it loose for now. Don't point it at anyone, for Christ's sake. Just hold it. Got it?"

"Yeah, I got it." Leal raised the gun, swinging it in a slow arc, left to right, sighting along the barrel, taking aim through the trees.

"You want to fire it, you've got to slide the top of the barrel back till you hear it click. Like this. There, now. It's all ready to go."

"I didn't say I wanted to fire it," Leal said. "Here, you take it."

But Saul took a step backward, both hands in the air.

"I'll gladly take it back after you've fired off a round or two."

"That's okay. I've changed my mind."

"Here, hold it out steady."

Leal held it, but his arm started to shake. Standing behind him, Saul placed his hands over Leal's on the grip, helping him aim.

"That's it, nice and easy. Just breathe in and out, in and out. You've got it. You're a natural."

Releasing Leal's hands, he took a step back.

"All yours," he said.

"What do I fire at?"

"What do you think? At the dummy, dummy."

Leal looked at the mannequin, sitting on the log. Sunlight streamed through the canopy of leaves, warming the ground in soft, yellow splotches.

"Can't I just shoot at a tin can or something?"

"It's a little more lifelike this way. It's like a real-life situation. Just pretend she's an intruder."

Leal let out a little laugh at this. He couldn't picture a burglar sitting on a log, naked, all beige. Except for the wig, she had a generic face, eyeless, noseless. Her breasts were plain, too, without nipples.

Saul seemed upset.

"All right, then. Maybe she's your wife, let's say, and you just caught her in bed with someone."

Leal didn't laugh at this. He lined up the mannequin along the barrel.

"Take your time," Saul instructed. "Just squeeze the trigger nice and easy."

"Is there a kickback?"

"Sure, there's a kick. Just a little."

Leal aimed the gun straight at the mannequin, but then his arm started to tremble. He felt a band of sweat form around the back of his neck. He lowered the gun and stared at the ground.

"Here," Saul said. "It's easy. I'll show you."

He took the gun from Leal and raised it. He fired one bullet after another, six shots in quick succession. *Bang, bang, bang! Bang, bang, bang!* Leal counted them with his fingers.

When Leal opened his eyes, Saul was walking over to the mannequin. Leal followed slowly. He watched Saul bend over her where she had fallen backward off the log. His aim hadn't been perfect, just fifty-fifty. Three small entry wounds had punctured her breast. Sawdust trickled from one of the holes.

"And that's how it's done," Saul said. "But just to be on the safe side." He held the gun an inch from the mannequin's temple and fired another shot.

Leal's head started to swim. His head felt light, a balloon about to float from his shoulders. Trees spun green and yellow circles around his head.

Thuster took the ringlet of purple and yellow flowers, their stems intertwined, and placed it on the mannequin's broken head. He lowered it like a funeral wreath.

Then Saul broke the silence.

"You ever get in any trouble, I want you to come to me."

"What kind of trouble?" Leal asked.

"Any kind. Doesn't matter. I just don't want anything bad happening to you, the way it happened to me when I was your age. I told you I was an acolyte, didn't I?"

Leal nodded his head, but Saul put a hand on his shoulder.

"I mean it," Saul said. "You come to me, first thing."

And all Leal could do was stare back.

*

Leal looks at Selena for her reaction.

He focuses his attention. He waits for revelation.

She knows he's waiting for her to open her mouth, to say something, but she's still processing his story by matching his description of events with the mannequin she's found in the woods this morning. She considers it a little too coincidental, his telling this story on the same day he led her through the woods—she has no doubt it was him—to arrive at the same mannequin. Except she was strung up by a rope, not sitting on a log. And she had Diana's trademark tattoos—another element missing from his story.

It's possible the mannequin is something he himself found. He's already admitted to hanging out in junkyards, picking up scrap pieces of discarded rubbish for kicks. She can easily imagine him hauling his find to the clearing by the lake, coloring her with magic marker, stringing her up to a tree. But what about the gun?

"Leal, I need to ask you something. It's just a standard question I'm required to ask all my patients …" who are a potential danger to themselves or others. "Is there a gun in your home? Does your mom own a gun?"

"That's two questions," Leal notes. "But the answers are 'no' and 'no.' My mom doesn't like guns. She disapproves."

Good, Selena thinks, exhaling relief.

"Well, then," she says. "I'll see you this Thursday, as usual. OK?"

"That's it?" he asks, standing. He seems a trifle disappointed. "Oh, wait!" he says, brightening on his way toward the door. "I almost forgot. I picked these for you." He reaches under the chair he has just vacated and retrieves a bouquet of flowers that appear in his hand as if by magic. They're violet and yellow and tied with a bow.

***

Dear Henri,

It is starting to feel like we are playing a game.

Chapter 7

It started to become a game that they'd play.

On the drive back to town with Jay, Diana and Leal would make up a story that explained what they did that day. Sometimes Jay would throw in a detail or two, just to make it sound more believable. And then Diana and Leal would repeat the story over and over until it sounded completely natural and their stories matched like gloves.

And this is what Leal would tell Saul if he came across him that day. He would tell him whatever story they made up.

Sometimes it was something simple, like a walk through the park or a trip to an ice-cream stand. But other times it was more difficult, like a visit to the local zoo for orphaned animals, where he'd have to tell Saul about the cougar without a front paw, the barn owl missing a wing, the hyena with a skin condition. Sometimes, it was only that he helped Diana work in her garden, or they volunteered for a walkathon for kids with muscular dystrophy, or they dropped off some used clothes for the Salvation Army. Or attended an afternoon matinee.

They would have fun imagining what the movie was about based on the title and poster and coordinating the details of the plot to keep their story straight until Saul would throw up his hands, shouting, "Spoilers!" Making up plotlines was much more fun than reading synopses online, so they were taking a chance on Saul expressing interest in seeing the same movie. Fortunately, he hated leaving his house at night.

Saul might be away on business for days at a stretch. But there always came a time when they would find him at home, reading the newspaper or pruning a tomato vine or feeding his chinchillas. He would ask how their day went when they stepped through the door or into the yard, finding a way to question them separately, privately. Diana might go upstairs to change, and this is when Saul would turn to Leal. And Leal would tell him the story that he and Diana invented.

Then Saul would smile and nod and say, "Isn't that nice." But he could tell that Saul was always a little disappointed in the stories he told. "Is that all?" he would ask. "Nothing else? You didn't happen to meet anyone? Talk with anyone?" And then he would go back to his newspaper or tomato vine or chinchillas.

He never thought Saul believed him—not truly.

Just as he knows that Selena doesn't believe him. Nobody does. The police didn't believe him either. They hadn't looked closely enough for evidence, for clues. Sure, they looked through church records, scanned missing-person reports. They even interviewed parishioners whose blank stares confessed their ignorance of such a child. But they failed to do one thing. They hadn't dredged the lake.

His school counselor, Ms. Jacobson, didn't believe him. That's why she sent him here, to these sessions with Dr. Harris— Selena. That's what she wants him to call her. She wants to bond with him, like a parent or a friend. But how can he bond with her if she doesn't believe a word he's saying?

Oh, she pretends to believe him all right. She nods her head. She smiles. She takes notes from time to time. But he knows she doesn't really think he's telling the truth. He can tell by her eyes, by her questions, the way she asks him to repeat certain parts of his story.

She says it's his choice to keep coming back, but he likes coming here. He likes being in her office. It feels comfortable. That's a word she likes using. She always wants him to feel comfortable. More than this, it feels safe. At the end of each session—he can't tell her this—he doesn't want to leave. He would like so much to sleep overnight on her couch, the way he used to at Father Mac's.

*

Now Selena is asking him something from her side of the office. He has to make his mind focus hard on what she is saying.

"How are things going at school?"

Her voice sounds far away, as though funneled through the coils of a seashell.

He forces himself to answer.

"I don't know," he says.

"Do you like school, Leal?"

He doesn't want to think about school, doesn't want to talk about it.

"I guess it's okay. I mean, sure, I know it's important. If you want to make something of yourself someday."

"Have you thought about what you might want to be when you grow up?"

Why is she asking him these questions? She never asks this many questions—not in a row.

"Do you have any ideas?"

"No, not really. I mean, I'm past the age when you want to be a fireman or a cowboy or circus clown. But I don't really know what I want to be. My father was a salesman, but I don't think I'd like to go into sales. I was thinking I might try to be something more practical—like a lawyer or a doctor. But I don't think I'm smart enough to be a lawyer. Maybe something else. Maybe a mechanic. Something like that. But it's too early to say for sure."

"Do you think you'd like working on cars?"

Another question. When will she stop asking questions? He doesn't want to talk about his future. He wants to talk about his past.

"I don't know. I only know what I wouldn't want to be."

"What's that?"

Leal takes a deep breath.

"The manager of a residential care facility for disadvantaged boys."

*

It was difficult having a conversation with a woman in the nude—this is one thing Leal was learning.

As soon as Diana took her seat, Jay took up his brush and started painted straight away, brushstroke after brushstroke. Once he got an idea fixed in his head, he painted steadily, as though whitewashing the side of a barn, only occasionally looking up at his subject. And his subject was always an unclothed Diana.

Leal told her about Father Mac's plan—how he wanted to send Thuster away. He wanted to take him to some kind of orphanage in the suburbs of Chicago—a residential care facility for disadvantaged boys.

"What's wrong with that?" Diana asked.

"I'm just not sure that's what he wants," Leal said.

"What who wants? Thuster?"

"Who else?"

Diana stretched her hands over her head. She took in a long breath. Her breasts heaved along the top of a sigh.

"I don't mean to sound rude. But how do you know? How do you know what he wants or doesn't want? From what you've said, it doesn't sound like it would be an awful place for him."

"I'm not saying it would be awful."

Diana scratched a nail along her thigh. Leal traced with his eyes the red line it left behind.

"He has to go somewhere. From what you've told me, Father Mac can't hang onto him forever. He can't take Thuster to Florida with him, right?"

"It's just that there would be all these kids. All these other kids around. About twenty-five of them."

Diana shifted her body weight. She propped an elbow on the arm of the chair. She placed her chin in the palm of her hand. Her hair fell in long strands across her breasts. Jay didn't seem to care that she kept changing her position.

"That's a good thing, isn't it? He would be around other boys. The same kind of boys. Boys that are like him."

Jay paused with his brush at eye level, a glob of yellow-green paint clinging to it.

"I think Diana's making a valid point," he pitched in.

"I just hope he'll be happy there," Leal said.

"Everything changes," Diana said. "Nothing's constant."

She crossed both legs and folded her arms beneath her breasts. Her nipples popped free like raspberries.

"I know," Leal said.

"What do you think he wants?" Diana asked.

Leal thought about it—but only for a second.

"A family."

Jay's brush fell against the canvas, a yellow-green streak moving down the side of one of Diana's painted legs.

Leal looked out at the lake. He watched Thuster, standing along the gray strip of beach, hands at his sides, swaying like a willow strand with the slight breeze.

"Maybe you could—" Leal didn't finish his thought. He couldn't complete the sentence. He already knew what the answer would be.

"What did you say?" Diana asked.

He looked at her reflection in the window. Her body arched long and white and bare.

"Maybe you could adopt him. You and Saul."

Silence. He didn't hear a sound, not even the slithering slide of a brushstroke. Turning around, he looked straight at Diana, eye for eye. He needed a level of eye contact for playing hardball. Negotiating. Saul had taught him that.

"No, Leal. I couldn't."

"Why not?"

"It just wouldn't work out. You must realize that by now."

"Why wouldn't it work out? It would be perfect."

"We've tried. Saul and I have tried to have a baby—produce a child. We thought about adopting, but we're past the point—past the point in our relationship—where it would work out for both of us."

Jay's eyes ran back and forth along the top his canvas, keeping score.

"But it's what he really wants. I know it."

"What who wants?"

"Thuster. It's what he keeps hoping for. I can see it in his eyes."

"What makes you think that? I don't mean to sound hard on you, Leal, but do you really think you can read his mind?"

"No, but I can read other things. I can see how he acts around you. I'm not blind. I know you're not blind to it."

"I'm sorry. It's just not—feasible. It wouldn't work. You have to trust me on this. I just don't want you walking around carrying this wild idea inside your head."

"What's so wild about it?"

She reached out a hand, palm up—a peace offering.

"I'm sorry, honey. I really am."

They looked at each other across the room. All Leal could see were her eyes: a staring contest to see who would blink first.

"Well," Jay said. He set his brush aside. "I think it's all right if we break a little early today."

*

Selena switches off the recorder.

"We went a little longer today than normal," she says. "I have a patient waiting."

Leal stands slowly from the couch.

"It's what my mom's always threatening to do too," he says.

"What's that?"

"Send me away to a boarding school. Or someplace worse, place me in foster care."

"But not seriously," Selena says. "I'm sure she wouldn't do that for real."

Parents make all kinds of idle threats that their children take seriously. It's half the reason the kids who come to see her are so messed up.

Leal shrugs.

"It's because I'm so difficult," he says. "Half the time, I think she might really go through with it."

***

"How are you feeling today, Marla?" Selena asks, as her next patient takes her seat.

"I'm fine," she says, "but I don't know about that boy."

"What boy is that?"

"The boy who just left."

"What makes you think he's not all right? You mean emotionally?"

"No," Marla says, "financially."

She hands Selena a business card. "Here," she says. "He left this behind."

Selena notes it's double-sided, which in itself is unusual, aside from the fact the two businesses seem unrelated. On one side it advertises:

BETTER LIFE CHOICES
Financial Consulting

On the other:

BOOT CAMP FOR BOYS
Faith-Based Residential Care

Curiously, the phone number is the same for each. No street address or website, which is odd, just city and state: Evanston, Illinois. She knows the suburb well.

Selena has a rule against engaging in small-talk about other patients, but in this case, she can't help herself. "Do you know him?"

"Everyone does at the middle school, sure." Marla scrunches up her nose as though she smells rotting eggs. "Leal the Eel." She squirms in her seat to show her repugnance. "He's icky."

Selena tries to remember. Don't girls at this age think all boys are "icky"? Or is Leal ickier than average?

"Paula feels the same way about him as I do."

"Oh, that's right, you're friends, I forgot."

"Besties," she concurs, hooking her pinkies together to show the depth of their relationship. "How is she doing, anyway? They won't let anyone visit who's not family."

"Well, I'm not seeing her as a therapist anymore, but I understand she's still stable."

"Stable, huh? Well, that's still better than Leal. He's about as unstable as they come." She rolls her eyes around her head to underscore the point.

*

Selena tries the 1-800 number between patients.

The phone rings ten times without going to voicemail. She's just about to give up, when a woman answers with a bright, crisp voice, albeit out of breath, as though she had to sprint a hundred meters to reach it.

"Better Life Choices. Boot Camp for Boys. Which one are you interested in?"

Selena ponders the question for a moment.

"Both," she answers.

"That's not unusual. Many of our clients, after they've placed a child with our residential facility, find they have all kinds of money left over to make investments they never thought possible. Can I get your name, please?"

Selena gets as far as the "S," emitting a sibilant sound through her teeth, and then, driven by an impish impulse, her mind switches gears and she sounds out "S-s-s-andra."

"Sandra? Sandra Porter?"

"Uh-huh," Selena acknowledges, surprising herself by this bit of play-acting she's putting on.

"It's me. Madeline—Madeline Kahn. You know, just like the actress, except pronounced different. 'If anyone can, Madeline Kahn,' ha-ha. Don't you remember? I was the one gave you the tour. You were with a priest, a Father Mc-something. Hang on, it'll come to me."

"MacDougal. You're right." That she is continuing the act surprises her. She's not typically this deceitful.

"I have to say, you sound so much different over the phone. The paperwork's still on file, in case you were wondering. We haven't given up hope on our end, ha-ha. And remember, because we're church-affiliated, we're tax-exempt, meaning virtually no cost to you."

Selena finds she can't formulate a response to this proposal. Recovering her voice, she wends her way carefully.

"I'm still having some doubts," she says softy, slowly.

"That's understandable," Madeline chirps like a songbird on

a spring morning. "It's common for parents—especially mothers—to have second thoughts. After all, it's a big decision, giving up custody of a child."

"Yes," Selena agrees, "it is."

She's starting to feel sick inside, her stomach churning. Plus, the baby has decided to perform cartwheels, which make her double over her desk.

"Well, tell you what. If there's anything I can do to ease your mind, just let me know. Oh, I know! Next time you come up, bring your son along. Leland, isn't it?"

"Leal," Selena answers, wondering how long she can hold out before she needs to rush to the toilet she shares with the dentist across the lobby.

"Right, I forgot, he goes by Leal. Such an interesting name. Scottish, isn't it?"

"Yes, I think so." Actually, Selena had looked it up in her book of baby names. "It means trustworthy, loyal."

"Helpful, friendly, clean, reverent, and all the rest. My son was a Scout, ha-ha, so I know the motto backward and forward. Anyway, be sure to bring him up and let him get a feel of the place. Often, by the time a boy finishes the tour and sees all we have to offer—all the activities and sports and rec facilities and even an indoor pool—well, the tour makes his mind up for him. It'll be all you can do to keep him begging you to sign off on the paperwork."

"Thank you," Selena says, her voice a mere murmur, "that's very helpful."

"Well, it's been nice talking to you again. You've got our number. So don't ever hesitate to call."

"Don't worry, I won't."

"And remember," Madeline adopts a more maternal tone, "whatever decision you make, it's all for the greater good—yours and his."

"I'll keep that in mind." She can't help tacking on an addendum, perhaps out of spite: "Ha-ha."

As soon as she hangs up, Selena plops her forehead against the desk, waiting for this spell of biliousness to pass. If she were on a boat, she would blame seasickness. As it is, there's only one thought that goes through her head, anchoring her concentration in place.

Betrayal, she thinks.

How awful Leal must have felt, if he had known of his mother's tentative plan to put him away, lock and key, to be so betrayed by someone he loves.

***

Sometimes, after a difficult day at the office, it's nice to curl up in a comfy chair and watch other people sort out their troubles, especially if their main worries are whether there is an extra bedroom for an office, or the counters are genuine granite and the appliances stainless steel, or the en suite has a jacuzzi.

Often, she watches the channel with her father, as she does tonight. They place bets on which house the couple will select. Will the husband hold out or will he cave to his spouse's wishes? It's a study in psychology, which her father rather enjoys. By profession, he's a number-cruncher. Give him a cubicle with a digital adding machine, and he can go for hours without human contact. He's always plied two trades, back to back, a CPA during tax season, helping clients find loopholes in the tax code, and a tax attorney in the off-season, helping these same clients survive IRS audits.

Tonight's episode features a couple of island-hunters, Canadians with a $10 million budget looking to escape the subarctic cold by buying their very own island.

"Imagine it, Dad. Your own private Idaho."

"I thought they said 'Tahiti.'"

"It's just an expression."

At ten o'clock, her father, surprisingly still awake, requests the nightly edition of the local news, and after the First Watch warning of inclement weather, a commercial comes on showing a stout, middle-aged man with a five-o'clock shadow wearing a royal ermine stole with slicked-back hair held in place by a chintzy crown, a chinchilla on his shoulder.

"Turn the channel!" her father insists.

"No, Dad, wait a minute."

And in that minute, a young woman prances onto the screen from stage left wearing a white string bikini, a white winter hat, white gloves, and gleaming-white vinyl calf-high boots that only half conceal the squiggle of an orange snake.

"Why, here's our little Snow Bunny, right now!" Saul Solomon, the Chinchilla King, announces.

"Snow bunny, my ass," her father says with disgust. "That's got to be his third wife to date."

"Aren't you cold, little bunny?" Saul asks, and Diana nods her head with an exaggerated shiver, crossing her arms over her ample breasts, although one can still see the purple butterfly peeking above.

Saul waves his scepter and there's an explosion of confetti. When the confetti settles, there's Diana, donning a fur coat.

"Oh, Saul," she says, performing a quick catwalk to show it off, "my hero!"

"You can be that special someone's hero today," Saul claims, as Diana spins and twirls. "Come on down to Saul's Chinchilla World and take advantage of 'our buy one get one half-price' deal. What are you waiting … fur? Get it?"

"Yes, Saul," Diana pitches in with a roll of her heavily mascara-etched eyes. 'I'm sure they get it."

"That man's nothing but a crook," her father alleges, switching off the TV.

"You've had dealings with him?"

"He's come to my office a couple of times trying to sweet-talk me into doing his taxes, but I wouldn't give a guy like that the time of day. Everyone in the industry knows King Saul keeps a double set of books, one for his cronies, and one for his investors, to hide the fact he's hemorrhaging money faster than flint through a goose."

"Dad," she interrupts with outstretched arm, trying to calm him down.

"I'm surprised the bum hasn't gone belly up by now."

"Dad?" she inquires. "Have you taken your meds?"

"Stop in, soon!" Diana had said, by way of concluding the commercial. Maybe it was time Selena took her up on her offer.

***

Dear Henri,

It is all so real in his head. I am sure of that now. I believe that Leal believes his own story about his involvement with Saul and Diana. But there's something you should know: I'm starting to believe it too.

Chapter 8

According to the girl's mother, when Paula emerged from her coma, she looked around the hospital room. Everything was in white: walls, bed sheet, curtains, lights. She plaintively asked, "Is this heaven?" Her mother brought her down to earth gently: "No, dear. It's far from heaven." The daughter felt betrayed. She looked at her mother with accusing eyes. "Then give me more pills!"

Selena took up the mother's invite to visit the psych ward where her daughter had been transferred for extended observation.

"Dr. Harris, I'm so glad you're here. I hate to admit it but—"

She confessed she had been wrong to take her daughter out of therapy prematurely, and now look at what's happened. The mother broke down in heaving sobs and Selena suppressed an "I told you so" knee-jerk reaction to console her. Not that more therapy would have prevented a recurrence, Selena surmises. She'll have to wait until the girl is released from inpatient observation to see where things stand. In the meantime, it wouldn't hurt to review the safety plan for home care.

"Personally," the mother said, once she recovered, "I think she's been reading too much Sylvia Plath."

Selena doesn't have to feign surprise.

"Are kids still reading her these days?"

"Her English teacher—some pseudo-hippie leftover from the '60s—introduced his class to her. You know the type, still clinging to a past decade, idealizing a bygone era. I could kill him, but it's probably more practical to report his outdated teaching methods to the school board."

Selena couldn't be sure if this was meant to be a joke.

"It would be so nice if you could suggest something more uplifting—something by one of your people."

Your people.

"What?" Selena retorted. 'Like Maya Angelou?"

Apparently, she hadn't injected sufficient sarcasm for the patient's mother to detect it.

"Why, yes. That one about the caged bird. I should have thought of it myself."

Other than Paula, Selena is experiencing a series of strikeouts with her patients. Each week, she meets with twenty-some patients, mainly adolescents, and five of these require more than one weekly visit. Aside from the girl with a predilection for suicide attempts, there are three other cases that worry her: a boy whose recent shoplifting spree for laxatives was finally stopped by a plainclothes security officer, a girl whose insomnia is fueled by nightmares involving her deceased twin, a young woman whose addiction to abusive boyfriends has produced welts on well-hidden areas of her body.

And then there is Leal.

***

She asks her standard opening question:

"How are you feeling today, Leal?"

"I'm fine."

"That's good."

This isn't, of course, what she wants to hear. She wants to hear truth: I'm miserable, I'm scared, I'm nervous, I'm depressed, I'm traumatized. If he is fine, truly fine, then there is no point to his presence in her office.

"But *you* don't think I'm fine, do you?"

Here is something new: a verbal reflex, as though the tap of a rubber mallet has produced a nervous twitch in the opposite knee.

"Well, I'm not sure. That's what these visits—these sessions—

are about. To find out if you're fine or not."

"You think I'm making it all up, don't you?"

"Your story, you mean? What you've been telling me?"

"It's all right if you do. Everyone else thinks I'm making it up."

"Have you told anyone else what you've told me? I mean, aside from the police."

"Well, the police. They didn't believe me. And Ms. Jacobson. She didn't believe me either. I guess that's why she sent me here. Right? To see if you believe me or not."

"I guess you could put it that way. Yes—in a sense."

She watches his eyes. They stare at the floor. They flit to the window, roam the office, look anywhere, everywhere—except at her.

"I've noticed you haven't talked about one thing yet."

He raises his eyes. They focus on the Monet.

"I've noticed that you haven't—well, except for that first meeting—you haven't talked about the drowning."

They could be in an art museum, it becomes so quiet: the bowels of a cave.

"It's all right if you don't want to talk about it. I was only hoping that at some point you might."

She counts to ten—no response.

"Did you not want to talk about—what happened that night?"

"No. I mean, I can't."

"Is it because someone told you not to talk about it?"

"No. I just can't."

"That's all right, Leal. I've said this before—I don't want you to feel pressured to talk about anything you're not comfortable with."

"I can talk about Thuster if you want. I can talk about him when he was alive. I like talking about him when he was alive."

"That's fine. If you want—"

"It's funny, really. Out of all the people who knew him. I'm thinking right now of Diana and Saul and Father Mac. Out of all these people, it was Jay who got to know him best."

*

Leal remembers coming back from the lake, with Thuster behind him, a pull toy on an invisible string. Diana, wrapped in a gray painter's frock, sat in the purple armchair, hugging her knees. Having cleared a space on his table of paints to make room, Jay began pouring goblets of wine.

"Leal," Jay said, "you're just in time. We're celebrating."

Leal accepted the half goblet of wine from Jay and took a shallow sip. He couldn't remember the last time he was offered wine. He couldn't remember the last Sunday he took Holy Communion, even though grape juice was substituted for kids his age.

Taking the glass Jay poured for Thuster, he handed it to him carefully so it wouldn't spill.

"Have a seat." Jay motioned toward the floor, and Leal sat crisscross applesauce in a small square of sunlight. "There's something I want to ask you."

Accepting a goblet from Jay, Diana slid off her chair in an easy motion, joining Leal and Thuster on the floor.

"I'm getting very close to the end of the series of paintings I have in my mind to do of her," Jay said. "Very, very close." He took a long swallow of wine. "Diana's been very patient, but I feel it's time to give her a little break." He waved his hand at the painting drying on its easel, then to the stacks of canvases leaning against the walls under the windowsills. "I've been giving some thought to a new subject, something fresh."

"Hey," Diana said. "You're making me sound like leftover liverwurst."

"Something a little different, then."

"That's better," Diana said.

"Anyway, I've been thinking about it, and I was hoping, if it's all right with you. What I mean is, you seem to be acting as his guardian."

"What Jay is trying to say," Diana said, "is if it would be okay, do you think, to have Thuster pose as a subject?"

Leal took another slow, careful sip of wine. He felt the blood rush into his temples. He looked at Thuster holding his glass, peering inside it, as if it contained gasoline.

"Sure," he said, "why not? It's fine with me, if it's all right with Thuster. I mean, if you can get him to pose for you."

"Oh, I think I can manage that all right," Jay said.

It came to Leal as an afterthought.

"He can keep his clothes on, can't he?"

*

The painting grew over three afternoons, three perfect days, all in a row. Looking back on it, he wishes it could have been more. He wishes it could have been a week of perfect days, a year. He wishes they hadn't stopped.

He stayed inside all the time now to watch Jay work his canvas. He didn't go out onto the beach. He didn't hike around the lake through the woods. It wasn't that he didn't trust Jay or that he felt the need to constantly look after Thuster or that he thought anything was going to go wrong. It was just that he liked watching Jay work.

He liked seeing the way he squeezed globs of oil onto his palette. He liked watching him mix his paints, squirting thin gleams of linseed oil onto the colors like starter fluid for a pile of charcoal. He liked watching him dab his brush onto the canvas, sometimes in long, clean lines, sometimes in wide patches forming a mosaic. Other times, he worked in careful dots and dashes, a private Morse code. Diana spent her time reading a book, doodling in her journal, wading along the beach.

"Want to go for a swim?" she'd ask.

"I'll stay here," he'd answer.

"There aren't many swimming days left this summer."

"That's okay. You go ahead."

"Suit yourself."

For all he could tell, Thuster was just being Thuster. He sat on the chair where Jay had placed him, taking Diana's place, staring straight ahead into nothingness, as if he had X-ray vision and could see through Jay's canvas. He kept perfectly still, as though holding his breath for the hours it took Jay to work. He could tell when Jay was finished for the day, because he would set his brushes aside in an empty Mason jar, then take a single step back from the easel with his hands on his hips. Thuster wouldn't flinch, wouldn't move.

"It's like he isn't real," Jay said. "There's definitely some—unreality—about him. He's breathing. I know he has to be breathing, but I can't tell that he breathes or when. His nostrils don't flare, his chest doesn't seem to rise or fall. I've never known any model to sit so still. I don't understand it. I can't even catch him blinking. I know he must blink, it's only natural. But he must do it whenever I'm not looking in his direction. And the lighting. He absorbs it somehow. He retains the shadows of the room in and on himself, I can't even explain it. They cover his face like a veil. It's uncanny. It's like he knows what I want before I even know that I want it. It's as though he anticipates each brushstroke, each shade of paint. If I didn't know any better, I'd say he was an inanimate object. He's like a still life, a perfect still life—a still life in dungarees."

Leal liked it when Jay talked about Thuster that way. No one had ever talked this way about Thuster before. It made him seem important. It gave him a touch of class. He was no longer just this little kid who didn't know how to talk or pretended not to know how to talk. Everyone else just seemed to look at him as some kind of problem, a puzzle to be solved. But Jay saw him as something different, not just a freak of nature, but something worthy of study, something gifted and noble.

"You can go unfreeze him now," Jay said.

Diana walked in from the lake, dripping water on the floor. Leal thought it strange she was wearing a swimsuit. He wondered if she had brought it from home.

He took Thuster's arm and slowly unbent it at the elbow. He did the same for his other arm, then his two legs at the knees.

"There's a lot going on inside him, isn't there?" Jay said.

"What do you mean?" Leal asked.

"Well, he's a contradiction in terms. For one thing, I sense an utter calmness, a freedom from any anxiety whatsoever."

"I could sure use a dose of that these days," Diana said, drying her hair with a towel.

"It's like he's in touch with the source of all knowledge," Jay said. "If there is such a thing."

"You're being melodramatic," Diana told him. She nudged his ribs with her elbow as she moved to his side of the canvas.

"No, I'm not," Jay said, taking offense at the jab. "But then there's this undercurrent, like a pool of stagnant water in a deep, dark well. Something you can sense deep inside him. This undercurrent of—I don't know how else to label it—this undercurrent of anger."

"Anger?" Leal said. He had never thought of Thuster being full of anger before.

"Stop it," Diana said. "You're going to scare the boy."

*

Anger. Selena jots the word on her notepad. She adds an exclamation point. She underscores it twice.

Here is something she can use. Anger—suppressed anger. It makes perfect sense. If anything, Leal seems calm on the surface, polite, well mannered.

If anger is what fills him, motivates him, imperceptibly, undetected by those around him …

She reflects on her conversation with Madeline of the Boot Camp for Boys. She believes it might be the one thing, nothing else, that would make her patient angry.

The question, though, is whether or not Leal knew about his mother's tentative plan to send him away—for real. And if not, she doesn't want to be the one to break it to him. But maybe she can lead him there, bring him to a trough to see if he might be inclined to take a long, cool drink.

Selena suspends this line of thought. She needs to concentrate on what Leal is and isn't telling her. She needs to read between the lines.

"You said earlier. You said just a little earlier that you weren't sure you could trust Jay."

"I did? I don't remember saying that."

"Well, you're right." Selena flips through her notebook. "You said something to the effect that you stayed by Thuster—you watched Jay paint—not because you couldn't trust him, but because you liked watching him paint. But let's just talk about that—just that one thing—for a second. That element of trust. What did you mean by that?"

She waits for a response. Leal slumps in his couch, stares at the floor.

"What I mean to ask is, are there others—other adults—is there anyone whom you don't trust?"

She isn't making herself understood. Or maybe it's the opposite, she's making herself understood all too well.

"Let me phrase it another way. Why wouldn't you trust an adult? What might an adult do to you? Or to Thuster?"

Leal looks up from the floor, looks into her eyes—briefly,

then away. Eyelashes flutter like bird wings.

"Okay," he says. "I sort of see what you're saying. Well, I guess all I must have meant is that, you know, when it comes to strangers, you can never be too sure."

"But Jay wasn't a stranger. Was he? You had been going to his cottage now—well, you had been visiting him throughout the summer. Isn't that right?"

"Yeah, that's right."

"So he really couldn't be labeled a stranger. Let's think of it a little differently. Let's think of it this way: Are there adults whom you know, adults who know you well—are there these kinds of adults you can't trust?"

"I don't know. I—I can't really think of anyone. Not right now."

"Well, let's think of the adults that you know. Let's think of some adults. Okay?"

"Okay."

"Let's start with your mother. Do you trust your mother?"

His eyes glaze over. Selena can tell he has gone somewhere else, if only for a moment, as though he has entered a sort of trance.

"Leal?"

And then he snaps out of it, as if no time has elapsed at all.

"Yes. I mean, of course I trust her. What's there not to trust?"

"What about your counselor at the school? Ms. Jacobson—do you trust her?"

"Yes."

"How about your teachers? You mentioned Mr. Birch?"

"Yes."

"What about Father MacDougal?"

"Father Mac?"

"Yes. Do you trust—did you trust Father Mac?"

Leal stares out the window. A tree limb crosses the pane. Its leaves have turned red, outlined with rust. Mid-October sunshine bleeds through the leaves, illuminating the edges like pieces of stained glass.

"Leal? Did you trust Father Mac?"

"I can't think about him right now."

"Why is that?"

"I don't want to think about him right now."

Leal shifts his gaze to the floor. Then softly—a murmur.

"I didn't like what he was doing. I didn't like what he was doing to Thuster."

***

Dear Henri,

The HS reunion was an absolute bust—just as I knew it would be.

I wanted to get drunk as quickly as possible, so I pretended my glasses of 7-Up were laced with bourbon.

But in the end, I'm glad I went. As it turned out, I found out some vital information from an unexpected source: Leal's mother.

She suspends her typing, studies the keyboard for a long while, contemplating, considering, reconsidering, then picks up her phone and presses the appropriate speed dial number of favorites. Some stories just don't translate well in print.

"Henri? I didn't wake you I hope?"

"Selena! How wonderful to hear your voice. Genevieve is abed, but I'm still awake. This isn't an emergency, is it? Should I prepare myself for awful news?"

"Nothing like that," Selena laughs into the speaker. "Can you spare a few moments? I thought this is something you might like to hear."

*

It was a small class to begin with, and just under half showed up. You'd think more would have made it for a 20th anniversary, but maybe they're holding out for the 25th. In any case, a lot of people have left town since graduation. Leaving for college, other towns, other jobs. Selena was one of them, remember. Not many return—she is a definite exception.

You know how small towns are. Gossip. Rumors. Conservative values. Anything you've heard is 99% true. As soon as she entered, she took up a post in a corner of the reception hall, a lone wallflower behind a white paper-covered table most of the night, but even so, she's at a stage where her pregnancy is hard to conceal. She's already gone up three pant sizes.

"Come on," Lori encouraged her. "Let's get out and mingle."

Selena begged off, claiming swollen ankles. Besides, she was Lori's designated driver for the evening, so she didn't think she'd have much fun being the adult in the room.

"Have it your way," Lori sang to the tune of an outdated Burger King jingle and jounced off making an arrow for the bar.

Selena felt she was doing a pretty good job staying incognito until three tall white women from across the way spotted her and performed a charade of a fast break, fake dribbling and passing a ball until they were within an imaginary three-point arc, when the shooting guard tossed her the ball, and she raised both arms in imitation of a slam dunk, even though she couldn't make her feet, ensconced in flat-bottom penny loafers, leave the floor if she had wanted to.

"Score!" the one shouted.

"Our old center, back in action," another said.

"Just like old times. Remember that final second of the regional semifinals?"

"When Selena blocked the winning layup? Who could forget?"

"Good to see you again." A pat on the shoulder. "How you been?"

"Never mind asking," another observed. "Just take a look at her."

"Round as a B-ball. When are you due?"

Of course, they each had to take a turn touching her stomach for luck. And just like that, she was joshing and jostling with her old squad of starters. They hadn't aged equally. One had put on a pound or two, another had let her hair turn prematurely gray, while the third looked just the same except for an obvious nose job gone awry. But she would have recognized them in a check-out line from a distance of a hundred yards, and in a way, she was glad to reunite with them. They had a way of accepting her just as she was.

"Where's Shawty?" Selena inquired.

Shawty, aka Marissa Tompkins, had been their point guard. Just as Selena had felt implicit pressure from coaches and team-mates to live up to stereotypes associated with her color, Marissa had put in extra effort to overcome a disadvantage in height. She was ferocious on offense, and she and Selena had developed an almost telepathic bond when it came to her being in the right place, hands stretched from a leap toward the hoop, at just the right moment in her trajectory, as Marissa fired the ball in her direction.

"You don't know? You hadn't heard?"

"You're not going to believe it."

"She did it! She finally did it!"

"Did what?" Selena asked, completely befuddled.

"Why, she maxed out her credit cards and moved to Tonga."

"Just like she always said she was going to do."

"Her lifelong dream, don't you remember?"

"Oh, yeah," Selena recalls. "Wasn't that her yearbook caption?"

"*Most likely to place first on Survivor.*"

"Her favorite show."

"Here's a postcard she sent."

"You got one too?"

Passed around hand to hand, the postcard showed a set of

palm trees bookending a hammock, the hand of an otherwise invisible recliner raised with a cocktail in a coconut mug topped with a miniature umbrella. Wifi must be spotty in the middle Pacific, Selena concludes.

On the back, a simple scrawl of a message: *Living the life! Come visit!*

"If she can do it, who's the say we can't do the same?"

"Talk about early retirement."

"Whaddup, home girls?" This was Lori, plugging her face into the circle, her mouth, already heavy on the lipstick, outlined shockingly red by the gallons of rum punch she'd consumed.

"Why, look who's here?" the small forward exclaimed.

"Our very own cheerleader," the power forward recognized her, too.

"Give us a cheer, Lori!" the shooting guard begged.

"Go-o-o, Otters!" Lori shouted, throwing out her arms, but so unsteady, Selena reached out to catch her, until two bystanders took over. Thankfully, Lori was too drunk to continue the cheer. She could hardly stand unsupported, much less perform a cartwheel or split.

"Hey! You know what?" Lori slurred. "We should have your baby shower tomorrow. Now that everyone's back in town. All your friends, I mean. We don't even have to send out invitations! Where's a microphone?"

"Lori, no," Selena cautioned, pulling her away from the group.

"*Psst!*" Lori hissed in her ear. "Let me know when I get too embarrassing."

"It's a little past that," Selena said soberly.

"In that case," she smiled, her mouth as grotesque as a clown's. Before she could stop her, Lori rushed to the DJ's booth and took over the mic.

"Ladies and gentlemen," her voice boomed, overriding the

music. "Wait a sec, just the ladies. You're all invited to my dear, dear friend Selena's house first thing in the morning to shower her baby, I mean to baby her shower—oh, you know what I'm trying to—"

Selena grabbed the microphone before her friend could say anything more incriminating.

"Come on," she said. "As your DD, I insist it's time to go."

She insisted and kept insisting, but Lori counter-insisted and clung to the party well past closing time, when she finally pried her friend free of last call, a drink still in her hand.

Selena thought to drive her passenger straight home, but Lori knew of an all-night diner where she could get a cup of coffee. Throwing a tantrum, she stomped her feet and faked a crying fit, until Selena circled the block and found a space out front of the plate-glass window. The scene looked straight out of *Nighthawks*, only a couple of loners at the counter, another in a booth, so she thought, *What the hell?* She could use a cup of mocha herself.

Inside, only one waitress was on duty, early thirties, face drained and wan beneath stringy hair tied back in a bun. Her nametag read "Sandra," so Selena knew exactly who she was.

"We meet at last," Selena said, when she arrived at their table to take their orders.

"Excuse me?"

"You're Leal's mom, aren't you?"

"And you must be Dr. Harris. I should have guessed. You sound just like you did over the phone."

She gave a listless smile and smoothed her apron.

"And this is—"

No introduction was necessary. Lori had already passed out, her forehead pressing against the table, her arms drooping at her side like worn-down pendulums.

"Late shift?" Selena asked.

"A double."

A few idle words of chit-chat before she doubled back with a pot of coffee and the conversation turned to Leal.

"You're all Leal ever talks about. It's too bad you can't see him the whole school year through," Sandra said. "He's been a different boy since he's been seeing you. But all good things come to an end."

"Not *too* soon?" Selena asked.

"I just hope it doesn't take you much longer to make your determination. You know, before his visits run out."

"Right." Her father's been assisting her with billing, but Selena recalls her insurance plan. Waiting tables doesn't provide much in the way of secondary coverage, and Medicaid allows only so many behavioral health visits a year.

"Leal won't hear of it, of course. He's already threatened to make my life a living hell if I take him out of therapy."

"Really?"

"No offense, but I've already contacted the school about transferring him back to his guidance counselor before these sessions of yours get too expensive."

"Lori? I mean, Ms. Jacobson?"

"Yeah, that's the name."

"You've never met?"

"No, but I should have, with all the times he's been sent to her office."

Apparently aroused by the smell of fresh coffee, or the mention of her name, Lori raised her head, threw a bewildered look around the restaurant, then led a cavalry charge to the restroom. Unisex.

Selena used her absence to her advantage.

"I've been meaning to ask you something."

"All right, but make it quick." The entrance bell jangled, admitting a fresh posse of customers. "With the bars closing, this gets to be our busy time."

"That woman you described. The one who found your husband?"

Not the merriest of faces, Sandra's deepened into a scowl.

"What about her?"

"I was wondering if you know her name."

Sandra bent closer, setting the pot of coffee on the Formica table, lowering her voice into a whisper, her eyes turning into narrow slits as though carved by a steak knife.

"You don't think I didn't track her down after the cops were through grilling her? But it's like I said before. She had an airtight story. Just passing by, huh! That didn't explain the fact that her room was right next door. An adjoining one, too. You could pass through, one to the other, through a double set of doors. You ask me, they let her go too easy. No evidence, they said. All circumstantial. The only fingerprints were those of my husband and son. Now if you'll excuse me."

When Lori finally emerged from the toilet, a stench of vomit on her breath, Selena told her not to bother sitting back down. It was time to go.

At the register, Sandra was more conciliatory. Lori had already stumbled ahead to the curb mumbling something about Newtons—Fig or Wayne, it wasn't clear.

"Quite a case, your friend," Sandra said.

"And this is one of her good nights," Selena joked.

"I'm sorry," she said. "Earlier. I didn't mean to go off on you like that. It's just—that whole episode. It's something I want to forget."

"I don't blame you," Selena said, and as Sandra gave her back her change, she noted a curling vine strung with purplish blue flowers beginning at her wrist. Selena could easily imagine the vine traveling up through her short sleeve and winding down around a breast as though to ensnare it, just as it was immortalized in the series of paintings that Sid the landlord had shown her at the lakeside cottage.

A moment passed—and Sandra coughed politely.

"Uh, Dr. Harris? Your change?"

"Sorry, I just noticed your tattoo. Violets?"

"Clematis, actually."

"Pretty."

"Yeah, just something I had done back in my wild and crazy youth."

"And the significance?"

"Oh, right," Sandra smiled. "Your chance to psychoanalyze me, huh?"

Actually, Selena had a dozen questions on the tip of her tongue: Where, when, and how did you meet Jay? Did he talk you into painting you nude or did you propose that yourself? How long were you seeing him? What was the nature of your relationship? Did Leal tag along to these painting sessions? Was he allowed to watch Jay paint you unclothed? Do you know where he moved to? Are you still in touch?

But Selena also remembered what she'd learned from her father who taught her how to play Texas Hold'em from a young age. Right now, they were still determining the size of the buy-in. To ask these questions point blank would be like going all-in for a showdown before any cards had been dealt. Plus, Sandra would know she'd been snooping.

"—and that's how come I came to choose clematis."

"Because it's your mother's name," Selena echoed from a recording in her memory bank.

"That's right. I was afraid for a moment you weren't listening. That's your job, isn't it? To listen?"

"Sorry, I was thinking it might be a nice name to add to my list." She gave her stomach a pat. "That is, if it stays a girl."

"My bad, I should have noticed. You're expecting."

Selena only wished her belly wasn't preventing her from peering over the counter to get a second look at Sandra's ankles. She suspected one of them being wrapped with the tattoo of a chain.

*

"And Henri," Selena forges ahead breathlessly, "you're not going to believe this, but the next morning, with Lori passed out on my couch, I heard the doorbell ring. Who should be standing there but a woman I'd met at the reunion the night before. She'd been sitting out dances, as I had, just another wallflower, except in her case it wasn't voluntary. She was a true shrinking violet. In her hands, she held a small pink box wrapped with blue ribbon.'

She has a moment of uncertainty as the phone connection sounds dead.

"Henri, are you still there?"

"Yes, my dear. I'm here."

"You haven't been listening to a word I've said, have you?" she accuses him lightly. "You've been multitasking." *As usual,* she thinks.

"I confess. Guilty as charged. Just a few items cluttering my desk. But I assure you, I have hung onto every word. Please, won't you proceed?"

"All right, but you better be paying attention. So anyway, she says to me, 'I wasn't sure if it's a boy or a girl. Am I early?' She poked her nose through the front door to scope out the setting."

"So you invited her inside?" Henri asks. "You see? I was listening."

"What else could I do? She was standing right there. If I'd jilted her, her self-esteem would have plummeted into negative numbers."

Another moment of silence, except for a rustling of papers in the background—the click of a pen? Is he taking notes?

"A very humorous story," Henri comments drily. "You know I am very interested in the progress you are making with your young client."

Or lack of it, Selena thinks, in Leal's case.

"But tell me something, Selena. What about you?"

"Me? Little ol' *moi*?"

"How are things going with you? And I do mean, really."

Selena takes a deep breath.

"I'm fine—really," she emphasizes the adverb, hoping her rejoinder sounds convincing.

"And your meds? Do you need refills? The prices in Canada are so much less expensive than in the States, are they not?"

Chapter 9

They take their respective seats, eyes fencing across a slender rectangle of carpet, as usual.

Selena decides to break the silence.

En garde!

"Last time you said you didn't like what Father Mac was doing."

"I did?" *A subtle parry.*

Redoublement … renew the attack. She flips through her notes.

"You said you didn't like what he was doing to Thuster. What did you mean by that?"

"Did I say 'doing'?" Leal disengages, stretches his hands over his head, crosses his feet on the floor. *A feint?* "I meant 'planning.' I just didn't like what he was planning for Thuster—the way he was planning to take him away. I didn't like his whole idea of putting Thuster in a home for boys. No matter how good he tried to make it sound, it always came off like a prison."

Selena retreats but recovers her *riposte* stance. You can never let your guard down—not with this boy. She keeps her eyes and ears alert for an opening within which she can lunge.

*

Daylight was fading, as Leal walked through the opening in the chain-linked fence of the basketball court across the street from St. Mary's. Thuster was sitting on the sidelines, staring up at the rusty metal rim as Father Mac took his shots. He tried a jump shot, but it bounced clean off the backboard, so Leal chased it to the other end of the asphalt court.

"Leland," he said, out of breath. "Thank you for helping out an old man of the cloth. You saved me at least a dozen steps toward an early grave. I'm just not the man I used to be at this game, I can safely tell you that."

"How about a game of H-O-R-S-E?" Leal suggested, throwing him the ball, a dead-on bounce pass.

"What shall we play for?"

"Thuster," Leal answered.

"It isn't wise, betting on the souls of the living."

"You win, you take him to the boys' home in Chicago. I win, you let me keep him here—in Ovid."

"Leland," Father Mac said, cradling the ball like an infant, "I just want you to know, you were always my first choice. I've always thought that you and your mother—the special relationship you have with him—but then I've talked with your mother about it, and it just isn't feasible, economically. It's always economics that makes the worst of best intentions. That isn't to say your mother isn't a good woman, a very good woman. Her heart's in the right place."

Father Mac tossed the ball back to Leal.

"All right, then." Leal changed the bet. "I win, you take him with you to Florida. I'll start," he said before Father Mac could form an opposing argument. Leal tried a standard set shot. It banked off the backboard, angling through the hoop.

Dribbling in preparation, Father Mac braced his legs for the same shot, but it missed the rim altogether.

Leal tried a hook shot that fell short by an inch. For his turn, Father Mac tossed the ball in an underhand arc that slid through the rim, a perfect swish if there had been a net. Leal tried the same shot, but it fell short. He wasn't used to shooting underhand, it was so very old school.

"H to H," Father Mac kept score. "Here. We'll bend the rules a little. Take another shot."

Leal tried his luck from the side court. His shot rose in a high arc behind the backboard and landed with a thud.

Leal glanced at Thuster, sitting silently, unmoving, a passive spectator on the sidelines. His legs were crossed. Unblinking, his eyes stared at the rim of the basketball hoop, even though the ball was resting between Father Mac's feet. Sports weren't exactly his forte.

"I think he would be happy there, as happy as a boy with his condition can be," Father Mac stated.

Leal crossed his arms.

"You mean the boys' home?"

"He would be with others like him, and he would be watched, cared for, around the clock, by a team of professionals, who live with the boys."

"You know that, for sure?"

"There would be therapists who would work with Thuster—closely. He would be provided with everything he requires, all in one package: education, counseling, therapy, and even—down the road, so as not to be a far-off possibility—employment. In fact, it isn't unusual for boys like Thuster to grow up to be fully functioning adults, able to take their place in society."

"You've already decided?"

Raising the ball over his head, Father Mac attempted a feeble jump shot that swirled around the rim and fell through. Leal tried the same shot. It looked easy, but he missed it. He missed Father Mac's follow-up hook from the corner as well.

"H-O-R to H, I believe," Father Mac said. "It looks like you have some catching up to do."

Shadows grew long, and streetlights flickered. Surrounded by a halo of green light, Thuster blended with the darkness. On the brick wall of the church, neon graffiti glowed orange and yellow, boasts of local gangs.

"I'll be taking him there next week," Father Mac said. "Possibly as early as Monday, for what they call a preliminary interview. If it goes through, as I think it will, with shining colors, they can accommodate him in about two or three weeks, just as long as it takes to fill out and submit all the paperwork. Bureaucracies, you know. We live in a world of red tape. Even the Church is not exempt."

Father Mac passed the ball to Leal. He fired it at the hoop, but it hit the rim hard, rebounding into his arms. He wasn't prepared for the rebound. It smacked his chest, knocking the breath out of his lungs. He bent over with hands on knees, trying to get his breath back.

"I was hoping you might like to come with us," Father Mac said, placing a hand on Leal's shoulder. "Just so you can see what kind of a place it is. Your opinion, your approval—it is very important to me that I have your approval on this. And I know Thuster would like it, too, if you were to accompany us."

"Well," Leal said, breathing more easily. "Maybe. I mean, I'd like to see what kind of place it is."

"Leal, I know you wanted your mother to adopt him. I know you're disappointed." Leal noticed he used "Leal," not "Leland," this time. Father Mac ran his hand through Leal's hair. "I only wish I could continue taking care of him, but I can't. I can't take care of him anymore. The parish has already found a replacement, so I'll be moving as soon as Thuster is properly settled."

"Not if I win!" Leal reminded him. He threw the ball to Father Mac, but the priest placed it on the asphalt where he stood guard over it with long legs.

"Let an old man catch his breath for a second, if you would."

Father Mac held his hand over his chest. He squinted his eyes, as though in pain.

"Father?" Leal came up to him. "Are you all right?"

"That's enough for tonight, don't you think?" Father Mac said. "Let's call it a game. We can always pick up where we left off next time."

"Okay," Leal said. He was feeling out of breath himself.

"But for now," Father Mac said, gazing fondly into Leal's eyes, "it looks as though I'm ahead."

*

"So you felt bad for Thuster," Selena summarizes.

"Yeah," Leal confirms. "I guess I did."

"You felt sad that Thuster was leaving. You felt sad that Father Mac was moving away."

"Oh, no," Leal says. "I don't think I felt sad. I wanted him to go."

"You mean Thuster?" Selena asks.

"No," Leal says. "Father Mac. But I wanted him to take Thuster with him."

Selena waits for Leal to continue, to elaborate, to explain, but he stares out the window. A mild breeze flutters the red and brown leaves on the tree limb stretching across the pane. It seems their session is at an end.

"Don't forget," she says, standing. "I won't be able to meet with you next week."

"Oh, yeah," he says. "Your conference. Right?"

"That's right," she says, escorting him toward the door.

"What kind of conference is it?"

"To tell you the truth, they can be a little dull. They mainly consist of academic types reading boring papers."

"It sounds like school."

Selena laughs.

"Yes, in a way. That's a good analogy."

"Why are you going?"

"To present a paper—a paper of my own."

"What is it about?"

"I'm not sure you'd care for it. It's really dreadfully dull. I'm sure I'll put half my audience to sleep."

Leal pauses in the doorway, turns to face her.

"Well, if you want to know. It's called 'The Link between Schizotypy and Schizophrenia in Preadolescent Borderline Cases.' I know that probably doesn't mean a lot to you. But it's about magical thinking."

"Magical thinking?"

"It's when you make strange associations in your head. Let's say you push a button in an elevator and a fire alarm goes off or someone in the elevator faints. You might feel responsible. You might think that every time you push an elevator button, something bad will happen. So from that point on, you avoid elevators. You might always take the stairs, even if it's a hundred-story building."

"Sounds kind of crazy." He takes a few steps and then stops.

"Here," Selena hands him a business card. "I want you to have my number. If you ever feel you're in trouble, if something isn't going right, or if you just feel you need to talk about something—I want you to be able to get in touch with me."

Leal takes the card, wedges it into a back pocket.

"Have a nice trip," he says on his way out.

As she watches him go, Selena wishes again she could get hold of Father Timothy MacDougal, but the alternate number the diocese gave her keeps going to an automated voicemail account. Maybe she can't contact the priest, and maybe she can't track down Jay, who presumably has returned to his life in Chicago. But there are two people she can contact who are not only available but right here in town. In fact, one of their commercials invited the viewer to "make sure and stop by soon." Maybe she would just have to accept their invitation for a visit.

***

A woman answers the door dressed in a pink bathrobe and house slippers: soft features, long-flowing auburn hair. Inside the neckline of the woman's bathrobe Selena detects the purple wings of a butterfly pressed against white flesh.

"Mrs. Solomon?" Selena asks.

"It depends on who wants to know."

Selena introduces herself as a therapist. Could she spare a few moments? She has a couple of questions about one of her patients.

Reluctantly, the woman invites her inside. Feel free to call her Diana. A single floor lamp illuminates the living room, strewn with newspapers. A set of spaghetti-stained paper plates with plastic forks and knives sits on a coffee table in front of a plaid couch. A TV set is playing at low volume. So this is how local celebrities live.

The "lovely Diana" invites her to take a seat, but Selena declines. She won't stay long. She doesn't want to take up her evening. Does she know a boy she is treating: Leal Porter?

Diana gives her a slant-eyed quizzical look, then calls up the stairs.

"Honey, do we know a boy named Leal? Leal—" She turns her head to Selena.

"Porter," Selena says.

"Porter! Leal Porter?"

"Who is it wants to know?" a gruff voice travels back down the stairs.

She hears a toilet flush. A set of footsteps clomps down the steps.

The man who descends is wide, but tall, with dark hair held in place with gel. He wears a polo shirt, a maroon horse embroidered on the chest, dress pants with plaid socks, no shoes. He confronts Selena with an unsmiling stare—so unlike the friendly salesman's expression he uses in his commercials. Yes, Selena thinks, he must be Saul, although she has trouble recognizing him without his TV makeup and costume. People, she gathers, look so much different in real life than on television.

"This woman," Diana says. "A Dr. Harrison."

"Harris," Selena corrects her. "Please, Selena."

"She's a psychologist. She's seeing this boy named Leal."

"Leal," Saul repeats. "Leal Porter. Wasn't that the name of our newspaper boy?"

"Yeah," Diana agrees with a smug smile. "I think it was."

"Is that all you wanted?" Saul asks. "You only wanted to know if we knew this boy or not?"

"Yes," Selena responds.

"Well, then, it looks like you got what you came for." He takes a seat on the couch, picks up a newspaper and spreads it with a loud rustle, concealing his face.

"There is one other thing," Selena says.

Saul lowers his paper, peers at Selena over its top edge.

She asks if they know of a man named Jay, an artist. He rented a cottage by a lake for the summer.

Diana looks questioningly at her husband.

"No," she says, tentatively, as though testing the water, "I don't believe so. His name isn't ringing any bells."

He might go by a different name: Gerald.

No, Diana is sorry. She doesn't.

Selena divulges certain details of Leal's story. She asks Diana if she ever posed as an artist's model before.

"Is that what he told you?" Diana asks. "That I posed? Well, I'm flattered by the compliment. I can assure you. But no, I've never posed for a painting before, if that's what you mean. I used to be a dancer. I'm used to men's stares. But that was awhile back. In Chicago."

As Saul hides behind his newspaper, Selena presses Diana about her relationship with Leal. Had she ever spent a significant amount of time talking to him? Maybe when he was collecting for the paper? If so, what did they talk about? Was there ever anyone with him? A young boy? Silent? Probably autistic?

Saul sets aside his paper, stands up from the couch.

"Look, lady, I think we've answered enough questions for one day. I pay lawyers to answer questions like this for me. And I don't see no lawyers present. So if you don't mind—"

Selena apologizes again for her intrusion. She is already standing at the threshold, so it's an easy matter ducking out the door.

As she gets in her car, wedging herself behind the wheel, she wishes she would have called first. What was she hoping for with a face-to-face? A phone call would have been much less intrusive.

*

Three intersections away, she spots headlights in her rear-view mirror. They stab through the twilight like dragon's eyes. She doesn't pay them notice, until they come up close behind her, disappearing below her rear windshield, as she waits her turn at a four-way stop. She has four more stop signs to go before she can turn onto a thoroughfare that leads to her home.

On her way to the next stop sign, the headlights hang back, far behind, then race ahead, so they are right behind her again when she makes her next stop. This time, the horn blares, too. She lurches in her seat. She rolls down her window partway and makes a brief wave of her hand, acknowledging the other driver's impatience, to feel free to go around her, but the car stays in place, revving its engine.

At the next intersection, she feels a slight tap. The vehicle behind her continues pushing her rear bumper, nudging her forward. She floors the gas pedal, races to the next intersection, but the car comes up behind her again. She doesn't stop, powers through it. Her pursuer doesn't stop either but speeds around her, a dark streak that comes to a sudden halt, forcing her to apply her brakes, hard, to avoid a collision. Her wheels bounce onto the curb, and she hits her head against the side window. The engine goes dead.

She watches the figure of a large man approach in silhouette. He moves quickly through her headlight beam. She locks both doors with the push of a button and turns the ignition key, but the car won't turn over. Saul comes up beside her and places his hands on the window, thick fingers curling over the edge. His face leers a lurid green in the glow of the dashboard lights.

She keeps both hands on the steering wheel, a cold, white grip, and stares straight ahead through the windshield. She knows the rules of conflict: do not initiate eye contact, do not speak, do not engage.

"Listen," Saul tells her thickly. "I didn't do any damage to your car. You could step out, see for yourself. Technically, I didn't do anything wrong. It was just a love tap, let's say. Nothing too serious. Nothing to waste taking up a police officer's valuable time. Here—" He removes a hand, digs in his pocket, then feeds a few slices of paper money through the window that flutter onto her lap. "That should cover the cost of a little touch-up paint."

She waits, frozen in place, maintaining her forward gaze. She doesn't look at his face, but she can smell his breath, heavy with drink. She contemplates picking up her phone, threatening him with a 911 call, but she's afraid of how he'd respond. Same thing with the window. She reconsiders powering it up the rest of the way, crushing his fingers.

"You come into our house. You snoop around. You ask questions. How am I supposed to react? All right, so you got this boy in your office, this kid—Leal Porter. He used to be our newspaper boy. Now he's in your office. He's telling lies about us. Making up stories. Put yourself in my position. How am I supposed to feel about that?"

She doesn't respond. She feels consumed by fear, feels it as a primal force, paralyzing her, keeping her from reacting. It's a fear, she realizes with a sudden jolt, not so much for herself as for her baby. She has experienced confrontational patients promising assault—one who menaced her with a switchblade even. But these threats were different. They felt more sanitized, clinical, possibly because they had taken place in her office, within reach of a door, a lobby, the dentist across the hall.

Saul takes his fingers from the window edge and straightens up, cracking each set of knuckles in turn.

"You know I've got two court cases pending? One in county, another in federal. Now, this one in county, all they're going to do is make a motion to turn it over to the federal prosecutors— consolidate both cases. They got all kinds of evidence. They got their witnesses all lined up in a row—former employees, CPAs."

A car moves slowly around them, through the twilight. Selena tries to make her hands move, her arms. The moment passes. In her peripheral vision, Saul's head turns, his face half in shadow. He smiles, half waving, as though caught in the act of playing good Samaritan, assisting a woman whose car has broken down, jumped the curb.

"Last thing I need," Saul says, turning back to her, "is one more witness against me, some little punk of a kid showing up in court, disparaging my character, saying God knows what about me. You understand what I'm saying?"

Selena nods her head. She understands. She knows exactly what he's saying.

"Good. Then we got ourselves an understanding. I don't know what all goes on in your office. I don't know nothing about shrinks' offices. But if it's anything like a lawyer's, then you got such a thing as confidentiality. Am I right?"

Again, Selena finds she is just able to nod her head.

"Now, this confidentiality, I want you to make sure you keep it confidential. Understand?"

He doesn't wait for her to nod her head this time.

"Anything leaks out of your office—this boy you've got—he shows up in court. He testifies. I wouldn't want to say what might happen." He's leaning in so close she feels a spray of saliva splatter her cheek. "I'm riding on a wire. You got to know that. I'm riding on a wire, and if I go down, I don't think I'd stop at taking anyone else down with me."

He stands back from her car. Out of the corner of her eye, he gives her one last, hard look. Then he walks back to his car, a royal blue Lincoln Town Car in her headlamps, casually, as though out for an evening stroll. Still she can't relax. She doesn't feel any sense of relief, not even when he closes his door and drives off.

It takes her several attempts to restart her car.

***

At home, she finds her father in the kitchen, where he is playing a hand of solitaire.

She pours herself a Scotch. Just one drink, she tells herself. One stiff drink shouldn't hurt the baby. She takes a seat at the table. She brings the glass to her lips. Her hand is still trembling. She finishes her drink in one swallow, pours herself another.

"You all right?" her father asks.

She doesn't want to worry him.

"Yes," she says, "fine."

Her father plays a red jack against a black queen.

A sudden booming noise makes her jump. It emanates through the floorboards, vibrating her feet, shaking the walls, becoming a steady, throbbing beat. She takes another swallow of her drink. She forgot her brother has dropped in to use her father's basement as a place to practice his bass. She knows he's into reggae now. Last month, it was grunge a la Kurt Cobain.

Next month, who knows? Maybe back to cool jazz.

"He wants to move in," her father says. He smacks another card against the table, adding it to a growing column.

"He does?" Selena asks.

She shouldn't be surprised. Every few months, her brother is always moving back home, whenever things with his latest girlfriend aren't working out, or a job falls through, or a move to a new town leaves him bankrupt, or he's trying to kick partying without going through rehab.

"Permanently? What did you tell him?"

"I told him I'd have to check with you first."

She pictures unused plates in the sink, bandmates sleeping on the couch, ashtrays filled to the breaking point.

"What about his music?" Selena asks. "Won't it drive you crazy?"

Her father folds up the columns of cards and reshuffles the deck, but he stops midway dealing out another hand.

"I don't want you to feel like you have to take care of me," he says. "I don't want you to feel you're stuck here. Forever."

He finishes out the rest of his deal, but Selena stops him, lightly touching his fingers.

The bass pulses with a syncopated beat, threatening to loosen the floorboards, unhinge the doors.

"How about a game of gin rummy?" she asks.

Chapter 10

The morning of her flight to Montreal, she studies the divorce documents at breakfast. Everything seems in order. Their lives have been neatly divided in half, as previously agreed. All that's required is her signature.

She can picture Thomas opening the return package in L.A., sharing his joy of permanent and perpetual release with his lover, susy-q. His life would be in perfect order, while her own life …

At the breakfast table, her brother, dressed in pajama bottoms and tank top, advises her to take a harder line. Fifty-fifty is too damned generous. Plus, there's the baby to consider. She should screw the bastard for all he's worth.

"You're supposed to be taking me to the airport in an hour," she reminds him.

"Yeah, I know. I'm ready."

"In pajamas?"

"It's not like I have to escort you to your gate."

She's glad the conference arrived when it did. Another couple of weeks, and her OB-GYN would ban her from flying.

Their father flips through his Facebook feed, letting his coffee cool.

"I never liked Thomas in the first place," her brother says. He raises his cereal bowl to his lips and slurps the remaining milk. "He's too damned conventional. He made you conventional, too."

"Conventional?" Selena asks, smiling inwardly at his use of the term. *Conventional* has always been her brother's code word for being too "white"—like their mother—not "black" enough to match the contours of an image he holds in his head.

"He's a lawyer, for Christ's sake."

"Dad's a lawyer. Have you forgotten?"

She watches him cram a triangle of buttered toast into his mouth. She studies his milk moustache.

"You were never *that* conventional growing up. Isn't that right, Dad?"

Their father eyes each of them in turn over his cup of coffee.

"What's wrong with being conventional?" he asks.

But her brother is wrong. She had never been footloose, carefree—comfortable in her own skin. Not the way her brother is: rootless, aimless, restless. She is unable to comprehend his lifestyle, the way he moves from job to job, gig to gig, living arrangement to living arrangement.

She knows he won't last long at their father's house. It is only a temporary haven, a place to recoup his energy before setting off for a new locale, a new scene. Is it coincidence his hashtags are all #BlackLivesMatter while hers are more #MeToo?

Still, there had been her affair with Henri. Had that been reckless?

Her brother rises from the table with a parting word of wisdom: "It's boring," he says. "You might as well be dead."

"Your mother was conventional," their father says.

"Christ, Dad, I didn't mean her."

"I'm conventional," he adds.

"No you're not," her brother retorts. "You shouldn't underrate yourself. You were a 'playa.' Think of where you grew up."

"South side of Chicago, and what of it?" Their father turns back to his smartphone. "Why do you think your mother and I moved here, to Ovid, to start a family? It wasn't because I was a 'playa,' as you call it."

Finishing her yogurt, Selena reviews the document, studying spaces requiring her signature, others needing only a set of initials.

She looks everything over one page at a time.

"Just sign already," her brother advises. "You've been studying the damn documents all morning."

Her brother is right. All she has to do is sign.

****

After school, on the afternoon he would normally attend his counseling session, Leal pumps his pedals through the park past the fountain of mermaids. He passes a playground, where two children swing side by side, seeing how high they can go.

He pedals past the town limits sign to a crossroads. He enjoys the freefall of the steep hill that takes him past Jay's now-empty cottage and curves along a gravel road that leads to the far side of the lake. Leaving his bicycle on the shore, he walks through an opening in the trees.

In fading daylight, the trail is hard to follow. Roots and stones trip his every other step, even though he has made this same pilgrimage before, weekly, since late summer. Clouds hang low and gray, propped above treetops like the canvas of a tent. He feels a drop on his cheek. He doesn't look forward to the prospect of riding home in the rain.

Sitting on a log near the shore, Leal stares over the water, random raindrops dimpling its surface. As the sky darkens, he suppresses a feeling of dread. The clearing begins to feel eerie, a haven for witches, a meeting place for ghosts.

"Thuster," he murmurs.

Rain falls harder, mottling the surface of the lake. Leal tilts his head toward the sky with open mouth.

"Thuster!" he shouts at the storm, voice swelling with defiance.

"Leal?" he hears a voice say in return, a distorted echo.

A shadow steps into the clearing. Leal stands up to face it, backing against a restraining wall of briars and nettles.

"What are you doing here?" he asks. His voice sounds meek, soft. He clears his throat, as the shadow takes another step and becomes the figure of a woman.

"Are you not glad to see me?" she asks, coming closer.

"How did you find me?"

The rain falls even harder. She opens an umbrella, spreading it over both of them.

"I followed you from school. I was worried about you."

Holding the umbrella, she reaches down, selects a blade of grass, maybe a fallen twig. Then she rises back up, looking at Leal with soft, searching eyes.

"Go away," Leal says, his voice catching in his throat.

"Go away?" she says, pouting. "Don't you like me any-more?" On her finger is a ladybug. It crawls to her fingertip and spreads its wings. "Ladybug, ladybug, fly away home …"

She breathes gently, and the ladybug leaves her finger, flying out into the rain, spiraling to dodge the heavy drops. He thinks of the purple butterfly, concealed within her yellow slicker, the orange snake slithering up her calf.

Leal feels saliva rise in his throat. He feels weak. His head sways. His legs give way, and he collapses onto the ground, knees bending into a pretzel, as though he has planned it.

"What are you doing here?" he manages to ask again.

"The real question," she says, kneeling next to him, "is what are you doing here? Out in the rain."

Leal looks at the muddy ground between crossed legs.

"Thuster," he answers, so softly he can barely hear his own voice.

"Oh," she says, huddling under the umbrella. "Is he out here somewhere? In the lake maybe? He's picked a bad day for swimming."

She makes a slight laugh, as though to let him know she is

only making a joke.

Leal doesn't turn his head. He can't meet her eyes.

"I guess so," he says again, quietly, as though to himself.

Cold water swirls around his jacket collar and down his back. Rivulets run through the grass, beneath his legs, seeking stronger currents. He lets his chin sink into his chest.

"Do you think he's going to come swimming out of your imagination? Like the Loch Ness monster?"

No, Leal thinks: like a frog. Like a frog out of a fairy tale.

Lights go on in the cottage across the lake, drawing their attention.

"Looks like somebody new has moved in," Diana says lightly.

She tips the umbrella against the slant of rain, blocking for a moment their view of the cottage.

"Word is you're seeing a psychologist."

At this, Leal lurches, involuntarily, but says nothing.

"Are you not seeing her today? Your psychologist?"

Leal shakes his head.

"She's at a conference."

"Do you like seeing her?"

Leal shrugs.

"I guess so."

Facing him, she places a hand on his shoulder.

"What are you telling her?"

Leal tries to turn his head, but she pulls him around, gently, so he has to look at her.

"Nothing. I'm not telling her anything."

The rain falls heavily through the canopy of leaves, slashes along the surface of the lake. A steel curtain, it hides from view the opposite shore, dimming the lights of the cottage.

"That's good," she says, looking out from under the umbrella.

"It's Saul, you know. Saul's worried. He's afraid you're making up stories about him—about us. He has these court cases—it's complicated. But he has a business to protect. A reputation. You know how it is." They listen to the rain falling. It sounds like it's letting up, just dribbling on the umbrella. "I'm sure your mother's told you, it's not polite, telling stories behind other people's backs."

She stands up. She raises her umbrella. Water drips from the edges, splashing against Leal's cheeks and eyes.

"We had a good time last summer," she says, looking down, as Leal stares up at her. "Didn't we?"

Leal lowers his head, nodding.

"Too bad it had to end," she says, reflectively. "But you know what they say—what goes up ..." She gives a slight shrug of her shoulders. "It's that way with everything. You'll see."

"I miss you," he whispers, speaking toward the ground.

"Here. Take my hand."

Leal looks up. He looks into her eyes. He contemplates her outstretched fingers.

He reaches up his hand and lets himself be pulled to his feet, as though being lifted to safety from the edge of a cliff, a dark abyss.

"Come on," she says. "I'll take you home. I'm pretty sure your bike will fit in the trunk."

∗∗∗

In Montreal, the third night of the conference, Selena waits for Henri in the hotel bar.

The atmosphere of the barroom is old guard, sartorial. Mahogany tables. Padded leather chairs. Waiters in tuxedos. Oil portraits of bearded gentlemen hanging in stern disapproval.

She is having a drink by herself at a table, waiting for an opportunity to speak with Henri—alone, just the two of them. So far, they've encountered each other on only three occasions—speaking briefly each time. At present, though, a number of admirers, mostly women, encircle him at the end of the bar.

Genevieve must place a great deal of trust in her soon-to-be husband, now that they've finalized their wedding plans, leaving him with such obvious temptations as congregate at the bar in backless evening gowns with daring cutaways revealing beckoning cleavages.

They've exchanged a few glances across the room, but when she looks back over, Henri has disappeared. Now she worries she won't have a chance to speak with him, after all, as the conference will conclude the next morning. Leaving a couple of Canadian bills on the table for a tip, she walks to the elevator. When the doors open, Henri appears inside. He takes a step toward her. Maybe he has only forgotten something from his hotel room—his billfold, for instance.

"Sorry I've been so delayed," he says.

He gives her a hug, a kiss on each cheek, which she returns.

"I was starting to give up on you," she responds.

He takes a step back with his hands clasped to her shoulders, covered and padded, unlike those of the other women in the bar.

"I'm sorry I missed your paper."

"Oh, well—you didn't miss much. Besides, you've already read it." And critiqued it, with virtual red ink, just as he had done as her dissertation director.

They go to a table where he pulls out a chair for her.

He leans close to her from behind as she takes her seat.

"I think you've forgotten to tell me something," he says.

"I have?"

He goes around to his side of the table. He leans forward from his chair.

"You're expecting?" he asks.

She studies his eyes. He seems to wish to avoid looking too directly at her. His pupils keep drifting away like a pair of dust motes on a laboratory slide.

"Yes," she says simply.

"How long?"

"Seven months now—thereabouts. I should keep better track." She lets out a laugh.

She can tell he is making a calculation in his head, based on their last encounter, shortly after Thomas abandoned their home—his wife—in Oakland Park.

"You never told me. Why haven't you told me?"

The waiter comes up and takes their orders.

She can tell he is still making the same calculation.

"It didn't go over very well, I'm afraid."

"What?"

"My paper."

"No?" He reaches out to pat the top of her hand. "I'm sure it was fine. You need to have more confidence in your abilities."

This is nice—just nice. Maybe it's better this way, she thinks. They are friends now, not lovers. They are just friends, sharing a drink before going their separate ways: she back to her father, Henri back to his fiancée. No amour, no ardor, just a neutrality of emotion—clinical, but not cold.

She brings up the subject of Leal. This is the one patient giving her the most agitation, discomfort. At night, she feels like the princess lying atop a stack of mattresses, disturbed, far beneath, by the chafing of a pea. Does Henri have time?

He checks his watch. Sure, but it's getting late.

"Genevieve?" Selena asks.

Henri nods.

"She's expecting me to call."

"She isn't here at the conference?"

"I left her at home. She finds these sorts of affairs stifling. Still, she likes it when I call in every night." Henri smiles. "You know how it is with young brides-to-be."

"Yes, I do. I was a young bride-to-be once," she replies.

It will only take a minute. She promises she won't keep him.

The waiter delivers their drinks.

She sips a safe seltzer, Henri a not-as-safe Tom Collins.

"I feel like a surgeon," Selena explains. "I'm probing. Always probing. And I don't even know for what. He is like a patient complaining of a stomachache. And I'm digging, searching with my scalpel. I'm looking for a hidden bullet. A tumor. I don't know. He doesn't know. I just feel I'm not getting anywhere. I'm only making a bloody mess. I just wish I was done with it all— the etcetera."

"Pardon?"

"It's an expression Leal's mother likes to use. I think it's a euphemism for, well, you know, for bullshit."

"You are underestimating your own expertise," Henri assures her, reaching out a hand. With his other, he takes a large swallow of his drink, examining her over the rim of his glass. "Well, there is this. He'll soon run out of his story—or his bullshit, if you prefer," Henri adds with a smile. "He'll run out of material—in his narrative, he is fast approaching the end of 'What I Did Last Summer'—and arrive at the present moment. I would imagine at that point—when he has no more to say about this imaginary friend, this Thuster—you will then know what's going on inside, what's really bothering him."

"You're sure he's imaginary?" Selena ponders. "He seems so real."

"It's an interesting choice of name."

"How so?" Selena asks.

"I looked it up. I thought I had run across it before. In my grad school days. It's Middle English."

"Middle English?"

"It means 'darkness, shadow.'"

"Would a boy like this know Middle English?"

"No, presumably not. I found it in a poem, though: *Hymn to the Virgin*. Want to hear it?"

Before Selena can answer, he unfolds a sheet of copy paper out of his pocket and holds it as though to deliver a speech.

"You'll have to excuse me. My Latin is a little rusty."

Again, she feels as though Henri is viewing her more as an object of study. He coughs into his fist, self-consciously.

"All this woreld were forlore
Eva peccatrice,
Till our Lord was y-bore
De te genetrice.
With 'Ave' it went away
Thuster night, and com'th the day."

He pauses to clear his throat once more—symptom of nervousness?

"Dark night," he translates, then proceeds.

"*Salutis*
The welle springeth out of thee
Virtutis."

"May I?" Selena inquires.

Henri hands over the printout of the poem and finishes his drink.

She'll have to Google translate the Latin. Henri's Latin may be rusty, but hers is nonexistent. Her French is passable, her Spanish atrocious. Unlike Henri, languages are not her forte.

He waves at the waiter walking by with an empty tray. When the waiter stops by, he asks for their check.

"On me," he tells Selena.

Then he leans across their table. He takes her hands. He smiles.

"Shadow or not, he's killed him off once—with his confession. Now you will have to get him to kill him off again."

Selena's phone vibrates.

She checks the number: unknown caller but same area code as her own. It could easily be a progress report on Paula. Selena had handed her off to a psychiatrist, who was trying to get her Zoloft level right. It could also be any one of a half dozen high-risk patients to whom she had given her number in case of emergency. Somehow, though, she knows it's Leal.

"Excuse me," she says. "I'll be right back."

"Of course." Henri stands up to give her room to get by. She feels even more self-conscious as she leaves their table. She has bought a loose-fitting tunic especially for this trip, but she fears it fails to conceal the rounded heaviness of her 3X pants, as she finds a quiet nook in the lobby from which to talk in private.

"Is there an emergency?" she speaks into her cell phone.

"No," Leal says. "At least, I don't think so." He sounds nervous, agitated.

"Is something wrong?"

"I just wanted to see."

"See? See what?"

Silence, static. Someone is talking in the background. His mother? The radio?

"See what, Leal?"

"I just wanted to see if your voicemail worked. I didn't mean to bother you."

"Are you sure that's all?"

More silence. A gunshot.

"Leal? Are you watching something?"

"Just something on TV. A cop show."

Another gunshot. Or maybe the slamming of a door.

"Leal?"

"It's my mom. She doesn't want me seeing you anymore."

"No?"

"Something about her insurance. It will only cover one more session. Isn't that what you call them—our meetings?"

"Yes, that's right. Are you sure?"

She had kept track, of course, and knew Sandra's insurance allotted more visits than that.

"I just thought I should warn you, that's all."

The phone goes dead in her hand.

When she reenters the bar, she finds their table empty. Henri has left. In his place, she finds his business card pinned beneath his tumbler—a quick scribble on the back of it.

Sorry—had to go.
Love, H.

Beneath that, his room number has been etched in careful jags and blocks.

Odd, now that she thinks of it, that he booked a room here in the hotel rather than commute from his house. Maybe it's too far to go. He lives downriver in Saint-Sulpice. Still, leaving Genevieve at home when she's less than an hour away …

It takes her nearly that long to make up her mind. If only she could have been nursing a gin and tonic all that time to steel her resolve.

When she knocks on his door, she's about to turn on her heel and flee, but it opens within seconds. Usually, Henri reserves an entire suite, but this is an ordinary room with a single king-size bed. Or, as Henri might phrase it, *un lit digne d'un roi.*

"You're not room service," he notes with a smile.

"Do you always greet room service in your sleeping clothes?"

"You mean pajamas?'

"Bottoms only," she observes. His chest is bare. For an older man, he is very fit, his abdomen not quite as taut as a six-pack but well short of a mini keg. His biceps and pecs are well formed. The only flaw is the pallid skin tone. It's obvious he spends his spare time indoors, but she won't hold that against him. After all, Quebec isn't exactly the Riviera.

"Give me a minute to change," he tells her.

"That won't be necessary," she responds. She takes a step forward, pulling the door closed behind her. Another step and she is enfolded in his embrace, an awkward one that makes room for her pregnancy, as though there were a large parcel they are trying to balance between them while standing.

One final step, Henri moving backward, she forward, and they reach the destination she desires, where they tumble onto the covers, the bed still made, not yet turned down for sleep. A hidden mechanism, something Henri must have left on as he answered the door, is causing the mattress to undulate, making it easy to imagine they are on a life raft at sea.

"I didn't hurt you?" Henri asks solicitously.

"It's okay," she assures him with a whisper. "I'm tired of feeling so fragile." And vulnerable and alone and afraid, she might add. "So don't worry about hurting me."

"But gently," he advises.

"Yes," she agrees. "But gently."

Chapter 11

Leal studies the clock, as he takes his seat. He follows the second hand, tracing it about the face.

"Only one more hour," he murmurs, his voice slow, sluggish, sad. "And that's it, isn't it?"

"Not necessarily," Selena counters. "I looked into what you told me on the phone, about your mother's insurance running out. I'm planning on giving you—your mother, I mean—a special deal. A reduced rate."

"Oh?"

Leal raises his head, eyebrows forming hopeful arcs.

"That is, if you want to keep coming here."

He gives Selena a rare, direct look, mouth creased into a crooked smile.

"Of course I want to keep coming back. I like coming here. It's important I keep coming here. Isn't it?"

"Important?" Selena echoes.

"I better tell you what happened with Saul," Leal says eagerly. "I mean, just in case your deal falls through."

*

One morning, stopping by his mom's diner, he was surprised to find Saul sitting at the counter, his mom pouring him a cup of coffee. It was like a YouTube clip of *The Twilight Zone*. Leal generally knows how to read the signs that portend that strange, surreal realm, where reality and nightmare merge. Still, he didn't know how to take his part in this episode. He wasn't sure what role to play.

"Leal!" his mom exclaimed, as he walked in.

Saul spun around on his padded stool.

"Well, there he is," Saul said. "How you doing, champ? We were just now talking about you. Come on, have a seat." He invited Leal with a pat of the stool beside him. "I just delivered a certain present we were talking about to your mother, who, I must add, is quite a delightful woman. No words you have used to describe your mother could do her justice."

Leal watched his mom blush, and this was a first. He doesn't believe he had ever seen his mom blush before.

"Mr. Solomon's told me all about it," his mom said.

"Uh-uh," Saul corrected her. "Saul, remember?"

"How you've been helping him around his house. Odd-and-end projects. And how, instead of asking for payment, you asked for a special gift. For me. You shouldn't have, Leal," she gushed, holding up a fur coat wrapped in cellophane. "You really shouldn't. You know I'm allergic to fur."

"Normally," Saul said, "I would have had one of my salesmen—I should say, I also employ a saleswoman—I would have had one of them deliver it. But I thought I would deliver it in person, as a sort of special gesture of good faith."

"Aren't you going to take a seat?" his mom asked. Reluctantly, Leal went ahead and sat down next to Saul, leaving an empty stool between them.

Saul reset his watch against the clock on the wall.

"I was just discussing with your mother the prospect of a fishing expedition," he said. "Just the two of us."

"Fishing?" Leal felt as tongue-tied as a knot in a fly reel.

"I've been working just a little too hard lately. I think it's time for some R & R. I thought maybe you could stop by the house tomorrow, and I'll take you out fishing. Just the two of us."

"Tomorrow?" Leal asked.

"Or the day after, you're too busy tomorrow. It's not like I'm pressed for time. I've decided to take a couple weeks off."

"It turns out we know each other," his mom said. "I thought I recognized Mr. Solomon—Saul—when he came through the door. He used to be one of my regulars. Before he became such a celebrity."

"That's right," Saul said. "It's been quite a long time. But that's what happens when you become the president of your own business and you don't have to spend as much time on the road anymore. It only took one cup of coffee to bring back all of the memories, late nights at the diner. But I'm very glad we made the effort. Your mother, Leal—she hasn't changed one bit."

"Leal is in need of a role model," his mom said. "He doesn't have a father, as you probably know."

"Then it's settled," Saul said, rising from his seat, creaking the stool, or else his knees. "Leal, I want you to stop by my place at seven tomorrow."

"A.M. or P.M.?" Leal found himself asking.

Saul laughed. "That's a funny one. I'll have to remember that one. A.M., of course. Bright and early. It's the early bird, they say, that catches the worm. Or in our case, we'll be digging them up before they have a chance to fight back. Well, I better be on my way. Mrs. Porter—"

"Please, call me Sandra."

"It's been a pleasure, a genuine pleasure, I can't tell you."

He took one of his mom's hands and kissed it, lips grazing the knuckles. His mom blushed once again—for good measure. Saul seemed to keep pressing a hidden button that made her blush over and over, like a specially equipped Barbie doll. Even her knuckles were tinted a light red.

"Leal, I'll see you tomorrow. Come by the house."

His eyes followed Saul out the door, down the sidewalk, past the plate-glass window. And then he realized what was different about Saul. This was the first time he'd seen him out of his normal costume: dark suit and narrow tie. He was wearing a bright blue Hawaiian shirt—splotched with yellow parrots and green palm trees—and beige shorts and sandals. His mom pocketed the dollar tip Saul left behind.

"What a nice man," she said. Lifting his coffee cup, she wiped the countertop with her towel. "You wouldn't happen to know if he's unattached. I didn't see a ring."

"No," Leal said, evenly, keeping his expression as neutral as he could make it, "I wouldn't."

"Hopefully not to that trollop in his commercials. What's her name again?"

"Beats me," Leal said and made a dash for the door.

*

Seven o'clock came early.

Diana was wearing a blue silk bathrobe. She greeted Leal at the door, and he heard Saul's voice booming from the kitchen, singing a sea shanty: "Fifteen men on a dead man's chest. Yo ho ho—"

"And a bottle of rum," Leal pitched in quietly.

"Here," Diana whispered. She handed him a small pink envelope. Nothing was written on the outside, no address, no stamp. "Make sure he gets it."

"Who?" he whispered back. Her eyes were sleepy. She looked at him through half-closed lids. A fresh scratch slanted above her right eyebrow.

"Who do you think?"

Saul's shadow fell through the doorway.

"Is that Leal?" he shouted. "Is Leal here?"

"Yeah," Leal said, using his normal voice. He didn't feel up to shouting. "It's me."

"Good," Saul said. "Be out in a minute."

"Just give it to Jay, okay?" Diana said. "If you see him today."

"How would I see him today?" he wanted to know.

Her eyes focused on him like he was some strange breed of mammal.

"You'll be at the lake," she whispered.

"The lake!"

"Don't worry. It was my suggestion."

*

"Thuster wasn't with you?" Selena observes.

"No, not this time. Just the two of us, me and Saul."

Note to self: So there are times when Thuster is left behind—intentionally. Not just missing in action. Interesting. She has been nursing a pet theory that Leal and Thuster are one and the same.

*

Leal followed the low beams of the headlights along the familiar stretch of country road, past the wide-open field on the right, thick patch of woods on the left, then descending the long winding curve into wisps of fog. The headlights glanced off Jay's mailbox. No lights on in the cottage. The road narrowed into a thin gravel path, a line of weeds between tire marks, under overhanging willows.

"I was looking for a place we could go," Saul said, "somewhere private, with the county map all opened up on the kitchen table, and Diana—she pointed out this little blue dot. The lake—it doesn't even have a name. You can't get much more private than that. She said she just had this hunch it would be a good place. I'll tell you something, Leal, I've always been one to go along with a woman's intuition."

Trees swept back from the shoulder to expose the wide strip of a muddy shoreline, and Saul parked the car.

They dug in the soft earth for worms, which were easy to find. It didn't take long to fill up a bucket. In the dim light of dawn, Saul showed Leal how to hook a worm, then how to cast out. Leal's bobber made a small splash. Otherwise, the surface of the lake was calm as a mirror.

"Well, now," Saul said, "let's see if Diana's hunch pays off today."

They sat in two lawn chairs Saul brought out from the trunk of his car, along with a cooler of beer. Saul offered him a can of his own, but Leal fished out a Gatorade instead. They reeled their lines slowly, over and over, until the sun climbed above the line of trees on the farther shore. They didn't have any luck at this spot, not even a nibble.

"It's too wide open," Saul explained. He crumpled his empty can of beer and tossed it into the water. "Any fish worth his salt can spot us a mile away."

Leal resisted the urge to tell Saul it was a freshwater lake.

They folded up the lawn chairs, reeled in their lines, moved into the woods to their left, walking carefully along a narrow trail. Leal carried the cooler, along with the bucket of worms, while Saul managed the tackle box. Several more casts, a couple more beers, and still no luck. They picked up their gear, moved down the path, and Leal's line got tangled in the branches of a tree. Saul cut the line and retied another hook. He let Leal spear the worm on his own this time, but Leal can't say he was grateful for the experience.

"The nice thing about fishing," Saul said, leaning back in his chair, "is that it teaches the virtue of patience. Infinite patience. There's a fish in this lake, I can sense it. We just need to find the right spot."

They continued their trek down the shoreline, under the trees, looking for the right spot until, by the time the sun had risen halfway into a cloudless sky, they emerged at the edge of the gray narrow strip of beach leading all the way to Jay's cottage.

"Looks like the end of the rainbow," Saul cursed, throwing down his pole. "What's the sign say? Private property?"

"No trespassing, keep out," Leal read. Was Saul's eyesight that bad?

"If we don't find anything here, looks like we're going to come back empty-handed. Won't that be an embarrassment? What'll Diana say about that?"

The lakeside door of the cottage opened and Jay emerged with his easel under an arm, screen flying shut behind him with a bang.

"Civilization, at last," Saul said. He stood up, waved, shouted, "Hello the house!"

Jay stopped short with his easel. He looked in Saul's direction, straining his eyes—tiny black marbles—along the shore. Saul marched a few steps down the beach, and Leal tagged along like a faithful dog.

"Sorry to be bothering you." Saul said, moving closer.

Leal cowered behind Saul. For his part, Jay pretended not to know him, and Leal knew to keep mum, afraid his voice would give him away.

"I was just wondering if you could tell me and my friend, here, are there any fish in this lake at all? We've been at it half the day now, and the only bites we've gotten are from mosquitoes."

Jay froze in place. He might have stopped breathing.

Saul introduced himself, holding out his hand, until Jay set down his easel. Saul gave him a bone-rattling shake. Then he introduced Leal. Saul turned around to look for him, but Leal stayed directly behind him until forced to show his face.

"This your property, I take it?" Saul asked.

"No," Jay sputtered. "Just renting."

"Nice cottage," Saul observed. "Nice, solid structure. What style is it they call this? Cape Cod?"

"I wouldn't know. I'm not an architect."

Saul looked at him over the top of his sunglasses. "You here to do some fishing, too?"

"No. Painting. I'm a painter."

"Yeah, I can see that. Never any fishing, huh?"

"No. I'm afraid that's not my forte. My field. But I have seen them—fish, that is. I've seen them jumping, out in the middle. I guess that proves they're out there. They exist."

"Well, that's the best news I've heard all day. Means we're not wasting our time, at any rate. They're just making it a challenge for us, sounds like."

Saul glanced at his wristwatch, looked up at the sky. "Listen," he said, "I hate to bother you, but I was wondering if I could make a phone call. I can't pick up a signal for the life of me." He unpocketed his cell phone as proof. "Technically speaking, I'm on vacation, but you know how it is—you're running a company, you've got to stay on top of business. When the cat's away, you know."

"I'm sorry." Jay looked relieved. "I don't have a phone."

"No phone, huh? But that's a phone line running to the cottage?"

"Yes, I suppose so. But it's out of service. Landlord's kind of stingy that way. Sorry I can't be of more help."

"No cell phone of your own?"

Jay shrugged. "Same issue. Signal's intermittent at best."

"Not a problem. Not a problem. Listen," Saul said. "I hate to be a pain in the you know what." He dropped his voice into a hoarse whisper. "You wouldn't happen to have a little boy's room, would you?"

The blood stopped circulating in Jay's head. His face looked deathly white, with an undercoat of olive green.

"I mean, if it's not any trouble. One thing I hate to do is inconvenience anyone. Ordinarily, I'd find the nearest tree, but you know the saying, 'If a bear shits in the woods.' Only I'm not a bear."

"No. No. It's no trouble." Jay led them in silence to the cottage, opening the door to invite them inside. "Up the steps. To the right."

"I'm afraid I'm going to owe you, buddy, when everything's said and done. I'm sorry, I didn't catch your name."

"Gerald," Jay said, swallowing hard.

Jay and Leal watched Saul trudge up the steps. They waited until he shut the bathroom door. Then Jay turned his head to face Leal. His eyes suggested he wouldn't mind wringing his neck like a little bird's.

"Here," Leal whispered. He held out the pink envelope, crumpled from being carried around in his back pocket. "It's from Diana."

Jay took the envelope, tore it open. He removed the letter on pink paper. His eyes went narrow, then wide.

"No," he said, a little moan coming out of his throat. "No." His eyes scanned the letter like balls of mercury. "No. No. No."

The toilet flushed, and Saul emerged, lumbering back down the steps, his keys and loose change jingling. Jay folded the letter, stuffing it into his front pocket before Saul reached the foot of the stairs.

"Thanks a million," Saul said. He took a quick survey of the living room, scanning the rows of paintings leaning under the windowsills.

"These all yours?" Saul asked.

Jay looked carefully at Saul out of the corner of his eye. He nodded his head slightly.

"You do nice work," Saul said. "Who's the broad?"

"I'm sorry?" Jay said.

"The woman," Saul said. "Anyone in particular?"

"Oh. No. No. Not at all. I work completely from my imagination."

"That's really quite an imagination you have. Me—I wish I had an imagination only half that good. Hey, would you take a look at this one?" Saul pointed at a painting hanging above the mantle of the wood-burning fireplace. "What do you think, Leal? This one looks like that friend of yours. You know, Thuster. A very close resemblance."

Jay and Leal didn't allow themselves to breathe until Saul let himself out through the door back into the daylight of beach and lake, trees and sky.

"Well, thanks again for use of the bathroom. Leal, ready to go track down a couple of fish? Or you want to call it a day? We can always buy a couple trout from the supermarket on the way back into town, so we have something to show for ourselves."

Leal followed Saul along the beach back into the woods. He looked over his shoulder at Jay standing all alone and empty-handed in front of the cottage.

"Funny thing about painters," Saul said. "They come across as such nervous, sensitive types."

*

Selena escorts Leal to the lobby she shares with the dentist.

He faces her before descending the stairwell to the street below.

"I hope I see you again," he says.

"I hope so, too," Selena responds.

"I'll talk to my mom again. I'll make sure she gives you a call."

He turns to go, but Selena calls after him.

"Leal?"

He pauses at the top of stairs.

"There's something I've been meaning to ask you."

"Yeah?" he says brightly.

"Those paintings of Jay's. Was it always just the one woman? Diana?"

Who's the broad? Saul had asked in Leal's story. But if this is something he had to ask, surely he didn't recognize the purple butterfly, the orange snake. There must have been a different set of tattoos. And this is something Leal must have been alluding to without saying it directly. Or had it been a lapse in his narrative—a slip? The paintings couldn't have been of Diana. They must have been of someone else. His mother, for instance. But she can't ask about her point blank because then Leal would know she knows for sure. He has to be the one to tell her.

"Were there others?" she asks.

No answer. His face drops. His eyes fall to the floor.

He turns on the stairwell, hand on the rail.

"Leal? Wait."

He pauses but doesn't turn around.

"Did Jay paint other women? The same way he painted Diana?"

"Maybe," he mumbles. "I can't say for sure."

"Were any of the others women you knew?"

"I've got to go," he says, his voice subdued, apologetic.

"Leal?" she calls after him, "one more thing." He turns at the bottom landing, looking back up at her, waiting. "No matter what happens with your mother, I'd like to see you again—at least one more time."

A smile crosses his face.

"You would?"

"Sure—next Tuesday. Same time, same place. OK?"

***

The phone rings at home, disturbing her sleep.

Selena glances at the clock on her dresser: 1 a.m.

It's Leal's mother on the line. Did she wake her? Oh, then, is it all right if they talk?

She wants to know how Leal is progressing.

"Favorably," Selena responds. She chooses this adverb carefully.

Leal's mother—Sandra—brings up the issue of payment.

"I don't mean to sound crass," she says. "But I've already told you. I'm a waitress, as you know. I don't have a great insurance plan to begin with. And now with my insurance running out, I can't afford to use up any more sessions."

"So it hasn't run out yet?"

Selena already knows the answer, but lets silence fill the gap. "Sandra?"

"I thought you should know I'm seeing someone too. A counselor."

"Oh?"

"Rehab," she confesses without elaborating.

"Recovering?"

"Recovered. I'm trying to stay clean."

"I understand," Selena assures her, thinking of her own bad habit. She's heard it said giving up cigarettes is as bad as trying to quit heroin. Turning the conversation back to Leal, she decides to take a risk on turning him into a charity case. "I'm willing to go pro bono."

"Free of charge?" Sandra sounds skeptical. Selena was afraid Leal's mother's dignity would get in the way of such a proposal.

"I thought it unfair of the school board making you pay for Leal's treatment to begin with."

"Well, that's how it is, isn't it, when levies don't pass and you have a guidance counselor that can't do a thing with him."

Of course, she means Lori. Not for the first time, Selena feels a pang of embarrassment for her friend.

"Now I don't mean to sound rude," Leal's mother says, "or uncaring. But is there any sort of end in sight? Or is Leal going to keep seeing you two times a week forever?"

Selena advises her that it wouldn't be a good idea to reduce the number of weekly sessions—not at this point. Privately, she feels they are close, very close. If nothing else, Leal's narrative, as Henri foretold, is running out of material.

Then Sandra asks a surprising question. At least, her question takes Selena by surprise. She isn't prepared for it.

"What are you getting out of this, anyway?"

Selena buys time. She claims she doesn't understand.

"Why are you so interested in my son? Why him? Why are you cutting us these special deals, these favors? You don't do this for any of your other patients, do you?"

Selena explains that yes, she does, occasionally, cut deals, as Sandra phrased it, for other patients—when she feels there is a chance for a breakthrough, for closure.

"And you feel that way about Leal? You feel you're close to a breakthrough?"

She tells her the truth—she feels she is only beginning to dig beneath the surface, to get at what is troubling him. She explains that therapy isn't as glamorous as it is portrayed in the movies. Perhaps "breakthrough" is the wrong choice of word. It isn't that her patients experience some sort of epiphany, that they are miraculously cured or healed—not overnight, in any case.

"Are you saying you can't heal my son? That there isn't a cure?"

"No, that isn't what I'm saying. I'm only saying that a 'cure,' if you want to think of it that way, is not always what occurs. Usually—in fact, most of the time—it's more a matter of a patient gradually coming to terms with an issue or problem or worry. Learning new coping skills. The patient begins to see it from a new perspective. In a new light, as it were. And then the patient can hope to become more adept at dealing with it—strategically."

"So how close are you to doing this with Leal?"

"That's just the problem, Mrs. Porter."

"Please. Sandra."

"I'm not exactly sure what we're dealing with yet—Sandra. I

don't have a good idea as to what Leal's issue really is. And what's making it difficult is that I don't think he knows either."

Sandra remains silent several minutes. Selena worries she might have ended the call, but the button on her phone is still green, the seconds adding up on the screen.

"Let me think about this," she says.

"Of course," Selena responds.

"I have to think about what's right for Leal. I have to think about what's in the best interest of my son."

"Of course you do."

"I'll let you know tomorrow."

***

She has trouble falling back asleep, so she goes to her keyboard. She stares at her computer screen. Her wallpaper shows a red sand beach in Maui. White foam recedes from a small, secluded cove, creating a private lagoon with lava-rich cliffs rising to meet a dense fringe of jungle—a paradise for two.

She opens a blank email screen for fresh correspondence.

Dear Henri …

She takes a deep breath, begins typing, her fingers moving fast. There are so many things she wants to tell him, so many memories of their last night together she wishes to recount. So many sweet nothings she wants to express.

She stops mid-sentence and presses DEL until it all vanishes, every last letter and punctuation mark. Better if she keeps her correspondence impersonal, polite—professional. She concentrates on what she now thinks of as her special case. She is only seeking advice from a colleague, a specialist in borderline cases. This relationship between them—he, her former mentor; she, his former student—this is all it can ever really be.

Chapter 12

Another day, another hour.

Selena waits for Leal to take his seat.

"I haven't heard from your mother yet."

"You haven't?" He looks confused. "You mean about me coming here?"

"Yes."

"About coming for more treatment?"

"That's one word for it." She thinks for a moment. "Have we ever used that word before?"

"What word?"

"'Treatment.' I don't think we've used that word, have we?"

"Oh. Maybe I heard someone else use it."

"Like who? Your mother?"

"No. Maybe those kids at school—the ones I was telling you about."

"Are they still teasing you?"

"Yeah—sometimes. Not very much."

"How does it make you feel? The things they say about you?"

"Oh, I don't know. I mean, it would be different if I really liked them or something. Then it might be a little different."

"You don't feel angry?"

"No. I wouldn't say I feel angry."

"You never get angry, do you?"

"I don't know. Maybe. Sometimes. It's like my mom says, 'Why get angry, when you can get even?'"

Well, there's a fine life lesson for an impressionable boy.

"What makes you angry? Can you think of anything that

might make you angry?"

"No. Not really. Sad, maybe. But not angry."

"Sad? Did someone make you sad?"

"Not someone. Something. It was sad seeing Diana for the last time. That's something that made me sad."

Finally, Selena thinks, breathing an inward sigh of relief. *Maybe we're finally approaching the end …*

*

There was one day when everything was just like it was before.

The mermaids were dancing in the fountain. The water sparkled along their green bodies, splashing from their tails, and Thuster reached his hand through the water to steal another person's wish. Leal stopped by the library and picked up a book, then went to a bench in front of the courthouse and started to read while Thuster stared at the slow movement of the minute hand around the face of the courthouse clock.

Everything was the same, but Leal somehow knew it would all end. He knew when the bells chimed, it would sound as though they were signaling the end of summer. It would seem as though summer had never been, or else it's like Father Mac says, everything always goes around full circle, and the world is nothing more than a clock, and all the little people are on a huge treadmill—talking, walking, eating, sleeping away the time that isn't even theirs to begin with.

And then it was like nothing even mattered. It didn't matter that Father Mac was leaving for Florida with his bags packed, ready to go. It didn't matter that Leal's mom had a new chinchilla fur coat in her closet that she would never wear because it made her sneeze. It didn't matter that Thuster was going to a strange, new home in Chicago, because Leal didn't even think he would notice the difference. And it didn't matter that Leal would never see Saul or Jay or Diana again.

Nothing mattered except that everything seemed exactly the same as when the summer started—for this one day, this one hour, this one second—and anything less than a second that could be squeezed like a lemon into no time at all. But then it's like Diana told Leal one time, nothing lasts forever, and Leal knew exactly when forever came to an end.

*

"So," Selena muses, "this was when you saw Diana?"

"No," Leal says. "This is when I ran into Jay."

*

Ten minutes till three, the red, clanking Mazda pulled up in front of their bench, and Jay stuck his head out the window. Leal knew that anything that was good and calm and silent and true had just flown out of his life like any blackbird trapped inside a house might find an open window.

"You don't know what it's been like looking for you," Jay said. "This town. It's no Chicago. I mean, it looks small from the outside, but when you start driving around, deliberately looking for someone."

Jay held a yellow rose, twirling the stem. He took a seat on the bench, beside Leal.

"Listen," Jay said. "You've got to do me this one favor. I'd go to the house myself, but I know he'll be there. I've already driven past it a dozen times. I don't even know if she wants to see me again. That letter. That note." He looked between his knees at the sidewalk, shaking his head. A couple of people walked by—an old man with a cane, a woman in plaid skirt and tennis shoes. "I know she didn't mean it. It didn't even sound like herself. I know she feels as if she has no other choice. I don't blame her. Now that the paintings are done—finished—I mean, there's no reason, of course, to—"

He pushed his hand through his hair, brushing it clean off his forehead. His eyes held a restless, wild look, like a starving hyena's. His face was unshaven, too. He just didn't look like himself. Every other time Leal had seen him, he'd always looked so calm and confident, as if he owned the world—the world of his vision, at least. But now, he seemed a changed man. He truly looked like a starving artist. If this is what love does to a person, Leal didn't want any part of it.

"If you could just deliver this rose to her house, make sure she gets it. Just like you somehow—I still can't believe it quite— just like you were somehow able to deliver her letter to me, right under her husband's nose." He shook his head, twirling the rose. A yellow petal fluttered from the stem to the ground, like the wing of a flightless moth.

He dug in his shirt pocket and brought out a sheet of yellow, blue-lined paper torn from a legal pad. "This goes along with it." He handed the rose and the paper to Leal, but Leal didn't take either one. He still couldn't believe Jay had found him. It seemed like the earth was getting ready to split in two all over again, right under his feet. "Leal, aren't you going to take it? Ahh. I know. I'll make it worth your while."

He pulled out a wallet and took out a dollar bill. "Here's something for your trouble." But Leal still didn't take the rose. He didn't take the notepaper either. "Oh, okay. Here. Here's another dollar for your friend. Maybe you can go to the dollar matinee." But he still didn't take the rose. "Okay, here," Jay said. "This is all I have." He counted out three more dollar bills, then pulled a five from his shirt pocket. But he still didn't take the rose. "I think I've got some pocket change, if that'll make a difference." He began to dig in his pocket.

"Wait a second," Leal said.

"Thank God, you can talk," Jay said. "I was beginning to think for a second there—" He threw a glance at Thuster sitting still and silent on the other side of Leal, staring up at the clock, waiting for the hour hand to circle its face again, now that the bells had chimed the hour.

"You'll do it, then?" Jay asked. "You'll do this one little favor for me? You don't know how much this means to me, Leal. You don't know how important it is. You're my only hope."

Like Obi-Wan Kenobi, Leal thought. He didn't take his offer of money but agreed to deliver the rose, along with the note. One thing he was learning about the adult world was how everything always had to seem so goddamned important.

***

Her phone's ringtone interrupts Selena's nightly correspondence with Henri.

"It's that patient of yours," Lori's voice snaps in her ear. "The little bastard got me suspended."

"Slow down. Suspended? What are you talking about?"

"He's evil, I'm telling you. Pure, unadulterated evil."

"Leal?" Selena says. "I wouldn't go that far."

"Who do you think finked on me? He came into my office yesterday afternoon. Smelled alcohol on my breath—or so he claimed. Reported it right away to the vice principal, the little snitch."

"Would he do something like that? It just doesn't sound like something he'd do."

"He did it—I swear. It was just one harmless little drink. At lunch. You know me—I wouldn't let myself have more than one drink. One's my limit. Especially during work hours. But then they just had to conduct a search of my office."

"Oh?" Selena arches an eyebrow.

"They found a flask. In my desk drawer. God's truth, I have no idea where it came from. I wouldn't be surprised if he planted it."

"Who? Leal?"

"All because I told him he needed to wrap things up with you and your sessions."

"Why did you tell him that?"

"The school board's getting antsy."

"Antsy?"

"They want a determination, Selena. An assessment. I can only stall them so long. They're like a bunch of hungry hippos wanting answers. If they don't get one soon, they're going to expel him anyway. As a safety measure. You know, keeping students safe."

This is news to Selena. She has no direct contact with the school board herself. Lori has always been the intermediary, so she has to trust what she says.

"Well, I wouldn't sweat it too much," Selena tries to reassure her. "You've got a good track record with HR, don't you?"

"Impeccable," she insists. "Fifteen years. I've given fifteen years of my life to this school district—thirty if you count all the overtime take-home work they don't pay you for. I should just scrap it all. Pack up and move to Trinidad. Or Tobago. Why is it called Trinidad *and* Tobago anyway? Can't they make up their frickin' mind?"

"Why there?" Selena asks to ground the conversation in something real. She is starting to grow concerned over her friend's mental state.

"Oh, I got one of those time-share invitations. You know, free dinner, free door prize, everything free? Maybe you got one too?"

"The one that says free consultation, no obligation?"

"You want to go in on one together? Except in my case, it won't be temporary, I have to warn you. Once there, I may never come back!"

"Oh, hush," Selena tries to calm her friend's frayed nerves.

She tries to sound sympathetic. Surely she will be reinstated.

"I wouldn't count on it," Lori says. "That little shit. He ruined my career."

Chapter 13

Leal shows up as usual—right on time at the top of the stairs. He walks through the lobby and into her office—she's left her door open at the end of her last session—plopping himself on his couch before Selena even invites him inside.

Selena slowly lowers herself into her seat. Her office chair feels uncomfortable. The baby—she is starting to think of it as more than a fetus, now that she's firmly entrenched in the middle of her third trimester—has moved into an awkward position.

She wants to ask him about his mother—why she hasn't returned her calls—but he surprises her by taking the initiative instead.

"Are you going trick-or-treating tonight?" he asks.

"I'm a little too old to trick-or-treat," she replies.

"I meant with your kids. Do you have any other kids to take trick-or-treating?"

"Other kids?"

He stares at the balloon of her stomach, and she understands. Her other patients have already asked about her condition—some directly, others obliquely. She has been wondering when it would be Leal's turn to inquire.

"Oh," she says. "No, I don't. This will be my first."

She shifts in her seat. She can't seem to make herself feel at ease.

"What about you?" she asks.

She wonders what he would dress up as: vampire, ghost, skeleton.

"No, I'm a little too old for trick-or-treat, too."

He smiles.

Selena leans far back in her office chair. Then she shifts to one side.

"You know, I really shouldn't be meeting you today. Not without your mother's consent."

Now it's his turn to shift in his seat.

"It's all right. I'm sure she wouldn't mind."

"I can't seem to get hold of her. She hasn't returned any of my calls."

"I'll talk to her again. I really will."

Something occurs to her.

"Do you ever talk to your mother, Leal? The way we talk? The way you talk to me?"

"Sometimes, sure. Not always." He bends over to tie a shoelace. "Normally, we text or just leave notes for each other."

"Notes, huh?"

"Sort of like the note Jay wanted me to deliver to Diana."

Selena can't help rolling her eyes. As she learned from their previous session, no amount of prompting will spur Leal's story toward its conclusion, which, apparently like a fine wine, will not be ready before its time. He will always come up with one installment after another—a perfected stalling tactic.

*

Saul answered the door, pulling it open an inch, staring through the crack.

"Leal," he whispered. "Hello. I see you've brought Thuster. That's good. Listen, you'll have to be very quiet. Diana isn't feeling very well."

"That's okay," Leal said. "I just wanted to give her this."

He showed Saul the rose—or what was left of it. It had lost another two petals on the way over.

"Come in, come in," Saul said. "She'll be glad to see you. It might do her a world of good. I just don't want any germs coming in. You know, from outside."

Diana lay on the couch under a blanket, two pillows propped under her head. A magazine was spread across her lap.

Holding the rose as delicately as he could, Leal handed it to her, a few wilting petals on a trembling stem.

She sat up. "For me?" She sneezed, violently, three times in a row. "You haven't caught me looking my best." She wiped her nose with a tissue. "It's lovely. Really."

"Here," Saul said. "I'll take it. I'll go find a vase. I'm telling you, if Leal was just ten years older, I might have to feel a little jealous." He clomped into the kitchen, opened and shut cupboards. Tap water poured from the spigot. Diana sat up a little straighter on the couch.

"Here," Leal said. He slipped her the yellow, blue-lined piece of paper from Jay. "This goes with it."

She took the note and hid it inside the magazine, as Saul bounded back into the living room.

"I couldn't find a vase," Saul said. "I set it in a glass of water. Fresh out of the dishwasher. There's a little more light in the kitchen." He turned to Leal. "Diana's been sicker than a dog the last few days. But I've been taking good care of her, playing nursemaid."

Diana blew her nose in another tissue, nodding her head, and tossed the used tissue onto a pyramid overflowing a wastebasket nearby.

"Hell of a way to spend what's left of my vacation," Saul said. "Here, let me take this from you. What is it? Another *Glamour*? You've been reading it all morning. You need your rest."

He grabbed hold of the magazine on Diana's lap, but she grabbed hold, too, beginning a tug of war as Saul pulled in one direction and Diana the other. Finally, Saul tugged a little too hard, and Diana fell right off the couch, rolling onto the carpet. The magazine landed in the middle of the room, but Diana was all tangled up in her blanket, a pinioned croissant, her pupils peeking out like raisins or poppyseeds.

"What were you thinking?" Saul asked. "What on Earth were you trying to do?"

Helping her back onto the couch, he fluffed the pillow behind her head, tucked in the blanket all around her.

Leal was all set to give Diana back her magazine, but Saul took it from him like a prize possession, clutching it by its spine as though he had won a trophy in a Battle Royale.

The yellow letter fell out of it, fluttering like a rare butterfly onto the floor. Everyone's eyes went to the yellow scrap of paper: Leal's eyes, Diana's eyes, Saul's eyes. Everyone's eyes except Thuster's. Leal looked around to see what happened to Thuster's eyes.

"What's this?" Saul reached down for the paper, and Diana's arm shot out at the same time, hand falling short of Saul's wrist.

"What's what?" Diana said.

Saul picked it up. He unfolded it slowly, eyebrows forming a V.

"It's nothing," Diana said. "Probably just a grocery list."

"This don't look like your handwriting," Saul said, bringing the note close to his eyes.

Diana glanced away. She turned her head to the back of the sofa, facing the wall.

"Here," Saul said. He handed the letter to Leal. "You read it. I can't make out the lettering without my glasses handy."

Leal looked over the letter. Diana turned her head around slowly to focus on Leal. Her eyes moved back and forth like the beads of an abacus. Saul kept his eyes on Diana, as Leal made a preliminary cough, straightened his body, and started to read.

"*Dear Diana—*" he began.

Dramatic pause, glancing at Diana. Then back to the letter.

"*I just want you to know that I love you. I have never loved anyone else. I think of you night and day. I dream of you each and every night.*

Your face is always in my—I'm sorry," he said. "I can't make it out."

"Keep reading," Saul commanded.

"It looks like *mind*. I'll just say it says *mind*. Anyway, *I can't live without you. You are my moon and sun. Without you I am as good as dead*."

Saul's eyes grew narrow. The space between his eyebrows formed a deep trench. Fists clenched, unclenched. Sweat built a bridge across his forehead.

"*Love*," Leal announced. "*Love* … Leal."

A moment of silence, absolute calm. Saul turned to face him. Diana's eyes were disbelieving, questioning, wide.

"Diana was right," Leal said. "It sounds like a grocery list."

Saul's face broke into a long, leering grin. The grin gave way to a guffaw. Then the guffaw turned into a genuine laugh—loud, hoarse, dark. "Ha, ha, ha, ha, ha. Ha, ha, ha, ha, ha, ha, ha, ha, ha. Ha, ha, ha, ha, ha, ha, ha." He placed an arm around Leal's neck, hugging him to his side, putting his head in a headlock, rubbing his scalp raw with his knuckles. Then he pushed him away and clamped his hands hard on his shoulders. Squinting his eyes, he finished the rest of his laugh, the way Leal imagines an undertaker might button the collar of a corpse.

"So," he said, "you have a crush on my Diana, do you? How old are you, anyway? Twelve? Thirteen?"

"Almost fourteen, sir."

"And you've already got a one-hundred-percent American, no-nonsense, schoolboy's crush." The laughter caught in his throat, and Saul spun him around, swinging a heavy arm around his neck from a fresh angle. "Can you believe it?" he asked Diana. "Delivering love notes right under my roof? Hell, right under my nose? Unbelievable. Just unbelievable."

Leal took the letter and folded it in thirds. He ran the edges between thumb and forefinger, pressing hard with his nails. Then he handed the note back to Diana for safekeeping.

"No, you keep it," she said with a smile, her face drained, but looking terribly relieved.

She opened her mouth to say something else, but an explosion of glass from the kitchen stopped her. The sound was followed by a meek, mild cry, like the mewing of a kitten.

They ran into the kitchen—Saul first, then Leal, Diana a distant third.

Thuster had fallen back onto the white and yellow linoleum squares of the kitchen floor. Shards of glass encircled him like a wreath. A splinter of glass had lodged in his forehead, leaving a jagged, deep gash when Leal removed it. The blood spilled out in thick red bubbles, running down the side of his nose, dribbling onto the linoleum, forming a red puddle in one of the squares, where he sat like a pawn in a game of chess. But he found what he wanted. He was holding the yellow rose in his small, tight fist.

Saul knelt beside him, taking a closer look, tilting Thuster's head one way, then the other, under the overhead light. Diana grabbed a dishtowel and handed it to Saul, and he pressed it against the wound. Thuster sat calmly, cross-legged, as though nothing had happened. He was only happy to be holding Diana's rose. He twirled the stem around and around between his fingers.

"How is he?" Diana asked.

"It looks pretty bad," Saul said. "I think he'll need stitches. Well, one thing's for sure, his blood's red—not green."

"What are you talking about?" Leal asked.

"He's not an alien, like I thought. He's human, after all."

*

Selena releases a sigh.

"Leal," she says, "we're almost out of time."

"Can I tell you what happened next?"

"Yes, but I feel it's only fair to warn you. This might be our last session together."

"I'll talk to my mom. I'll make sure she'll give you a call."

"It's not just that, Leal. It's just—well, how can I put this without seeming to offend you? It's just that I don't feel we're making any progress."

"Progress?"

"I don't have any other word for it. Advancement. A feeling of getting somewhere."

"Oh. You mean with my treatment."

"Well, yes and no. I mean, we can't really call it treatment, can we? You haven't yet told me what you need me to treat."

"Can't I just tell you this next part?"

"We're almost out of time, Leal."

"It won't take too long. I swear. It's important."

"If you want."

"Are you sure?"

"Yes."

"I only want to tell you if you're sure."

"Okay."

"Are you sure you want to listen?"

"Yes, Leal. I'm sure."

*

Using his flip-phone in the waiting area, Leal called Father Mac.

The nurses—they wouldn't admit Thuster without Father Mac, so they had to sit tight. Leal could tell that the examining nurse wasn't sure how to deal with Thuster. He held a sucker out to him, but Thuster didn't take it. He just kept holding the yellow rose, flecked with drops of blood, clenched inside his fist.

Thanks to any number of clean, white handkerchiefs Saul applied to Thuster's forehead, the bleeding had slowed to a trickle. He kept pulling them out of his pocket like a magician.

Thuster's forehead—it was still seeping. It just wasn't Old Faithful anymore. Diana—she must have handed over a bunch of them—handkerchiefs—from Saul's dresser before they left. Saul left her at home—Diana. He wouldn't let her come along. He told her that there were more germs in a hospital ward than in the open air. He made sure she was tucked back under the covers on her couch before they left.

*

"Five minutes, Leal. I can only give you five more minutes."

*

Father Mac and Leal's mom entered the emergency room at the same time.

Father Mac—he took a look at Thuster's wound. Then he went to the nurses' station to fill out some paperwork and answer a couple of questions as his guardian.

Finally, Thuster was escorted through a set of double doors, and Father Mac followed, hands clasped behind his back. Saul took a seat next to Leal's mom, placing the last of his bloody handkerchiefs in his pants pocket. He put a gentle arm around her shoulder, assuring her everything was going to be all right, everything was going to be just fine—as though Leal had been the one rushed to the hospital, not Thuster.

*

"I wish you could have seen her, Dr. Harris. My mom smiled up into Saul's face and nodded her head and placed a hand on his knee, and I kept waiting for her to melt into a puddle of water on the floor, the way she kept looking at him all bleary-eyed."

"All right, Leal. It's time."

"Saul kept telling my mom what a good boy he thought I was, and my mom told Saul that she thought I was a good boy, too—"

"Leal, it's time."

"It took all of two hours for the doctors to finish up with Thuster, from the time we walked through the sliding glass doors to the time Father Mac came wheeling him out in a wheelchair. Thuster's eyes were closed. And it was funny, too, that his eyes were closed. The doctor—it was this older woman with gray hair—she explained to us that they decided to put him under, completely sedate him, rather than just give him a shot, because they weren't sure how Thuster would react to a hypodermic."

"Leal—"

"Father Mac seemed proud of him, and Saul—well, he was very impressed, too. He thought nine stitches were very impressive. They'll leave a nice little dueling scar, he said. But the doctor—she said, no, they would heal up just fine. They would look like just another wrinkle on his brow—when he gets to the age where he starts having wrinkles."

"Leal, please. We have to stop now."

"So we all went our separate ways. Saul went back to his house. He said he would have to go back to playing nursemaid as soon as he stepped through the door. This night wasn't over, Saul said. Not by a long shot. And Father Mac—he ended up refusing the offer of a ride from my mom. He said he would take Thuster back by taxi. A taxi would work just fine. He had to apologize. It was waiting on an Uber that had made him a little late coming over in the first place."

"Leal—"

"And then my mom—she dragged me through the double doors, and I looked back through the glass, and I saw Thuster, with his eyes closed in his wheelchair, and Father Mac standing beside him with his hand on Thuster's shoulder, and it was the saddest sight I ever saw in my life—I can't tell you how sad it made me feel—and I knew right then—"

"Leal—"

"I knew right then that it would all end up horrible. I knew it, just looking at the two of them through the glass—I knew it would all end up bad."

Selena leans forward in her chair, while Leal sinks back in his couch.

They stare at each other, across the space of the carpet, as though looking through an invisible wall.

"I'll see you next week, won't I?" Leal asks.

"I don't know," Selena says. "It all depends."

***

This time, Selena doesn't need her nametag to identify her.

She takes note of the tattoo running along the inside of her arm, disappearing into her sleeve, doubling back below her neckline, peeking out of the V in her shirt: a vine with an indigo string of clematis, as Sandra pours her a cup of coffee at the counter, where Selena has managed to seat herself on a high rotating stool.

For her part, Sandra doesn't seem too surprised to see her.

"I don't suppose you're here to see a menu, are you?" she asks. Her smile appears friendly, genuine, and is something she sustains while pouring Selena a cup of coffee, leaving room for a smidge of cream. Sandra apologizes for not calling. She's been suffering a string of migraines lately.

Plus, she has a black eye, flesh noticeably puffy and blue, impossible to conceal.

"This?" She notices Selena staring. "I could make up something, tell you I collided with a doorframe, but the truth is more interesting. It was my ex, a guy I'd been seeing."

She sounds almost boastful. They got into a grand finale of fistfights, but Sandra assures her, he got the worse of it.

"And Leal?" Selena steers the conversation back to the reason for her dropping in.

Yes, she's thought it over and wants to continue her son's

therapy. But not pro bono. She doesn't want to be a burden.

"He's as much as threatened me physical harm if I keep him from seeing you."

They compromise on one session a week, at the reduced rate of $30 per session—in psychiatric terms, virtually free of charge. The only thing they don't do is shake hands on the deal.

Selena bides her time while Sandra takes the orders of three new customers—teenagers—seated at a booth. On her return trip, she notes another tattoo wrapped around her ankle, a chain of gray-green links punctuated by barbed wire.

Sandra asks if Selena would like something to go with her coffee. Piece of pie? She points to the display case of pies preserved under glass: pumpkin, cherry, coconut cream. Selena is tempted but shakes her head. No, just a refill is fine. Besides, there's a fly flitting from slice to slice that's apparently escaped Sandra's notice.

"Sandra—I want to ask you about something—about something Leal mentioned today."

Sandra warms her cup of coffee, sets out two extra creamers from her apron pouch, waits for Selena to proceed.

"He described a trip to the emergency room. He said it took place sometime over the summer."

"Yeah," Sandra says, setting the pot back on its burner. "That's right. That would have been—let me see. I think it happened around the end of August. Right before school in fact."

"He said it was because of his friend."

"Which friend was that?"

"Thuster."

"You mean, he's still talking about Thuster? Oh, Dr. Harris—" Sandra lets out a laugh. "You haven't made much progress at all, have you?"

"Please," Selena says. She invites Sandra to call her by her first name.

"Well, then, Selena. Let me tell you what happened. It wasn't imaginary. It wasn't something that happened to this 'friend' of Leal's either. It was something that happened to Leal himself. I don't know what he told you about Thuster, but it was Leal who went in for stitches. It was something that happened when he was visiting Father MacDougal."

"Father Mac?"

"That's what they call him—the boys."

"What happened?"

"Father Mac took him to the emergency room and called me from there. That's where I met them. Leal needed nine stitches in his forehead. Father Mac said it was an accident, and I believed him. He said he turned while holding a kitchen knife just as Leal was passing behind him. I saw no reason to doubt the word of a priest."

"No, of course not."

Selena takes another sip of coffee. She waits while Sandra clears a plate at the counter. She watches her pocket a fifty-cent tip. Then she goes to the corner booth, delivering two ice teas and a diet Pepsi to the three high-school kids.

When she comes back, Selena asks her about Leal's relationship with Father Mac.

"He's a godsend," she says, "no pun intended. I'm sorry. I should put that in the past tense, shouldn't I, now that he's retired? What I mean is that he made it easy for people like me, people in my situation—single mothers with kids. I know what they say about priests in the papers, but Father Mac was different. Grandfatherly. He took care of them during the day in the summers. He coached them on the basketball court. He fixed them dinner. Sometimes, due to my work schedule, Leal would spend the night."

"He spent the night?" Selena asks, feigning surprise, secretly pleased to be receiving corroboration of Leal's account from an independent source.

"After Leal's father died, I was having a rough time making ends meet. I wasn't in a position to afford an all-night babysitter. And it wasn't just Leal. Other children spent the night, too. It was like he was running a boarding house for teenagers—adolescents."

"Did *you* approach *him*?" Selena asks out of curiosity.

"Oh, no. He was a wonderful presence after Leal's father died. The way he consoled the family—well, Leal and me—and offered to help in any way he could."

Selena takes slow, careful sips of her coffee, while Sandra makes the rounds with a fresh pot. By the time her cup is half empty, she's decided on a different tack—something more direct.

"Did you know Jay?" she asks, as Sandra returns to refresh her cup a third time.

"Jay?" Sandra pauses with the pot of coffee at a tilt.

"He's an artist Leal's talked about. You might know him as Gerald."

"I know who he is. I just can't believe Leal's mentioned him, that's all." She wrestles her arms into a fur coat she grabs from a hook on the wall behind the register. "He promised he would never talk about him in your office. I made him promise, and he agreed."

"Wait! Where are you going?"

"I'm late for my break."

"I haven't paid."

"It's on the house," she says and passes through a door behind the counter into the kitchen. Selena rises from the stool as fast as she can, which isn't very fast at all, and follows in her footsteps, drawing the eyes of two short-order cooks in her wake. She finds Sandra pacing in the back alley, inky dark except for the wavering light of a streetlamp angling near the entrance, so it takes her a moment to perceive her smoking a cigarette with quiet fury.

"Maybe I should have told you before," Selena says, catching up with her.

"Damn straight," she says, blowing out a stream of smoke through clenched teeth. "So now you know."

"Look, I'm not judging you." Selena reaches out as though to stop her from running away. "I wouldn't be one to judge."

"How can you say that?" Sandra says, lurching back around and stopping short. "How can you say that, knowing what you know?"

What can she say to ease her mind? Commiserating with her is like trying to tame a savage beast.

"As far as I know, posing unclothed as a painter's model isn't a crime."

This checks her movement mid-pace. She turns back around to face Selena, giving her a curious look as though to solve the last few twists of a Rubik's cube.

"That's all he's told you? That I was posing?"

"Actually, he didn't even tell me that much. All he told me was that he made visits to Jay's cottage."

This seems to calm her. She takes a last drag on her cigarette, tosses it to the pavement, squashes it like a bug with her heel, as though performing a pivot on a basketball court.

"I needed the money. There was an ad on Craigslist. I responded to it."

"That's as far as it went?"

"No," she admits, drawing another cigarette from her purse. "It went farther. But it doesn't matter now. He's gone."

"Do you know where?"

She shakes her head side to side. Inside her fur coat, she could be an Inuit out for a stroll.

"Back to Chicago, I think," she says with a sneer. "Alcatraz, for all I care."

Or some other island, Selena imagines, sunny and sultry and tropical, far, far away, where mermaids sing each to each.

"Were there others? Other women he painted?"

"Maybe. I don't know. Probably. If there were, he never mentioned them. I never saw any other paintings." She throws her cigarette to the ground, even though it's only half-smoked. "I'm sorry, I need to get back."

"Just one more question." This holds her in place, her hand clutching the handle of the steel door to the back of the diner. Selena can't wait for a better combination of cards in some future deal. It's time for a showdown, all cards on the table.

"How well do you know Saul Solomon?"

"The Chinchilla King? From the commercials?"

"That's a chinchilla fur coat you're wearing, isn't it?" she bluffs. Personally, she wouldn't know fox from ermine, she's so anti-fur, just as her politically correct, environmentally conscious mother raised her. She wouldn't be surprised to learn her mother harbored a can of spray paint in her purse for impromptu protests of fur-clad women she might encounter.

"So what if it is? I don't think I like the implication. How would I know someone like that? It's not like I'm out running around with half the married men in town."

She holds herself steady, arms at her side, but Selena notes the closed fists. Sandra may be small, but she's feisty. There's no doubt in Selena's mind who would win a wrestling match, despite her advantage in height—and weight.

"I didn't mean to imply—it's just that I'm worried about Leal."

"And I'm not?" Her breath is rapid and short through flaring nostrils, and Selena knows she's pushing her luck.

"I think he might have got into some sort of … entanglement, for lack of a better word, over the summer."

"With who? Saul Solomon?"

"And his wife."

Sandra blinks away what might be an incipient tear.

"The 'lovely Diana'?" she asks with scorn, quoting the commercial.

"And Jay. I think he may have got caught up in some sort of lover's triangle."

"You don't think I would know that? You don't think I would know if something like that was going on with my own son? You don't think I keep better tabs on him than that?"

Selena realizes she may be misreading her opponent's breaths. Maybe it's not anger they're holding in check, but tears.

"Oh, honey," she coos, experimenting with the same sugary tone her mother used to adopt when having a girl-to-girl talk with her whenever she was in a bad way. "This isn't about you or your parenting skills. It's about Leal, your son. I believe he underwent something traumatic at the end of the summer. I think he experienced a great deal of trauma. And all I'm trying to do is figure out what it was."

She waits as Sandra heaves her shoulders once, twice, and then they collapse, and her face melts like a Jell-O mold gone soft.

"I just want it to be over with," she whimpers, eyes sad and round as a scolded puppy's, her cheeks glistening in the slant of light from the streetlamp at the alleyway entrance.

"The etcetera?" Selena asks.

Sandra lets out a snort, half laugh, half cry, and then it all comes out in a gush.

"I'm so tired of it all. I don't know how to be a mother to him anymore. There are times I don't even recognize him as my son. Half the time I'm actually scared of him—not *for* him, but *of* him. Isn't that terrible? Being afraid of your own son? I had him too young. I think that's part of the problem. I had him just too goddamn young."

"It's all right," Selena shushes her, taking a step forward, reaching out a hand. "It'll all be okay."

Sandra looks up through wet strands of hair that have fallen against her forehead.

"You think so?" she asks. And then, without warning, she wilts, and Selena folds her up inside her arms, fur coat and all, and holds her, like giving a wild animal a bear hug, while Sandra lets break a series of sobs. "I just don't know how to do it anymore. If I had the money, I'd send him to a boarding school or a military academy. I'm just a terrible, terrible mom."

"Surely, you're being too hard on yourself?"

"No, it's true," she says, sliding out of Selena's embrace. Selena doesn't have the wherewithal to prop her up as she slithers against the brick wall and ends up sitting on the cold cobblestones of the alley. "You don't know this. I never told you. But I was planning on giving him up."

Selena is actually glad to hear this   the truth, for once, confirming what she already knows—but she's careful not to betray her private knowledge with the slightest of expressions.

"Like for adoption?" she nudges her confession along.

Sandra looks up with a wet-eyed look, mascara running down her cheeks.

"A boys' home. A home for boys. Father Mac knew of one. I let him pick it out. We even went up there together. I thought if maybe Father Mac were to come along, it would be okay. Leal trusts him. I thought maybe he would make it all easier. Just his presence would smooth things over. The transition."

"Does Leal know?"

Sandra shakes her head.

"I never told him. It was just something I was thinking of. It's been so hard, a single mother and all. And with Leal the way he is, always getting into trouble at school and so hard to manage at home. I just thought—"

She breaks into a fresh torrent of tears, head bobbing as though she's a marionette on a string. Selena wants to console her but knows better than to kneel. She wouldn't be able to get back up without the help of a crane.

"Am I evil?" Sandra asks, face buried in the collar of her fur coat, her question muffled by sobs.

"Is it still something you're thinking of doing?" Selena asks. She has to know.

Sandra shakes her head.

"No, not anymore. Father Mac was supposed to help, but he's gone. So it's no use my trying to take him there on my own."

Now it's Selena's turn to shake her head—in disbelief. She can't imagine it, suffering through all that labor, raising a child until he's thirteen years old, waiting all that time to just get rid of him.

The morality of it is questionable to begin with, but the fact that Sandra's decision hinges on a technicality makes it seem even more cold-hearted.

"You won't tell him?" she asks, throwing a nervous look, as she raises her hand for assistance.

"No, I won't tell him." It would be unethical to divulge something so monumental she learned outside her office. Besides, she's pretty sure Leal has already found out and has been letting her know in his surreptitious way. Anyway, she doesn't believe this is the only trauma Leal is concealing.

"Help him," Sandra pleads quietly, as Selena takes hold of her hand. "Please, do what you can."

"I'll try," Selena says. "That's all I can do. But—"

"But?"

"I'm afraid you're going to have to help *me*—if you want me to lift you up, that is."

***

It's half past ten o'clock when Selena comes home. As she pulls into the driveway, the headlights of her car slice through long streams of toilet paper hanging from the branches of the front-yard trees. Her brother is filling black garbage bags full of toilet paper, while her father pulls it from the branches with the prongs of a garden rake. Whoever it was has done a thorough job.

She would pass it off as a Halloween prank, except for what her brother points out to her. A poster-sized message is hanging on their front door. Its letters have been cut out of newspapers and magazines, pasted together. The message is clear enough, crude as it is:

LeaVe LE al ALOne
I'Ll Be WAtchINg

Below the words, a crudely drawn black-and-white representation of a hangman's noose.

"Who's Le-al?" her brother asks her. He pronounces it as though it's two names: Lee and Al. But she doesn't bother correcting him.

"No one," she says. "A patient."

"You want me to call the police?" her father asks.

"It's just toilet paper, Dad," her brother tells him.

"I'm sure it's just a prank," Selena says.

"So who's this Le-al?" her brother asks again.

***

Dear Henri,

I am no longer standing on the outside of Leal's narrative, looking on in the role of spectator. I feel myself becoming ever more involved—being pulled inside.

There is one more thing I should mention. It's something I learned about myself from my encounter with Leal's mom.

Apparently, I'm allergic to fur. My forehead's broken out in a lovely rash. Plus, my eyes wouldn't stop watering and I couldn't stop sneezing all the way home.

Chapter 14

Dr. Harris isn't talking. After a brief "hello" at the door, she hasn't said anything from the moment he walked into her office and they took their respective seats. She contemplates him with a blank stare, a stare he can't read. He can't see what is going on in her mind, behind her eyes, and this unnerves him. He has a sense of unease.

"I told you it would all work out," he says.

She doesn't respond. She doesn't answer.

"I told you my mom would come through for me. She cares about me. She wants me to get better."

He doesn't look out the window, doesn't look at the clock on the wall, the Monet. He looks directly into her eyes.

"Didn't you miss me?" he asks. "It's been a whole week."

This isn't right. This isn't her normal routine. She hasn't even asked how he is feeling today—her standard opening question.

"Aren't you going to talk to me?"

Leal shifts in his seat. He crosses his legs. He folds his arms. Anxiety worms through his intestines.

"I get it. The silent treatment, right? You're not going to answer me, are you?"

This has to be it. She must be trying something new—a new approach. He lets himself feel a momentary sense of relief.

"It's all right. I don't mind. I'm used to it—people not listening to me. People not taking me seriously."

More silence. An inquisitive, curious stare. He feels like an amoeba on a microscope slide in science class.

"Is something wrong?"

Leal feels the corner of his mouth twitch. His foot, resting on his knee, begins to tremble.

"Aren't you going to say anything?"

Selena relaxes her shoulders. She lowers her chin.

"What do you want me to say?" she asks.

Her words excite Leal. He feels a warm wave flood his mind.

"I don't know. Anything. Why are you being so quiet?"

Selena sighs.

"Well, in strict psychotherapy, the therapist never says a word. You come in. You say your piece. Then you leave. No words are exchanged at all." In fact, there's a joke—she thinks it's Woody Allen—about how he was in psychotherapy for six years before he realized his analyst was dead. "Now, as you know, I'm not a psychiatrist. I'm a psychologist. There's a difference. However, in your case, Leal, I feel I've been interfering too often. Interrupting too often. I just want to see how this will go if I don't say as much."

Leal unfolds his arms, places both feet on the floor, leans forward.

"But I like it when you talk. I like it when you ask questions."

"I know you do. That's just the problem."

"So what do you want me to say?"

"Whatever you want to say."

He searches his mind for images. He pictures a tire swing, mermaids in a fountain, a purple butterfly.

"You mean I can talk about anything? Anything I want?"

The silent treatment again. It reminds him of his confession at police headquarters. The detectives—a blonde woman in a stained blouse, an older man with a goatee and a loosened tie— had met with him across a table. The male detective jotted down notes. The woman stared at Leal sternly with folded arms.

"I'm not sure I like this very much. I'm not sure I like what you're doing."

They had put Leal in a holding cell with two other kids—

juveniles accused of vandalizing public property. They asked him what he was in for. "Murder," he told them quietly, under his breath. They didn't talk to him after that.

"How do I know if you're even listening?" he asks. "I mean, how do I know you're not thinking about something else? For all I know, you could be thinking about a foreign country or making up a grocery list."

They had kept him in the cell all that afternoon. He had never felt so lonely, but at the same time, he had never felt so safe. He was almost sorry when they released him later that day.

"It's all right. No one ever listens to me, anyhow. No one ever wants to hear my side of things."

The detectives who interviewed him weren't there to greet him upon his release. A woman in uniform escorted him to the lobby, where his mom was waiting. He tried asking the officer what the detectives had found out. Had they dredged the lake? Had they found the body? Had they located Thuster? He really needed to know.

"You probably don't want to hear about this," Leal says. "You're probably tired of hearing about it."

Closing his eyes, he waits for the images to surface. He lets his mind go, relapsing into a dream, until he can see it, until it all becomes real.

*

It came as afterthought, waking.

He thought he was dreaming—all of those noises. He thought it was just a dream. But then he heard Saul's voice booming up the stairs: "Is Leal here? I have to speak to Leal." His voice sounded like the long, whining wail of a police siren.

He climbed out of bed, put on his clothes. He looked at the clock: one-fifteen. He heard his mom say something downstairs, but her voice was too soft, like a pillow. It was overpowered, smothered, by Saul's voice. "I need to talk to Leal. Where's Leal?"

He buttoned his shirt, tucked in his shirttails. He held his shoes by their laces, one in each hand, flopping at his sides. When he reached the bottom step, he turned the corner slowly, peering into the living room.

Saul took up center stage, pacing figure eights on the thin carpet. Leal's mom was a spectator at an ice rink, watching a giant polar bear glide on a pair of skates. As he paced, Saul looked up at the ceiling or down at the floor or across the room into the mirror above the fake fireplace. Over and over he said, "I'm so sorry. I'm so sorry." But no other words came out, until he caught sight of Leal. He bounded across the room. "Leal! Thank God! Leal!" He reached out his hand and grabbed one of his tennis shoes. Saul looked at the shoe, as though afraid he'd torn Leal's hand from its wrist and the laces were tendons, ligaments.

"Leal, I'm so sorry to bother you. This time of night. I wouldn't have come over, you know that. Not unless it wasn't something awfully important. Not unless it was an emergency situation, and it is, Leal, it is an emergency. She's gone!"

Leal stared at him. He couldn't think of anything to say, even though his mom kept looking at him, prompting him with her eyes.

"Mr. Solomon," his mom said, "I don't want you to worry at all about the hour. But won't you please have a seat?" She offered him the armchair. "Please, it might be better for you to sit down." Saul sat hunch-shouldered. He took up the bulk of the armchair, filling it to capacity. "Let me fix you some coffee. And then you can tell us all about it."

Saul shook his head. "No thanks. Not coffee."

"Then how about a beer?"

"Sure," Saul agreed, "a beer. A beer's just what I need, if you don't got anything stronger."

"Leal, go see if we have a beer in the fridge for Mr. Solomon."

"Saul, remember?"

"Of course," his mom agreed.

Saul's voice followed Leal into the kitchen.

"I'm so sorry," Saul wailed. "I know how this must look, me coming over so late and everything, knocking down your door. But you don't know, you just don't know how it is to be missing someone."

"There, there," Leal's mom said softly. "Now, who is it you're missing?"

"I went out for cough syrup from the local CVS—the one on Henderson and Firth. You see, she's been sick with the flu, and the bottle had run dry, so I went out to get a refill at her request, and when I got back, she wasn't there. The lights were all on. But she wasn't there on the sick couch in the living room when I opened the door.

"At first, I thought, well, maybe she's gone up to the bathroom. So I didn't call upstairs right away. I sat down and looked at the newspaper instead. But then, when she didn't come back down after a while—well, I went ahead and called up the stairs.

"When she didn't answer, I thought maybe she just fell asleep on the bed, so I went up and looked in the bathroom and the bedroom. I even looked inside the chinchilla room. But I didn't see her in any of those places. So then I told myself, 'Saul, don't panic. Maybe she's in the kitchen and didn't hear you come in.' So I was going back downstairs, but then I remembered seeing hangers. Hangers, lying there on the bed.

"That made me go back into the bedroom, so I went back in and turned on the lights, and everything—everything in her closet was gone. Along with the suitcases, two American Touristers, all leather, I'm telling you she couldn't carry both them suitcases together, not if they was heavily packed.

"So I drove down to the bus station, and they were just

sweeping up. And I say to one of the janitors what time the last bus was that left, and he says a bus just pulled out fifteen minutes before the hour for Kansas City, and I'm thinking, she doesn't know anyone in Kansas City. So why would she go to Kansas City?"

"Of course not," Leal's mom said. "No one in their right mind would take a bus to Kansas City at this hour. Not if they didn't have to."

"So that's when I thought I'd come over here. I'm sorry again it's so late. I hate to keep having to say I'm sorry. I know you must have all been asleep. But Leal here is my last resort."

Leal stepped out of the doorway to the kitchen, where he'd been eavesdropping, and handed Saul a Bud Light, his mom's brand of choice. Leal's mom gave him a strange, quiet look.

"Leal," his mom said, "what do you know about this?"

"What do you mean, what does he know?" Saul said, snapping the tab from the beer can. His jugular pulsed a thick purple. "He's only been my right-hand man this whole summer, him and that little sidekick of his."

"Sidekick?" Leal's mom asked.

"Thuster," Saul grimaced.

"Thuster," Leal's mom echoed.

"Thuster," Leal repeated, under his breath.

"I just thought if anyone might know anything, it would be Leal, or Thuster, maybe. Except he don't ever talk—not when I'm around."

"No," Leal's mom said, "he wouldn't."

Saul took a deep, long swig of his beer, then wiped his mouth clean with the back of his hand.

"Tell me something, Mr. Solomon—Saul," Leal's mom said. She had a very concerned, a very worried look on her face—very motherly. "There's something I don't understand."

Saul took another gulp of his beer with a loud slurp. "Ahh," he said, tipping the can back level, "just what the doctor ordered. See, I told you this was going to turn into a longer night than what I expected, didn't I?"

"Why would my son know anything about this missing person?"

"Well, I'm figuring he was with her every minute of a working day, most nearly. Leal was what you might describe as my hired hand, a sort of babysitter, so to speak. I know it sounds odd, a kid looking after a grown woman. All I'm saying is I thought if anyone would know, he might have seen her talking with someone, you know, laughing or joking—having fun. Spending time with some-one in a special way, if you know what I mean."

Taking a final swig of his beer, Saul crumpled the empty can in an iron fist.

"Good to the last drop, so they say. Well, obviously the kid don't know nothing, or he would have told me by now, isn't that right?" He gave Leal a friendly punch on the shoulder that tipped him off balance, like a roly-poly clown.

"Well, like I was saying, I hate to bother you like this about something that isn't even really anybody's business, I guess, but my own. I've already taken up way too much of your time. I'll ask around town tomorrow. I know a couple people I can ask. I'm sure someone or other has seen her, can help me out. After all, we're not talking about that big of a town. Or who knows? Maybe she'll change her mind and turn back up. Women have a way of changing their minds, don't they?"

"Well," Leal's mom said, "things like this, they always have a way of working out for the best."

"Anyway, thanks for your trouble, Sandra." He gave her a quick nod. "Leal, you'll let me know the first sign of her. I mean, let's say she looks you up on the sly, okay?" Another friendly punch on the arm, same sore spot, then he made his way toward the door. Leal's mom followed him across the carpet, a foot-bound servant.

"Saul," she said, holding the doorknob. "Could you please answer me just one question before you go?"

Saul turned at the door. He gave her a broad, warm, winning smile. "Certainly."

She took a deep breath as if to brace herself. She would probably have taken a deeper breath if her pack-a-day habit let her.

"Who exactly is it we're talking about?"

"Excuse me?"

"This person, who seems to be missing, temporarily."

"I'm sorry. My mistake. I just thought you would have already known about her. You've seen my commercials? Didn't Leal ever mention her to you? Diana. Her name's Diana."

Saul sighed, hand on the doorknob.

"Diana," his mom whispered, and Leal could tell by her eyes she was spinning the combination of a lock to a safe.

"Nothing else, maybe she'll come back to me in my dreams."

After he left, Leal's mom turned slowly in the doorway to face him, as though her feet were glued to the top of a music box.

"So it was *that* Diana," she said quietly, almost to herself.

Leal waited for the inevitable lecture. He closed his eyes. He hoped the penalty wouldn't be as bad as he imagined. Maybe he'd only be grounded for a year, maybe two. After all, his mom could only keep him confined to the premises, under house arrest, until he turned eighteen and was legally free to pursue his own way in the world. He couldn't even say he minded the upcoming pun-ishment. In fact, he was looking forward to it.

It would feel nice having some kind of rule, some regulation, to keep him inside and safe, where he didn't have to worry about what Saul or Jay or Diana was going to do next. It was only the hollering that would be bad. If only she would skip all of the yelling, then it would be easy. But she surprised him altogether. She didn't say anything for several minutes, for as long as he held his eyes closed.

"It's late," she said. "I'm sure we can both use our beauty sleep."

Leal's mom took the crumpled can of beer from the mantle, checked her appearance in the mirror, carried the can into the kitchen.

Leal took his time climbing the stairs. The whole march up the stairwell, all he could think about was how he'd never seen his mom looking so weary.

*

That night, he dreamed of Diana carrying two suitcases down to the shore of a lake. She was wearing a black trench coat. A black babushka covered her head. She kept looking behind her. It was apparent she was being followed.

She set the suitcases down on the beach. It was night. The lake was a dark surface of black glass, the shore a long strip of gray sandpaper. When she opened one of the suitcases, a thousand pieces of black clothing flew out at once, like a murder of crows flapping wild wings, except that she managed to grab one piece before it could fly away. It looked like a bra, a black brassiere, struggling, flapping in her hand. Then she reached down and opened the other suitcase, and a million pieces of paper flew out. She snatched the last piece of paper from the air above her head, just before it was able to fly away. It flapped feebly in her hand, as though with broken wings.

She took the black brassiere and pressed it against the sheet of paper, and when she opened the paper and showed it to Leal, he knew he was supposed to see a hidden object, a sign in the two black splotches of ink. But before he could even take a guess, two gunshots rang out.

Diana looked down at her chest, where two small, dark holes

oozed twin streams of black ink, and then Saul appeared, wearing a cowboy hat and spurs and a black handlebar moustache, holding his gun, with a terrible evil smile on his face. As Diana collapsed, she turned into a painting, complete with wooden picture frame, and Leal picked her up by the top of the frame and carried her away, into the water, where he floated the painting like a raft, pushing it into the deeper water, into the middle of the lake.

*

"It was a very strange dream," he admits.

Selena sits still, perfecting her silent treatment.

"How come you never give me any of those inkblot tests? Isn't that something you should have given me? What are they called again?"

"Rorschach tests," she says.

"Rorschach tests," Leal repeats. "Hey! I thought you weren't going to answer me anymore. But it's good to know you're still listening."

"That's something they do more in the movies."

"Oh, right," Leal concedes. "TV shows. I should have known."

He waits for her to say something further, but she only stares at him with level, steady eyes.

*

"Here's to every woman who ever jilted her lover."

Saul raised his glass and tilted his head, downing the liquor straight down his throat. Then he poured another glass to the brim. It seemed to Leal to be a little early to start drinking, but he could see he had caught Saul at the conclusion of an all-night drink fest.

Three empty bottles lay at his feet, along with two empty cartons of orange juice and an ashtray overflowing with cigarette butts. It looked like Saul had spent the night creating mayhem.

"Here's to any woman who ever broke a poor guy's heart in two."

Saul raised his glass in toast once again. A row of knickknacks had been swept from their shelf with what must have been one violent slash of a backhand. Another shelf of sports trophies had been upended, the necks of miniature athletes snapped in two.

"Here's to every trophy ever won and lost," Saul said. "And here's to the woman who made me lose them."

Sheets of newspaper littered the room. The cushions of Diana's sick couch had been tossed about, outcome of a one-man pillow fight. Her blankets twisted like snakes through piles of trash. Saul must have emptied a dozen garbage bags onto the rug. The floor lamp was bent at an angle, light bulb shining through a torn shade.

"Here's to every woman who's wrecked a lifetime of plans and promises." Saul raised his glass again.

"Skoal," Leal said this time, waiting patiently.

The liquor slid down Saul's throat like maple syrup. He brought his head forward, wiping his mouth with his shirtsleeve. He tried to make his eyes focus on Leal, but each pupil had an idea of its own which way it wanted to stare.

"What was it you were trying to tell me, Leal?" Saul asked.

"You wouldn't know him," Leal said. "He was just someone who came by from time to time."

Saul sank into his armchair, chin on his chest.

"What was his name again?" he mumbled.

Leal told him the man's name.

Saul turned the name over and over, concentrating as though to bring a kaleidoscope into focus. "So what is it about this guy? Fill me in."

Saul downed the last drops from the bottle, upending it above his mouth.

"Nothing," Leal said. "Except that you wanted to know if I remembered anything, and this is just something I remembered. Whenever he would come over—"

Saul peered into the empty bottle, rotating it against his eye like a spyglass.

"Right," Saul said. "He came to the house?"

He lowered the bottle. His eyelids drooped to half-mast. Leal was afraid he was going to fall asleep in his armchair. But then he opened his eyes. "Hey, Leal, why don't you go see if you can find another bottle or two of—what is this again?" He turned the bottle, searching for the label.

"Captain Morgan," Leal said.

"That's right," Saul said, "and see if you can hunt down an extra shot glass. I want you to join me in a toast. Maybe a round of toasts."

Leal went into the kitchen.

"Well," Leal said, searching for the bottle, yelling through the kitchen door. "Every time he came over, he would come down the stairs straightening his tie."

"Straightening his what?" Saul shouted back.

Leal brought the bottle and a glass back into the living room.

"His tie," he said.

"He was straightening his tie?"

Saul's pupils drifted off to the side, moved into his forehead, stared down at his lap. They looked everywhere around the room except directly at Leal, and Leal couldn't help but take it person-ally—his almost complete lack of attention.

"In the house? In my house?"

"Yes," Leal affirmed.

"Unbelievable. I can't believe it."

Again, Saul tried to get up from his armchair but sat right back down. He looked around the room. He threw a heavy-lid-ded look at the stairs, as though to catch Diana and the man Leal had described descending the stairwell, hand in hand.

"That's right, sometimes for a half hour or more. And then he would come down the stairs, straightening his tie."

"Let me get this straight. He was coming out of the house—coming out of *my* house—straightening his tie?"

Saul opened one of the bottles and poured the liquor into two glasses, filling each to the brim. He gave Leal a glass, and Leal stared down at the contents, tilting the glass one way and the other, watching the yellowish liquid climb the sides.

"Here's to every guy with a tie who comes out of a house straightening his tie," Saul proposed, lifting his glass in salute, and Leal followed suit.

Saul tilted his head back, but all Leal could do was to take a shallow sip. "I can't believe it. Right here in the house. Straightening his tie." Then Saul gave Leal a sharp, sudden look. "He was straightening his tie?"

"Yes," Leal said, "he was straightening his tie.'"

"Unbelievable," Saul said, shaking a heavy head. "Hey, Leal, what's wrong that you're not drinking? Come on. Down the old hatch, so we can have another toast."

Leal took another short sip of his drink, but then Saul gave him a severe look, and he went ahead and drank it all the way down. It felt very warm going down his throat, and then it felt very hot. It made his head feel very dizzy and alive. It was very sudden how dizzy and alive it made his head feel.

"I can't believe it," Saul said, refilling their glasses. "Straightening his tie." He raised his glass in mock toast. "Here's to every no-good son of a bitch who runs off with a fella's wife after straightening his no-good tie. Cheers!"

Leal clinked his glass against Saul's, then tilted back his head quickly, the glass brim at his lips. He felt the same slow burn, as though he'd just swallowed a potion whose chief ingredient was gunpowder.

"Anyway," Leal said, trying to make the room spin back to the right, taking a close look at the slanting floor, "I just thought you should know."

"You're damn right I have the right to know what's going on in my own house when I'm not around. Some strange guy straightening his tie. Leal, do your duty." He waited for Leal to refill each of their glasses, half emptying the bottle.

"Say, where does this guy live, anyway?' He leaned out of his armchair, wrapping an arm around Leal's shoulder, holding his mouth very close to his face, so he could almost taste the liquor sliding out on his breath.

"Not that far," Leal said calmly, flatly.

Saul rose to his feet, pushing himself out of the armchair. He left his glass on an end table, and Leal set his aside, too.

"Can you take me there?" Saul asked. "Can you show me where this son of a bitch lives?"

"Sure. You want to go there now?" Leal asked.

"I want you to ride shotgun. This could get ugly. I can't believe it. Straightening his tie."

*

Leal stops talking and looks up at the clock.

"Almost out of time," he laments.

"Actually," Selena informs him, "my next appointment cancelled." She can't believe she's suggesting this, but she wants him to continue. He can't stop now. She needs to find out just how "ugly" this next part is going to get. "So, if you want …"

"You mean you want me to keep going?"

He perks up as bright-eyed and bushytailed as a meerkat popping out of its den.

"As long as I'm not keeping you from anything."

"Not that I can think of. But won't this cost my mom more money?"

"We'll just consider it part of a normal session."

"She's a little worried about the money this is costing."

"There won't be any added expense. I promise. This one's on me."

"Okay." Leal settles back in his seat, folding his arms behind his head, stretching out his legs and crossing his feet, as though reclining in a hammock. Talk about adopting a comfortable pose. "As long as there won't be an extra charge."

Chapter 15

Suburbia.

Saturday morning.

Birds chirruping.

Houses low and long and white, with green shutters, brick walkways, red and blue and yellow doors.

Lawns spread out like a rolling green carpet, dandelion-free.

Young men and women in jogging suits rustling by on the sidewalks.

Old men walking their toy terriers on long leashes.

New mothers pushing strollers full of blinking kids.

Sprinklers churning, water spiraling like silver glitter.

People washing and waxing their cars dripping in driveways.

"Turn here," Leal instructed Saul. He pointed outside the windshield, to a side street.

Saul veered left, then swerved too far right to compensate and bumped over the curb, narrowly missing a car backing out of its drive. A horn blared, but Saul blared his own horn right back.

"Son of a bitch," Saul said. "Keep going?"

"Yeah," Leal said. "I'll tell you when. Just a couple more blocks. Watch out for this stop sign."

Saul stomped on the brakes and came to a screeching stop in the middle of the intersection. Fortunately, traffic was light this morning.

"Okay," Leal said, "right turn."

"Here?" Saul asked, his eyes darting into the rearview mirror. They were sagging circles of dull red.

"Right. Here. Now."

Saul spun the wheel hard right, the front tire squealing along the curb like a newborn baby.

"This it?" he asked.

"Yep, the house on the right."

"You sure?" Saul said.

"Yeah. That's it. Number 269." At least, that's how it was listed in the phone book.

"You wait here," Saul said, throwing the gear into park. "I'll be right back."

He left the car idling outside the white, two-story, frame house.

Leal leaned back in his leather seat. The interior of the car was so big, it was like waiting inside a doctor's lobby.

Saul tucked in his shirt, shifted his bulk, and staggered up to the front door, where he gave the frame of the aluminum screen a rattling knock, even though there was a doorbell in clear view.

Saul knocked again, louder, if louder was possible, as though his intention was to shake the rest of the neighborhood awake. He kept knocking until the door was opened by a small, wiry, bald-headed man with horn-rimmed glasses wearing striped pajamas that made him look like a convict. It's hard recognizing someone in pajamas, because you just don't see them dressed this way every day, but Leal was sure this was the right house.

"Can I help you?" Leal heard Mr. Birch say. He used the same, small, squeaky voice when teaching math, furiously working out a problem on the whiteboard, his thin chest heaving like an exhausted canary's.

Saul didn't answer Mr. Birch's question but pushed him back inside the house with both hands against his chest. He turned his head side to side in the doorway, looking up and down the street, before stepping inside and quietly closing the door behind him.

The street was quiet except for a solitary bird in the branch of a tree chirping merrily, as though nothing out of the ordinary was happening, and it didn't share the same sort of cares of Mr. Birch at this moment, which it wouldn't, if what our Lord Jesus Christ says is true about sparrows. Leal found a cigarette from Saul's glove compartment to take the edge off his nervousness as he tried to picture what was taking place inside the house.

The cigarette was his only gauge of time, and he had just flung the butt onto the sidewalk, where it continued to burn a white needle of smoke, when Saul finally came out of the house, wiping his palms against each other, but Mr. Birch didn't appear to escort him off his premises. Saul gave Leal a long, sheepish grin as he retook his seat, heavily, behind the wheel. His foot pressed the gas pedal even before he gave himself a chance to close his door, and the car rolled slowly down the street, like the lead car of a funeral procession.

"Nice try," Saul said. "Nice try."

"What do you mean?" Leal asked. He tried to make his words sound natural, normal, but his jaw was starting to quiver. It's hard trying to make your words sound normal with a quivering jaw.

"He doesn't know anything. He's actually a pretty nice guy, pretty decent. You could tell by his eyes. Very nice eyes. Honest. If he would have known anything, he would've talked."

"What did you do to him?" Leal had to ask. He had to know the answer, so he could take it with him into eternity, so he would know how to answer for himself at the Day of Atonement.

"We had a conversation. I asked him a couple of questions. Point blank and simple."

Saul pulled to the curb to make room for a squad car flying down the road, its red and blue lights swirling, siren blaring. Before Saul could step on the gas, he had to brake again to let an ambulance flash past.

"Okay, okay," he said. "So I roughed him up just a little bit.

If you must know. But put yourself in my position. I thought he had it coming."

Leal shrunk down in his seat, pulling his baseball cap over his eyes. He felt tiny, very small. He couldn't look at Saul. And he knew he was going to have an awfully hard time looking at himself in the mirror whenever it was he went home.

*

"Will I go to hell for what I did?" Leal asks, leaning forward anxiously, a far cry from the ease of his starting position.

He sounds sincere, but the question tempts Selena to turn her frown into a smile. She tries to recall early Sunday School lessons. Which commandment was it: thou shalt not rough up thy math teacher?

"You were trying to create a diversion," Selena says. "You were trying to protect Diana."

Leal nods. He seems relieved.

"Maybe you didn't foresee how far Saul would take things?"

She holds her breath, hoping this is the truth, but Leal doesn't answer. He doesn't strike her as the kind of kid who would seek revenge on a teacher simply because he had been forced to attend summer school.

"Thanks," he says, rising slowly from the couch.

"For what?"

"Listening. You're better than a priest. You know, hearing confessions."

"Maybe I've chosen the wrong profession."

They exchange grins as Leal makes his way to the door.

Selena glances at her desk calendar.

"You'll remember our new schedule?"

"Yeah, sure." He jabs at his temple. "It's all in here."

"All right, then," Selena says, rising from her chair. "See you in a week. Oh, and Leal?" Leal turns on the threshold, the sound of her voice making him pause, a siren song holding him fast. "Try and stay out of trouble, okay?"

***

At home, Selena finds her brother has invaded her bedroom—her private space. He sits hunched in front of her computer screen, typing at the keyboard. A sense of outrage makes her feel she has regressed thirty years. Nothing has changed. It is as though he were once again playing with her dolls without permission.

"What gives you the right—" she starts a surprise attack from behind.

Her brother holds a hand over his head, beckoning restraint.

"I needed to access my bank account. I don't trust doing transactions by phone. I didn't think you'd mind."

"That still doesn't explain why you've invaded my PC."

"Sorry, mahn. Simple curiosity. It will be my downfall someday."

She wasn't aware her brother ever had enough money to bother with banking. Most of his transactions were cash under the table.

"How did you break in?" she asks. "How did you know my password?"

"Truly, it wasn't that hard, mahn," her brother says, still staring at the screen.

Mahn—Selena wants to snort in contempt. Part of his reggae phase.

"But how—?" She stops herself short, takes three deep breaths.

"You're a name person," he explains, his back still toward her, vulnerable, exposed. "I tried out all of the baby names you've been considering."

"And you just happened upon the right one?"

"That, and it was taped to your computer." He hands her a Post-it note with the name "chantal" inscribed in lower case.

"What's the point of a password if you leave it lying around? Is that the name you've settled on?"

"You should have asked me," she says.

"You wouldn't have let me," he answers. "I know how you are, mahn."

"Cut out the 'mahn' business. You're not from Jamaica." Although she has to admit, the shoulder-length dreads are a nice touch.

"I'm not sure I'd go with Chantal, though. It was the name of the hurricane that wiped out our vacation that one summer. Remember? All those jellyfish washed up on the beach?"

She remembers crying and crying, she had been anticipating the ocean so. But her brother, four years her junior, had shrugged off the letdown by clearing a space in the sand where he could build castles with his pail and shovel.

"Thanks for the association," Selena comments drily, crumpling the Post-it and tossing it in the trash. Why tempt fate twice over?

"Speaking of names, who's Henry?"

"Henry?" Selena repeats. "You mean Henri?" Accent on the second syllable, "h" soft, not hard.

"What is he, French?"

"Canadian." She sits on the edge of her bed. She feels exhausted—mentally drained. "How do you know about Henri, anyway? What did you do, breach my email account, too?"

"Sorry, you left it wide open. I couldn't resist. You've let a lot of emails to him pile up as drafts."

"Please don't tell me you sent them!"

She can't seem to catch her breath. The wiring in her brain feels strained to overload.

"Of course not. What do you take me for?"

Gritting her teeth, Selena chooses not to answer.

"At least now I know who this Leal character is, anyway."

"Listen carefully," Selena says. She is finding her bearings, relocating her sense of self. "I don't want you using my computer again. Not without my permission. Got it?"

"Sure, Selena, sure," her brother says, putting on an easygoing front.

"Ever."

"No problem," he says, backing away from her desk. "By the way, who is this French-Canadian dude, anyway?"

"No one. Someone helping me with my patient."

"With Leal?"

Selena nods, taking a seat on the edge of the bed.

"I'm just not getting very far with him," she admits.

"With Henri?"

"No, with Leal."

"Henry—I mean, Henri—thinks you should try hypnosis. At least, that was his latest suggestion."

"I don't need hypnosis," Selena says, feeling defensive.

"He doesn't mean you. He means with Leal."

"He probably meant 'hypnotherapy.' That's one of his specialties." Not to mention CBT, DBT, ACT, and a slew of other acronyms.

"Sounds like the same thing."

"Hypnosis is more a carnival act for the stage. *Hypnotherapy*," Selena persists, "if you want to get technical, is meant to help subjects overcome phobias, obsessions, addictions." She gives her brother a meaningful glance. "Deal with trauma."

"Semantics," her brother insists with a shrug. "Mom tried it."

"True." Their mother, an oncologist, had advocated self-hypnosis to alleviate the pain of cancer, her own included. "But I wouldn't be very good at it." For one thing, she's been feeling too tense, too uptight, these past few weeks with the baby coming on strong to feel relaxed herself, despite keeping up with her yoga twice weekly.

"You're probably just out of practice."

"That's just it: I've never practiced. It came up in grad studies, but there was a lot of debate about its effectiveness. Plus, I'm not licensed." And with Leal, she's wary of planting hypnotically induced memories, as documented in hundreds of false-memory accusations of sexual abuse by hypnotized children way back in the '90s. "The most I've ever practiced is mindfulness." She uses it from time to time to help some of her younger patients focus, especially the ones with ADHD.

"Again," her brother says, "semantics. From what I've read, it's just the power of suggestion. If you get your victim—"

"Victim? Don't you mean 'subject'?"

"—to think they're undergoing hypnosis, they'll play the part of how they think someone undergoing hypnosis acts."

Selena can't help feeling skeptical.

"It's just like sales. You've got to believe in your product, even if it's a load of crap. The more sincere you seem, the more your customer—"

"I've never been good at sales," she snaps, cutting him short.

"Or music. It's just a matter of getting your patient into the right groove."

"What, like New Age?" A refrain by Enya springs immediately into her mind: *Sail away, sail away, sail away ...*

"Or maybe one of those whale-song CDs."

Picturing a beluga spread out on her office couch, Selena lets go a laugh.

"If you need a guinea pig, I'd be a willing—subject," her brother volunteers, taking his leave. "It would be like old times. Just like when we were kids."

With that, it all comes back to her: how she used her brother as a surrogate for anything she was interested in doing but unwilling to be the first to try: jumping off a cliff into a quarry, crossing a street against the walk signal, borrowing money from their dad's wallet to attend a matinee.

"Just promise you won't make me act like a chicken." And then he adds as a postscript: "Mahn."

***

Dissociative syndrome: the feeling of being dislocated from one's body, the sensation of having no body, of floating in air.

Selena feels this, lying on her bed.

It was the dentist who had pointed them out to her: several magazines on a coffee table in the waiting room they shared above the hardware store. The dentist is an older, friendly man, his sunless face topped by a high bone-white dome of a forehead. Two years past retirement and counting, he has confided, all for lack of a younger version of himself, a graduate fresh out of dentistry school, to take over his practice.

Usually, she doesn't come across him in person, the only evidence of his existence the high-pitched whine of his drill behind a not-thick-enough door transmitting the occasional groan or scream from his patients. More than once, when she has encountered him, he has commented on the "loveliness" of her smile, forgetting he has offered the same compliment before, often capping it with a query: "Did you ever wear braces as a child?" That her answer is negative always surprises him.

On her way out the door, it was Selena's turn to be surprised. He held up two magazines—old, mildewed issues of *Time* and *Cosmo* meant for his patients—one in each hand, by their edges, letting the pages unfurl limply, as he might show off two dead rabbits, trophies of a hunt.

"Seems we have vandals on the premises," he remarked.

"Oh?" Selena responded, taking a step forward for a closer look. She saw what he meant. The pages in question were missing squares, rectangles, circles, ovals, surgically removed. Some of the cutouts were still hanging by a single fiber, chads clinging to a punch card.

"And it's not just these." He pointed to others lying about on the low table all opened to pages showing the same signs of purposeful mutilation. "Any idea who?"

Selena shrugged, but she had an idea. It was an idea that made her swoon. The dentist dropped the magazines and helped her to one of the frame-and-canvas chairs, guiding her with a surprisingly strong handhold on her upper arm into a seat that felt as though it might collapse from under her at any moment.

"It's just as well," he said by way of consolation. "They're most of them all outdated anyway." He gave her a long, wistful look as though to add, "like me."

Now, stretched out on her bed, mummified in a blanket, she lies completely still, her mind buoyed by warm currents of air from the heating duct. She feels weightless, light, as immaterial as a jellyfish in a warm salt sea.

A series of kicks brings her back to reality.

"There, there," she says aloud.

She wonders what dreams will come tonight. A woman in a lake? A boy in a tree?

***

During the day, four buses lumber like Indian elephants along the streets of Ovid. At night, only one bus makes a final round, picking up and dropping off a handful of passengers who work late shifts at packing plants and warehouses on the outskirts of town.

Leal is too tired to ride the rest of the way home from the lake on his bicycle. Besides, it's raining. It seems like it's always been raining the past few days. He locks his bike in a vacant lot and waits in the rain for the bus. It takes ten minutes for the Number 3 to arrive with a hiss of airbrakes, and he boards it with fifty cents leftover from his weekly allowance.

He moves down the aisle as the bus lurches forward. Only two other passengers are riding the bus at this hour. They give Leal empty, lifeless stares as he shuffles past them. He takes a seat near the back, gazes out the window at the receding lights of houses, the rolling darkness of yards. As they approach the center of town, the bus makes another stop, in front of St. Mary's, and a passenger takes a seat across the aisle.

"Leal?" she calls sweetly. "Leal, is that you?"

The voice belongs to Sister Sophia, a nun Father Mac had introduced him to before he moved away. She seems young for a nun. She wears a light trace of lipstick, an even slighter hint of mascara. Leal wonders whether makeup violates the rules of her order.

"Hello, sister," he says.

"Dear me," Sister Sophia responds, "you're all wet. You're soaked, head to foot. You're going to catch your death of pneumonia. Don't you have an umbrella?"

An image, like a dream, swims into Leal's consciousness. A network of roots from a willow droops over a cleft in the shore, obscuring his view. He wades through water, up to his waist. The water feels numbingly cold. It pinches his groin, travels along his spine. Bending, he peers into the darkness of the recess behind the roots, where he sees an eye, gray and shiny, like a marble. It stares at him, accusingly, pleadingly.

Leal blinks the vision out of his mind. He contemplates the slight, hooded form of Sister Sophia, who continues to stare at him, expectant, half-smiling.

"What were you doing that you were out in the rain so long?"

"Fishing," Leal says. He turns away his eyes. He had brought a coil of rope, long enough to wrap about the trunk of a tree. Even using the tree as a pulley, it had been heavy going, pulling the bloated torso to shore. It was like a game of tug-of-war, but he knew he couldn't let go of the rope. He knew he couldn't be on the losing side. He willed himself to win.

"Fishing?" Sister Sophia asks. "On a night like this?"

"Yes," Leal says. He stares out the window. He doesn't want to talk anymore. "Don't you know, Sister? Fish bite better in the rain."

Chapter 16

"What's with the church clothes?" Selena observes "You're all dressed up."

Leal is wearing a striped tie against a white shirt, dress slacks over polished shoes.

"My mom's birthday," Leal explains.

"Well, send her my well-wishes," she bids him sincerely.

They take their respective seats, falling into the routine of therapeutic interaction.

"How do you like our new schedule?" she asks.

"It's fine," he says.

"Once a week is all right for you?"

"Sure. I mean, I guess I can get more homework done this way."

Selena laughs. "That's a good point."

He sits with knees apart, fingers interlaced on his stomach. He seems relaxed, comfortable. Privately, one of Selena's goals is just the opposite—to make him ill at ease, uncomfortable.

"Leal, do you know anyone—do you know of anyone who wouldn't want you to continue with this?"

"I'm sorry. With what?"

"With these sessions? With your therapy?"

Leal leans his head against the back of the couch and stares at the ceiling.

"No, not that I can think of. Except for maybe Father Mac. But he wouldn't care about it—not now, of course."

"He doesn't like the idea of therapy?"

"I don't think he cares much for psychologists."

"What makes you say that?"

"I just don't think he would … approve. He believed—he

believes everything could be solved—all problems can be solved through Christ."

Selena keeps working her needle, applying a subtle pressure, like acupuncture. She doesn't want to let up—not yet.

"Do you believe that?"

"Yes. Of course. I mean, of course I do. I have to."

Leal lowers his head to eye level.

"My mom," Leal says flatly.

"Really? Your mother?"

"She doesn't like me being here. She didn't want me to see you in the first place. She's only doing it because of the school. The principal called her about it. She's always asking me what we talk about. She's always making sure I'm not talking about Thuster."

"She is?" Selena asks. *Or Jay, or Diana or …*

"Or Saul," Leal says flatly.

"Saul?"

"He wouldn't like what I'm doing in here either. He wouldn't like it that I'm telling you about what happened."

"Have you seen Saul lately?"

"You're talking to me," he observes.

"I'm sorry?"

"You're talking to me again. I was afraid you weren't going to talk to me."

"Do you like it better when I talk to you? Some patients—they don't like it when I talk. They like it better when I'm quiet. They don't even want to know anything about me. My private life."

"Are you glad to be having a baby?" Leal asks. The question takes her by surprise.

"Yes. I am. Very."

Is she? she has to ask herself. *Truly?*

"But you're not married, are you?"

She can tell he is studying her ring finger, the empty space where her ring used to be.

Selena inhales. She lets out her breath.

"No, Leal. I'm not—not anymore."

He knows her hot buttons, seems to have a knack for invading her worry zones.

"You like working with kids, don't you? You like seeing—oh, how did you say it—adolescents?"

"Yes, I do."

Somehow, he has reversed roles. She is supposed to be the one asking the questions. She is supposed to be the one learning more about him.

"What about you?" she asks to regain the initiative. "Is there a part of you, maybe, that doesn't like coming here? That would rather be left alone?"

This time, she thinks she's needled a nerve.

Leal looks at the clock on the wall. He checks it against his wristwatch.

"We still have plenty of time," Selena observes. "Last time, you left off at Saul's."

"I remember."

Leal shifts in his seat.

"I just wish—I just wish I could have done something more. You know, to keep it all from happening."

Selena waits. She doesn't want to lose this line of thought.

"It's all my fault, really. What happened. I wish—I wish I wasn't so goddamned weak. I could have stopped it. I could have stopped it all from happening."

"Maybe you couldn't," Selena suggests.

Leal looks her in the eyes. His eyes are wide, lambent, light green.

"No. I could have. I could—"

"Maybe you shouldn't blame yourself."

"You don't understand. There isn't anyone else to blame."

"Do you want to talk about it?"

Leal lets a few seconds go by. He takes a deep breath. And then she knows he will return to his story. She thinks about his narrative in a new light. It isn't just a defense mechanism. It gives his life, at least the 50 minutes of his life he spends in her office, some measure of control—maybe even comfort—the pleasure principle at work.

*

After the episode with Mr. Birch, he escorted Saul back to his house. Saul dropped his ring of keys a couple of times on the welcome mat and had to sort through them fresh each new time he picked them back up. Giving up, he handed the keys to Leal, but the door swung open as soon as he touched the key to the lock. Saul pushed his head through the door, leaning his big hands against the frame, and called softly into the house, with a small, pigeon voice: "Diana?" But of course there was no answer.

Leal took him inside and led him up the stairs. He helped him undress, leaving him in his underwear and socks. He didn't look half so intimidating in just his underwear and socks. He went through Saul's drawers, looking for a pair of pajamas. But he found Diana's drawer full of lingerie by mistake. And then he found another drawer that contained Saul's gun, the handgun he had used in the woods, giving him lessons on how to shoot.

By the time he found the right drawer, Saul was already asleep, mouth open, emitting a series of rough snores. He closed the bedroom door behind him and walked down to the living room. He thought vaguely about helping clean up, to make the room nicer for Diana when she returned—if she returned. Part of him worried he would never see her again.

That's when he saw the blinking red light of the answering machine. He had never encountered technology this ancient, but he could guess what the blinking light meant. Someone—maybe several someones—had left a message. Maybe Diana.

He pushed play, and the first couple of messages were telemarketers—not even real people, robocalls. The third message was a voice he recognized all too well.

"Hello, Mr. Solomon—Saul. This is Sandra—Sandra Porter. You were at my house last night."

Leal thought it amusing she felt the need to remind Saul of his whereabouts. He wasn't that drunk at the time. He had only had the one beer.

The next part he didn't find amusing at all: "I have a pretty good idea of where your wife went, where she disappeared to. I have a shift at the diner, but you can always reach me on my cell."

Aside from leaving her number, that was it, the message followed by a beep that startled Leal out of his reverie. Erasing the message was easy: a simple push of a button. But what would prevent Leal's mom from calling again? He knew she disapproved of his friendship with Diana. She would no doubt go to great lengths to disrupt it.

*

Leal leans forward, elbows on knees, staring at the carpet.

"I thought with the way he was when I left him, all passed out, I'd have lots of time."

Selena presents a sympathetic look that's wasted on his hunched-over form.

"Time for what?"

"To get there ahead of him."

"At the cottage?"

"I thought it would be my big chance," Leal says, lifting his head.

"What big chance? To play the hero?"

Selena can't keep from sounding a little skeptical.

Leal turns his gaze out the window as though to study the shapes of cumulus clouds.

"I thought I would warn Diana. Let her know Saul was on her trail."

"You thought she might appreciate that—being rescued?"

"I thought if she knew there was no going back to Saul, she would run away with us. I thought we could all run away together."

Selena leans forward.

"Us?"

"Me and Thuster. You know I couldn't leave Thuster behind. But like I said, it was a crazy plan. I thought we could all go away somewhere together. We could go somewhere new. Start over. You know, be a family."

"Jay, too?"

"Yeah," Leal says, sinking back in his couch. "Jay, too."

*

In the basement of the parsonage, Leal had found Father Mac up to his ankles in muddy, murky water. His pants were rolled around his knees, his shins showing long and white. He held a heavy plumber's wrench like a scepter. Leal walked down the stairwell, a poor serf on pilgrimage, stopping on the next to last step, keeping above the water line.

Thuster sat at the top of the stairs, pants rolled, too, in imitation of Father Mac. Nine dark-green stitches slanted across his forehead, giving him a nice Frankenstein's monster look. If he ever decided to talk, they would give him bragging rights, for sure. Leal would have to come up with a new backstory, however. Getting skewered with a drinking glass because you're reaching for a rose isn't the most glamorous of accounts behind a scar. A fencing match with a German veteran of World War Two, an officer of a Wehrmacht or Panzer division—that's a much better account.

"I wouldn't label this a major emergency," Father Mac said,

surveying the water level. "It's not life-threatening, for instance—nothing like the Johnstown flood. Still, it is one of life's unfortunate mishaps, when one of your water pipes splits in two." He used the heavy wrench as a pointer, indicating the problem. A set of gray pipes ran end to end of the cellar along the ceiling, one of them bubbling water. "It's because they're made of lead. This parsonage was built back in the '20s when lead was in common use."

Leal looked at the rows of wooden beams propping the planking of the upstairs floor. Cobwebs threaded the joists; a naked light bulb radiated a yellow halo from its porcelain socket.

"The plumber should be on his way by now," Father Mac said. "I just thought I'd try and see what I could do, maybe beat him to the punch. Save the church a little money. But it looks like the water's backing up through the sewer from the street at the same time, so I'm in what you might call double jeopardy."

"Father, is it okay if I steal Thuster away for the rest of the day?" Leal asked.

Father Mac sloshed through the water, wading without lifting his feet.

"As long as you promise to have him back by nightfall. We have a big day planned tomorrow."

"Right." He hadn't forgotten about the trip to the residential care facility—the boys' home in Chicago.

"Leland, have you decided if you'll be coming with us? I know Thuster, in his own special way, would appreciate your presence. It would help him settle in."

"I'd have to ask my mom," Leal said.

He turned to go, pulling Thuster by the hand at the top of the stairs. Father Mac came up halfway to see them off.

"And Leland," Father Mac said, giving Leal a steady look with his set of graying eyes. "Please make sure nothing happens to him this time around."

"You be careful too, Father," he cautioned him. "You never know. You wouldn't want to slip and hit your head and end up face down in the water."

"No," Father Mac agreed with a smile, "I can safely say that is something I would not very much prefer."

*

Leal stops his story. He gives the clock on the wall another look.

"We still have some time left," Selena says.

"I know."

"Did you want to keep talking?" she urges gently. "Did you want to keep telling your story?" *To the bitter end*, she thinks, *the part where you drown your friend …*

"No. Not right now."

"No?"

"This next part is hard."

"What makes it difficult?"

Silence. No words.

"Leal? What makes it so difficult?"

More silence.

Odd, she thinks, for her patient to put on the brakes with time on the clock.

As Leal takes his leave, Selena follows him to the door. She touches him lightly on the sleeve of his jacket.

"I need to tell you," she says. "I won't be able to meet you next week."

"You won't?" Leal asks. His voice sounds neutral—not hopeful, not sad.

"No," she confirms. "I'm sorry."

"Why not?" he asks.

"I have to take a trip."

"To Montreal again?"

"No, not this time. I'm going to Chicago."

"Why there?"

Leal pauses on the threshold. She waits for him to take a step through the door but doesn't want to hurry him. She almost divulges the real reason—the court hearing with Thomas, but …

"Sightseeing," she fibs. "There's a lot to see in Chicago. Have you ever been there?"

"Once, I think, when I was little."

"You should get your mother to take you sometime. There's a giant Ferris wheel and an aquarium and planetarium. And they have a wonderful museum of art you shouldn't miss."

"I doubt my mom would ever have the time to take me."

"Well, you can watch a movie all about it instead if you get a chance. There's this one called *Ferris Bueller's Day Off*."

"Yeah?"

"It's about a kid, not much older than you. He plays hooky and takes his friends all around the town."

He continues to hesitate on the threshold. She can almost hear the gears spinning.

"So," she says. "I'll see you week after next."

"OK," Leal replies.

*

He doesn't look at her on his way out the door. As he crosses the lobby, he thinks about going back, though. There is something he didn't tell her, and he thinks maybe he should. The thing he didn't tell her about was Saul's gun. When he found it in the drawer, he didn't leave it there. He took it with him. He wonders if this is something he should divulge. Maybe next time, he thinks. There is always next time.

***

Selena hasn't stepped inside a church in years, with the exception of two or three special occasions since her wedding: baptism of a collegiate friend's infant, bridesmaid for a close colleague in Chicago.

She stares at the steeple of St. Mary's, a slender fingertip tracing strips of thin clouds in a darkening sky. She enters the nave. The parishioners are kneeling for vespers, so she takes a seat in a rear pew. She counts a handful of white-haired heads seated near the front of the church. The priest, a young man with a red face in a wrinkled black robe, leads a prayer. The service doesn't last much longer—a final hymn sung off-key.

She crosses her breast in harmony with the other members of the congregation making ready to leave. The priest has moved to the exit, shaking hands with parishioners as they depart, and Selena makes sure she is last in line.

"Father," she says, when he takes her hand in his. He eyes her gently, releasing her hand. "You're the replacement for Father Mac—Father MacDougal?"

"Yes," he answers, his eyes tender, whites like soft-boiled eggs. "I have that privilege—for the time being."

"I was wondering if you could help me." She explains she is treating a patient, a young boy who served Father MacDougal as an acolyte at the church. It would help her greatly if she could learn a little more about him—Father Mac, that is. Has he completed his move to Florida? "Ft. Lauderdale, isn't it?"

"My understanding was a small out-of-the-way parish in one of the Keys."

So maybe that explained it. She's been having trouble reaching him. Does he know of a different address than the one the diocese gave her in Ft. Lauderdale?

Sliding his forefinger around his neck, loosening his collar, he escorts her down the concrete steps. He looks up at the evening sky. Two parishioners, an elderly man and woman, antique salt-and-pepper shakers, stand on the sidewalk, pretending not to eavesdrop.

"I'm afraid I can't really help you there," the priest says. "I only met him once or twice. And that was several months ago." He looks at her more carefully, more guardedly, under lowered eyelids. "We were colleagues in Christ. Unfortunately, we never had an opportunity to become more than mere acquaintances."

She looks down at her feet, picturing a small boy: dark hair, vapid eyes.

"You wouldn't know," she says, looking up. "You wouldn't know if he had been a foster parent?" She hopes she isn't asking an ignorant question. Are ministers—priests—allowed to become foster parents?

"He was very good with children," the young priest says. He starts to climb the stairs back to the church, but hesitates, turns. "That is, from what I understand. It was a pleasure to make your acquaintance, Miss—"

"Dr.," Selena corrects him. "Dr. Harris."

"Maybe we'll see you back here someday," he says. "We welcome all denominations."

As he ascends the remaining steps, Selena makes one last attempt before he reenters the lighted arched doorway.

"That's the parish house next door, isn't it?" she calls after him. "Will you be going there after you're done here …" doing whatever it is priests do to tidy up after a service? "I was hoping to take a peek inside."

He stares at her as though she has posed him a *Jeopardy* answer.

"It's my patient," she tries to explain. "It's a place he keeps describing and I thought, if I could just take a look. You know, to corroborate the features."

The young priest's eyes narrow. He takes a handkerchief and wipes his forehead dry, even though the temperature has only made it into the low 50s today.

"I'm afraid I can't help you out there either, Miss—Dr. Harris. Being only temporary, I don't reside in the parsonage. In fact, we're doing our best to get it ready for the next tenant."

And with that, he takes his leave, pulling the heavy wooden door closed behind him.

At the bottom of the steps, an elderly gentleman—one of the salt-and-pepper shakers—grabs her by the elbow, stopping her progress. He squints into her eyes. He talks in a whisper. Spittle leaves his lips.

"There was an investigation," he hisses.

"Alfred," his consort says, taking him, pulling him, by the arm. "Please. Leave the nice lady alone."

"There was an investigation," he repeats.

"Alfred," the old woman begs.

"An investigation?" Selena asks.

The man swivels his head one way, then the other. He ignores the pleas, the pulls, of the old woman.

"Gestapo," he whispers.

"Alfred," the woman complains. "That's enough. It wasn't an investigation. It was a party. A farewell party. That's what you remember." Then to Selena: "Don't pay any attention to him, miss. Oh, I mean, doctor. He hasn't been the same. Not since his stroke."

Selena knows just what she means.

"Do you work with stroke patients," the woman asks hopefully.

"I'm not that kind of doctor," Selena explains. But maybe the woman has overheard. Does she know anything about a little boy—a boy who had been in Father Mac's care? A silent boy, black hair—probably autistic? He went by a nickname: Thuster.

The woman thinks for a moment. No, the name Thuster doesn't sound familiar. There were a lot of boys, she explains. They were always running in and out of the parsonage. Father Mac had been very good that way. He had taken care of them— a Good Shepherd watching over his flock.

"Have you heard from him?" Selena asks. "Has anyone

heard from him?"

"No," the old woman replies. "Not yet. He is enjoying his semi-retirement, I'm sure. Once he is settled—perhaps then. With the older members of the congregation—how can I put this?" She turns her eyes inward for inspiration. "With us, he was never so good as he was with the children. He didn't form lasting commitments."

"Gestapo," the old man insists.

Selena thanks the woman, then takes her leave, noting a janitor with mop and bucket on wheels emerge from a door to the right of the cathedral and ascend the stairs to the vestibule.

As though she's a detective in a crime novel, she decides to case the joint. This is the exact phrase that pops into her head as she studies the parsonage from across the street: "case the joint." *Apparently, my life isn't dramatic enough*, she thinks. *I've got to play-act private investigator.*

***

The lake is a perfect mirror of the sky. Small, white clouds drift like lily pads across its still, calm surface. The sun has dipped below the trees. Mallards swim along the shore. A frog croaks among cattails.

Leal finishes his work with the trowel, a small triangular spade. He empties a shovel of moist earth onto a shallow oval mound near the water. He plants a fistful of artificial flowers—yellow daffodils he bought at a thrift store—at the base of the mound.

He folds his hands, lowers his head. He mumbles a few words under his breath, then stands silently. He closes his eyes. An image comes into his mind, that of a small boy floating down through the cold, dark water of the lake. As he descends, his body revolves and revolves, showing a different face every time. Sometimes it is the face of a boy, sometimes that of a man. Maybe it is the man he would have become had he lived. Maybe it is another person's face altogether. Both faces contain a jaundiced eye that glares at him accusingly.

"I'm sorry, Thuster," he whispers in lieu of a eulogy. "I truly am."

***

There's a perfect little shop on the corner where Selena sits at the plate-glass window with a coffee and donut.

At 6:30 p.m., she phones her father and leaves a voicemail to let him know she'll be running late this evening. She isn't too worried about him. Her brother is home to attend to his needs. He can zap a microwave dinner as readily as she can. As a safeguard, she texts her brother, just to be sure.

By 7:00 p.m., she has consumed three donuts and two cups of coffee.

At 7:27 p.m., feeling she has overstayed her welcome, she relocates to a bus stop bench on the corner, first buying a paper at a newsstand for the purpose of avoiding detection. If only she had brought a pair of sunglasses, her disguise would be complete.

At 7:55 p.m., she promises herself just five more minutes and she'll go.

At 8:00 p.m., she makes the same promise, holding out for some activity inside the parsonage, but the windows remain dark, the door closed. She'd already tried it a couple of times and found it locked, as airtight as Lazarus' tomb.

At 8:12 p.m., she hides her face behind the paper as the young replacement priest descends the stairs of the church. She watches over top of the finance pages as he climbs into a Mercedes along the curb and pulls away with a rev of the motor into traffic. Priests' salaries must be pretty good these days.

By 8:32 p.m., she's been back to the donut shop three times since: twice to pee, once for a refill of her Styrofoam cup.

Only till 9:00 p.m., she avows, and not a moment past. Thus, she's grateful when, with ten minutes left on her mental meter, she sees the janitor emerge from the church and transport his mop and bucket to the front door of the parsonage. He climbs the three steps with difficulty, his hip causing obvious trouble as he pulls the bucket up after him. This could be her chance to run to his aid, to assist, but she doubts he would let her inside to help mop floors or clean tables or scrub toilets.

She crosses the street stealthily and takes an inconspicuous spot on the corner with a lamppost for cover. As soon as she sees a window toward the rear of the parsonage light up, she hurries up the stairs—waddles, more accurately—and tries the door. Finding it unlocked, she pushes through to a brightly lit kitchen with burnished pots and pans gleaming unused on the stove.

So this is where Father Mac brewed his infamous Irish stew. She isn't sure what she's actually looking for: certainly not a recipe book. But what? Left-behind documents, letters?

There's an archway between stovetop and fridge, and she hears the janitor whistling a merry tune from a room down the hall to the right. She ducks into a darkened room to the left, a bedroom, she realizes, when she bumps her shin into a bedframe. The whistling stops, and she finds a closet she can duck into, fitting her bulk neatly inside like a parcel bound for shipping.

Not a moment too soon, as the light switches on with the flick of a switch. Through a slim space between door and frame, she watches the janitor take a feather duster to a dresser top, nightstand, picture frame containing the silhouette of a boy against a pale sky looking up at the heavens.

She notes with alarm the snail shell of a rolled-up yoga mat shoved partway under the bed, stripped of its covers, exposing the floor beneath its frame.

As he turns out the light, the janitor shakes his head and lets out a *"Phew!"*

A series of limping steps, the creaking wheel of the bucket, and she hears the front door close. She's more or less been holding her breath all this time, and when she takes in a gulp of air, she realizes what the janitor meant. She hadn't noticed it when she entered, but this room of the parsonage is filled with a foul odor that gets stronger when she leaves her closet hideaway. It appears to be wafting through the ventilation grill in the floor.

Not risking a light, she proceeds down the hallway by feel until she comes across a flight of stairs going down to a cellar. She finds a switch at the top of the stairs and decides to descend into the gloom. What better place to look for skeletons in a closet?

It's easier breathing through a leftover COVID mask she finds in her purse. With only a single naked incandescent bulb giving off any light, it's like descending into a dungeon complete with cement brick walls splotched with mold and mushrooms sprouting through cracks in the concrete floor. But these aren't the chief culprits behind the smell, which has a flavor of something rancid, a combination of sewer water and spoiled meat.

She notices three large stalls, as though built for horses not restrooms, along one wall of the basement, separated by partitions of plywood, but each is sealed by a gate made of chain-link fencing and clasped shut with padlocks. As far as she can tell from the feeble light, they don't contain anything of value.

In the first is a treasure chest of crucifixes and incense holders and brass candlesticks and collection plates she would label "miscellaneous" if put in charge of the yard-sale sign. The second holds towers of cardboard boxes stacked haphazardly. The contents of the third cage are hidden by a plastic tarp, a painter's drop cloth perhaps, and it's from this general area that the smell is most intense.

"*Phew!* is right!" She makes a face behind the tissue-paper fabric of her mask. In the corner, a large, black hole, the opening of a well, bubbles with dark fluid like a witch's brew. So this is the true offender: an inadequate sump pump. And offensive it is! It looks to be brimming with fecal matter, a frothy jetsam floating on the surface.

She turns on her heel to leave, but the overhead bulb flickers once, twice, and then goes out with a *Pfft!*

"No!" she cries out, then digs for her cell phone. It takes a few seconds rooting around to fish it out of her purse, by which time she is thoroughly panicked. Something about the darkness and the odor converging on her senses throws her off balance. She feels nauseous, ready to retch.

Finally, the bright glow of the screen reassures her, and she aims it toward the floor to light her way. A creak on the stairs gives her pause. Surely, no one is here. She takes a step but stops when she hears another creak. The janitor returning for unfinished business? She switches on the flashlight app to see farther. It helps, but the gloom is all encompassing.

"Is someone there?" she risks calling out, aiming the phone toward the stairs.

She hears a footstep behind her and spins around, but no one is there. Another noise to her right, a clicking sound, as of someone trying to ignite a lighter, but same thing: nothing where she aims the light. Just blackness beyond the spread of the beam. Is someone playing games with her? Here, in the dark?

Keeping her flashlight aimed toward the corner where the smell is foulest, she begins backing slowly toward the stairs, as though escaping a creature from a black lagoon. She tries to settle her mind. How far back was that movie made? Who starred in it? Weren't they supposed to do a remake of it? Whatever happened to that?

"Dr. Harris?"

She spins around, her phone lighting up a face with a bluish tint, a ghoulish, cavernous mask with deep eye sockets and hollow cheeks. She is so startled she drops the phone and opens her mouth to scream, but no sound comes out. Her baby lurches deep inside her, as though sharing her terror, and she doubles over, stomach hurting, like she's been stabbed. Has she been stabbed? Oh, my God! What fresh hell?

"Dr. Harris? Are you okay?"

A light clicks on overhead, and when she glances up, she sees Leal, standing there, holding onto a string that dangles from a socket screwed into the joists. He reaches out to her, but she flinches, waving her hand in front of her face as though to ward off a vampire.

"Leal?" she gasps, trying to catch her breath. Deep inhale. Deeper. Her throat feels like it has closed off the passageway, but air starts to come through in a wheeze. One breath, two breaths, three. There now, easier and easier. "What—are—you—doing here?"

"I was going to ask you the same thing," he says calmly, giving her a look as though she's the oddity in the room, out of place.

She straightens slowly, clutching her belly, as though to cradle the baby to give it comfort.

"I was—I came in—I—" But she doesn't have a reasonable explanation.

"Was it the priest? The new one? Did he let you in?" She isn't sure, but it seems he's trying to give her an out.

"Something like that." She nods her head uncertainly. "How did *you* get in here?" she asks, turning the table.

He digs in his pocket and holds up a key.

"I've kept it ever since Father Mac left. He let me have it. As a spare."

"But why? What are you doing here?"

"You already asked that. I like to come here sometimes. At

night. Sort of like a vigil. You know? Just to visit."

"Oh, I see." She tries to gather her thoughts. "You must miss him."

Leal nods his head, looks down at the floor, goes silent, sees her phone and retrieves it for her.

"Thank you," she says, accepting it as she might a peace offering, noting that the protector glass has fractured.

Once more, she takes into account how tall he is for his age—skinny as a rail, but tall. The crown of his head approaches her shoulders—and she has always been considered tall for a "girl." In the darkness, the shadows cast by the single light bulb make him seem grotesquely taller.

"But the smell," she crinkles her nose. "How can you stand it?"

"Oh," he says, shrugging, "you get used to it after a while."

"Come on," she says. "How about we both get out of here?"

"Okay, but I'll have to turn off the light from down here. The other light went out. The one that turns on at the top of the steps."

"Yes, I know."

He switches off the light, and everything goes black again. She feels his arm tuck itself within hers, like an usher in a darkened theater.

"Hang on," he says. "I'll guide you."

Letting him lead, she follows him up, one slow step at a time. At the top, he turns on the hall light and she notes he's still wearing his dress clothes, except they're splotched with dirt. Mud on his shoes is leaving tracks everywhere. The janitor isn't going to be happy with this state of affairs when he returns.

Leal's right about the smell. You get used to it. Either that or it's dissipated with the fresher air upstairs. She doesn't feel as nauseous; neither does she feel completely settled. The baby has done a number on her insides with a series of martial arts moves.

"There's a donut shop on the corner," she suggests, removing her mask. "What do you say I buy you a hot chocolate?"

"Really?" His face beams with gratitude. "You'd do that? It's okay? You won't get in trouble?"

"I owe you one," she says with a smile, ruffling his hair. "For rescuing me."

"But I scared you half to death."

"Yes, you did. But without you," she offers half in jest, "I never would have made it out of that basement alive."

Chapter 17

Vaguely, like an afterimage on the negative of memory, Leal remembers tall buildings. They cluster like ship masts, an armada advancing across the landscape of his imagination, as the freeway bleeds like a yellow-brick road toward the towering fortress of the city.

To finance his trip, he has borrowed his mom's tip money that she keeps in a sugar bowl. Technically, it isn't stealing. He has left a promissory note in the jar—an IOU. He just hopes his mom wasn't saving it to pay the next installment on their mortgage.

When he steps off the bus—a Greyhound—he doesn't feel nervous being alone in a strange city. He feels uncannily at ease.

He walks along Lake Michigan until he comes upon a peninsula that advertises a planetarium. A grown man falls asleep beside him beneath the darkened dome. Leal finds his snores amusing, even though they disturb the audience in their seats—soft, cushioned armchairs with reclining headrests. Faces turn in silhouette. Leal calmly watches the planets careen across the black canopy of the virtual night sky, purposefully oblivious of the whispers, the giggles, the wake-up coughs of those around them.

He is reminded of nights in the parsonage, when he had stayed overnight, in the spare room. Father Mac would stretch out beside him on the bed, above the covers. They would lie, side by side, staring at the ceiling, in the dark, and Leal would listen to the murmur of Father Mac's voice, spooling philosophy on a bobbin of slumber. On most occasions, Father Mac would be the first to fall asleep, and Leal would listen to the wheezing snores of the priest's exhales, until oblivion, in its own slow way, would overtake him.

A picture hung above the bed—a picture of a boy lost in shadow, his face obscured by darkness, shrouded in mist.

"Tell me about him," Leal had beckoned. "Tell me who he is."

"Thuster?" Father Mac responded. "You want to know about Thuster?"

"Yes," Leal replied.

Father Mac emitted a longwinded sigh.

"Thuster is the dark part inside all of us. We each have a Thuster."

"Do you?" Leal asked. "Do you have a Thuster?"

"Oh, yes," Father Mac sighed. "I have a Thuster."

"Do I?" he wanted to know.

"Yes, of course," Father Mac assured him. "If anything bad happens to you, it isn't you it's happening to. It's Thuster."

He wanders the city, looking in amazement at the towering buildings. He is sure he has seen them before—when he was younger, just seven years old. His father used to bring him along on his sales trips. But he spent most of his time in the hotel room, while his father was out and about.

He remembers he would watch TV, leaf through Gideon's Bible, doodle on the motel stationery, playact a shootout at the OK Corral with the hair dryer. He loses himself in thoughts of Superman leaping spires in a single bound, King Kong beating his chest while clutching an aerial. The amplified voices of passersby drone through his ears like the buzzing of bees.

Worries slip away. They are just images, words, inhabiting his mind, his imagination. It is as though his story no longer exists. Chicago has interrupted it, in transit. He has stepped off the moving train of his discourse, and now stands in awe of a fountain, large and beautiful and loud. Wasn't it by just such a fountain he had first met Diana? Only this fountain is so much bigger than the one in the park of his hometown. It has many more levels and platforms, geysers and streams. It looks like a giant birthday cake. But it has seahorses instead of mermaids.

He likes the one in Ovid, because of the mermaids. They remind him of Diana, even if she hadn't said anything to him that first day he came across her. He had watched her from the other side of the trickling water. He felt sorry for her because he could see that she had a black eye. When she left the park, he followed her down the sidewalk. He found out where she lived. He would go to the fountain, day after day, waiting to see her again. Except she never came back. After that one wish she had made, she never returned.

He had scooped up her nickel though. He had put it in his pocket, where he carried it still. And he would walk all the way back to Lambeth Street. He would hide behind the catalpa tree, spying on her house, trying to think of a reason to knock at her door.

Later that afternoon, he finds the art museum Selena had mentioned. He has never been to an art museum before. Leal sees paintings of Diana, brightly exhibited in his imagination. He could picture Diana posing, Jay working his brushes furiously across the canvas. But then painter and poser dissolve, the cottage shrinks into a playhouse for dolls, and Leal is only sitting under the strands of a willow by the shore of a lake. No one else is around. The shoreline is empty.

He was not allowed inside the cottage this day. It was his mom's turn to pose. A breeze stirred his hair from his forehead. He noticed, in the distance, across the lake, peering out of a clump of bushes on the farther shore, a young boy with dark features. He waved, and the boy waved back, using his left hand instead of his right. He could have been a mirror image, but Jay clamped him on the shoulder and told him they were all done for the day. His mom just left for the diner. Would he like to take a nap in the loft?

The lions at the entrance to the museum seem larger cousins of those guarding the entry to the library in Ovid, where he has checked out so many books over the summer. He remembers he was at a bus stop, across from the courthouse, leafing through the pages of a book of verse Father Mac recommended. It was a difficult book. The footnotes failed to enlighten him. The language seemed harsh, foreign, old-fashioned. He read aloud, whispering the words, as they crawled across the page. He turned his head. A shadow sat beside him. He came across that word again: 'thuster.' He looked for the footnote, and the shadow evaporated into the humid, shimmering air.

He followed it down a sidewalk, along an alley, through the gap in a fence. A small boy was in a backyard, helping his mother hang clothes on a line. He pulled damp shirts out of a laundry basket, handing each in turn to his mother, who clasped two clothespins in her mouth, pressed between her lips. They seemed so content—mother and son. Was this the shadow he had followed? Had it turned into the form of this tiny boy? And then he recognized the boy. He was the same boy he had seen across the lake. Now that he thought of it, maybe it was the other way around. Maybe it was the boy who had been following him all these years.

Inside the museum, he climbs the marble staircase to the upper galleries. Some of the women in the paintings are naked, wrapped loosely in falling garments or sheets. They pose in voluptuous nudity: round thighs, ample breasts, sensuous hips. They don't look like Diana's version of nudity. She had been so thin. Her hair had been long and dark. Her breasts, though, had hung full and ripe and white. But in his imagination, she begins to fade, as well. She is on a doorstep in a bathrobe. Leal has brought her the newspaper, personally, to her door. He rings the doorbell.

"Oh," she says, "is it time to collect already?"

She will be right back. When she returns with a fistful of change, she drops a quarter on the welcome mat. She and Leal reach for it at the same moment. Their heads clunk, hard—but this only makes her laugh. As she stoops, bending low for the quarter, her bathrobe comes undone. It falls away, and Leal can peer through the opening at her throat, widening toward her navel. He can see her breasts, swaying into full view. She seems to know it, too. She knows Leal is looking. It must give her a thrill because she doesn't stand up right away.

She lets her bathrobe hang loose, allowing Leal a full stare. A purple butterfly with yellow-veined wings peers out at him. After what seem minutes, she slowly stands up. She smiles warmly at Leal, as though happy he has enjoyed her private show.

And then a man appeared behind her through the screen. He recognized the face from TV: the slicked-back hair, the rectangular jaw, the thick eyebrows. The only things missing were his scepter and crown. As soon as he saw them together, he knew who they were. Side by side, they looked just like they did in their commercials. But Saul the Chinchilla King wasn't smiling his award-winning smile. He had a dark shadow of a beard and an even darker scowl. And the "lovely Diana" seemed nervous.

"You're not our paperboy, are you?" he said, growling the words.

"No, sir," Leal answered, backing away from the door.

"Then what are you here for?" he wanted to know.

"Stop it, Saul," Diana said. "You're scaring him."

"A job," Leal blurted.

At this, Saul laughed. Diana, he could see, was smiling, too.

"What kind of job?"

"Any kind," he said.

Saul stood there a while, behind the screen, rubbing his chin the way he might pet a chinchilla.

"Come back tomorrow," Saul said. "I might have something you can do around the house."

"Yes, sir," he said, and as he turned on the mat, Diana gave him a wink.

On an upper floor of the museum, he comes upon a huge painting. Up close, Leal can see it is made of hundreds, thousands, of points and dashes.

Leal sits on a bench in front of it. The painting is so tall and wide that it fills a wall of the viewing room.

It is a pretty scene—a scene by a lake. A woman holds a parasol, even though it is sunny. People recline on a lawn. Others navigate a small sailboat. Men and women converse, like mannequins caught deep in thought. It is all pinks and yellows and blues and greens. Leal likes the painting very much. If only it were possible to step through the frame, to pass from one world into another.

"Do you like it?" a gallery guide in a red uniform asks Leal, coming up behind.

The question startles him.

He sees the face of a man in the hallway, standing behind his mom, another one of a string of men she has brought home for the night from the diner. Except this time it is a face he has seen before: the long, sallow face of the artist, eyeing him for his reaction.

His mom turned on his bedside light. She wanted to show him something: a painting she was holding. At first, he couldn't tell what it was. It looked like a bunch of squiggles and dots. But then he could make out a face and a body below the face. He could tell who it was by the tattoo of a vine stringing purple flowers up her arm and across her shoulder and down and around her breast—a breast he hadn't viewed since intruding by accident on one of her bubble baths.

His mom sounded excited, and the artist, coming up behind

her, was smiling in the half darkness, his face in shadow.

"Do you like it?" she asked.

He felt embarrassed—for himself, for his mom. He turned his face away.

"Yeah," Leal admitted, "I do."

"It's called pointillism, the technique," the guide explains. He is elderly, grandfatherly. With his full white beard, he could double as Santa Claus.

"It must have taken a long time to paint," Leal says to keep up his side of the conversation.

"Shouldn't you be in school today?" the guide asks kindly.

"They let us out a little early," Leal lies.

The guide walks away, but Leal knows he hasn't deceived him. He would have to leave the museum. He would have to leave the painting behind. He would like so much to be able to leave this world of hopes and cares, worries and dreams. It would be so nice to enter a world of perfect forms, where everything is what it is, where there is no guessing, where nothing ever changes its shape.

Not yet, Leal thinks. He likes the painting. He doesn't want to leave. Just a little longer.

But he would have to leave soon. He would have to find the Greyhound station to board the bus taking him back to Ovid.

***

For the occasion, Selena has dressed in beige slacks with a wide elastic band to accommodate her paunch, a flower-print blouse that feels the size and shape of a pup tent. She wears a long, bulky overcoat, even though it is warm for November, sunny. She carries no briefcase, no traveling bag—only her purse, a small leather packet on a strap. And the package, of course, tucked under her arm: white cardboard Fed-Ex folder containing the documents that will end her marriage to Thomas.

So many marriages being dissolved. The hallway resembles a square dance, a hoedown, men on the left, women on the right, rows of wallflowers, some alone, others seated with their lawyers. A few of the clients converse softly, under their breath, last-minute conferences, detailing their statements, rehearsing their lines. Others sit quietly, their lawyers paging through documents, papers. One-by-one or two-by-two, and sometimes four-by-four, they are called into the courtroom by their case number. Husband-lawyer, wife-lawyer—till divorce court us do part. Last call for mending differences, healing wounds, venting issues, exposing scars.

Selena plays a game in her head. She tries matching husband and wife before the bailiff summons them with her loud, abrasive voice. She has arrived an hour early, just to be safe, sure. When Thomas arrives, she wants to be the first party present, her position secure. She wants Thomas to feel a sense of unease, of disorientation, as he makes his approach. She wants to greet him sitting down. He won't have a lawyer. He prefers to manage all legal affairs on his own.

Of course, it won't work this way, she thinks, as his footsteps stroll the checkered tile of the hallway, as though pacing the requisite number of steps in a duel. Thomas comes right up to her, briefcase in hand. He eyes her steadily with calm, emotionless pupils. Hadn't he always eyed her so, as though searching for flaws, blemishes? Had they ever known love, true love?

Now it seems to Selena that their relationship, their engagement, their marriage had been a series of steps in a business arrangement. Everything in their lives had been preplanned, prepackaged. They had always been so careful, for instance, waiting until Thomas had passed the bar and Selena had finished her graduate coursework to get married. They had found the perfect home in Oak Park. They had found the perfect jobs, selected perfect furnishings, curtains, carpets, cars.

The only problem that had marred their perfectly wedded bliss had been her failure to produce the perfect child. Had that been it? The still birth followed by a miscarriage—one succeeding the other—five years apart? And during those five years, all the subtle coaxing and cajoling—not continuous, of course, but intermittent, surfacing like a whale on anniversaries, for instance, only to plunge below the surface, but just barely below, leaving his dearest hopes unspoken—trying to persuade her the still birth had been an anomaly, a fluke. They owed it to each other to try again.

When she had finally, after five long years, agreed—how the miscarriage must have destroyed him from the inside, a house of cards come tumbling down. Even as it confirmed her worst predictions.

"Selena," Thomas says coldly.

"Thomas," she responds. She doesn't stand. He doesn't sit, doesn't offer his hand. She doesn't offer hers. "You had a nice flight?"

"You didn't bring a lawyer," he observes.

"No," she says. "You didn't either?"

"Funny," he says, shaking his head.

"Here," she says, handing over the Fed-Ex envelope.

He eyes the envelope suspiciously, as though it might contain anthrax.

"The papers," she says before he can ask. "They're signed."

Thomas takes the envelope. He sits on the bench, leaving space between them.

Thomas pages through the slim sheaf of paperwork. He verifies the initials, the signatures, the dates.

"You signed these a week ago," he remarks. "Nine days, to be exact."

"Yes," she replies.

"I don't understand." Thomas stares at her with narrow eyes, dark eyebrows accentuating his disapproval. "You made me fly all this way. You agreed to a hearing."

"Thomas," she says gently. She places a hand on his knee. Thomas flinches. His leg jerks. He brushes her hand aside as though it's a poisonous snake. "I wanted to see you," Selena explains, still searching his eyes, although they have turned away. They look at his watch. They look at the envelope. "One last time. I wanted to tell you—"

Thomas stands up, turns away from her. He pats down his suit coat against his hips, adjusts his tie.

"Tell me? Tell me what?"

Selena chooses this moment to stand, as though acting on cue. She unbuttons her coat, slowly, then spreads the edges as though opening a curtain on a circus sideshow.

She waits. He spins away from her, and she watches the back of his neck turn red—a familiar sign of mounting anger, impatience, irritation. He takes a deep breath. He tilts his head toward the ceiling. Then he looks at the floor. Finally, he turns back around, taking in her bulk, sizing her as though with an invisible measuring tape, eyeing her up and down and around. He lets out a slow, agitated whistle between his teeth.

"Goddamn it, Selena. How long?"

If he hadn't unfriended her on Facebook, he might have found out how long. He has the lost, confused look of a little boy—a look she has never seen before in all their years of marriage.

She reaches out her hand, but he shrugs it away so that it slides down his sleeve toward her side.

"Mine?" he asks.

She lowers her voice, forcing a whisper: "I don't know."

People lining the hallway are staring, enjoying the drama— witnesses to the death throes of a failed marriage.

Thomas takes a seat, and Selena sits beside him. He leans forward, elbows on knees, staring at the floor.

"This changes everything," he says.

She moves her jaw to respond, to counter, resist. Bubbles of saliva escape a corner of her mouth.

"What does it change?"

"I suppose you'll want a paternity test."

He turns his head but doesn't look at her. His eyes drift from hers. They sink to her belly. They fall to the floor.

"I just wanted you to know," she says.

The bailiff barks out the next order of business. Her voice echoes harshly down the hall.

Thomas straightens his tie. His neck cranes out of its collar like that of a heron. He seems eager for the proceedings to begin.

***

When she leaves the courthouse, it is already late afternoon. She had in mind to call a couple of college friends, a colleague or two, but she isn't in the mood.

Neither does she feel like going home—not yet. She needs to ease her mind. She wants to view something beautiful. She finds herself wandering the Loop, like a somnambulist, toward the Art Institute.

As she approaches the entrance, she finds him sitting on the museum's concrete steps. A knapsack rests on the step below his feet. He doesn't look up until her shadow covers him entirely in the late afternoon sun, slanting through the spaces between buildings.

Somehow, in the back of her mind, she isn't surprised—not at all.

"Leal?"

"Oh," he says, looking up. "Hello, Dr. Harris. Selena."

"What are you doing here?" she asks. "Is it a field trip or something? Is there some reason you're here?"

"No," he says. "No reason."

"Are you here all by yourself? Is there no one else with you?"

"Yeah, I guess," he replies calmly, neutrally.

And then Selena knows. She knows she has made a mistake divulging her destination. She would have to be more careful in the future. She would have to make sure to keep her life private: no admittance, no trespassing.

She doesn't feel angry. Just sad. Sad for herself. Sad for Leal.

"How did you get here?" she asks.

"By bus." He stares up at her, squinting through the sunlight.

"How were you planning on getting home?"

*

Neither speaks much more than monosyllables on the drive from Chicago. Leal spends his time staring out the passenger window, observing silos and barns, counting horses and cows, arranged on green hillsides like plastic animals, unmoving, immobile. For her part, Selena stares through the windshield, her eyes focused, intent, on the double yellow lines of the roadway since they left the interstate. Selena contemplates her analogy: a field trip. She knows this particular trip could be viewed as a violation of her ethical code as a practicing therapist. For one thing, the distance between her and her patient, so carefully measured out in square yards of carpet in her office, has been reduced to a gear shift between the seats of her Honda Accord. She tries to justify their journey as an experiment in the therapist-patient relationship: a test of silence.

Sitting beside Leal, she thinks how tall he is for a boy his age—in silhouette, almost adult. Thin but tall. He eludes categorization. During the course of his treatment, she had considered and discarded any number of personality disorders: paranoid, antisocial, borderline. She supposes he could be classified as schizoid. To a degree, he is withdrawn, passive, prone to daydream. Even on this

one-hour trip, she can sense his preoccupation with an inner vision, a private demon or shadow. Not so much by the things he
says, or doesn't say, but by his body language: the scratching of his
scalp, the rubbing of his palms together, the crossing and uncross-
ing of his legs and arms, the shifting of his eyes.

Selena returns her gaze to the road.

Even now, she thinks, he is engaged in the great struggle. He
wishes to relinquish his story, his narrative. He would like so
much for it to evaporate. And she knows what is required of her.
She must give him the means necessary to finish his story. She
cannot let it disappear, stall into freefall without a denouement.

Chicago blues give way to Country-Western, and she turns
off the radio. Ovid appears on the horizon, church spires bris-
tling on its hilltop like toothpicks, thin wires. The highway, four
lanes while passing a shopping strip anchored by a Wal-Mart,
narrows to two as it approaches the heart of town.

As they pass the town limits sign, Leal breaks the silence,
without looking at Selena, without turning his head.

"Are you all right?" he asks.

"Yes," Selena answers.

"Are you sure? You haven't been talking."

"Sometimes, it's nice just enjoying the quiet of your own
thoughts, don't you think?" She turns her head and smiles. "Did
you have a good time? On your own? In Chicago?" She hopes
the question doesn't sound sarcastic. She doesn't mean it to be.

"Yes," Leal answers truthfully. "Yes. I did."

"It must have cost you a pretty penny. How did you finance it?"

"A loan."

"Oh, from a bank?" she jokes.

"My mom's tip jar."

A few moment later, she pulls up to a drive-thru ATM.

"How much did you take out?" she asks.

Leal quotes a figure that makes her eyebrows arch.

"That much, huh? And nothing left over?" She can imagine it draining his allowance for years to come.

"You don't have to," Leal tells her, slumping in his seat.

"That's all right." She's already fed her bank card into the slot and pushed English as her language of choice. "I don't want you getting into trouble with your mom."

Anymore, she thinks, *than you already are.*

"Well, I'll pay you back. I promise," he says, as he takes the money tentatively, then folds it and stuffs it into his pants pocket.

"That's OK, really. I feel partly responsible. You wouldn't have gone to Chicago if you didn't know I'd be there, am I right?"

Leal nods his head, as she pulls her car back into traffic.

By the time she arrives at Leal's house, a thought has come to her.

"What do you know about hypnosis?" she asks.

"You mean, getting hypnotized?" Leal pauses with his hand on the door handle. "Would you make me flap my arms like a chicken?" he asks, grinning.

Why is this the first association everyone makes when they hear the word "hypnosis"?

"Yes, Leal," she answers in mock seriousness. "That's exactly what I would do. Turn you into a chicken."

"Then count me in!" he says, gleefully, and hops out the door.

***

It is dusk when Selena pulls into her drive. She had waited until Leal stepped inside his house and turned on the lights. Of course his mother wasn't home from the diner to ask where her son has been.

The lights of her father's house are off—except for the porch light. Her brother's car isn't parked in its spot on the curb.

The front door is locked.

She finds a note taped to the door where she would spot it, first thing. It's in her brother's handwriting. At first, she thinks it's one of his lyrics, waiting for her critical commentary, her review.

Texts wouldn't go through. Sorry.
At hospital.
ER.
It's Dad.

That's it. No further message.

She hops back in her car, speed dialing without an answer. She ignores stop signs, runs red lights. At the hospital, she learns her father has been placed in intensive care. He suffered another stroke. His condition is stable.

Her brother is in the room with him, sitting by his bedside. His look conveys a mixture of anxiety, relief, guilt. A tube runs from a bottle into one of her father's arms, another tube empties into a plastic bag below the bed. He breathes through an oxygen mask. His heart pulses across a monitor, steadily beeping. His eyes remain closed.

Her brother stands to give her a hug, but Selena releases him, pushes him away. He sits back in his seat, his head down.

"How is he?" she asks.

"It's all my fault," her brother says.

"How is he?" she wants to know.

"I fell asleep. He fell asleep. I missed his pills."

Selena bends over her father. She whispers into his ear: "Dad?"

"When I woke up, I couldn't find your directions. I mixed them all up. He took them like he knew what he was doing."

"Dad?" she whispers. "Can you hear me?"

"The doctors have been checking on him. They need to perform a bypass, but they can't until his condition stabilizes. They can't risk anything—not right after a stroke."

Please, Selena thinks. She closes her eyes. *Don't die. We're strangers. I don't even know you—not really. We don't know each other. Listen*, she pleads within herself. *I need to know who you are.*

Chapter 18

Dear Henri,

Visiting hours end at 9 p.m. No exceptions—not even for family members. He seems in good spirits. His condition has stabilized—or so the doctors say. You know doctors, though. They always come across as so patronizing. I feel like I'm in first grade all over again.

Dad regained consciousness five days ago—over the weekend. For now, he's being retained in the short-stay unit for observation. They had to perform a special procedure called a carotid endarterectomy—there's a spelling-bee ball-buster for you—to prevent further hemorrhaging in the brain. As easy as spooling a thread through a needle, I was informed. It is sad, and frustrating, trying to communicate with him. The left side of his face is paralyzed, but he is able to speak out of the corner of his mouth, with difficulty. He recognizes his daughter. He recognizes his son—my brother. He told us he loves us. But he wanted us to run the dishwasher; he thought it was full. Then he asked if his wife, our mother, would be stopping by to see him. I let him believe her still alive.

The doctors said the stroke was mild. He may improve over time, they said. At present, they are more concerned with his heart—specifically, an arterial blockage they plan to circumvent with angioplasty, not a bypass after all. The irony is even this procedure may dislodge platelets that can cause a stroke! They are continuing to feed him intravenously. They are monitoring his condition. Our father is doing as well as can be expected, they have assured us.

My brother continues to harbor a measure of guilt, even though the doctors consoled him by saying the stroke was inevitable. It was in the cards, all a matter of time. He is lucky, they said. He is lucky my brother was there to call the ambulance. Time is what saved him. But this news does not go very far toward comforting him.

As for my client, Leal. I met with him this afternoon after my daily visit to the hospital. I am not competent to judge whether the mindfulness worked its magic. I do believe it put him into a relaxed, dreamlike state. His discourse was even more lucid, more free-flowing, than usual.

Was it unethical of me to allow him to think he was undergoing hypnosis rather than participating in a mindfulness activity? Perhaps, but as my brother pointed out, a subject who believes he or she is being hypnotized is likely to act in the way he or she believes a hypnotized subject should act. And so I allowed Leal to believe he was being put into a trance rather than simply a relaxed, more focused state of mind.

Chicken jokes aside, I explained our goals for the session—not to make him do odd things or act in odd ways that he wouldn't perform normally but to help him remember. That this was more of a memory exercise to help him revisit the events of that fateful day, when he tried to reach Diana ahead of Saul. Except this time in a safe space where no one could hurt him, with someone he trusts, someone who can guide him to discover what is going on beneath the surface, in his subconscious.

I decided to take my brother up on his suggestion of music, so beforehand, I went to the expense of purchasing a DVD player with high-end compact speakers so as not to risk commercial interruptions on my smartphone. To let him feel some measure of control over the exercise, I gave him an option of several CDs: yes, one of them was whale songs, if you must ask. Another was tropical rain forest sounds, but he selected ocean waves, which I admit produced a gentle, soothing rhythm of ambient noise. So effective, in fact, they almost put me to sleep!

Next, I asked if he was into any roleplaying games, like Dungeons & Dragons, or online games with friends—I understand a videogame called Skyrim is popular with kids his age—and he answered no, he does play computer games, but solo ones, like Minecraft or chess against the computer, now that Father Mac isn't available to sit on the other side of the board.

I told him that this would be like a roleplaying game, but one he would perform solo as well.

I turned off the lights and closed the blinds against the afternoon sun. I asked him to stretch out on the couch, eyes open, and he readily complied.

He told me it was just like a sleepover.

I asked if he had many sleepovers, but he said no, just the one, and he had never been invited back.

This made me feel oh so sad, you wouldn't believe.

I set the laser pointer I had used for my PowerPoint presentation in Montreal— my boring lecture that put everyone to sleep—on my desk, aimed it at the darkened ceiling, and asked him to focus on the bright red dot.

He was keen on the laser—the novelty of it—and once he settled down with his questions, I coached him on his breathing, in through the nose, out through the mouth, asking him to not worry about counting his breaths, just in and out, in and out, inhaling and exhaling, feeling his breath enter his lungs, expanding his chest and belly, then letting it out again, over and over, just enjoying his breath … in and out … in and out … (Are you still with me, Henri? Have I put you under yet?)… until I felt we were ready for the induction phase.

The transition wasn't exactly smooth. There was a lot of squirming— true to his nickname, he's slippery—and he had to overcome a couple of spasms of giggling, but eventually he got into a rhythm, his breaths matching the lapping sounds of the waves.

We persisted until I thought he was calm enough to ask him to close his eyes and imagine he was in a costume shop.

*

"Like for Halloween?" Leal asks.

"Yes, that's right," Selena replies. "You're browsing through the store, walking up and down the aisles, until you come across a costume that you would like to try on."

Selena isn't sure what to predict: disco 70s guy, pirate, surfer dude, Batman.

He ends up selecting a suit of armor, which seems appropriate for someone wanting to play the hero.

Next, she leads him to a bubbling fountain and asks him to select one of several cups that are sitting there on its rim. He chooses a golden chalice, which makes sense: Galahad selecting his Holy Grail. Selena tells him the fountain is a fountain of memory, that dipping the chalice and taking a long, cool, soothing drink will take him back to the time when he set out to forewarn Diana. She waits until he sets the chalice aside, then positions him in front of an open door.

He hesitates at the threshold because he can't see what lies on the other side. Selena encourages him to keep focusing on his breathing and to only step through when he feels ready. Or not to step through at all if he feels too threatened.

"OK," Leal says after releasing a pent-up breath for courage, "I'm through."

"Where are you?" Selena asks. "Can you tell me where you are?"

"It's dark," he says softly, his voice a low murmur. "I'm standing on a road."

"Is anyone with you?"

"Yes," he answers.

"Who's with you, Leal?"

"Thuster."

"And what is Thuster doing?"

"He's just lying there. Lying in the middle of the road."

*

He wishes he knew the answer to why Thuster is lying there in the middle of the road with twilight spreading over him so quiet and still. He wishes there was someone there to ask. He would pull at their belt loops, he would step on their toes, just to get an answer. But there isn't anyone there. Just the sound of the wind in the trees.

Doesn't Thuster realize how important it is to arrive at the cottage ahead of Saul? Doesn't he understand the peril Diana is in? But Thuster doesn't respond to Leal's urging. To Leal's prodding. He lies there stiff and silent in the middle of the road leading to Jay's cottage on the far side of the lake.

Twilight darkens into night, and the moon floats into the branches of a tree overhead. Shadows fall across Thuster like a net—soft and beautiful, like velvet thread. He wishes he could be like Thuster, so calm and peaceful without any worries. He looks asleep, but his eyes are wide open. He looks dead, but his chest rises and falls.

He can hear a car coming. It rumbles through the darkness. It is a black spot on the hill. Against the sky. There are headlights that flash up and down like twin beacons.

Thuster doesn't seem to hear it. He doesn't flinch at the sound, the way others would flinch, the way Leal has flinched. He stares into the branches of a tree, but he stares farther than the tree. He stares inside himself. But it isn't the same way that Leal stares inside himself. He is not looking at anything outside or inside himself. He is not looking at anything at all. He is not looking.

Leal thinks he should move him. He thinks he should try to move him. But he doesn't, and he wonders why he doesn't.

The car is not going fast, but it is going fast enough. Leal doesn't look at the lights. He doesn't look at Thuster. He looks like a lump of rock in the road under the headlights. He is a shadow, and Leal averts his vision. He looks into the branches of the tree at the moon. He waits. The car is going fast enough. He waits, and the car is still coming. He waits.

His ears burn hot. The tips of his ears are burning, but he doesn't touch them. He knows not to touch hot things. The wind feels cold on his back. It feels cold on his face.

The moon hangs cold and white in the branches of the tree.

He hears the crunch of brakes. There is the engine, but there is not the moving car. It is a long car in the dark. He hears a car door creak open, and a man moves into the headlights, bending over Thuster. He hears him say something: "What the hell?" He picks up Thuster. He carries him upright. He has trouble placing Thuster in the back of the car. He lays him across the back seat, like a length of lumber. He puts the car in gear. He goes around a curve in the road. The taillights disappear behind the trees.

Leal runs out of the bushes. He runs after the taillights, moving farther and farther away, like a pair of red eyes. Then he comes to a standstill in the middle of the road. He is quiet. He waits a long time, and then he sees the car lights behind the trees. He hears the engine along the shore. It bends around the lake. He follows the lights through the trees. He can see the cottage with its yellow light. It burns softly in the upstairs window. The car lights shut off. He can hear the slamming of a door. It comes softly up the hill through the woods. More lights go on in the cottage.

And then Leal knows what he has to do. He starts running along the dirt road in the dark. It isn't Diana he has to rescue but Thuster. He has to rescue Thuster.

*

There is a long moment of silence.

"Leal? How are you feeling?" Selena asks, quietly.

More silence, just the ambient sound of the waves. His eyes remain closed, but his body seems tense, his fists loosely clenching and unclenching, his breathing a small measure more rapid.

"Do you want to stop?"

She lets more silence wash by, a few more breaths.

"Do you want to go on?"

A slight nod of the head.

"Are you sure?"

"Yes," he answers softly, his body seeming to relax as Selena encourages him to continue focusing on his breathing.

"Where are you now?" she asks after a time.

"Outside the cottage."

"What are you doing?"

"Looking through a window."

"What do you see?"

"Thuster. Sitting in a chair."

*

He is sitting in the purple armchair, where Diana used to pose. He is sitting upright like he's been propped in place. Not blinking. He looks lifeless. Wooden. Like a puppet.

Saul is pacing around the room. Jay is standing behind his easel holding a blank canvas, not a dab of paint on it. His eyes follow Saul as he paces. Saul stops in front of one of the paintings propped against the wall under the windows. It's a painting of Diana. She's nude in the painting.

"Look at this," he says. "Just look at this. What do you call this, anyway?"

"A painting," Jay says.

Jay stays in place. He doesn't turn his head. He doesn't twist his neck.

"Painting," Saul snorts. "What are you, a wise guy?" He waves his hand around the room. "These look nothing like her. Nothing like her at all. They could be anyone, the way they're all disfigured, deformed."

Saul fixes his gaze on another painting. Leal looks through the window at Saul. He holds his breath. Saul's eyes are yellow. Full of acid.

"You've turned her into a cripple," Saul says. "She could be one of those women in a wheelchair you see outside a Salvation Army. Why did you need her to pose for something like this, anyway? You could have just kidnapped someone from a homeless shelter. A nursing home, just as well."

"I paint what I see," Jay says. He says this calmly. His eyes follow Saul around the room.

"What the hell are you talking about, you paint what you see? What the hell does that mean? That day I was here. Even without my glasses, I could tell you were a terrible painter. You can't paint worth a damn what's in front of you. You're totally blind. You've got no appreciation for beauty."

"I paint what I see," Jay says again.

Saul brings his fist down hard on the table. Tubes of paint go flying. The paintbrushes scatter—like pickup sticks—onto the floor.

"God damn it. Will you quit saying that? What does that mean, anyhow? It doesn't mean anything."

Jay takes a deep breath. He keeps his eyes on the floor. He lets out a deep breath. "All I mean," he says, "is that my vision— my inner vision—"

"Inner vision," Saul scoffs. "What are you talking about, inner vision? What kind of bullshit mumbo jumbo is that?"

"All right," Jay says. "My imagination—"

"Imagination," Saul says. "That's a little better. I know what you're talking about when you say something like that—imagination."

"I sensed she was trapped—confined—imprisoned—"

"Trapped—in what possible way was my Diana trapped? She had all the freedom she could ever want—and then some. I've never known—ever—a more free person in my life. Trapped. Next thing you're going to tell me is that I was the one trapping her—like some kind of prison warden—for Christ's sake."

"No—no—I wasn't going to say that. She was—is—trapped inside—inside herself. I'm not saying you were—are—the one responsible—"

"What are you, anyway, some kind of shrink? Are you a licensed psychologist or something? I don't see no psychologist's license hanging in a frame gives you the right to shrinkwrap my Diana."

Saul pulls out a cigarette, places it on his lower lip, unlit. His pacing comes to a standstill in front of Thuster.

"This kid here," he says. "I just don't get it. Here I am, driving down the road to get here, hoping beyond hope she's here, based on a tip I received, but at the same time hoping for anything in the world she's not here, and I almost run him over, this kid, this Thuster. It doesn't make any sense. And that's another thing."

Saul turns around. He faces Jay. "First time I was over here, I saw that painting of a kid above the mantle, and I knew, I knew I had seen him before. I should have known right then, I should have known right at that point it was Thuster. I've been taken for a fool. Set up. This whole goddamn summer long. Believing it all. Believing everything—the line of bull his friend, babysitter, nanny—whatever—kept feeding me. The gall of that kid, concocting story after story. If Leal was here right now, I don't know what I would do, God help me."

Leal backs away from the window on his hands and knees. He tries standing, but he can't. He can't bring himself to stand. He feels sick inside.

Saul says he's through talking. He stands in front of Jay. He crosses his arms. He asks Jay where Diana is.

Jay doesn't say anything. He stares past Saul's head.

Saul shoves Jay backward, into his easel, and Jay crumples onto the floor in a tangle of wooden legs.

"I'm going to give you one more chance to come clean. You tell me she's not here, one more time, we're going to take a little tour of the house—inspect every corner. She's not in the house, we're going to search the premises. She's not on the premises, fine. No harm done. You have my fullest apology. She turns up here, somewhere in the house, down by the lake maybe, well, I'm afraid I'm not going to be able to take responsibility, anything that happens after that. No offense, you understand?"

Jay doesn't move. He doesn't nod his head. His breathing sounds rapid. His chest rises and falls. Sweat breaks out across his forehead. Little beads of white glue.

"So, let me ask you one more time," Saul says. He leans toward Jay. He drills holes into Jay's eyes. "Where's Diana?"

Jay waits a second. He whispers, "I don't know."

Saul stands back. He smiles. It's a wide, slow smile. "You're saying she's not here?"

"That's right. That's all I'm saying."

"All right." Saul rolls up his shirtsleeves. "Up off the floor. We'll settle this mano a mano."

Jay doesn't move, he doesn't sit up.

"On your feet, I said! What are you, hard of hearing?"

But Jay still doesn't move. His eyes are focused on the fallen blank canvas, unblinking. He is as still as Thuster.

Saul pulls his foot back and gives Jay a hard kick in the ribs. The air rushes out of Jay's lungs. Leal wants to cover his ears. He wants to cover his eyes. He wants to cover his mouth. But he can't move his hands. They stay at his sides.

"Goddamn it, I said, 'Get up!'"

Saul kicks at Jay another time, a hard shoe in the stomach. Jay starts gasping, wheezing, for air.

Looking through the window, Leal crouches, steady, unmoving. His body tenses into the starting block of a sprinter's stance, his fingers tucked into fists, knuckles set hard against the ground.

Then Leal hears a small, quiet voice from above: "Saul ..."

Saul pulls his foot back for another kick.

Then this small, quiet voice again: "Saul ..."

Saul looks around the room. Then he looks up, and Leal

looks up, too. There's Diana, along the balcony of the upstairs loft. She's leaning over the railing. She's wearing a man's dress shirt. The sleeves cover her hands. The tails of the shirt droop low along her thighs. Her thighs are bare.

"Diana?" Saul says.

Saul takes a small step away from Jay. He moves toward the open stairway.

"Saul, you big, stupid hunk of salami. You big, stupid bull moose. Jay's innocent. He didn't do anything, except give me a place to stay for the night. I was hoping if I stayed hidden long enough you'd give up and leave. But I'll go back with you, if that's what you want. Just so you leave him alone."

"You expect me to believe that? You expect me to believe nothing happened. Look at you. Look how you're dressed. How can I believe you when you're dressed like that?"

"No, I don't. I don't expect you to believe anything. It's just what I'm telling you."

Diana starts moving down the staircase. She takes one slow step at a time. Her feet are bare. She makes no noise at all.

"How could you? I don't understand." Saul moves to the bottom of the steps.

"What's there to understand?"

"I gave you everything. I took good care of you." Saul drops his arms to his sides. They hang like sausages.

"What did you give me? Name one thing you gave me, Saul." She stops halfway down the steps.

"I was a good provider." Saul droops his head. He stares at the floor. "I put a roof over your head."

"It leaked, Saul. The roof leaked. It's been leaking into a bucket for three solid years now." She takes another step down the staircase. Only four more steps to go. She keeps her eyes on Saul waiting at the bottom of the staircase.

"I was going to fix it. You didn't give me any time to fix it. I was sensitive, wasn't I? Sensitive to your needs? To everything you always wanted. I made you a celebrity. I dressed you in furs."

"I didn't like wearing them. I'm not the kind of woman who likes wearing furs. And as for flaunting myself in those little string bikinis you make me wear …" Another step, then another. She is only two steps above Saul. Her head shows above Saul's head, chin seeming to rest on his crown.

"I was there for you. I was always there for you. I took good care of you."

"Saul, you're such a child. You're such a naive, stupid, little child. Did you think you were taking care of me, all this time?"

"Yes, I took care of you. When you were sick. When you needed help."

"It was me, Saul." Diana takes one more step down the stairs. Her head becomes hidden by Saul's, eclipsed from view. "I was the one taking care of you."

Saul shakes his head from side to side. "That's not true. That's just not true."

"Think about it, Saul. Just think about it, would you? I was your little showgirl, your little prize possession. Something that gave you hope when your little world was falling all apart. Some-one who always came running when you called. Someone who wiped your ass whenever it got dirty. Someone who didn't laugh when you couldn't get it up when you were so full of worry—"

The slap comes hard and fast. It is very loud. Saul draws back his arm and knocks Diana to the foot of the stairs. Saul gets down on his knees. He bends low over Diana, but she's not mov-ing. She's completely still, lying on the floorboards. Her head is turned to one side.

"Diana? Diana?" Saul shakes her shoulder, but she just lies there. She doesn't move. She doesn't open her eyes. "Diana? I'm sorry." Thuster rises from his chair and goes over to Saul. He stands next to Saul leaning over Diana. He pulls at Saul's shirt. He pulls at Saul's arm. Saul swipes the back of his arm back hard, sending Thuster sprawling across the floor.

Now Leal is inside the room. He doesn't even know he has left the window. He charges into the center of the room. He pulls out the gun—the one he took from Saul's bedroom drawer—from under his shirt. He trains it on the back of Saul's head.

"That's enough," Leal says. His voice is very even. It is deep. Steady.

"Son of a bitch," Saul says when he sees him.

"Leave her alone," Leal says. "Step back."

"She's hurt, you little shithead punk," Saul barks, glaring at Leal. It's hard to tell if he even sees the gun Leal is holding, both hands wrapped around the butt. "Can't you see she's hurt?"

"Just step back," Leal says. "Away from her."

Saul stands up. Leal keeps the gun aimed at Saul's chest. He waves Saul away with the barrel, and Saul takes a slow step backward. Then Leal points the gun at Diana. She is still on the floor, unmoving.

"Go see if she's all right," Leal says to Jay.

Thuster is lying face down, and Jay is still lying curled up on the floor. But now he rolls over onto his hands and knees, and crawls over to Diana. He kneels next to her and takes her arm, feeling with his thumb for a pulse at her wrist.

"She's alive," he says. He looks up at Leal, still holding the gun. "Someone should go for a doctor. I don't have a phone."

"You see," Saul says, "it isn't that bad. I didn't hurt her that bad. I knew it couldn't be that bad." He takes a step forward, and Leal holds the gun straight out with stiff arms. He points it directly at Saul—at his head, his face. Saul stops. "Now, son. Just put down the gun, okay? Be a good boy. I know you don't want to hurt anyone."

"Just stand where you are," Leal says. "Don't move."

"Someone should really go get help," Jay says. "She isn't moving. It could be her neck is broken."

Saul takes another step forward. Leal raises the gun to eye level. He sights along the barrel, just as Saul taught him, feet apart, forming the base of a triangle with the gun as its apex.

"Just put the gun down, like a nice boy," Saul says. "That's the whole trouble with your generation. Kids today— they think everything can be solved with a gun. That's not the way it was back in my day. We used our fists. We used our fists to settle an argument. That way at the end of a fight, everybody got up, shook hands. Walked away."

"Shut up," Leal says. "Hold still."

"Isn't anyone going to get a doctor?" Jay wails from the floor. "What's wrong with everyone?" He holds Diana's wrist. He strokes her hair lightly.

Saul takes another tentative step, and Leal backs away. He hears everything—Saul's footsteps, Jay's breathing—ultra loud. Everything is edged hard in black and white, and the noises, the words—they echo off the walls and ceiling. Leal feels suddenly larger than his body. His body doesn't feel like his body at all.

"You heard him," Saul says. "She needs help. What are you going to do? Keep her from getting the help that she needs?"

But Leal no longer belongs to his own body. He watches everything from above. He floats along the archway of the ceiling. He looks down and sees everyone, like still lives in a painting. He can see Jay kneeling alongside Diana. He can see Saul and Leal—the old Leal, the Leal he used to be—confronting each other, eye to eye, as he trains the gun on Saul. He can see Thuster getting up from the floor, and then everything unfreezes.

It all happens very slowly. Saul lunges for the gun, holding his hand out to grab Leal's wrist. Thuster again comes up to Saul, sweetly, silently, taking hold of Saul's shirttails. Saul turns his head, falling forward, reaching for the gun, missing Leal's wrist with his open, clawing hand, and Leal's finger pulls back on the trigger, ever so slightly.

The gun makes a sharp popping sound. Then it leaps upward, flying out of Leal's hand in the softest, loveliest arc, flying up and up, to where Leal—the new Leal, the out-of-body Leal—is still floating, against the ceiling. It seems he should be able to just reach out and grab it by the handle as it twirls and twirls, end over end, just under his nose, even as he looks at the scene below.

Saul has fallen sideways. Jay looks up from Diana. The gun falls away from the ceiling, twirling and twirling, butt over barrel. It lands with a thud at the old Leal's feet. And then he is in two places at once. He is still floating against the ceiling, but he is also looking down at the gun on the floor, and he watches himself looking down. He watches the whole scene from above. Everything seems so still, so peaceful.

He wishes it could last like this forever. He wishes time didn't have to move forward, and he wishes he never would have to come back into his body. The world seems so distant and small and unimportant, but then he feels a slight tug at the base of his neck, and everything goes into regular motion again, so hard and so fast, his head is dizzy and dazed. But he has enough presence of mind to reach down and pick up the gun from where it has skidded along the floor, coming down.

Saul rolls over. He squirms on the floor like a worm. He lies on his back, clutching his shoulder. Blood leaks through his shirt. His eyes are clenched closed. He just keeps shouting, "I'm hit, I'm hit, I'm hit."

Diana starts shaking her head back and forth. Jay helps her sit up, his arm behind her back to brace her. Her face is streaked red. The imprints of knuckles are still fresh along her cheek, and her mouth bubbles blood. Her jaw opens and closes, painfully. Thuster walks across the room. His arms swing lamely at his sides. His eyes are bright and cold and dark, staring straight ahead. He brushes past Leal and goes out the doorway into the night, trailing drops of blood on the floorboards.

Leal just stands there, holding the gun, trying to keep his hands from shaking.

Diana crawls over to Saul, where he's still lying on his back, clutching his shoulder. She pries his hands away and tears his shirt, ripping it from the wound. She wipes the blood away with her palm and eyes the wound closely.

"Saul, Saul," Diana says. "Look at me, Saul." But Saul keeps rolling his head from side to side on the floor with his eyes squeezed closed. "Saul, you big, hairy ape, listen to me. It's just a nick. It's nothing. Do you hear me? It grazed your side. That's all. It's nothing." And then Saul starts crying, sobbing, and she lifts his head and drops it on her lap, cradling it, sitting cross-legged on the floor. She brushes her hand through his hair, whispering, "There, there. It'll be all right. There, there. Let me take care of you."

Jay rises slowly, staring at the two of them, disbelievingly. His hands feel their way up the wall. He presses himself flat against the plaster. Then Diana looks up. She looks right at Leal with wide, blank eyes, but he can't read the look in her eyes. It isn't a look that says anything, and so Leal turns away and moves out the door. He goes all the way down to the beach, taking the gun with him as a precaution. He can't be sure Saul won't seek him out for retaliation for the part he played in Diana's attempted escape.

And then he sees Thuster. There's a thin carpet of light from the cottage rolling down the beach. There's a white hook of a moon glazing the water. Thuster is down at the boat shed, pulling at the rope attached to the rowboat, trying to drag it down the beach and into the water.

Leal knows what he has to do. If he can just row Thuster across the lake, he can leave him there on the opposite shore, where he can tend to him. It would keep him out of danger. It would keep him safe.

*

Selena observes Leal's body begin trembling, hands shaking, eyeballs rolling beneath fluttering lids, and she knows the time has come to stop.

"Leal? I'm going to count backwards. I'm going to count backwards from three. I want you to walk toward the doorway. It should be brightly lit now, from the other side. Do you see the doorway?"

"Yes. I see it."

"Good. I'm going to start counting. And when I reach number one, you will be through the door and fully awake. Three … two …"

"Mom?" Leal asks. He opens his eyes and props himself up on an elbow, looking around the office. "Mom?"

Selena opens the blinds, suffusing the room with soft streams of sunlight.

"Where am I?" he asks, groggily.

"You're here with me. In my office. You fell asleep."

"I'm sorry. I didn't mean to."

"It's all right. It's fairly common with this kind of exercise."

"Did it work? Did I tell you anything? You know, like you said, from within my subconscious?"

"You started to, but then you sort of drifted off."

"What did I tell you? What did I remember?"

"Well, you talked about Thuster lying in the middle of a road at night, and Saul coming across him with his car, so you didn't get to the cottage in time to warn Diana. Then how you were looking through the window of the cottage and you saw Thuster sitting in a chair with Saul confronting Jay, and Diana nowhere to be seen. And then it got sort of fuzzy."

"Fuzzy?"

"You were sort of mumbling. Like you were talking in your sleep. Were you having a dream?"

"Yes, I think so." He draws his knees up into his chest, clasping them in place with his hands. "It was all very real. I tried to stop it all from happening. I tried to break up Jay and Saul. I tried to stop Saul from hurting Diana. But a gun went off."

"A gun?" This truly alarms her, even though it's part of his imagination, his dream.

"There was a gunshot. Thuster was wounded. And I thought I would take him somewhere, away from it all. I thought I would row him across the lake where I could keep him safe."

They sit in silence for a few minutes until his trembling lessens and he swings his body around and goes back to his standard position, feet on the floor, leaning forward, elbows on knees.

Selena turns on the overhead light and switches off the laser. She makes a move for the DVD player but Leal stops her.

"No, not yet. I like the sound they make. The waves."

"Are you sure you're all right?"

"Yeah, I'm fine."

"Do you think you would like to try this again next time?"

He eyes Selena through narrowed lids and tentatively nods his head.

"Are you sure?"

"Yeah, I'm sure. But next time, could we maybe try the whale songs instead?"

***

Reflection: I have to be honest, Henri, I wasn't expecting the continuation of Leal's narrative during this session. It seems real but also, at the same time, a little too good to be true. It sounded genuine, the parts that were verbalized. It's possible events occurred just as described—sans

Thuster, of course.. This doesn't mean, however, that I can entirely discard my initial hypothesis of schizotypy. This entire story may be an unconscious fabrication, part and parcel of a delusional syndrome.

On the other hand, this session revealed a central dilemma: Leal believes this version of his autobiography, whether fictionalized or no. It has penetrated the deepest layer of his psyche, except for one very important factor: he still hasn't reached the part of his story where he drowns his imaginary friend in a lake. We are getting closer. He is circling the central feature of his confession hawklike, zeroing in on his prey.

We are so close now, so very close—real progress indeed. Has the narrative replaced reality? Is this narrative Leal's new reality? I can only answer in the affirmative, with a vague hope that the traces of the 'real' reality can somehow be reclaimed. I still consider his narrative a stalling tactic. I believe it has a specific function: to keep putting off as long as possible the very real trauma it attempts to conceal.

***

The phone wakes her later that night. She answers it quickly, before it can go to voicemail.

It's the hospital. The doctor is very sorry. Her father has just died. She assures Selena his death was sudden, painless. Time of death was 2:17 a.m.

Chapter 19

Any man's death diminishes me,
Because I am involved in mankind …

Dear Henri,

I am sorry it has been so long since I've found an opportunity to write. It's been taking a while to settle my father's estate. And then there's the baby, of course. I've named her Jonquil, after the flower, a type of narcissus. I chose it as a near rhyme with "tranquil," and that's what I feel I need to sink into these days: a sea of tranquility. You'll understand why I was unable to attend your wedding or even respond to the invitation, although I appreciated receiving it. I truly thought that the night we spent in Montreal would constitute a last memory of our time together.

Dad was buried on a Tuesday. I was as surprised as my brother to see the number of friends who turned out for the service. His lodge paid the expenses. The service was nondenominational, held in a funeral parlor in the uptown, near Father Mac's church. He is resting next to his wife, our mother. They have only to etch in the final year of his life, and then his history will be complete.

For my part of the eulogy, I chose the Donne poem, the one about no man (or woman, I should add) being an island. By the time I got to the part about the tolling of the bell, it was all I could do to suppress a geyser of tears. Especially as I had synchronized my reading to coincide with the ringing of the church bells on the half hour: the bells of St. Mary.

It was on the Thursday following that I had my final session with Leal. I can understand your desiring the audio files for your research. But they've been subpoenaed. The trial has become big news, after all. I'm sure Leal would be amazed to learn his case has been reported as far away as Montreal.

As the court date is still pending, you can understand my high level of concern that the transcripts be held in strictest confidence. I would hate to come across publication of them in one of those professional journals that solicit your eloquent ability with the written word. You never know—there may be one police investigator, even in the small town of Ovid, who happens, as a hobby, to brush up on his or her French by skimming the latest psychological theories in Revue Francaise de Psychanalyse. *I would hate for it to be cause for a mistrial.*

I wish I could give you more encouragement to respond, but I am afraid this must be my last correspondence. I'll be going away soon with the baby after the trial. I promised Leal I would be there for him, even on days I am not scheduled to give testimony.

I feel there is nothing more I need to tell you. I am not so sure you would love to hear me say how I miss our late-night discussions. Our moonlit rendezvous at cafés under skies reminiscent of Van Gogh. On the other hand, you may want to snip off this last paragraph so as not to give your spouse cause for jealousy. Oh, and speaking of spouses, give my best to Genevieve.

***

Transcript
    Start: 4:17

    [Silence.]
    Do you see the dark doorway, Leal?
    Yes.
    I'm going to start counting. Let me know when you're through it. One ... two ... three ...
    [Silence.]
    I'm through.
    Good. Where are you?
    On a boat.
    [Silence.]
    What boat?

*

There is a splinter in his eye, and he tries to blink it away. It is like a small world in his eye, floating, clouding his vision. He pulls at the oars until they are in the middle of the lake. They glide through the water. The moon is gone from the lake. There is a cloud covering it, and the moon has disappeared. The lights of the cottage—they flicker in the lake like stars.

Thuster lies on his lap. He is stretched crosswise in the boat. His feet hang over the edge of the boat. His legs are stiff. His neck and arms are stiff, too.

He places his hand under Thuster and feels for an open wound. His hand comes across something wet and seeping. He pulls his hand away. He looks at his palm in the dark. There is a splotch of blood on his hand, but he can't be sure. He puts his fingers to his mouth. It tastes like blood, but he can't be sure.

He lets the boat drift. He does not raise the oars.

They come to a stop.

He looks toward the cottage. The lights are on, but there is no movement. Nothing is moving—inside or outside. The cottage has become very quiet and still.

He holds Thuster on his lap. Thuster's eyes are open wide. His chest rises and falls, but his eyes are dark and dull. It seems the life is slowly oozing out of him, and Leal knows there is little use trying to save him. It is too late for that.

The water laps in soft thuds against the hull. The water rocks the boat. It drips from the hanging oars.

He lets the boat drift. Crickets sing along the shore. The boat rocks. The night is still. The moon is in the lake again.

He looks around the splinter in his eye. He stares at Thuster a long time. The moon is in the lake. It is like a cold face in the water.

He crouches in the bottom of the boat. He puts his arms under Thuster. He lifts Thuster's head away from his lap. Thuster's feet hang over the gunwale. It is hard lifting because he is so long and big and heavy. His arms are tired from lifting, but he lifts.

It takes only a second to drop Thuster into the water.

Thuster slides into the water. He looks over the edge of the boat at Thuster in the water. Thuster's legs float like dark wood on the water.

He starts to count on his fingers. He watches Thuster glide away from the boat. His feet sink into the water, and now his waist … arms … shoulders … His head bobs in the water, spinning a circle, bobbing. The moon gleams white in his open eyes. Now his head sinks. Thuster is gone, hidden by the calm, unruffled surface of the lake that gleams like a mirror below the moon, but he is still counting.

He takes the oars and pulls the boat toward shore.

He floats through the water. He floats through the water until he is at the far shore across from the cottage. He raises the oars straight above the water.

He keeps count on his fingers. He looks back at the middle of the lake, holding his breath and counting on his fingers. He goes through both sets of fingers over and over. He cannot hold his breath any longer.

He pulls the boat along the shore. He steps out of the boat and looks back over the lake.

He walks under the shadows of the trees out of sight of the moon. He starts and stops to cry. He walks under the shadows. He looks out over the lake. He has lost count. He is sorry for Thuster because he has lost count. He doesn't know how many breaths it has been since he lost count of his fingers.

*

Selena lets a moment drift away.

Something doesn't sound right. It's as though she is in a trance herself, an echo hollowing out her ears.

Long and big and heavy.
This is the phrase that sticks in her mind.
Long and big and heavy.
This isn't how Leal has ever described Thuster in all their time together. He has never used these words before. Thuster was just a little boy. Not something long and big and heavy—to be lifted, heaved, dropped like an anchor.

*

Leal?
[*Silence.*]
Let's move backward. I want us to move back.
[*Silence.*]
Let's move back to the cottage. You are inside the cottage.
[*Silence.*]
Are you there, Leal? Are you in the cottage?
Yes.
Now let's go a little deeper. Okay?
[*Silence.*]
Is that okay, Leal? If we go a little deeper?
[*Silence.*]
Yes.
There is a doorway in front of you. Do you see it?
[*Silence.*]
Yes.
Leal, I want you to go through this new opening.
[*Silence.*]
Okay, Leal?
Okay.
The opening is getting closer. It is getting bigger.
[*Silence.*]
You are almost there.
[*Silence.*]

It is right in front of you. Now you are stepping through it.

[Silence.]

You have stepped completely through it.

[Silence.]

Do you see that you have stepped through it, Leal?

Yes.

Good.

[Silence.]

Can you see where you are?

Yes.

Where are you? Can you tell me?

[Silence.]

In a room.

What room?

[Silence.]

Can you describe the room, Leal? What room is it?

A bedroom. A loft. In the cottage.

Good. Do you see someone on the bed?

Yes.

Who is on the bed, Leal?

Thuster.

No, Leal. It isn't Thuster. Who is on the bed?

[Silence.]

Leal? Who is on the bed?

[Silence.]

I am. I am on the bed.

Are you alone?

[Silence.]

Leal, are you by yourself?

No.

Who is with you?

[Silence.]

Can you tell me what is happening? Don't be afraid. I'm right here. I'm right here beside you.

[*Silence.*]

He crawls onto the bed. He is beside me on the bed.

[*Silence.*]

Leal? Don't be afraid. I'm here with you. Now what happens? What happens next?

It's like a weight on top of me. It's like a weight. Pressing down.

[*Silence.*]

I can't breathe. It's heavy. It's like a weight. I can't breathe.

[*Silence.*]

He whispers in my ear. He tells me not to worry. He tells me I'm a good boy. He tells me I'm a very good boy.

[*Silence.*]

Leal? I'm right here. Don't be afraid.

[*Silence.*]

Leal? Now what is happening? Can you tell me what is happening?

There is someone else in the room. I can feel it. I see a shadow. It moves fast and silent.

[*Silence.*]

The shadow—it pulls him away. Someone pulls him off of me.

[*Silence.*]

I can hear her voice. In the dark. I can hear her shouting. In the dark.

[*Silence.*]

I crawl away. I crawl off the bed. The shadow is pinning him down. He is pinned down by his shoulders.

[*Silence.*]

I can hear someone crying. I can hear him crying.

[*Silence.*]

Leal? Don't go away.

[*Silence.*]

Leal? Are you still there? Are you still in the room?

[*Silence.*]

Yes.

What are you doing?

I am watching. I am standing there watching. She tells me to hand her a pillow. She presses down on the pillow.

[*Silence.*]

I can't hear the crying anymore. I can see his legs. I see his legs in the dark. They are kicking.

[*Silence.*]

She yells at me. She tells me to sit on his legs.

[*Silence.*]

Do you, Leal? Do you do what she tells you to do?

Yes.

And now what is happening?

I am sitting on his legs. His legs are kicking. Struggling. And then they go still.

[*Silence.*]

Everything is quiet. Everything is very quiet.

[*Silence.*]

You can wake up now, Leal.

[*Sound of crying.*]

Leal? You can wake up now. Whenever you want. Whenever you're ready.

[*Crying.*]

Trust me, Leal. Everything is going to be fine.

[*Pause.*]

Everything is going to be all right.

End: 4:42

*

He doesn't feel awake. His head still feels cloudy. It feels numb inside his head. He sits up on the couch. He sees Selena beside him. She is sitting next to him on the couch. Her eyes seem tender, sad. She is stroking his hair.

He can still see it. He needs to tell her something more. He isn't finished. He can still see it, so clearly.

There is a shadow in the room. In the corner.

He looks at the shadow. He waits for the shadow to crawl out from under the bed.

He can't talk. He can't make himself speak. He is sitting on the floor.

His mom bends over the body on the bed, fingers against the jugular, feeling for a pulse. She turns toward Leal, shaking her head, then comes over to him and sits beside him. She runs her fingers through his hair.

"Don't worry," she says. "It was just a bad dream. I'll take care of everything. I don't want you to worry. It was only a dream."

But she needs help. She can't do it alone. There is one more part she needs help with, and then it will all go away. She promises.

They will carry the body out of the cottage. They will take him into the middle of the lake. It is twilight. They will ferry him across the lake. They will take him to its deepest part.

If anyone finds the body, floating, it will seem like a drowning accident, that's all. This is what she tells him, to console him, to make it better.

But a shadow follows them down the stairs. It follows them to the shore. It is the shadow of a little boy.

***

She waited by the fire until nightfall, feeding it sticks and dry branches—a signal fire that Leal had instructed her to build, forcing her to recall her Girl Scout days, so he could find her in the dark. There were no lights, no yellow twinkling stars from the other side of the lake. Selena stared at the distant roof of the cottage. She could just make out the flat gray strip of shoreline, the long row of narrow windows, but there was no sign of life. It was possible to believe that no one had ever lived there, that it was an ancient hovel from a medieval romance.

The fire started to die, to fade away into dull, red embers, and the woods closed in dark and deep. Selena fed the fire, then sat still and silent, staring into the pulsating flames, until she could hear her own heart thumping like the steady beat of a drum.

She sat like a Buddha, straight-backed and rigid, cradling her belly within her crossed legs. She stared without blinking, without moving her eyes. She closed her ears to all sound, the raucous croaking of deep-throated frogs, the violin symphony of crickets. *There*, she thought. *If only I could stop thinking, then everything would be set, everything would turn out all right.*

A hymn from childhood came into her mind—

Abide with me; 'tis eventide.
The day is past and gone.
The shadows of the evening fall;
The night is coming on.

She tried blocking it out. But then she realized that all she had to do was let the hymn die away, let the strains fade into nothingness.

She is sure now she could have remained this way forever. There was little secret to it—first, the force of will of keeping that sterile position of eyes and heart and mind until the cement of being sets—and then the slow unbending of that same will until there is nothing more to ever be said or made or done.

There, she thought. Perfect.

Above and beyond, she heard, far away and behind her, buried deeply in the woods, the proverbial snap of a twig. She sat very quietly and unmoving, and waited, without turning her head, until she heard another twig snap, and then she was sure.

He walked slowly into the circle of light thrown by the fire. His eyes reflected the yellow and orange flames.

"You came," he said.

"Yes," she answered.

"I didn't think you'd be here," he said.

"Well, I am," she responded. "What is it you want to show me?"

Evidence is what she was hoping for. Some parcel of evidence. Without evidence, there was not much point accusing his mother with a crime alleged via pseudo hypnosis alone.

"Not yet. We have to wait for someone else."

"Someone else?"

He took a seat on the ground on the opposite side of the fire. He sat with his legs folded into his chest, his chin resting on his knees, as he contemplated the runes of dark veins running through the coals beneath the flames. Selena added fuel to the fire as the night deepened, and still she waited, holding her breath, as out of the trees crawled a shadow.

It moved closer and closer to the glowing bed of coals, without making a further sound, except that she could hear shallow breathing through the nostrils. The shadow came even closer until it too sat by the fire, just outside the perimeter of flickering yellow light, and she could feel her skin prickle with gooseflesh, and her heart leapt into her throat, and her own breathing stopped.

"You should have left him alone," a voice said, quietly.

Selena didn't respond. She stared into the envelope of

darkness, but she recognized the voice.

"You should have just let him be," it said.

"I couldn't do that," she answered.

The woman's body leaned forward, slicing into the edge of firelight, and her face glowed a leering orange, like a Halloween mask. In her hand she held a gun, loosely aimed toward Selena—her belly—the shaft reflecting a silver sheen.

They sat there, the three of them, as the flames of the fire flickered and faded into dark, red ashes, faintly illuminating the patchwork of rotting leaves and crisscrossed twigs, the autumn carpet of the forest floor. She could hear the water softly lapping onto the bank of the shore beneath the trees.

"Do you want to talk about it?" Selena asked.

"What do you mean?" Sandra asked in return. Her voice slithered slick along a hard edge in the darkness. She sounded alert, defensive, suspicious of a trick.

"We can talk about it," Selena suggested. "If you want."

"What good would that do?" she rebutted sharply. "I'm sure Leal told you everything you want to know. That's why you're here, isn't it?"

"It isn't like that," Leal said. He turned his head toward his mother, toward the sound of her voice, like a weathervane. "She can help us. She knows how to help us."

"What makes you think I want her help?" she asked. "Have I ever needed anyone's help?"

"Everything we tell her is private," Leal said, but then he paused, uncertain. He turned his head toward Selena, his eyes widening with his plea. "Tell her, Dr. Harris. Selena. Tell her how everything we tell you is private."

"That's only in her office," Sandra snapped. "Look around you. Does this look like her office to you?"

Selena waited with infinite patience. The world seemed

suspended in an amber of timelessness. She listened to the beating of her heart in her ears. She tried to slow the sequence of her breaths. She felt immobilized—by what she didn't know. By confusion. By blindness. By fear.

"What happened?" she asked.

"What happened? You want to know what happened? You find someone new—someone you really like. You bring him home. You go to his place. You spend time with him. You let your son spend time with him. And then you find out the only reason he's seeing you is to get close to your son—to-to-to molest him. You don't want to believe it. You don't want to believe your son's stories, but then you go over and catch him in the act."

Sandra brought her hand to her eyes, and Leal rose from the fire. Selena got up heavily. Ignoring his mother, ignoring the gun, she followed him through the woods. Sandra walked closely behind, in her wake.

"Leal?" she whispered. "What do you want me to see?"

He paused before a low, dark mound rising above the earth. She stopped behind him. She could make out the form of a cross, a makeshift crucifix made of sticks and twine, planted at the foot of the mound.

"Don't listen to him," Sandra said, following.

Selena waited, but she wasn't sure what the waiting harbored, what wish it embraced.

She heard Leal take a deep breath. She listened to a hard swallow in his throat.

And then she felt her body tighten with his response.

"It's where I buried him," he said.

"Buried him?" she prompted.

"I did it to protect him," Sandra said, her voice edged with exasperation. "You have to believe me. I only wanted to protect him."

"Buried who?" Selena asked again.

"Thuster," Leal murmured into the night, the darkness.

"No, Leal," she said. "Not Thuster. Who?"

"Jay," Leal said. "It's where I buried Jay."

"I'm sorry," Sandra said, and Selena turned to face her. She held the gun in front of her, aiming it, but unsteadily, her arm wavering, hand trembling.

"You don't have to do this," Selena stated, more calmly than she felt.

"I don't want to, believe me. But you've given me no choice. I have to protect my son."

"No, Mom, no!"

Leal leaped in front of her, arms wide, body rigid, unyielding.

"Honey, move out of the way," Sandra admonished gently, as though he was photobombing a picture, blocking Selena from view.

"Mom, no! I can't let you!" He took a step forward, hand outstretched. "Give me the gun."

"Leal, you don't understand."

"But I do. I do understand." He took another step toward her. "You don't have to do this. It's just like she said. If you're going to shoot someone, shoot me instead."

"Leal, listen to yourself. What are you saying? Do you hear what you're saying?"

Selena felt a movement inside her and let out a groan. Holding her stomach, she collapsed to the ground, legs folding under her.

"What is it?" Sandra asked. She still held the gun, but she lowered it to her side. Her face looked constricted, concerned.

Selena knew exactly what it was. It was her water. Her water just broke.

"I'm going into contractions," she told Leal's mother, looking into her eyes, searchingly, beseechingly. "I'm ready to have my baby."

*

The wind died away and the surface of the lake became very calm, as still as green glass. She sat by the shore, hands on her stomach, feeling the movements within coming more and more strongly now, so she knew it wouldn't be long. The farther shore of the lake became a distant world, foreign and invisible, shrouded in mist, and the stars of the night sky opened like holes puncturing the canvas of a wide purple umbrella.

When the contractions started, Sandra had grown alarmed. There would be no further intimidation with the gun. Maternal sympathy had taken charge. Taking her son, she said she would call 911 when she got to town or got a signal. Selena felt in no condition to move all that way to her own car parked alongside a gravel road.

As she sat there, waiting, counting her breaths between contractions, she transported herself to the end of the summer, and she could see it all very clearly in her mind.

She could guess at the stories that had been told and retold, or the stories that hadn't been told, that had been held secret, like jars on a shelf. She could see Leal's mother going back to her job at the diner. And Father Mac, lying on his bed, eyes closed, bags all packed, dreaming of the white beaches of Florida. And Saul and Diana going back to their lives, carrying on as usual with their chinchillas and their commercials. And Jay, his head bobbing in the lake, dead, cold eyes transfixed on a rotating sky, as though to encompass one final vision before closing forever.

And she could picture Leal, waiting patiently in the woods, hoping to see Thuster emerge. Eventually, he leaves the shore. He makes his way slowly around the lake to the now-empty cottage, and steps through the door into the studio. He looks around the room into eyes that stare back, all those sets of eyes, dazzled by their quiet, dark intensity, as they gaze from their solitary confinement. He contemplates the slender lines, the purple shadows, the blue mask of a face from which the eyes emerge.

And then his eyes settle upon a painting displayed all by itself, a lone work of art set apart, and he becomes transfixed by that deeper gaze, the hollow, haunted eyes of a little boy.

Chapter 20

"So, Dr. Harris. May I call you Selena? Yes? Very well, I understand you've been through quite the experience, to put it lightly. Would you care to talk about it?"

He has been studying the Manila folder she had given him to bring him up to speed. She's also aware he's been studying her out of the corner of one eye with somewhat more than professional interest. The folder is filled with news clippings and journal entries recounting events. But there's more, so much more that the papers and social media posts and newsfeeds left out, so much more they didn't know, that they failed to grasp—that she had failed to grasp until it was much too late.

"That's why I'm here, isn't it?" Selena says this without smiling. She doesn't mean it as a joke. She's not in the mood for humor. Hasn't been for months. Ever since ...

The therapist smiles, as though to deflect the barb. He is an older man, this side of sixty, with a shaved head polished to a brilliant sheen so that she can almost see her reflection. He would remind her of her father except for the accent, heavily flavored with an Islander inflection.

This isn't quite the island paradise she had pictured. She could sue her imagination for false advertising, never mind the hype of an Airbnb ad. On the tourist side of the island, the sand is as white as sugar, pristine, combed free of debris, dotted with lounge chairs and tiki bars.

On her side of the island, the beach is sandpaper coarse, the ebb tide littered with the detritus of nightly escapades: needles, condoms, cigarette butts, marijuana stubs. The houses are small, thatched affairs with corrugated tin roofs and bamboo doors, raised high on stilts to stay clear of the flooding during hurricane season.

On the plus side, the rent is very affordable. She could easily live here a year without working, tapping only marginally into her portfolio. But she feels restless, unsettled, even though she's been here for a couple of months. Her brother has been pestering her by text to visit, but she's not ready to see him yet. She doesn't feel balanced enough to entertain visitors.

Thankfully, the therapist's office is a lightly built structure, all open air.

"Where would you like to start?" he asks, setting the folder aside.

Selena takes a deep breath as though instructed by a doctor pressing a stethoscope to her chest. She reflects on Leal's narrative, the story he told her in her office that took almost three months—an entire season—to unfold in its entirety. And even then, there had been more to divulge. She hadn't been prepared for it. She should have read the subtext. It would have kept her on the alert, her senses a perpetual code orange.

"At the end. I think in this case it would be better if I started at the end."

"Well, then, let us proceed. Can I get you a juice? Lime, lemonade?"

Selena shakes her head. She just wants to get on with it.

***

'Twas two nights before Christmas, when all through the house, not a creature was stirring, except for Jonquil, of course. Selena's brother had moved out shortly after the estate sale, mentioning a friend in New Orleans—or, as he pronounced it, "N'awlins." Only tacky tourists pronounced it this way. The correct way, Selena informed him, was to sound out the syllables: New OR-lee-yuns. But her brother had only laughed at her, labeling her the linguistic equivalent of a "grammar Nazi."

This left just Jonquil and her in a medium-sized suburban home that was gradually being stripped of her father's identity, as Selena sorted through his belongings, conducting triage among trash, thrift store donations, and treasures to safeguard.

Regarding Jonquil, Selena was amazed and pleased how easy a baby she was so far. All her vitals were up and running machinelike. She had taken to the breast as naturally as though she had read the user's manual. Selena had only recently begun supplementing breast-feeding with a bottle, using the pump from time to time to give her nipples a rest—if she were to put it bluntly. In fact, Selena thought Jonquil a better baby than she was a mother.

Maternal instincts didn't come naturally. She thought her body too angular—like one of those surrogates made of wire in experiments with baby monkeys—to be a comfort to her child. Before she did anything new with the baby, she consulted the appropriate pages of the *What to Expect* series. She wished there was a book from the baby's perspective: *What to Expect from Your Mother.*

Jonquil had popped out of the womb with a wild shock of hair, all curls, which Selena anticipated would pose a challenge to her pruning skills. From the moment of birth, she had a wise, steady look to her eyes, as though she were evaluating the world she had been born into to check if it was up to her standards.

It had all happened so quickly—the ambulance ride to the hospital, the rush through the ER doors, the trip down the hallway on a gurney, the push, push, push in the delivery room, with only moments to spare. The police arrived shortly afterward to ask if she had any idea where Leal and his mother might have disappeared, what escape route they had taken.

Understandably, she hadn't wanted to go through the delivery alone. She hadn't time to call her brother. He would arrive much later. The one person she wished to be at her side was Henri.

And now, two days before Christmas, he arrived like one of the calling birds from the interminable song. She was a little irked at the short notice: just the briefest of texts that morning asking if she was going to be home, only three hours before he dropped in, as though afraid she might fly away like a nervous turtledove before he arrived.

He had been texting her biweekly with voicemails in between. He just couldn't accept that Selena's last email was the absolute final word on their relationship. Of course, he had an excuse for flying in from Montreal. It wasn't just to see her. He was conducting some intercollegiate business with her alma mater.

It was the bombshell that broke the week before that gave them something to talk about over dinner. The news had even made it into the *Tribune* and *Sun-Times*. Father Timothy MacDougal had finally been located. He hadn't made it to Florida, after all. His body was found compartmentalized in one of the holding pens that Selena had observed in the basement of the parsonage. He was found as the place was being readied for the new priest.

It sickened her to think that his body was stored there, in the basement, wrapped in a tarp along with his luggage, in a puddle of water, where it had already spent a considerable amount of time decomposing. It seemed a day couldn't go by without some mention in newsfeeds of the Crime of the Century—at least for a small town like Ovid where murders occurred as rarely as a full blood moon. Obviously, there had been foul play. All detectives lacked were a motive and a perpetrator.

"Any more murders, and you will be ranked with Chicago," Henri said, wryly.

"It's not officially a murder until the autopsy comes out," Selena reminded him.

"And Leal?" Henri inquired. "He is being looked after?"

"Yes, he's a ward of the state. Until the trial concludes. It seems unfair being forced to testify against his own mother."

"You can do that in the States?"

"This state, apparently. If it's a criminal trial."

"That's got to be rough."

"I stop by every now and then to check on him. He's with a foster family. They seem nice enough. Cleared by Social Services, but you know how that goes."

"And his mother?"

"Still in jail, awaiting trial." For the murder of one Gerald Fitzgibbons, Esq. (aka Jay) lately of Chicago, she might have added. The bond was set too high for her to afford her release. The judge considered her a flight risk, whereas her son was regarded as a victim in his own right for the trauma he suffered—absolved of judicial consequences by his mother's full confession, claiming she acted alone with Leal as an innocent bystander.

After the funeral for Father Mac, Selena had arrived at his foster home to find him in T-shirt and jeans, socks without shoes, feet propped up on the coffee table playing a video game hooked to the TV. The game was older, '80s-style, involving a lot of jumping and pummeling and kickboxing.

"Leal? You weren't at the cemetery."

"No, ma'am," he answered without glancing up. "It looks as though I wasn't."

"You remember what we said about calling me 'ma'am.' I think we've progressed a little further than that." She smiled, but he kept playing his game, so she turned to leave.

"Do they know what killed him?" he asked, pausing with the buttons on the console.

"You mean what he died from? No, not yet. They're performing an autopsy, though. Is it important to you to know how he died?"

"No, not really," he mumbled and went back to punching and jumping and kicking. That's how some people deal with grief, she reasoned. By continuing their normal everyday activities, as though nothing had happened to distress them.

"How are things with your new therapist?" she asked, more out of politeness than interest.

"Okay, I guess. He's not the same as you, though."

"Oh, well. I'm sure you'll be fine."

She had become too involved to remain his counselor. Standard operating procedure, not to mention her code of ethics, demanded she keep a professional distance. She wouldn't have been able to keep seeing him even if she had wanted to.

Before telling him goodbye, she confided she probably wouldn't see much more of him before she left.

"You're leaving?" He looked away from the TV monitor to catch her eye. "For good?"

"I've made plans for a vacation." *A much needed one*, she added in her head. *A long one*, she tacked on for good measure. "But not until after the New Year. So if you ever need me for anything, you know how to get in touch till then."

Despite Henri's degree of sophistication—as he aged and grayed, he reminded her of the Most Interesting Man in the World of Dos Equis commercial fame—he had agreed to a popular local pizza joint that boasted Chicago-style slices with a touch of Ovid, which turned out to be thin crust instead of deep and tavern-style squares instead of wedges—so not traditionally Chicago at all. But the restaurant served Selena's purpose. Its red-and-white checkered plastic tablecloths and bright lights evaporated any hint of romance, thus ensuring the Platonic. It even had a TV bracketed in a corner above their booth.

Henri had cooed over the baby, and held her, and coddled her, and even helped change her diaper, and Selena had laughed when he averted his head and pinched his nose and asked for a clothespin to close off the smell. He offered to undergo a paternity test, an offer Selena declined. If the results of such a test were to come back positive, though, Jonquil would be his first.

"She has your eyes," he observed. "But—" And here he paused for dramatic emphasis. "I believe she has my nose."

"Oh, I hope not!" Selena had blurted. Henri's nose was thin, long, and aquiline. If it were any thinner or longer it could slice paper.

And so they had stepped out to dinner and left things at that—only a vague, ill-defined sense of the part that Henri would play, if any, in Jonquil's upbringing. Genevieve was understanding, he declared, despite Selena's skepticism. She was willing to let Henri interact with his presumed child, this visit included.

Paula's arrival precluded discussing the situation at home.

"Are you sure it's a good idea, leaving Jonquil with a patient?" Henri inquired.

"I'm no longer seeing her," Selena answered. "She's hooked up with a psychiatrist. Besides, this is good therapy for her—*post*-therapy, if you will. Her mother swears by her babysitting skills, so this will just add to her self-esteem—knowing I have confidence in her."

"Well, you're the doctor in this case."

"Besides, this isn't the first time she's babysat for me. She and Jonquil are already well acquainted. They get along fabulously."

"This just in," burst out of the TV above them, like the herald of a hovering angel. Selena angled her head to take in the Breaking News announcement.

"'Well acquainted,' you say? Why, she's not even two months—"

"Sh-h-h!" Selena shushed him.

"I'm sorry if I've said something to—"

Without responding, Selena rose and reached for the volume control of the television. On cue, Henri craned his neck as well.

"Hey! Turn that down!" a patron boomed, but she remained transfixed by the TV. The screen was showing a gray, bleary view of St. Mary's cathedral in the background with the headline "Priest Murder Confirmed" in block letters scrolling beneath.

"—result of blunt trauma to the cranium in the autopsy report released by the diocese just moments ago. The injury was too severe to have been produced by a natural fall. Cause of death has been officially ruled a homicide, making it the second murder of the year in the small town of Ovid. More on the story on News at 10."

"Well, there you have it," Henri said, reaching around her to turn down the volume. "Case closed."

But Selena continued to stand there, staring at the screen, which had ironically enough returned to an airing of a *CSI* episode.

"Are you feeling all right, dear?" Henri asked, helping her back to her seat at the booth. "I know the news is upsetting. However, it was already known the cause of death was suspicious, no?"

Selena couldn't respond. She kept replaying the news report over and over in her head, as a memory worked its way into her consciousness.

She recalled a session with Leal, sitting with legs outstretched, as casual as though he were attending a picnic, mentioning his last encounter with Father Mac in the basement of the parsonage. The basement had flooded, and Father Mac, she remembered from the story, was involved with a wrench—a heavy plumber's wrench— in stopping the leak, pants rolled up his shins.

"You be careful, too," Leal claimed to have told him as a parting message—maybe not his exact words. Selena would have to doublecheck her notes. "You never know, you might slip and fall and crack your head open and drown."

You never know …

But Leal knew. He already knew. He must have known. It wasn't a note of caution he had uttered but an admission of secret knowledge of events that had already transpired.

Selena stood up so suddenly, she rattled the table.

"What is it, love?" Henri asked, taking hold of his goblet of cheap wine to keep it from teetering.

"I have to go."

"What? Already? The evening is just getting started."

"It's Jonquil," she lied. "I shouldn't leave her so long."

Henri checked his watch, an elegant smartwatch with gold band.

"Surely, she's fine," he said, rising. It's barely seven thirty. Besides—" He sidled up to her, taking her by her shoulder with one hand and whispering in her ear. "I thought, if it's okay with you, I would spend the night. We have some catching up to do."

"Henri, no," Selena said, more firmly than she intended, breaking away from his grasp. "I can't. You know I can't. I appreciate your coming down and all." She knew she was sounding as impersonal as a business associate after a power lunch. Then she softened, studying him as though he were a wounded animal, the way he stood there, frowning. "Think about Genevieve."

"I see," Henri said, lowering his head. "May I drive you home at least?"

Now she wished she had been the one to drive. But it would seem impolite, at best, to refuse a ride in his rental.

She nodded, but that was as much body language as she was willing to communicate all the way to her house. She sat stiffly, face forward, eyes turned within herself, so she didn't see the holiday decorations on the houses they passed as anything more than a blur of lights. She answered Henri's inquiries distantly, absently, with monosyllables.

"Is it one of your patients?"

Yes.

"Is it Leal?"

Maybe.

"Can I assist?"

No.

It was something she needed to do, and she didn't want to get Henri any more involved than he had been. His presence would only disturb the equilibrium she had established with Leal. Besides, it was probably nothing—just her imagination getting the better of her deepest worries.

"If it's anything, I'll call you," she said, speaking into the car's interior before Henri could run around to her side to open her door like a gentleman.

"Can I at least come in and say goodbye to—?"

Did it surprise him to see she hadn't gone into her house but had crunched through the snow to enter her own car? But she was on a mission, and she wouldn't be deterred or dissuaded.

She proceeded through town slowly, cautiously, afraid of what she might find at the end of her quest. She followed the map in her head to the right street—in a poorer quarter of town called the Bottoms—and crept along the curb, looking for the telltale sign of a trellis with dead vines anchored to the side of the house.

The porch light was off, but the downstairs windows were lit, so she rang the bell and knocked at the same time until the foster mom, a woman in her late thirties, her hair done up in a head scarf, came to the door holding a squalling infant on her hip and scowling with a look that could fling tomahawks until she saw who it was. Three other kids, older, were playing a board game on the carpet while watching TV.

"Oh, Dr. Harris. Please excuse the place—Leal? Why, yes. He's upstairs in his room. He's been there all afternoon. In fact, now that I think about it, he missed dinner. Is it OK to go up? Well—"

That was enough of an affirmative response for Selena. She hurried up the steps taking two at a time.

"Second on the right!" the woman hollered up to her before Selena could even call down the question.

As she flicked on the light, she found the window open, the curtains blowing into the room like the skirts of a dervish, the temperature as chilled as a walk-in freezer.

"Leal?" she called out anyway. She checked the closet. She looked under the bed.

"He's not upstairs," Selena informed the foster mom when she trudged back downstairs.

"It's not like him to disappear like this," the woman said—a bit defensively, Selena thought. "Any idea where he might have gone?"

She's asking *me* this? Selena wondered. A bad sign.

"Yes," Selena said, hoping she was wrong. "I do."

***

Selena sits very still. She lets several minutes transpire. She has reached a point in her narrative where it will be a struggle to move on. Her own recollection of events is unnerving her. Her eyes transfixed, she listens to her own breathing, steady but shallow.

The sound of a baby crying—making a loud squeak, as of a squeeze toy being pressed—makes her jump. She has an instinct to leap out the window. *A baby is at risk! Her baby! Jonquil!* Then as the squeaking becomes repetitive, she relaxes gradually, lowering herself back into her seat, but she still clutches the armrests, while maintaining her gaze out the window.

"We have sloths in the nearby trees," the therapist explains.

"I didn't know sloths made any noise," Selena admits. "They sort of sound like a seal."

"It's the sound a baby sloth makes when it's exerting itself, climbing a tree to find its mother."

Selena listens to the squeaking until it stops: lost mother found?

"It is still early," the therapist says, sustaining a smile borrowed from the Buddha. "But we can always stop here if you wish."

Selena considers his proposition. *No,* she thinks. She came here for a reason, to unburden herself, to lighten her load, to empty some of the luggage she's been carrying around all this time.

She takes a deep breath, holding it for a count of three, then releasing it, listening to the wax paper whisper it makes through her lips.

"No," she says, a note of determination in her voice. "I need to keep going."

"As you wish," the therapist says and settles back in his chair.

Chapter 21

Pulling up to the curb, Selena took a brief moment to collect her thoughts. Surely, she was overreacting, jumping to conclusions. Leal was simply a lost and lonely adolescent. *He couldn't have, wouldn't have ...* But as she opened the front door, she wasn't so sure. The house was oddly quiet.

The times before, she had arrived home to find Paula with the television on as ambient noise while she coddled the baby or browsed her phone while she slept. Now there were no noises except from upstairs. Running water? She hadn't left instructions to give Jonquil a bath. Maybe she had soiled herself so badly ... but wouldn't Paula have filled the plastic tub by the sink?

A sickening feeling sunk into her stomach, product of a mother's intuition. She climbed the stairs hurriedly, beelining to the bathroom. The tub was overflowing, but that's not what alarmed her.

"No!" she shouted. "No, no, no!"

She found the babysitter, fully clothed, lying face down in the tub, her long curly red hair floating around her like strands of seaweed. Selena grabbed hold of the back of the girl's sweatshirt and heaved, yanking her halfway out of the tub—hard work since her clothes were weighing her down. Another hard pull and she tumbled over the edge, spilling into the inch-deep water on the linoleum floor.

Selena rolled her over onto her back and began CPR, not wasting time to check for a pulse. She pushed on her chest, performing compressions until a trickle of water spilled out of the girl's mouth, then tilted her head back and, pinching her nose closed, blew three long breaths into her open mouth. Repeat. Three chest compressions, three breaths through the mouth. She hoped she was doing it right. It had been several years since she had taken Red Cross classes.

"Come on, come on, come on," she repeated, with each push on her chest, but Paula wasn't responding.

Three more breaths, three more compressions.

How long had she been doing this? One minute? Five? Ten? Thirty? She had lost track of time, but she knew it was no use.

"My God, Paula. My God. Why?"

She sat beside her, stroking her wet hair, brushing the back of her hand down her cold cheek. She wished she had brought her purse with her phone, but 911 wouldn't save her. The faucet was still running, and she took a moment to shut it off, as though her former patient had simply finished bathing.

"Time of death, seven fifty-three," she heard from behind her, and when she turned, she saw Leal standing in the doorway, glancing up from his wristwatch with a horribly thin, strange smile on his face, twisted into more of a frown, as though he had consumed something sour.

The image was so unexpected, so incongruous, she screamed and screamed and screamed. The scream came out of her as something animal, primal, uncontrollable. She heard herself screaming as though it were someone else's voice echoing in her ear. When the screaming stopped, she sat there, panting, but lifted herself into a crouching position, as though to spring.

"Did you do this?" she demanded.

She was having trouble focusing, breathing. The room was a blur and she knew it was because of her tears—so many tears flooding her eyes.

"She told me not to. She begged me. She told me she would do anything if I left her alone. But we both know it's something she wanted. She's tried killing herself twice before, as you know. I just helped her along."

"Leal!" But this was all she could get out of herself, a single word. It was as though her brain was frozen, locked in place, all the gears corroded, rusted shut.

"Oh, yes. We mustn't forget about Leal. That scrawny no-account kid who talks to himself at his locker."

"Leal, what are you talking about?" She was finding her voice, her breaths becoming more even, but she didn't know how to proceed, what questions to ask.

"She was very concerned about the baby, you should know. When she saw it was inevitable, she asked me not to hurt the baby. And as you can see, I'm taking very good care of her."

And now Selena did see. She brushed her tears aside, and what at first she thought was just a lump, a bundle of dirty clothes from a laundry basket, she now saw was a carefully folded striped hospital blanket, forming a perfect burrito, and she had no doubt who was wrapped inside, even though she couldn't see the face from this angle.

"Leal, give me my baby!"

Selena stood and took a step forward, but Leal held the package closer to his chest, swaddling Jonquil within the eyrie of a cross-armed clutch. She took another step, but Leal took a step backward, into the hallway, the light from the bathroom illuminating his face like a waxen mask, affixed with that strange, lurid smile.

"Leal!" Selena shouted, finding her voice, uttering the command with an authority that was arising organically out of the situation. "Give—me—back—my—baby! Now!"

"You keep talking about Leal," he said, narrowing his eyes and giving his lips a curious pucker. "He got it all wrong, you know. Father Mac said that Thuster was something inside us that the bad things happen *to*. But he got it backwards. Thuster is also the something inside us that *does* the bad things."

Thuster, she thought, and the thought did more than unnerve her. It terrified her to think that the boy with a stranglehold on her baby wasn't who he seemed to be. Could she try reasoning with him? Should she try persuasion? She knew that he—whoever "he" was—was too smart to fall for psychological tricks. Hadn't he already proved that all those weeks in her office?

"Is that why you killed him—Father Mac?"

"I protest my innocence," the boy in front of her claimed, raising one hand in mock defense while maintaining his possession of her baby. "But I recruited someone who could."

Saul, Selena assumed, immediately, thinking back to the Chinchilla King's promise to come to Leal's aid if he was ever in trouble. But *had* he been in trouble? Or had he used this as another stalling tactic to steer Saul from Diana's scent? One that went too far—as it had with his math teacher.

"It's not like he didn't have it coming. He was plotting with Leal's mother. Conspiring. They were going to place him in a home for boys—as good as a prison for disposing of him. Then he was going to leave the next day, wasn't he? He was going to Florida without Leal. And I couldn't let him do that. Not after all they'd meant to each other."

She took another hesitant step forward, but Leal retreated backward down the hall, one step, two steps, three—until he reached the banister at the top of the stairs.

"Leal—stop!" It was time for a different approach. She could see her baby's little brown face poking through the opening in the blanket. She was doing that thing with her nose and mouth and eyes all scrunched together which meant one of two things: she needed to be fed or changed.

"There you go again, calling me Leal."

"What should I call you?" Dare she say it? "Thuster?"

"If you wish," the boy said with a heft of his shoulders to keep the baby in place as Jonquil began to squirm. This might be her chance. If Leal loosened his grip, even for a second, she could pounce and wrestle her baby free. But he seemed to sense her purpose and clutched the bundle even more tightly, making Jonquil let out a little yelp like a gasp from an accordion.

"But Thuster is good and kind and compassionate," she tried to remind him.

"And needy. You forgot needy. And impatient and demanding."

"And quiet, remember? He never says anything. He's silent!"

"Used-ter be." One corner of his mouth rose in a contorted half-smile like that of a stroke victim. That pun again—that terrible, godawful pun. "Not anymore." His eyes shifted, widened, stared—as though at a phantom, and a different voice broke through, a boy's voice, scared … Leal's? "I tried keeping him little. I tried keeping him small as long as I could but—"

"But you killed Thuster!" she shouted. "Remember? He's dead. You drowned him. Just like you murdered—" She was going to say Jay. She could have added Father Mac or Paula. But she ran out of words. She was running out of names.

"Leal only claimed to have killed him." *Leal again.* He was going back to talking of Leal in the third person, his eyes narrowing, his face hardening. "He knew if he boasted about something really shocking, something extreme, Ms. Jacobson would refer him to you. Everyone knew that you were where she sent all her difficult cases."

"Me? Why did he—why did you want to see me?" She was getting her pronouns all mixed up. She didn't know who she was talking with anymore.

"You're all Ms. Jacobson—Lori—you're all she would ever talk about." He put on a Wicked Witch of the West impersonation of his former guidance counselor. "'If you don't behave, young man, I'll send you to a real therapist. A real professional. She'll know how to handle you if you don't watch out.'" He paused as though to switch roles. "She even had a picture of you on her bulletin board, and when Leal asked about you, she said you were expecting and what a wonderful mother you would be."

So even then, Selena thought. *Even with our very first session, he was playing me.* Or was it the other way around? Had Leal been genuinely seeking help—trying to keep this darkness, *his* darkness, suppressed and at bay? Or possibly to eradicate it once and for all? Was he also a victim of Thuster?

"She was going to send Leal somewhere 'special,' too. A special ed school where he would fit right in with the other freaks, so she could be rid of him once and for all. It's not like she really cared about Leal's progress, anyway. The only thing anyone at that school cares about is test scores."

"Look," Selena said more softly, "I really need you to stop what you're doing. I need us to go downstairs where we can talk things through." And where she can make a phone call. If he'll let her make a phone call. If she can somehow convince him to give himself over to the authorities who will take him to a nice place where he'll be cared for and treated and diagnosed and medicated and confined and euthanized and …

"Talk, talk, talk. That's all Leal ever did was talk. I'm the one who did all the things that needed to be done. He wanted a family, he wanted a father. He was so pathetic, he actually thought maybe Jay and Diana would adopt him—at least take him with them when they left for L.A., which was their plan. 'City of Lights.' Isn't that what they call it?" With the epithet, his eyes take on an almost wistful look. "But that plan fell through. So I had to resort to Plan B."

"Plan B?" Selena was starting to put two and two together but kept ending up with five.

"After Diana went back with Saul, Leal thought it could just be Jay and his mother. He thought if there was a guy around the house—a father figure, isn't that how you phrased it?—she'd give up trying to send him away. Everything would be settled. But Jay wasn't going to stay put, was he? Marry Leal's mother? Be a father to Leal? Hah! He was going to abandon Leal, just like all his mother's other so-called boyfriends. And Leal needed something he could hold over his mother—for life. So she wouldn't ever think about sending him somewhere—to some sort of boys' home—ever again."

"Blackmail," Selena realized.

"When he told you he was the one being molested by Jay and how his mother came to his rescue? What he didn't tell you was I set it all up. I had Leal text a message from Jay's phone to his mother telling her to meet Jay at the cottage that night. He had something important to tell her. A proposal. Jay was in no position to resist after Saul was through with him that night, and before she arrived, I slipped into bed with him. When I heard her call out in the dark, I pulled Jay on top of Leal and yelled. So when she climbed the stairs, I made this accusation, and his mother just freaked. I was the one who pushed the pillow down on his face before Jay even knew what was happening. She was the one who sat on his legs and pinned down his arms at my command."

"But your mother confessed. She gave herself up voluntarily."

As soon as she says this, she realizes how inane she must sound. What mother wouldn't take the fall for her son if she could? Even if she subsequently pleaded "not guilty" by reason of temporary insanity.

"You mean *Leal's* mother, don't you? The whore."

Whore? This isn't the kind of language Leal ever used. This wasn't the tone of voice he would use either. She was beginning to let herself be convinced that this wasn't Leal after all. But Leal must be in there somewhere, if only she could find him again.

"Leal?" she began, softly, soothingly, as though buttering bread.

"And that's not to mention what I did to his father." His smile took on a smug look, to underscore his bragging rights. "Leal wasn't under the covers in the motel room like his mom told you over the phone." So … he'd been listening in? Eavesdropping? "Leal was in the bathroom holding the hair dryer. He liked feeling the warm air on his face, and his dad was in the tub yelling at him. 'What the hell are you doing?' he wanted to know. 'Put the damn thing down. I'm warning you. If I have to get out of this tub.' And that's what he started to do, so … I put it down."

His smile broadened, and Selena had no trouble picturing him committing the crime he was describing, even if he had only been seven years old.

"But it's true," he continued, "a woman came by to find him, and by then Leal really was under the covers. He was going to introduce them, his dad said. He was going to see how they all got along." The boy's face took on a dark turn with the memory. "He was going to divorce Leal's mom." As though this justified everything. "He wasn't the greatest dad in the world anyway. He didn't do nice things."

"Leal?" she prodded.

"Ah, well," he concluded, giving his shoulders a shrug that jounced the baby. "Accidents happen."

"Leal, listen to me."

"No! Not Leal! I told you!"

"Leal," she insisted, but gently. "You were little. You didn't know any better." She imagined rubbing his shoulders, massaging his neck, as though to sustain the illusion of friendliness, but the image became one of clasping her hands around his throat and choking him and choking him until he let go, until he …

"Leave—Leal—alone!" he said tersely, repeating the words of the handmade sign that had been affixed to her front door on Halloween night.

"But why? What's wrong with Leal? He's got to come out sometime, doesn't he? Leal? What are you doing here? What is it you want?"

"I'll tell you what he wants," the boy sneered. "He's got this crazy idea that you'll adopt him, take him somewhere, anywhere, away from here. Where you and he—where you can be mother and son."

She heard it clearly—a choking sob in there, stifled, suppressed, but still surfacing, interrupting. So maybe she was close to reaching him?

But before she could say anything else, the boy turned and stomped down the stairs, jostling the baby enough so that she started crying.

"Leal!"

She hurried along, sliding down steps, twisting her ankle as she turned at the bottom of the stairs, but not enough to slow her down. She hobbled after him, but he stopped short at the dining room table, where her laptop had been set up.

"Look!" the boy said, touching the keyboard so the screen lit up. He still held Jonquil tightly in his other arm. Again, Selena thought she might lunge and grab the baby, but she was afraid of knocking them all over. Bones might break, necks might snap—and she didn't want these to be Jonquil's. She glanced at the screen, not wanting to take her eyes off her baby, who was starting to fuss, poking her arms and kicking her feet as though to escape Houdini-style from a straitjacket. She saw he had brought up a webpage about adoption.

"Oh, Leal," she said, a note of sympathy creeping into her voice against her wishes.

"There're only ten steps to adoption, and we're already past number four: Search for a Child. You don't have to search. You have me. And then it's only a few short steps to number ten: Live as an Adoptive Family. Just you and me."

"You? You mean, Leal?"

A look of confusion contorted his features.

"Here," he said, abruptly handing over the baby, just like that. Selena took her quickly and decisively from his arms. "It's not her I want, it's you. Besides," he said, his nose crinkling, "I think she's messed her diaper."

Selena turned to flee. She only had to cross the living room to the front door, and she could rush down the street like a mad-woman, shouting for help. Or just make it to her purse where she had left it on the couch, although it would take time to dig out her cell phone. But Leal's voice advanced on her like a knife, along with a metallic ratcheting sound punctuated with a sharp click that made her stop.

"I'm afraid I can't let you leave."

Selena turned a few paces short of the doorway. She took in what she half expected to see: a handgun pointed in her direc-tion, the same sort of pistol with a magazine in its handle that he had described Saul teaching him to shoot. The slide was back in position along the barrel, primed and ready to fire.

"Not till you promise," he said calmly.

"Promise to adopt you?"

The boy—was it Leal?—nodded.

"And if I don't?"

"Here's how it will work. You'll tell the police that Paula drowned herself. They'll believe it based on her past history. And then you'll begin the adoption process."

"And if I don't?" she repeated.

"I'll follow you. I'll track you down. I'll never leave you alone till you do."

"And Jonquil? What about her?"

"She'll never be safe."

A shiver went through Selena. They had reached a stalemate in their negotiations. She knew from experience whoever talked first at this point would be the loser, so she kept her mouth shut.

The boy, however, opened his mouth to say something more—deliver another threat? An ultimatum?

But his eyes opened wide, as though he had just awoken in an unfamiliar room. His mouth trembled.

"Look, I really don't want to hurt anybody. I only want to—"

But before he could finish his thought, a voice called out from the top of the stairs.

"Dr. Harris?" it said weakly.

Glancing up, Selena was astounded to see the thin, drenched and dripping figure of her former patient wavering on the staircase, hand on the banister—impossibly, miraculously, very much alive.

"Paula!" she shouted, raising a hand. "Get back!"

At that moment, the door burst open without a preliminary ring of the bell or a knock.

"Selena? Are you all right? I saw through the window—"

Before she could warn him, a shot pierced the air. It sounded no louder than a cap gun—a child's toy. But Henri crumpled to the floor, sliding along the doorjamb, staring dumbly at his abdomen—that fledgling six-pack from a workout regimen he was always so proud of—that was revealed through his opened jacket, where a small red hole was spouting blood all over his white shirt.

"Henri!"

Selena knelt beside him, laid her baby carefully down on the carpet, and pressed her palms to the wound. As she did, she heard the sound of an object clanking against the floor and saw a shadow rush past in her peripheral vision, out into the night.

"'Tis merely a flesh wound," Henri said, smiling.

"This is no time for jokes," she reprimanded him.

She pressed ever harder. Her phone was in her purse—her purse out of reach.

"I take it that was your patient?" Henri said, matter-of-factly, searching her eyes.

"Yes," she nodded, tears building up once again.

"Well, I'm glad I finally got a chance to—"

And then, just like that, he was gone.

Epilogue

"Looks like we're out of time," Selena notes, glancing at a clock that has various tropical fruits in place of numbers. The big hand is on the pineapple, the little hand on the kiwi. She doesn't want to overstay her welcome in case there are other patients waiting to be seen.

"Yes, yes, so we are," the therapist says, letting an unprofessional note of disappointment underscore the observation. "Before we conclude, do you wish to discuss how you're feeling?"

"How I'm feeling?" Selena knows exactly what she's feeling, a sense of outrage rising in her throat like bile. "Guilty." So very, very guilty. If only she'd entered her house before trying to track down Leal, there was a chance she could have stopped it all from happening.

"Try not to be so hard on yourself," the therapist advises with a smile. "You are not to blame for events out of your control."

"That's just it. All of it—from beginning to end—all of it should have been under my control."

"Think about the things you can control in the present. You have moved to a new home here in the Islands."

"For now. It's only temporary." She has to keep reminding herself she has a life to get back to—someday.

"You have a beautiful baby girl. Do you know the Serenity Prayer? 'God grant me the serenity—'"

"'—to accept the things I cannot change.' Yes, yes, I know it by heart," Selena says, tiredly, shifting to the edge of her seat, preparing to rise.

"Please, before you go, we still need to determine a schedule. Now, if I can just take a look at my calendar."

"Oh, I won't be coming back," Selena informs him, an announcement that makes him slump back against the padding of his bamboo chair. The therapist keeps a couple of birds—brightly colored macaws—in a large bamboo cage in the vestibule, and these make disapproving clicking and clucking noises as though to criticize her decision.

Wouldn't it be nice to take over this therapist's practice? Selena wonders. Or go in as partners? But she isn't sure she wants to practice psychology ever again. She doesn't think she's very good at it, after all.

"No?" he asks with raised eyebrows, bushy and dark, like pieces of felt glued to the large black dome of his forehead. "But I haven't had time to make my diagnosis." He smiles, letting Selena know she can take this as a joke, if she wishes.

"Surely, you've made a preliminary one?"

"I'm sure, in turn, you already know your ailment."

"Post-traumatic stress syndrome?"

"Yes, yes, with a measure of survivor's guilt thrown in."

Survivor's guilt. Somewhat different than just plain, old *guilt* guilt. She hadn't considered this. Maybe there was some value in coming here after all, but her mind has pretty much been made up.

"Listen," the therapist says kindly, leaning forward, elbows on knees, as though to confide a great secret. "Many of my patients—and I'm sure yours, as well—start out this way. They start out by telling a story. But at some point, my dear. And this may be sooner or later, it's all part of the process, as you are no doubt well aware. At some point, you're going to have to tell—if not me, then someone—what's really troubling you."

Selena can't help but break into a laugh. She surprises herself. This is the first time she has laughed, never mind smiled, in months. She takes this as a promising sign, as she stands, opening her purse, and pulling out a checkbook.

"Did I say something amusing perhaps?"

"Perhaps," she says, filling out the check at a desk by the door.

"Please." The therapist restrains her with a gentle hand. "This first one's on me."

"Thank you," she says, sincerely, and walks through a corridor into the brightness of the day.

Private vans are always and forever stalking the beachfront, driving up and down in search of prey, so a short taxi ride brings her to the doorstep of her very own Quonset hut, a single-story structure with a rounded roof made of bamboo and clay.

It has taken her these past two months to get to the point where she's allowed someone else to watch the baby. Today marks the first day, in fact, that she has let Dahlia, the nursemaid who stops by every afternoon, take care of Jonquil on her own.

Little Jonquil is sitting restfully on her caretaker's lap, which in turn is propped up by an enormous rocking chair on the porch, and the baby appears pacified by the slow back-and-forth motion.

She's wearing a pair of loose-fitting shorts that show off her chubby knees and nothing on top, leaving her arms and chest and belly all bare. But they're in the shade of a pair of palm trees, so no threat of sunburn. She's so light-skinned, this is always a worry at this latitude with the sun so high up in the sky. She's wearing a bright yellow bonnet that with her brown face as a centerpiece makes her look like a pie-eyed daisy.

"Hello, there, little one," Selena sweettalks her, lifting her out of Dahlia's lap. The nursemaid sits up. It's obvious she has been lulled into a doze by the same rocking motion.

"Would missus like me to make her some lunch?" she asks, rising.

"Thanks, Dahlia. I think I'll just sit here for a moment with the baby. Maybe a little later. I'm not so hungry now. Do you think *she* is?"

"I fed her a bottle not long ago. If it's okay with missus, I'll go to market and pick out some fresh fish for dinner then. Maybe some ingredients for a nice mango salad, eh?"

"Yes, but not too tangy."

"No, no, never too tangy for American missus who has virgin taste buds."

"Hmm," Selena says, smiling. *Virgin*, huh? She'll have to think about this one.

"Oh, here, I almost forgot." Dahlia removes an envelope from a pocket of her apron and offers it like a calling card.

"Is it?"

"Yes, mum. Another one from 'the Boy.'"

This is their code name for him, once Selena forbade her from mentioning his name in her home.

In some ways, his threat to keep stalking her is coming true via postal delivery. This is the third letter in as many weeks. She had to report her change of address to the county psychiatric ward where Leal is incarcerated as well as the Ovid police department, but it is supposed to be protected information. Somehow, he's found a way to wheedle her address out of someone or other—an underling, a new orderly, a friendly nurse. He's slippery, after all—just like an eel.

The second letter was the same as the first: a hundred repetitions of "I'm sorry" followed by, "How can I ever make it up to you?" and "Please forgive me." She is fairly confident this third letter will be more of the same.

The saddest part of the first letter was the postscript:

I'm taking all kinds of meds now, and they're making me feel so much better—and together. Know what I mean?

The P.S. attached to the bottom of the second letter almost made her cave:

Why didn't you write back? You know where I live LOL.

She keeps meaning to write—she pictures him so solitary in his ward, a bird in a cage—but every time she brings pen to paper, her hand freezes, as though gripped by paralysis.

This third letter inscribes a single, terse message in the middle of an otherwise blank sheet of paper. As opposed to the hurried scrawl of the previous letters, this one has been written in neat block letters using a blue ballpoint pen:

JUST THOUGHT YOU SHOULD KNOW, I KILLED HIM. FOR REAL THIS TIME. HE'S DEAD! AND HE'LL NEVER COME BACK. I PROMISE!!!

Then underneath in an unwieldy cursive: *Please, please, please write. I miss you!*

The message makes her shudder, causing her to drop the letter as she might a poisonous snake, letting it slither to the ground.

She can't believe his psychiatric team would have prescribed suppression as a cure. It might seem to Leal that repressing disturbing thoughts, feelings, urges is the straightest route to relief, but she would be the first to tell him the road to recovery is long and winding, just like the song.

And paved with good intentions, remembering the poem.

"Missus? You all right?"

Dahlia takes the baby, and Selena stoops to retrieve the letter and tuck it back in its envelope.

"Yes," she assures her, performing an exchange. "Just place it with the others, okay?"

She thinks it important to maintain a record of correspondence, even if it's only one-way.

In hindsight, she wonders if she should have referred him to a psychiatrist early on for prescription meds. They wouldn't have prevented the two murders already committed over the past summer, which seems so long ago and far away, but maybe they would have stopped him from carrying out any further loss of life. Looking ahead, she knows he's in for years of intensive therapy before he'll be allowed to mix with the general population of teens in juvie—if he ever reaches that point.

She retakes the rocker, still slightly rocking. The baby cuddles and coos, snuggling against her, but her mouth isn't gaping, as it is wont to do, guppy-like, when she demands to be fed, so Selena is content to rock with her in the shade with the ocean in view. That is, if you look through the spaces between the new rowhouses that are being built along the beachfront.

Even so, she can hear the soft lapping of the waves, the inrush of water softer, gentler, on this side of the ocean that faces the mainland, the long, dark line of which you can just make out like a brush of eyeliner across the horizon, separating sky from water.

"And how is Miss Jonquil today?" she asks, taking her tiny fingers in hers and giving her hand a little shake. She has read that it is important for a child's development to be talked to as though she were an adult, thus making traditional baby-talk taboo.

But lately, she's thrown conventional wisdom under the bus. She'll talk to her baby any damn way she pleases, and this afternoon, with the sun still high in the sky, she chooses to sing her a lullaby she's picked up from the locals.

> *"There's a brown girl in the ring*
> *Tra la la la*
> *There's a brown girl in the ring*
> *Tra la la la la"*

Jonquil gives one of her newly found smiles showing off her gums, and then she lets out a little giggle.

"Did you just laugh, honey pot?" Selena asks in disbelief, lifting her high in her arms above her head, and then she does it again.

"Oh, you good, good, good little baby," she praises her, kissing her midriff where her belly button bulges with a loud raspberry, and this makes her laugh even more.

And so she keeps singing to keep them both happy.

"Show me your motion
Tra la la la la
Come on show me your motion
Tra la la la la la
You look like a sugar in a plum
Plum plum"

She twirls her in the air, and when she brings her to land on her lap, Jonquil wriggles and squirms, her mouth agape, so this time Selena knows she's hungry for real. She loosens the top of her blouse and lifts out a breast, which Jonquil latches onto with gusto. There's no need for self-consciousness, not around here. So Selena leans back in the rocker and lets her feed while still singing the song, but softly, under her breath.

"Skip across the ocean
Tra la la la la
Skip across the ocean ..."

*

She's not sure when she fell asleep, but it must have been before the end of the song. She was feeling so exhausted by her day, and all she had done was visit a therapist. Is this what has tired her so?

She's jostled awake gently and, without opening her eyes, she asks, "Dinnertime already, Dahlia?"

"Come on, love," she hears. Instead of the nursemaid's lilting twang, it's a man's deep baritone, with that characteristic French inflection she used to so adore. "It's time we were going."

Part of her knows this is a voice she shouldn't be able to hear, yet when she opens her eyes, there is Henri, in the flesh. But this shouldn't be such a surprise. Hadn't she been expecting him all along? Hadn't they made this arrangement?

"I'm not packed," she says, pulling her blouse closed, and cradling Jonquil as she stands with Henri's helping hand.

"Dahlia's done all that, not to worry."

It doesn't take long to arrive at the airstrip. Henri has his private jet, which they board at the bidding of a bright, young flight attendant. Just Henri's type if Selena wasn't assured he had eyes for no one else but her.

"Where to this time?" Selena asks as they squiggle into their seats. She straps Jonquil to her lap while Henri takes a seat across the aisle. It's a small plane with room for several other passengers, but there's just the three of them. She wonders if she should take a quick moment to change the baby before takeoff.

"You tell me," Henri prompts. "After all, it's your journey."

She takes a quick look to the row behind her, half afraid of encountering Leal, who has somehow sneaked aboard as a stowaway. She tries reassuring herself that he'll remain incarcerated until he turns 21. For now, he's as securely locked up as a marmoset in a zoo. But this doesn't prevent her worrying about files smuggled inside birthday cakes, lock picks crafted from paper clips.

"Iceland," she answers, as though only now making up her mind.

"I know you like island-hopping, but Iceland?" Henri's unibrow arches in surprise.

"It's the coldness. The whiteness. It helps clear the mind." She smiles. "Plus, they have natural steam baths."

Henri smiles in return.

"Iceland it is. Please inform the captain," he instructs the flight attendant.

Within minutes they lift smoothly from the runway, and the plane arcs above the clouds like a silver, pointed dagger puncturing a blanket of insubstantial cloth stretched out to the horizon like a veil.

The island disappears beneath a white, frothy carpet of clouds, and beyond and above is nothing but blue sky. It's a sky that promises to go on forever.

ACKNOWLEDGMENTS

A big thank-you hug to my three primary readers/editors: my spouse, Miona Jansen; my mentor, Katherine Burkman; and my mother-in-law, Pamela Caruzzi. Thanks also to Samantha Verba, Mia Altieri, Lucy Branch, Linda Thompson Sabo, Melissa Kraus Shockley, Clay Woomer, and Justin Simons for their feedback and support. And a special shout-out to Rusty Geiger for some last-minute fixes.

ABOUT THE AUTHOR

B. Robert Conklin (he/him/his) lives, writes, and works, not necessarily in this order, in Columbus, Ohio, where he helps his spouse nurture the creativity of their three Gen-Z kids, who seem determined to take less-traveled paths of their own. In his leisure time, he takes nature walks with his family's two ferrets and practices the craft of cartooning.

Visit him at brobertconklin.wordpress.com

www.ingramcontent.com/pod-product-compliance
Lightning Source LLC
Chambersburg PA
CBHW071230300726
48975CB00002B/351